Shabby Tiger

HOWARD SPRING, the author of fourteen highly-acclaimed bestsellers, was born in 1889 in Cardiff. At the age of twelve, when his father died, he left school: his first job was as a butcher's errand boy. After several other jobs he became a messenger boy for the *South Wales Daily News*, and by the time he left seven years later, he was a fully-qualified reporter. After working on other newspapers, he was 'discovered' by the *London Evening Standard* and became its book reviewer.

During this period he wrote his famous novel *Shabby Tiger* – recently serialized on television – followed a few years later by a sequel, *Rachel Rosing*. After the success of *O Absalom* (later re-titled *My Son, My Son*) in 1938, he retired to Falmouth, Cornwall, scene of many of his later novels. He died there in 1965 at the age of seventy-six, leaving his wife and two sons.

HOWARD SPRING

Shabby Tiger

Collins

FONTANA BOOKS

First published in 1934 by William Collins Sons & Co Ltd
First issued in Fontana Books 1954
Fifteenth Impression August 1977

Made and printed in Great Britain by
William Collins Sons & Co Ltd Glasgow

FOR MARION

CHAPTER ONE

THE woman flamed along the road like a macaw. A thin mackintosh, washed out by weather into pastel tints of green, was belted tight above the swaying rhythm of her hips. It was slashed open to show a skirt of yellow wool, and you could see that the rent was an old one, that this lazy slut had no use for needle and thread. Thrown round her neck with as much consideration as a dish-clout is thrown on the string stretched before the kitchen fire was a scarf of silk, scarlet, stained and mottled like all she wore, yet achieving a gay defiant beauty. The wind made it a pennon. A great lolloping black sombrero that had belonged to a man, and was now trimmed with a broken green feather, hid the flash of the woman's black secret eyes. She lugged a suitcase of scarlet leather, but because, like all about her, it was tattered and outmoded and insecure, a length of clothes line kept its jaws snapped on whatever was within, permitting no more than a glimpse of white, frilled protrusion.

Her ankles were like the ankles of a racing colt—slim and resilient, but with the strong resilience of tempered steel. She swung the bag with ease. It did not drag her a shade from the upright. The motley assembly of her clothes took on significance, achieved entity, though the entity of something strange and foreign flaming through the green mistiness of the Cheshire lane.

Interminably on her right ran the paling of split oak, hoary and lichened, low, permitting uninterrupted vision of the bluebells. Seas of bluebells, washing round the shores of the green land that ran on and on to the soft swell of a hill, crowned with the sober loveliness of a mansion. The evening light came level across the land, turning the windows of the house to flame, making the new grass look like heavenly pasturage, fit for Pegasus, and, coming among the trees whereunder the bluebells grew, it offered the bewitching alternatives of a vast mediterranean expanse or the isolated beauty of one spire picked out with each bell suspended above the next.

The trees were beech, dull silver their boles in that light, their leaves, newly born, like clouds of green butterflies that had not yet dried their wings. Here and there, where the paling was broken, the road stank of oil and petrol, and the flowers were trampled where marauders had waded into the blue sea, gathering armfuls, and beating down beauty into the rich residuum of a hundred summers that showed brown and loamy through the white, violated stems.

The woman threw her bag through one of the gaps. It plumped among the bruised flowers at the foot of a beech, and she followed it, kicked it aside and sat down. She stretched out her legs, stretched her arms above her head, threw her rakish hat to the ground. It was like taking the lid off hell-broth, so sombrely smouldered the light in her dark eyes. Up the middle of her head ran the white ridge from which her hair was pulled down on either side so smooth and tight you might have called it a silken skull-cap split with the painting of a freakish line. The parted wings of her hair met on the nape of her neck in a knob of ebony. The skin of her face was pallid, hard and healthy, clean as God made it, even to the lips, and it was stretched as tight on the bones of her cheeks as her hair was upon her head. She was beautiful.

From the pocket of her mackintosh she produced a crumpled paper bag, took out a heavy sandwich whose meaty contents bulged from the ends as her white teeth assailed it. She threw the rumpled paper among the bluebells, found one cigarette left in a crushed yellow packet, and, when she had lit it, threw the yellow packet, too, among the flowers.

She leaned back against the smooth bole of the beech, the cigarette dangling from her lip, her hands thrust down her thighs within the pockets of the mackintosh.

"And now," she said. "What the devil now?"

Blackbirds and thrushes poured melody upon her, but she heeded them no more than she heeded the beauty of the bluebells. She flicked the ash of her cigarette contemptuously in the face of all of it. "That to 'em," she said. "That to all of 'em. Holy Mother of God! What a life! Forward!"

She smashed the hat upon her head, rose and seized the

suitcase. "I could do with a drink," she said, standing among the broken palings and looking up and down the road.

The sound of a car slewed her head back in the way she had come. "It might be a lift," she said, "and that might be a drink, in the long run."

The brakes squealed when the driver saw her; and at the same time she saw him, slithered from the bank into the road, and strode defiantly forward.

"Anna!" he called after her. But she only spat out the fag-end of her cigarette and went on, humping the scarlet suitcase.

She heard the slammed door of the car and the sound of his overtaking feet. She turned and faced him patiently. He was not self-possessed like her, but broken up by a buffeting emotion that darkened his blue eyes and twisted his features.

"Where are you going to?" he asked.

"Along this road," she said, "and then along the next."

"Anna!" he cried. "You know you've got *no*where to go to."

"And not for the first time, either," she said. "But a girl can always fetch up somewhere. If you want to help, give me five bob. I haven't got a penny."

"Didn't you get your wages?"

"Yes, and I owed every bean to the other servants. I tried to get away with it, but they nobbled me."

"But, Anna, why were you fired out like this?"

"Stealing."

"That must have been a lie. You didn't steal."

"I did steal." She heaved up the scarlet suitcase, indicated the froth of delicate fabric that showed through its teeth. "One of your sister's night-dresses," she said. "There's more inside."

"Come back," he said. "I'll make it right with my sister. You shall stay."

"You're a good sort," she said, "but you're talking through your hat." And then, flushing to a sudden passion: "What in hell should I want to stay for, anyway? Look at it— damned great prison. I'm glad to be out of it."

She pulled off the sombrero and swept it with an impressive gesture towards the house on the hill.

The young man's eyes went towards the house. "It's beautiful," he said. "I am never so happy as when I'm there. And I've never been happier there, Anna, than since you came. Come back now."

"And in God's name," she cried, "what for? Is it a cheap mistress you're wanting, or what? Be honest with yourself. I'll give you the names of three of the girls, if you like, who'll be willing to oblige you. And one of them's a virgin, which is more than I am."

He mumbled her name and tried to take her arm, but she jammed on the hat with which she had been fanning her flaming face and shook him off.

"Well," she said, "are you going to give me the five shillings?"

He went back to the car with his head hanging, put the bonnet into a gateway, reversed and sped away.

She watched till the car was out of sight, picked up her burden, and went forward, whistling among the whistling birds. The middle of the road was cobbled, and on each side was a dirt track. She trudged through the dirt, upright as a young poplar, and the sun, going down before her, furraged its diffuse yellow light among the tangles of ragged robin in the ditches.

Then she came to a gate and beyond the gate was the whiteness of a tent, and over the gate some blankets were stretched.

She dumped the bag again and looked over the gate to see a man sitting on a log before a fire, toasting a sausage at the end of a stick.

"Whose are the blankets?" she shouted.

"There're mine," he said, looking not at her but at the golden glow that was spreading on the sausage. "They're out to air."

"Take them in, you fool," she said. "The time of airing's long past. It's dew they'll be getting and you your death of cold."

"Then fold them up," he said. "You can see I'm busy."

She threw the bag towards the tent and leapt over the gate as light as a boy. "I can fold them better from this side," she said; and when she had folded them she laid them inside the tent and the scarlet suitcase on top of them.

She sat on the log beside the man, and he looked at her out of the corner of his black eye; and she looked at the long hand that held the stick with the sausage and at the cruel flexibility of the fingers, tufted on the back joints with black hair.

"I hope there's another sausage," she said. "Why don't you fry them?"

"Because there's enough damned junk for one narrow back without carrying a frying pan," he answered. "Hold it."

She took the stick, and the man went into the tent, having to get down on his knees and crawl, so low was it. He came out with a plate and some bread and more sausages. He eyed her when he stood upright, she with her back to him, the hat with the broken green feather thrown to the ground, the hard knob of her hair shining like polished ebony in the sun's last light. He looked at the high angle of her cheek-bones and her thighs pressed broad by the log.

He took the stick from her, prised the cooked sausage from it with a pocket knife and gave her knife, plate and bread.

"You get on with it," he said, fixing another sausage on to the stick.

She sat upright, eating. He crouched low before the fire. "My name's Nick Faunt," he said. "Yours?"

"Anna Fitzgerald," she mumbled over a mouthful.

"You've left your bag in my tent."

"I thought it might stop there."

"I thought it was a mistake."

"No. I don't make mistakes."

"You're lucky."

There was only one plate, and he used it when she had done. With swift prehensile fingers he swabbed it clean of fat, using the last chunk of his bread. He threw some wood on the fire, took from the inner pocket of his coat a flat book and fished some pencil stubs out of a waistcoat pocket.

"Put on your hat," he said.

She did so, and he stood off from her and looked at her as though she were wood, and then, his eyes flashing up and down from her to the book, he drew.

Anna looked at the suit of green corduroy, none too clean, the grey flannel shirt—"saves washing," she thought—the battered boots. The face was of a half-starved hawk, piercing of eye, formidable of beak, altogether predatory.

"Let me see it," she said, when he had done. For answer he tore the pages from the book, crumpled them to a ball, and dropped them in the fire. He took from his pocket a packet of cigarettes, tossed her one, and announced: "I'm going for a walk. Turn in when you like."

She was tired to death. She had not known till he was gone how tired she was. She put out the fire with sand, crawled into the tent, and spread the blankets. She uncorded the scarlet suitbag and took out a night-dress, allowing her fingers to play caressingly over its samite texture. She laid it on the blankets, slipped out of her clothes, and sat naked for a moment with the loosed torrent of her hair about her. Then she put on the night-dress and pulled about her the blankets, smiling secretly at their rough avid smell.

She had not intended to sleep. She had intended to wait. But she slept. It was dark when a hand was laid on her shoulder and a voice reached her ears.

"Here, you've got both the blankets."

Nick pressed the trigger of an electric torch. She sat up with the light stabbing painfully her eyes.

"Come on, hand over."

She sat up, dazed, and Nick seized the bottom of a blanket and heaved. He backed out on his knees, shrouded in its folds. She saw the hungry glint of his eyes, the predatory curve of his beak, before the flap fell. He walked, with the blanket trailing behind him, towards a barn in the corner of the field, his eye filled with the round swell of a breast glimpsed through meshing hair.

CHAPTER TWO

WHEN Nick came to the tent in the morning Anna had already lit the fire. Alongside it, the scarlet suitcase was open and she was burning handfuls of its contents.

"That's an expensive way to cook bacon," said Nick, hunched into himself in the thin morning air, unshaved, his eyes cavernous for the sleep that had not come.

"I'm not cooking bacon," said Anna; "and I'm glad to hear there is some. Holy Angels, I'm starving."

"What are you burning the stuff for?" Nick demanded, snuffling a bit in the nose and morose as a sick vulture.

"I'm making room," she said. "That's a damned silly way to cook—on the end of a stick. We'll need a frying-pan. I'll buy it, and I can carry it."

"Thank you very much," said Nick, he hoped with irony.

He crawled into the tent to get his shaving things; and, crawling out again, was confronted by the spectacle of her, back to him, bending over the fire. She was without shoes and stockings, her legs were patined with the golden scales of buttercups' gummed to her skin by the dew of the grass she had swished through. The back of her skirt was pulled half-way up her thighs, and the sunlight showed him blue veins in the dimpled hollows behind her knees.

"It's a long way to get water," Nick said, "but across two fields there's a mere. I suppose you found it."

"You suppose wrong," she said. "I haven't washed."

"Then you'd better come with me."

It was very early and the air was full of birdsong. A lark was tearing his ecstasy to pieces and dropping the tatters. The sun was sucking up the dew from the long white run of a hawthorn hedge, a million tiny alabaster cups, each offering its pinpoint of drink to the flaming thirst.

She was wet to the knees when they reached the mere, still a little smoky with the quiet of the night. There was not wind to shake a hair of the willows that drooped their tresses from the bank. The sun was in the brazen bosses of the kingcups and on the gentle mauve of the cuckoo flowers. The moor-hens squawked and rowed on the water with their webless feet, their red bills jerked forward with each staccato thrust. In the middle of the mere, head coiled on back, a swan slept.

Nick pulled from a pocket a tin mug, dipped it in the water, and took from another pocket a safety razor and soap. He stuck a fragment of mirror at an angle against a tree root, and, stripping off coat and shirt, began to shave, kneeling. He wore no vest.

She could count the ribs below his pallid skin. A mat of black hair gave him a bear's chest. His arms were fleshless and sinewy, small muscles writhing like ivy stems round the thin saplings of his bones.

She watched him frankly for a moment, then turned and passed behind the willows. Her clothes fell to her feet and she considered her body, firm, flexible, hued like faded ivory, and esteemed it more beautiful than his. She tried the water with an arched foot, shivered, with crossed arms clutching her breasts, then slid in with hardly a ripple.

Only when she was embarked did she throw to him a glad cry that shivered the integrity of the morning like a pebble hurled through crystal. He turned and saw her arms thrashing like flails and the wake of her going lighting up in shining silver. Her body gleamed through the translucent commotion, and out in the middle of the mere the swan awoke, seemed on his great webs to stand on the water, his neck stretched in challenge to the sun and his wings extended like doors flung open to the glory of the morning. With diminishing beats of his pinions he subsided, till he was rocking over the broken image of his own majesty.

Nick soused his face and neck and chest in the cold water, rubbed himself down and threw the rag of towel beside her clothes among the willows. Then he strode away, taking a billycan of water with him.

He had roused the dying fire by the time she returned. The water was bubbling, and while he made the tea she toasted a thin rasher of bacon. It was all there was, and she made him eat it; herself ate bread and gulped hot welcome tea. She sat with bare legs crossed beneath her, wearing a skirt

of yellow wool and a green woollen jumper—tight as a
bathing dress, betraying the powerful upthrust of her breasts.
Her hair was down; and when they had done with their
scanty eating she took from her bag a hair-brush, backed with
silver heavy and elaborate, and bringing her hair up over her
head, allowed it to cascade down before the glow of the fire.
So she posed and brushed and brushed, while Nick, sitting
on a log, drew her twenty times.

When she had dried her hair she fixed it as it had been
the day before, and then with provoking ostentation drew
on her stockings.

"Will your father be at the races to-day?"

Anna's dark eyes opened wide. "I remember you," said
Nick, "and you don't remember me. And if your father
knows you spent last night in my tent it's a hell of a hiding
I'll get from him, and you, too. He's a grand little man."

"God rest his soul," said Anna piously. Her hands flickered
a cross upon her breast. "He's been dead this six months.
A kick in the guts from a horse finished him."

"I'm sorry to hear that," said Nick. "I saw him at
Tarporley races a year ago. You were with him, but you were
not with him when we cemented a great friendship in the
village pub at night."

"I went with him to Tarporley for five years," said Anna.
"There never was such a little man with horses. He was no
more than a groom, but he'd have made a grand trainer."

"I was at Tarporley drawing horses," said Nick, "and
there I met him, and we arranged to meet again this day."

"Holy God!" Anna exclaimed. "It's as if his ghost sent
me to keep the appointment."

"Be that as it may," Nick answered with phlegm, "I'll be
sorry not to meet the little man himself."

"Sir John Scriven was his boss," said Anna. "Sir John
trained his own horses. He had only a few, and devil a bit
of training he'd have done without Dad. Dad had a little
cottage all to himself. It was a grand time we had together.
And then Sir John bought that ugly swine that kicked Dad
in the guts. Six months ago."

Nick threw her a cigarette and she lit it with an ember. "What then?" he asked.

"Oh, the greatest kindness all round, I was called up to the house after the funeral, and weren't they grand orations about the old Dad! And old Dad's daughter was to be looked after and come to no want. I began to think I could hear a thousand pounds rattling in the till. And what did it all boil down to but a slavey's cap! No thanks, says I to myself. I'll see the dirty weather through, and then I'll be walking. D'you know these Scrivens?"

"Heard of them," said Nick. "Very ancient."

"Heard of young Toby? The baronet-to-be?"

"Yes. What about him?"

"Never mind him now. What are we going to do to-day?"

"I'm going to the races. You can do what you like."

"I'd like to come with you."

He turned on her with sudden fierceness. "Why the devil did you plant yourself on me?"

"I had nowhere else to go," she said simply. "Nowhere —nowhere at all."

"You had your place. Why couldn't you stay in it?"

"Because I choose my own place—even if it's nowhere at all."

She got up and rammed her sombrero upon her head, reached inside the tent for her tattered raincoat. "I was willing to pay for my lodgings," she said, and angrily snatched up her scarlet suitcase.

Nick sat with his head in his hands, staring at the embers, his fingers awash in the lank cascade of his forelock.

"Well, so long," Anna said jauntily; and then, dropping the bag, came swiftly to his side. "You're crying!"

"I'm lonely," he said.

"And yet you were trying to pack me off!"

He looked at her, and a smile transfigured his face to something she had not guessed. "Yes. What fools we are. I've got nowhere to go to, either. We can at least go there together."

CHAPTER THREE

THE tent was folded up into next to nothing. It and all else that Nick Faunt possessed went into an old army pack. Anna groaned when he slung it on his narrow shoulders. "Glory be to God," she said. "If you are Christian setting off to the Holy City, what a past yours must have been. You see I'm a well-read girl with a neat turn for allegory."

"You've got a hell of a tongue in your head," said Nick, "if that's what you mean. You'll never want for bread."

"I could do with a bit more of it at this moment," she said. "How are we going to get our next meal? I could pawn the hairbrush. I stole it. And we could put the money on a horse."

"Maybe we would," Nick answered, "if we could find a pawnshop in the heart of Cheshire. I'll do some sketches of horses, and maybe I'll sell them. And to-night I'll draw portraits in the pub. It's a grand life being an artist in this happy land."

They slogged it through the pleasant undulating country-side, Nick's shoulders pulled to pieces by the weight of the pack, Anna upright as a pole, swinging her bag with an easy rhythm.

"I had a good look at you when you were shaving this morning," she said. "There's nothing on your bones but skin and hair. You want someone to see that you eat your food."

"I eat my food all right when it's there to eat," Nick answered. "And don't start looking after me. I can look after myself. Let's have a sing."

"I don't know any hymns," said Anna. "Only songs like 'Don't 'ave any more, Mrs. Moore!'"

"That's no good for marching. D'you know 'I'm a hobo?'"

"I do. Open the throttle."

So Nick sang:

"I do love my boss; he's a good friend of mine;
And that's why I'm standing here in the bread-line.

Halleluiah! I'm a hobo.
Halleluiah, amen!
Halleluiah! put your hand down,
Revive us again."

Anna joined in the chorus, and taught Nick many verses
he didn't know. She taught him:

"I went down a lane with a virgo intact-
A, who wrote to the boss and that's why I am sacked."

They roared the words aloud to the outraged countryside,
and Anna said, "There's not a copper in all Cheshire could
run us in for it. It's wonderful to be a woman of superior
education."

They came to a hamlet, a cluster of black-and-white
cottages set behind a duck-pond that edged the road. A
home made bench was beneath a trim window, sparkling to
the sun and enriched with a gleam of narcissi behind the glass.
Anna flung herself down, broken with weariness, upon the
bench and turned her great black eyes, melting with misery,
upon the young woman who stood in the doorway.

"You'd not mind us resting awhile, I'm sure," she said.
"We're walking to Birkenhead, and my husband with hardly
a boot to his foot, but a job at the end of it, blessed be God."

Nick looked at her foolishly, and the young woman looked
at Nick's gaunt face and haggard eyes, and Anna said, "Come
on, dear, rest while you may. It's hard work walking on an
empty belly." She patted the seat beside her.

With charming reticence, the cottage woman withdrew
when she had placed food before them. They drank hot tea
and ate their fill of bread and beef; and on the pond before
them two white ducks scrabbled for food in the mud, pointing their behinds to high heaven.

"I would beg you," said Anna, "to notice that beautiful
attitude of derision. That's how a duck puts his finger to his
nose."

She piled the plates and cups and returned them to the

cottage door. "May God bless you, missus," she said, "and the little one, too, when it comes."

The woman blushed as Anna's piercing eye ran appraisingly over her. "May your time be easy," she said. "Come on, dear, before the roads are full of racing people."

But Nick was slashing away with a pencil, a rippling composition of ducks and water.

"Keep this, madam," he said, when he had done. "Some day it'll be worth more than the cost of a couple of meals. I've signed it."

He joined Anna down the road and, out of sight of the cottage, turned on her with blazing eyes. "What the devil d'you mean?" he raved. "I've never begged in my life, and I don't intend to start now. If you're staying with me, remember this: we earn what we eat."

"There now," said Anna calmly, "it's a grand thing to see you sparking up. That's the beef in your belly, that is. Damn it, man, you've been looking like a corpse resurrected for an autopsy. And take note of that grand word. You never know when a good word'll come in useful."

"To the devil with you and your words," Nick answered. "I can see, so long as you're about, there won't be many words left for me. No more cadging."

They trudged forward in silence through the strengthening warmth of the morning. Motor coaches and motor-cars roared by bound for the races, turning the pleasant road into a cañon misty with choky fumes. The fumes pulled at Nick's throat, and the straps of the rucksack pulled at his shoulders, and soon he sat down amid the tall wayside grass under the delicate green drip of the larches.

"Rest a minute," he said. "Then we'll find a way across the fields. To hell with the highroad on a day like this."

Anna threw herself down at his side; but no sooner was she seated than she had leapt up again, run into the middle of the road, and, with fingers in mouth, emitted a piercing whistle, directed towards a car bearing down upon her. There was a whine of brakes, shouts of death and damnation from the car; and then Anna was on the footboard baring her perfect teeth in a smile that embraced the two men the car contained.

"Begob," cried one of them, "if it ain't the Colleen Bawn! And where have you sprung from now? I haven't heard of you since the old man died."

"I'm tramping the world in search of my fortune," said Anna, "and taking my fancy man along with me. Nick, come and meet the fine gentleman who's going to give us a lift to Tarporley."

"Easy, easy," the fine gentleman answered. "And where the blazes d'you think you're going to find room in this old junk shop? Damn it, we're full up already like a corporation dust cart. Ain't we, Mo?"

Mo croaked in reply like a raven. "Yes. There wasn't no room not even for the extra beer."

"That's a good word, Piggy," said Anna. "I reckon a bottle of beer's just what'd set my old bloke on his feet."

Piggy grinned. "Come on, 'Oly," he said. "I reckon one wouldn't 'urt us."

He ran the car to the grassy verge of the road. "And while you're getting out the beer, Homo, you can take out all the junk," said Anna. "You're a rotten stevedore. I'll pack that myself so's there'll be room for me and my shadow. Ain't he a shadow, Piggy? Don't you think I ought to be ashamed to be seen walking about with such a man?"

Piggy stretched himself, rubbed his hands upon the crimson cummerbund that went like a broad equator round the great sphere of him, and said, "I reckon that if we split the difference we'd make a couple of good men, eh?"

He slapped his stomach with approval, threw a grey bowler to the grass and advanced a flaccid paw to Nick.

"Piggy White," Anna introduced. "Nick Faunt. And the other bloke who's a long time getting the beer is Holy Moses, clerk to the said Piggy White, bookmaker. Sometimes known for short as Homo, but never sapiens."

"What the 'ell's she talking about?" asked Piggy, wiping his broad red brow.

"It's a grand thing to be a cultured woman," answered Anna, "and to insult people in the dead tongues."

"Dead tongues, be damned," said Piggy White. "Your tongue was always as lively as a viper. Well, here's how.

And if you think you can pack yourselves in there, you'd better hurry up about it. I want to get to Tarporley."

Anna was soon embroiled with the cargo that Holy Moses had taken out of the back of the car—two poles with a red banner run between them, a leather satchel, a box, a black-board, a vast umbrella striped broadly in red and white, baskets of food, bottles of beer, binoculars, another box stuffed with books and papers. Holy Moses, thin as a thread, great coffee-coloured eyes still as pools in the white blank of his face, looked on, and now and then croaked a suggestion.

Nick was in, with a case of beer on his feet and a basket between his legs; everything was in except Anna and her scarlet suitcase. She was about to heave it up when a thought struck her. Opening it, she took out the silver brush. "Piggy, here's a bargain for you. How much?"

Piggy, one hand on the wheel, appraised the brush. "Pinched?" he asked.

"I had to get away somehow," said Anna defensively.

"No monogram. Pretty safe," Piggy pondered. "Ten bob."

"Hand over," said Anna. "And, as one Jew to another, I hope the favourite wins every race."

Piggy produced the note. Anna handed it to Holy Moses. "For the kid," she said.

Mo nodded sadly.

"He all right?"

"Yes."

"Good. Away with sadness. Let her go, Piggy."

They were soon in the crawling procession that writhed its way through the village of Tarporley.

"Put us on something good, Piggy," Anna cried. "It's an experience I've longed for all my life—to get a tip from a bookie, lay the bet with him and collect the winnings."

"Shut your face," said Piggy, ungraciously. "Sometimes you're indecent."

Nick and Anna lingered long enough to see Piggy become a landmark. His poles were jammed into the ground, and between them ran the scarlet legend: "Charlie White—Manchester." His black-board went up, and the box from which he preached his gospel went down. The satchel went round his neck, the binoculars went over the satchel, and Holy Moses, cowering in the shade of the mountain, gave some apprehensive attention to his ledger. Piggy swept the broad acres with his glasses, decided, it seemed, that all was well, and descended from his box to await the opening of the day's work. His moment was not yet; but the day's adours were already pressing on many souls. Nick and Anna strolled among them: tipsters who knew the infallible secrets of wealth, but were nevertheless clothed in rags; nigger minstrels strumming on banjos; evangelists shouting, " Jesus is the only dead cert. Back Him, and be safe for eternity." There were little booths full of steaming food and gipsy girls dancing in them; there were frank beggars shuffling along and whining their tale. There were lines of cars wherein the county was eating its caviare and drinking its champagne; and motorcoaches full of riotous towny trippers with lashings of food in paper parcels and bottles of beer. In the little paddock a few horses were being led round, shy and touchy creatures, looking as though they despised the contact of the herd about them.

Over all was the blue sky, and in it were the first swifts that Nick had seen that year; and rising from earth to sky was the glad heartening smell of the crushed grass.

Soon the bellow of the bookies added itself to the gay babel, rose through all other sounds, dominated earth and heaven. Piggy White's good-natured face, distorted beyond even its normally generous rotundity, became a wild and feral thing. The veins swelled in his neck, flesh obscured his small optics; he became a great noise storming its way out of a bloated incarnation. Holy Moses, seeming to shrink and shrink as Piggy swelled and swelled, worked furtively at his ledger, sniff, sniff, sniffing to stay the running of his nose.

Nick walked among the crowds, and the lightning of his fingers struck at his sketch book. Horses, men, dogs, rich and poor, layers and takers, went down before him. He had thrown the rucksack from his shoulders, and, trailing after him, silent now, Anna swung it in one hand and her scarlet suitcase in the other.

"Put 'em down," he said, "and keep still." And he got her on his paper, the sombrero at a raffish angle, the broken feather sagging upon it, the faded waterproof strapped boyishly round her taut waist.

"By God!" he said. "There's not a woman on the course to touch you. I've only just seen you. You make these Rolls-Royce dames look like tarts. You and the horses are the only things worth looking at."

He rested the rucksack on the ground, stuck some sketches to it with pins, and began to shout his wares at sixpence apiece.

"If we can sell four," he said, "we're set up for the day. A bob'll buy some food, and there'll be a bob to put on a horse."

"You haven't signed 'em," said Anna.

"I know," he answered. "That's the snag. But these fools don't know it."

"You seem to fancy yourself. Since when has your autograph been that valuable?"

"Probably since the day after to-morrow," said Nick. "There or thereabouts."

"You haven't pinned me up."

"No, and I'm not going to."

He did not answer. A slim youth paused before the rucksack, a youth smelling of good tweed, bareheaded, crowned with the golden curls of Adonis. His blue eyes darted from drawing to drawing.

"I'll take the lot," he said, and added, "What's the game?"

"No game about it," said Nick doggedly.

"I s'pose you wouldn't like to sign 'em?"

"Why should I?"

"They'll be more valuable."

"How do you know?"

"Damn it, man, I've got eyes in my head. What d'you want to sign 'em?"

Nick thought hard. "A guinea each," he brought out defiantly.

"That's a bit steep. Six guineas instead of three bob."

"It's a gift."

"I'll take one—this one—signed."

He handed Nick a note and a shilling. "And if you want that note to grow," he said, "put it on Roysterer in the three o'clock race. Can't lose. I'm riding him. Sir John Scriven's horse—my father."

Toby Scriven strolled elegantly away. Nick looked round for Anna to shout his luck to her. She was emerging from behind a Daimler. "He gone? 'Struth! What a shave!"

A crowd had gathered round the small flutter in futures; there were offers at sixpence a time, but Nick was not now a seller. He packed the sketches, humped the pack, and set off whistling towards ample beer and sandwiches.

CHAPTER FOUR

I

WITH the rucksack and suitcase on the ground at their feet, they leaned against the rough counter of the feeding booth.

"Did you ever hear of a horse called the Roysterer?" asked Nick, swilling down with a great pull at his beer a mouthful of pork pie.

"Ach, by the saints in glory," said Anna, "if Dad hadn't been kicked in the guts what a horse he'd have made of the Roysterer! Begod, 'tis a horse that can run all day and jump over a street of houses. 'Tis a flyer—a Pegasus."

"Toby Scriven's riding him—told me to back him."

"Do so," said Anna. "He's a dark horse. You'll get fifteen to one, and if he wins you'll break no bookmaker's heart. All the money'll be on Tobermory. Lady, I'll have a port."

"You'll have nothing of the sort," said Nick, "seeing that every shilling we have now may be fifteen shillings in an hour's time. Be satisfied with what you've had and have your port of the Roysterer wins. I've spent my last bean barring that pound."

"Now, Glory be! Isn't it a grand thing to find I've entrusted myself to a thinking man? Come on, then, and lay your bet before they rumble the Roysterer and the price changes."

Nick did, indeed, succeed in laying his bet at fifteen to one; and when he had done so Anna suddenly laid her hand over her heart. "Nick! That ten bob I gave to Holy Moses this morning! I'd never forgive myself if the Roysterer won."

"Put it on, and you'll never forgive me if he loses."

"Ach! Don't be a fool, man. What's ten bob now I've got you?"

"You may find that having me is the very thing that makes ten bob worth sticking to."

"Get away! And you a man with sixteen pounds in his pocket—as good as."

"It won't be there long—if it gets there at all."

"And why not?"

"Because I'm going to spend it—the fat end of it, anyway."

"What on?"

"To do something I've wanted to do for a long time—have an exhibition in Manchester."

"All the more reason why I should have my seven pounds ten. Here goes for Holy Moses."

At that moment the yell "They're off!" told that the two-thirty had begun and liberated Mo from his intensive work on the recording of bets. Piggy White, with binoculars glued to his eyes, was watching the race. Mo, completely un-interested, was sitting mournfully on the box at his master's feet. Anna dropped her suitcase on his toes and he jumped up, but without a word. He looked at her, dog-like.

"Mo, hand over that ten bob. I'm going to have a flutter." He gave her the note, and his fingers were trembling.

"You'll get it back, Homo, if there's anything doing," Anna said, "and perhaps a bit more."

The pools of his eyes seemed as though they sought to suck her down through the dark still mirrors of their surface.

"Please don't give me money," he said.

"Don't be a fool, Mo," Anna exclaimed impatiently.

"We've had that out before. It's not only you; there's your sister to think of."

"No, no," he said. "Rachel won't mind. I will earn enough money. We will look after the child—for you."

"Mo, you're a good old fool, but you know you're talking nonsense. What about when I settle down? I'll want the kid."

"Anna!"

"Oh, struth. Don't look at me like that, man," Anna began, when a crescendo of shouts told that the race was ending, and Piggy White's feet, dancing impatiently in their spats, suggested that the ending looked like doing him no good. And indeed, half a minute later, a swarm of claimants was like bees round a honeypot. Piggy received and tore up tickets, shouted to Moses the amount claimed, and with monotonous regularity Mo answered, "Right," and marked his ledger. Anna slid away.

Nick, sketching the horses as they came off the course, looked up and saw her coming, and was struck anew with the perfection of her form, the thoroughbred ease of her carriage. The green broken feather, flaunting askew in the old sombrero, gave her the look of something queenly indulging in a becoming masquerade. The hat darkened her features, dark already with the disturbing Spanish touch that lies in some Irish faces, and there was a slow, provoking indolence sleeping in the rhythm of her gait.

"Well, lath-and-plaster," she hailed him. "What are you staring at?"

"I was seeing you with nothing on."

"Many happy returns of the day. I see the Roysterer's down to ten to one."

At that price she laid her ten shillings.

"If this comes off," said Nick, "I'm going home. I've been on the road for a fortnight, and it's time I was back at work. We'll be able to take train."

"I'm sorry about that. I was looking forward to the wind on the heath, brother."

"You can take the tent and go."

"I'd rather stay. If you'd let me."

"Thanks for that. You're becoming gracious."

"Stay close around and see if it's contagious."

"You're a queer devil. I can't make you out."

"You don't have to. I'm only asking you to take me in."

"What d'you want out of me?"

"Don't be so grand with your wants, cocky. I give as well as take. I'm a bargain."

"Oh, to hell with you! Come on. They're going to the start."

II

They did not take the train, after all. The evening was well advanced when a motor-coach dropped them, with twenty pounds in their pockets, in the middle of Manchester. It had turned cold, and the arc lamps of Piccadilly diffused a violet luminescence through the aguish air. All around the great open space red trams were crawling slowly, their bells tolling on a rich funeral note. The islands of the mid-road were black with people watching the stately caravels that towered slowly past them and left a wake of shining steel. The pavements seethed and dithered with the anxious rush of thousands whose speed suggested escape from a colossal trap.

Nick with his rucksack on his back, Anna conspicuous with her black hat and green feather and scarlet suitcase, stood still and were jostled. It all glowed on Nick's palate like wine.

"By God, Anna," he said. "It's a grand town to come back to. I could poison anyone who runs Manchester down."

"Ach, that's the grand feeling you've got with a few quid jingling in your pocket," she said. "Wait till you're broke. And don't expect me to stand here gawping like a fool with this bag in my hand much longer. What are we going to do?"

"We're going to eat," said Nick. "Eat like the devil. Eat till we bust. It's a fortnight since I was outside an honest dinner."

"Don't talk, man. For God's sake act. Or the back of

my belly will glue itself to the front. Is it to be the Midland,
or Hill's Tripe Saloon?"

Nick held up his hand to a passing taxi. "It's to be
neither," he said. "Driver, the Stoat, in Hurlingham Street."

They wormed a way out of Piccadilly and shot between
the black facades of Portland Street warehouses, grim and
strong as prisons, silent, at that hour, as the grave. Left they
went into the light and movement of Oxford Street till they
came to the University's inky mass piled against the last of
the sunlight like education's redoubtable Bastille. Then
right they went again into a street of mean houses and mean
shops, and the taxi stopped. The Sahara would have promised
more excellent fare. Windows, none too clean, full of fly-
blown periodicals, cheap toys, soiled packets of cigarettes,
met Anna's dubious eyes. And among all these was one
shop, small as the others, displaying delicatessen in its
windows and flying a signboard on which a stoat was
depicted, elegantly shorn of all feral attributes.

There were half a dozen tables within, and all were
occupied. Behind a counter, piled high with food, was a
vast crop-headed Teuton whom Nick hailed as Adolf. Adolf,
who seemed to exude the goodness of a thousand meals,
extricated himself from his narrow prison and conveyed the
impression which a perfect host can give: that all through
a long and weary day, pestered with superfluous people, he
had waited for this one refreshing moment of personal
service. He shepherded Nick and Anna up a few steps at
the back of the restaurant, leading to a tiny room that was,
as it were, an enclosed dais. There he solicitously relieved
them of pack and bag and deployed before them his startling
erudition in the matter of feeding.

But Nick was all for a hearty filling meal, and Adolf
bowed himself towards the door, charged with the provision
of minestrone and Wiener schnitzel and a bottle of Burgundy.
"And then we'll see," said Nick.

"Sir George Faunt has been in," said Adolf, departing.

"I should have thought the Midland was more in his line,"
said Nick.

Adolf shrugged a shoulder which suggested that it's never

too late to mend. "He has gone on to the Palace," he said.

"He can go to the devil, for all I care," Nick said savagely.

No one else was in the small room. "Sir George?" said Anna.

"Shut up," Nick answered savagely, stabbing with venom at a roll. "There's no money in it."

Anna's eyes blazed at him across the table. "If we were in the street," she said, "I'd land you one in the gob for that. You and your blasted money! What d'you take me for? You looked the sort of bloke to get money out of when I picked you up, didn't you?"

Nick was contrite. "I'm sorry," he said. "Don't mention my family."

"Why not?" said Anna. "You and I have got to talk some day."

"Why?"

"Well, there it is. It's happened. You tell me about your family, and I'll tell you about my kid. You've got to know about that."

"I don't want to know about your kid—not now, anyhow. I'm starving, and thank God here's the soup."

The food brought them to a mellow silence. The Burgundy came with the Wiener schnitzel; and after that they delved into a capacious apple pie. Some Stilton cheese and coffee came along, and excellent brandy. The little restaurant below them had emptied; and they sat on, smoking and enjoying a warm intimacy that kept at bay the thought of the dark street and the dampish air and the question of a night's lodging.

But it had to be faced. "We've got to sleep somewhere to-night," said Anna, stubbing a cigarette in her saucer.

"I'm not going to blue in all my money on hotels," Nick answered. "This meal'll cost enough. We'd better hump the bags and find some rooms. There ought to be plenty. Any of the streets between here and the Infirmary."

"I don't care where it is," said Anna. "But it seems a long time since I crawled out of the tent this morning. I'm as tired as—Holy Mother! Now look at that! Thank God I'm a reading woman and know all about *Trilby*. Otherwise, I shouldn't know where it had sprung from."

It was a young man with the bluest of blue eyes, the silkiest, most corn-coloured of beards. A shapeless black hat flapped upon its head, a vast bow of crimson silk flamed through the fine strands of the beard like a poppy in a corn-field. Hairy tweeds, amorphous as a haystack, enveloped it.

"Glory be to God!" said Anna. "You call yourself an artist! You're only a lousy scarecrow. Look at that, now. There's an artist for you."

Nick grinned. "Ay, there's an artist for you. I know him. His name is Anthony Brown. But for the love of Mike don't call him that. He's living it down." He hailed through the open door of the small room: "Hi! Anton! Come up here, you old devil!"

Anton sprang up the stairs on small agile feet, sweeping off his hat to Anna as he came.—"Nick!" he shouted, and in his round and chubby hand seized the brown twigs of Nick's fingers. "I didn't know you were back." He looked interrogatively at Anna.

"Anna Fitzgerald—Anton Brune," Nick introduced them.

"Model?" asked Anton.

"No," said Anna. "Mistress."

Anton Brune blushed furiously. "Chuck it, Anna," Nick growled. "She's pulling your leg, Anton. Understand, Anna, Anton's a thoroughly respectable young man. Aren't you, Anton?"

"I don't see why an artist shouldn't be," said Anton briefly.

"That's right, that's right," Nick soothed him. "You're a model to us all, Anton. I shouldn't be surprised to find you paying super-tax one of these days. Still working hard?"

"Up to the eyes," said Anton happily. "I've just rushed along from my studio, and I'm going on to the Bassoon Club dance. I can't really afford the time; but a man must relax. Eh?"

"I should think so," said Nick. "You live at a great pace, Anton."

"I do, rather, you know," Anton admitted cheerfully. "But, look here. What about feeding? Have you people fed?"

"We have, and we were just thinking of finding a lodging for the night."

"Oh, you mustn't do that—not yet," Anton protested. "Stay and have a drink, anyway. And what about coming on to the Bassoon Club? Hi, Adolf!" Ineffectively he tried to click his pudgy fingers.

So they sat and drank as Anton Brune picked his way delicately through an elaborate dinner, and the close little room seemed more and more friendly as the wine warmed their throats; and to Nick the thought of lugging a pack out into the grey night, along the clangour of Oxford Street, and up and down its wretched tributaries, became hateful, definitely impossible. To hell with lodgings! They'd sleep somewhere.

"Right-o, Anton," he said. "We'll come on with you. Eh, Anna?"

"A pretty-looking pair of spectacles we are," said Anna. "to go dancing. Begod, it's some old gipsy and his doxy they'll take us for. We'll be chucked out, sure as eggs."

Anton, warmed with a couple of glasses of unaccustomed wine, answered her sharply. "There are two things to be said to that. One is that you go as my guests. That in itself would be sufficient."

"Amply, amply," said Anna, with a gesture that was becoming vague.

"And the other is," went on Anton, ignoring the interruption, "that we will be among artists and those who know what art is. I am not aware, madam, whether you know Nick Faunt well enough to realise what that means. Believe me, he will not have to explain his presence."

"Cheese it, Anton," said Nick briefly. "She knows damn all about me, anyway"

Then Anna was aware of a strange thing. The dapper Anton, clothed like several tiger lilies of the field, well-fed, manicured, elegantly shod, was leaning back in his chair, his eyes swimming with unshed tears as he gazed like an adoring dog at the gaunt face opposite him, at the rusty clothes and the glimpse of hairy chest where a button was missing from the shirt.

CHAPTER FIVE

IT is no great distance from the Stoat Restaurant to the Bassoon Club, but Anton insisted on a taxi.

"You needn't worry, Miss Fitzgerald," he explained, as they dumped in the pack and scarlet suitcase. "It's a free-and-easy hop to-night. Nobody'll be dressed."

A fine rain had begun to fall, putting a cloak of misery upon the bowed shoulders of the city. The façade of the Palace was blurred with light, and Nick put from his mind the thought of his father, comfortable within there, his behind in the most expensive seat, cigar smoke lapping him round.

The taxi switched to the left right under the towering cliff of the Pre-eminent Picture House—a cliff burning with a mighty vulgar opulence that was almost majestical. It was like a man wearing simultaneously the uniforms of a Lord Mayor, a Free Mason and a Field-Marshal.

"A farthing dip," said Nick, "would do to read your Plato or your Shakespeare, Anton, but by the Lord God they set the world alight to lead you to this shambles of tripe and offal."

Anton said nothing. He had a great fondness for the Pre-eminent with its downy seats and its organ that came up out of the depths of the earth, spewed its treacle and retired again like some obscene beast to its cave. He paid the taxi-driver and led the way into a dark entrance where Anna cursed sharply at stubbing her foot on one of a row of dustbins.

"Holy St. Bridget," she said. "And are these the halls of gaiety?"

There was nothing in the cramped hall save those accursed dustbins, the drab beginning of a stone stairway and the lattice gate of a lift.

"I know how to work this," said Anton proudly, swinging the gate open to admit the other two.

The gate clanged behind them, and, looking through its criss-cross bars, through the dank, tiny hall into the rain-

smudged gloomy streeet beyond, Anna thought she had never
met a more unhappy gateway to joy.

The lift shot upward, past several silent floors where life
had been hushed till charwomen should give it a lugubrious
awakening on the morrow, and finally came to rest in the
premises of the Bassoon Club.

The Bassoon Club, existing as a meeting-place for those in
Manchester who practised the arts or were interested in them,
was an eyrie perched over the tumultuous valley of Oxford
Street. Its walls were adorned with the work of its members;
it had a useful little gallery for public exhibitions. One
might pleasantly waste an afternoon playing cards and drinking tea or coffee brought up from the café on the lower floor;
but it had tended to wilt at night, being without the magic
enlivenment of a licence. The recent installation of a cocktail bar had helped to mitigate this reproach and accounted
for the more joyous rhythm of the occasion into which Anton
Brune conducted his guests.

The place was full. Dancing was going forward in the
gallery. The cocktail bar had many sedentary devotees.
They were a mixed crowd—a few journalists, a handful of
textile designers, commercial artists, one or two young and
optimistic people who hoped, God knows how, to wring a
living out of pure art, hangers-on who are to be found wher-
ever a social crowd gathers together.

Everyone seemed to know Nick. He was hailed on all
hands and pressed to drink. But Anton Brune took his arm
and drew him aside. "Presently," he said. "First of all,
Nick, I want you to meet someone. Come on, Miss Fitzgerald, you, too."

"Ach, to the devil with Miss Fitzgerald," she said. "What's
wrong with Anna? It's a girl he's going to introduce us to,
Nick. Can't you always tell? The poor man's all of a dither."

A dance was finishing, and as the couples came trooping
out of the gallery Anton pounced upon a tall young Jewess
and separated her from the man who accompanied her.

"Rachel, this is Nick Faunt—in the flesh at last."

Rachel held out a slim hand. "I could hardly know you
better, Mr. Faunt, if we had met years ago," she said coolly.

B

"Anton has talked so much about you. Are you really a demi-god, or just what you look?"

Nick's brown eyes searched the black pools of hers to discern whether this was ineptitude or insult. Rachel's eyes had almost an oriental slant under their thin arched brows, and in the heart of them was a hard spark of mockery.

Nick accepted her challenge harshly. " Just what I look?" he said. "Let us exchange confidences. Tell me what I look to you, and I will return the compliment."

The mellowness that food and drink had put upon him fell away, and he faced her like a lean and hungry hawk, all beak and glittering eye.

She was defeated. She answered, "I expected so much."

"Sorry Nick disappointed you, my dear," said Anna, emerging from the background. "God knows, 'twould be robbing the rag-and-bone man to take a balloon for him. But me, now—don't you think I'm looking bonny with my green feather and all?"

Rachel's eyes kindled with a recognition that had in it no pleasure.

"You, Anna!" she said. "How on earth do you find yourself here?"

"Ach, that's a long and complicated narration," said Anna. "It'll keep."

"I've known Anna for years—for five years now," Rachel explained. "Perhaps, as you know Anna, Mr. Faunt, you have met my brother?"

"We met him this very day," Anna butted in. "You know, Nick—Holy Mo."

"I prefer his proper name," said Rachel coldly. "Jacob Rosing."

"My God, Rachel, you're very posh all of a sudden," Anna exploded. "Anybody'd think you'd been used to art silk knickers all your life."

Anton's forehead burned a painful red. "Will you give me this dance, Rachel?" he asked, and whisked her swiftly into the gallery.

Nick found two cocktails and steered Anna to an empty settee.

"Tell me about that saucy bitch," he said. He was still fuming.

"And wouldn't you have known all about her already," said Anna, "if you hadn't shut my gob when I wanted to tell you about the kid? This was the way of it. I was a dear confiding child, and I had a baby when I was fourteen. Now, isn't that something to be proud of? Perhaps in the East, where the temperature is higher, it can be done younger. But it's good for the temperate zone. I've sometimes thought to write about it to the *Daily Mail*. You know— 'Is this a record?' But the old Dad was all against publicity. So he looked round for a chance to farm the baby out. That was before we went to Sir John Scriven's. He was a groom at the time in a stable in Shropshire. It was at Ludlow races that he poured his sad story into Piggy White's hairy ear. Piggy had just begun to employ Holy Moses. He and Rachel were getting on the dear knows how up in Cheetham Hill, and Rachel was glad enough to jump at the chance of a quid a week. That's what my curiosity cost the dear old Dad, may God rest his soul."

She crossed herself devoutly, then gulped her cocktail.

"I should have thought the child's father might have done something," said Nick.

"It was a Blackpool holiday," said Anna, "and therefore I doubt if the magistrates would have called it a case. I saw the man but one night, and would not know him again. And I would not let the dirty dog touch Brian with the end of a long pole, let alone with a fistful of money."

"That's a grand sentiment," said Nick, "but it can't have been helpful to your father."

"It was the Dad's sentiment, anyway, as well as mine," Anna answered. "He tanned my backside black and blue, and said he'd give me another if I brought that man within sight of his house."

"Miss Rachel Rosing doesn't look on her beam ends now."

"She does not, and for long enough she's been trying to shift Brian back on to me. But Homo won't hear of it. It's a slave he is to the child. But he's got to part with him, choose how. And won't Miss Rachel be glad. Look at her

now, the stuck-up bitch.   She's got your little dog Anton in
her pocket."

Anton steered Rachel past the settee towards the cocktail
bar.   Her dress murmured furtively by them, and a whiff of
scent remained in her wake.   She held high her long head
with its pale face and secret eyes, and gave no look in their
direction.

"Has that young bloke got any money?" Anna asked.

"He's the only artist I know who has," said Nick.   "He's
a clever, slick little devil and turns his hand to anything.
He'd design a new shirt pattern or the lay-out of an interna-
tional fair all in an hour.   Posters, ladies in cami-knicks, restaurant menu-cards—Anton never turns anything down.
I like him.   He knows his limitations and how to use his
appearance to bluff fools."

"Well, I suppose that's where Rachel's capital comes from.
You've only got to look at her to see she's slick with clothes,
and now she and another Sheeny have opened a tiny dress
shop in Market Street.   You'll see it if you wander round
to-morrow.   All plate glass and chromium plate, with one
dress in the window and ' Arlette ' over the door."

Another partner took Rachel in to dance, and Anton,
looking very red and apologetic, approached with three
cocktails.

Nick held his aloft.   "Well, Anton, here's to Rachel.   May
she and I become better acquainted.   Engaged?"

"No," said Anton.   "Not yet."

"Well, happy days.   Now I'm going to find a bed."

"But where?" cried Anton.   "At this time of night!
Why don't you look after yourself better, Nick?"

"Oh, shut up," Nick answered, yawning and scratching
his tangled hair.   "Anna and I'll lug round till we find somewhere."

"Leave it till the morning," said Anton.   "Use my studio
to-night.   I've got a shake-down there in case I'm working
late."

"Well, that's practical," said Nick, "and a sleep's all I
want.   Suit you, Anna?"

Anna was strapping on her old waterprooof. She straightened her clean, taut figure and grinned at Anton.

"Condonation," she said. "D'you know that grand word?"

"There'll be nothing to condone, my girl," said Nick. "Anton, you're a good old devil."

Anton rushed away to tell Rachel he would be back later. Then the three of them turned out, to find that the rain had stopped and that the sky was a race of ragged cloud. The theatres were all shut. Oxford Street was still and almost empty. The arc lamps lit the long rain-polished perspective of the street which looked, as Manchester does after 11 p.m., as though it had gone to bed early, too tired to put out the lights. In the emptiness of St. Peter's Square a few prostitutes prowled like cats, reluctant to turn home hungry.

Anton's studio was one large room on a top floor in Mosley Street. There was no lift. They went interminably up echoing wooden stairs, Anton leading the way with a pocket torch, whose light flashed burglariously at each landing on clusters of plates bearing names that looked forlorn as names on tombs, names of men long dead and buried and forgotten.

"How much farther?" Anna whispered. "This stillness gives me the willies!"

Anton had no nerves. "One more flight," he said; and there seemed something desecrating in his loud, cheerful voice. He was rattling a key in the lock now; and then they were all three in a barn of a room, lit only by moonlight coming through a big skylight. Anton touched a switch, announced, "Well, here you are. There's a gas-ring and everything for making coffee," and promptly shut the door and rattled away downstairs. The bang of the front door came to them with a hollow reverberation.

Nick looked about him. There was a model's throne, and there was a large screen. There was a camp bed in a corner, with a couple of blankets neatly folded upon it. Nick shoved the screen round the bed, took one blanket, and said: "Turn in. I'll get down to it in the corner." He slung the scarlet suitcase behind the screen.

Anna came to him and put a hand on his shoulder. "Nick," she said.

He looked down at her with a savage wariness in his seamed young face. "Well?"

"Thank you for looking after me to-day. Thank you for putting up with me, Nick."

"All right, Anna. Good-night."

When he heard the camp bed creak under the weight of her he took an old overcoat that was hanging behind the door and spread it on the boards. He used his pack for a pillow, and, throwing off his boots, rolled himself in the blanket without undressing. He could reach the switch from where he lay, but for a moment he left the room lighted and gazed at a half-finished portrait in oils on Anton's easel. It was a slick portrait of Rachel Rosing. "My God!" he murmured sleepily. "What a thing! Poor old Anton."

Then he switched blackness into the room, blackness suffused with a thin silver light from the moon at which he gazed through the skylight. It plunged among the ragged clouds like a haggard swimmer, distraught amid disastrous seas. He heard Anna stir restlessly and sigh on the other side of the screen.

CHAPTER SIX

I

THE trams that hammer their way out of Albert Square run level if they are going south or east or west. But if they are going north they soon begin to climb. They go east as far as Victoria Station, turn left over the railway bridge, and climb the hill to what the posters call the breezy northern suburbs.

You are no sooner over the bridge than Jerusalem lifts up her gates. The eyes that you encounter are the eyes of Leah and Jael and Ruth; the writing on the shop windows is Hebrew. Synagogues and Talmud Torah schools; kosher meat shops; wizened little bearded men with grey goat's eyes and slim olive children with heifers' eyes: these are what you see as the tram storms the oppressive breast of Cheetham Hill.

You have not gone far when the facetious trolley-boy shouts: "Switzerland!" and down the grim street that faces you is the Ice Palace, beyond the monumental mason's yard where Hebrew hopes and lamentations are cut into the white mortuary slabs. The street is called Derby Street, and all the other street names hereabouts are as undeniably Gentile. The Jew has settled upon the land, but he has not made it his own. It is a place of exile.

A little higher up than Derby Street you come to Stacey Street, and because it is higher it permits a grander view of chimneys and smoke stacks, a profounder apprehension of the melancholy of that region stranded upon a hill whose forehead is the target of all the winds that blow from the Cheshire plain, race across Manchester, and drop from their grimy wings the rich deposits of acid soot that eat into Cheetham's vitals.

While Nick Faunt was stirring from uneasy slumber in the studio in Mosley Street, Holy Moses awoke in No. 8 Stacey Street. Those morose, coffee-coloured eyes in his white and uneventful face searched the greyness of the room, picked out the rickety wash-stand, the dressing-table with its cracked mirror, the cane-bottomed chair on which his shabby clothes were spilled pell-mell.

He sat up, leaned right forward towards the foot of the bed, along which ran a cot, and called hoarsely: "Brian! Are you awake, Brian?"

There was no answer, and Mo got out of bed. He was wearing a long white night-shirt that whispered on the tattered linoleum as he padded towards the cot.

Brian was asleep. His face was of a dusky beauty, soft and bloomy as a dark grape. Dark curls were tangled on his forehead, and he wore the deceptive air of holiness and fragility that visits a sleeping child and twists the sensitive watching heart with premonition.

Such premonition smote Holy Moses. He bent down and gathered the child swiftly into his arms. He bore him to his bed and lay there clutching him to his heart. Brian opened his eyes, smiled, and slept again deeply as though drugged, nestling tight to Mo's side. The man stayed fiercely awake, protective, as the light strengthened in the dingy room.

"They shan't take you. They shan't take you!" he muttered. "Oh, Brian!   We'll have grand times some day!"

II

It had been late—very late—when Mo got home the night before. Tarporley Races had been profitable for Piggy White, and Piggy was inclined to jubilate. Jubilation detained him and Homo for a time at Tarporley, but they were back in Manchester by eight o'clock. Piggy garaged his car in Whitworth Street, and led Moses to the grill-room near by in which he was accustomed to expand when things were well with him.

In a cushioned nook near the welcome warmth of the grill they watched the steak sputtering on the coals; and Piggy, with his thumbs in his waistcoat armholes, spread his broad nostrils with the ripe appreciation of an Inquisitor snuffing the candent fat of heresy.

Steak and onions and lashings of chipped potatoes, with a pint of ale in a can—that was what Piggy called a meal; and with a napkin tucked by two corners into his cummerbund and hanging with the coyness of a Masonic apron, he got down to it. He ate his way through it with smacking relish, while Moses accompanied him with a mouse-like persistent nibbling.

Piggy mopped up residual gravy with a piece of bread, pushed back his plate with a satisfied "Theer!" took a quill toothpick from his pocket and a pair of old-fashioned pince-nez from their case. With these compressing his nostrils, he explored his teeth with one hand and with the other shook out the pages of the *Manchester Evening News*. He ran his eye over the front page advertisements.

"'Arlette et Cie,'" he read. "That's Rachel's show, isn't it, Moses?"

Mo nodded. "Wot the 'ell does et see mean?"

"French—and company," Moses explained.

"Gettin' a bit set up like, ain't she—our Rachel?"

"More than I like," said Moses.

"Ay, gettin' a bit above 'erself is that lass. Last Sat'day night I was at the Ice Palace. Not skating. No, sir, spectating. You can see as good a bit o' leg at the Ice Palace as anywhere in Manchester. As good as a Cochran show, an' a darned sight cheaper. An' there was Miss Rachel as large as they make 'em. Blue velvet, with fur round the hem and making a little V down to the doo-dahs. Swinging a leg with the best of 'em, too. She did a waltz with a ruddy little rabbit all dressed up like an artist. Wot-O!"

Mo's face was moon-like and melancholy. He did not answer.

"I tell you what, Moses me lad: it'll be Didsbury for her soon, where all the good Yids go to. Cheetham 'Ill won't 'old Rachel much longer. 'Ow d'you manage about the Colleen's kid now you're both away most days?"

"We have an old woman in."

"Makes it come a bit expensive, don't it? I reckon that don't leave you much change out of what the Colleen can afford."

Piggy became aware of a strange intensity in the brown eyes directed upon him out of Mo's impassive face. They looked like news of murder on a page of domestic trifles. He threw down the paper and snatched off his glasses. "Oh, well, you're a funny old sod, Mo. But no woman's worth it. Look at me! Free as the bloomin' air. Come on. Billy Bennett's at the 'Ippodrome. We'll pop in to the second 'ouse."

They did; and they met a reporter with whom Piggy had had business relations, and as the reporter had no intention of going home, they accompanied him to the Press Club, where Piggy was commanded to "tickle the ivories." He obeyed, and his songs became bawdier and bawdier as the circle joining in the chorus became bigger and bigger. They kept him well oiled, and his good humour swelled like a balloon till he felt ready to ascend to unimagined heights of scandalous improvisation.

Holy Moses did not ascend with him. Beer made him

more melancholy than was his wont; and he was glad when
Piggy White drained a final can and insisted, for no apparent
reason, on forming a circle and singing, "For old time's
sake, let us forget and forgive." Even Piggy's humour had
passed the zenith. The balloon had burst; he was rapidly
tumbling towards earthly, lacrymose sentiments. As he sang
"Let not your enmity live," there were oily tears in his eyes,
and he took Moses by the arm and repeated, "Let not y'r
enmity live. Go-see Rachel."

Moses protested that he could get home alone, that it was
almost as far to the garage where Piggy's car was parked as
it was to Stacey Street. "Soon gerover that," said Piggy. He
hailed a taxi and drove to the garage; and at 1 a.m. was
erratically bearing along Corporation Street towards Cheetham Hill.

He was a chameleon in drink, and now, to the song of the
wheel, re-discovered his mirth and melody. Corporation
Street became the Road to Mandalay; but the flying fishes
were tricky on the tongue, and he returned hilariously again
and again to their conquest.

When they had crossed the railway bridge he began to
bawl, "Sweeping through the gates of the New Jerusalem,"
and then he saw the taxi ahead, and accelerated. But the
taxi-driver, a prideful fellow, would not give place. He saw
it was a chase, and accelerated, too. Piggy hung to his back
tyre yelling, "Ten to one the field! Ten to one bar one!
Come *ahn*, Steve!" and honking violently.

Mo was sickened of the whole business. "Steady, Piggy,"
he shouted. "Next turning left is Stacey Street."

The two cars took the turning together. The taxi stopped
with a jerk at No. 8. Piggy, by miraculous intervention, did
no more than buckle its number plate and twist his own
front mud-guards. Rachel, helped from the taxi by Anton
Brune, caught one glimpse of Piggy White and fled up the
garden path, shouting good-night to her escort. Moses, too,
did not assist at the conversations which were now opening
between Piggy, Anton and the taxi-driver. He followed
Rachel, and got his foot over the doorstep in time to prevent
the door from banging in his face.

III

Confidingly as though the Everlasting Arms were about him Brian slept; but the rock in whom he trusted trembled.

Moses sweated with apprehension, thinking of last night's scene. Rachel had said nothing. By the time he had got inside the door she had turned up the point of gas that was burning in the passage and was half-way upstairs, her velvet cloak clutched tight about her, her silken ankles seeming to spurn the threadbare carpet, held in its place by old-fashioned thin brass rods.

A light glimmered under the kitchen door, speaking of the vigil of Mrs. Moss, who came in "by the day." It was half-past one. Like her ancestors on the first Passover day, Mrs. Moss was dressed for a journey. She had been so dressed since 11 p.m., which she considered the reasonable limit of servitude. Wearing a coat of shabby black, with her hat on her head and her umbrella on the table, she had passed from simmering annoyance to boiling indignation. Moses had not time to reach the kitchen door before Mrs. Moss was through it. "If it hadn't been for the child upstairs——" was all her wrath permitted her to say. The bang of the front door, she hoped, underlined it.

Moses sighed, hung his well-worn overcoat on the rack that was pushed against the varnished wallpaper of the passage, turned out the gas and made his way upstairs to the shabby, stuffy room he shared with Brian. The reckoning with Rachel, he knew, was postponed, not abandoned; and he had no doubt that Brian would be involved in it. Rachel had had enough of Brian—that was clear; the sooner Brian went the better Rachel would be pleased. And now, like a fool, he had given her an opening she was not the one to miss.

The cheap tin clock on the dressing-table pointed to seven o'clock when the door was shoved unceremoniously open and Rachel, holding a dressing-gown about her, looked into the room.

"I hope you'll be down to breakfast for once," she said.

"I'm generally out of the house before you've started your breakfast," Mo retorted.

"Yes, always before or after. Try and make it the same time to-day. I want to talk to you."

Mo grunted, "All right."

"I hate seeing that child in bed with you," said Rachel, and, waiting for no reply, she disappeared.

She was as slick and self-possessed as a mannequin when they sat down to breakfast, marvellously different from Moses, who had stayed in bed till the last minute and now appeared with his feet thrust into carpet slippers, his trousers hauled on over his night-shirt, and a dressing-gown that had begun as shoddy and was now shameful.

"When is Brian's birthday?" Rachel began, as though she had thought out her opening gambit.

"In a month's time."

"And then he'll be five. I suppose you've made all the necessary arrangements for him to go to school?"

Mo stared at her blankly.

"You know, don't you, that children have to go to school at five?"

Moses gulped the coffee that Rachel made so excellently. "I'll see about it," he said.

"You'll see about it! Don't you think it's time that girl began to see about her own baby? What are we getting out of it? We haven't had five shillings a week out of her since her father died."

"She gave me a pound yesterday. I met her at Tarporley."

"So I understand. I met her myself in the evening with her fancy man."

Mo's eyes smouldered, but he said nothing.

"And did you ever see such a creature!" Rachel went on. "Green corduroys, no tie, dirty as a dustman and as starved-looking as a dog in the gutter. Another charming addition to our circle of friends. Anna herself told Anton she was his mistress."

"And Anton was fool enough to believe her. Look here, Rachel, you know Anna as well as I do, and you know she talks the first nonsense that comes into her head."

"They spent the night together in Anton's studio, you may be pleased to know."

"Not so pleased as you are to tell me."

"I'd be pleased to tell you anything that'd make you finish with that whole gang. Jacob—my dear—what's the good of it? I want something better—for you as well as myself. Last night—I was ashamed—I ran in so that Anton shouldn't see I knew that awful man Piggy White. Didn't you feel ashamed, too?"

Mo hung his head. "Yes," he said at last. "Piggy's always doing things that make me ashamed, but I like him. He's kind and generous. And Anna does things that make me ashamed, but I love her. And you do things that make me ashamed when you try to take me away from all I've always known and grown up with—all these dirty old ugly houses and broken-down people, and Piggy and Anna. But I love you, Rachel. And I love Brian. He's the only thing that never makes me ashamed. And I won't let him go."

Tears swam up to Rachel's great dark eyes. "Jacob," she said, "you're good. You're better than I am. But I think a person who is not very good might help one who is very good indeed. I want to help you, Jacob. People put on you. I want us both to go right out of this place. Give up Piggy White. You can find another job. And let Brian go back to Anna."

Mo was touched. He was not used to being pleaded with. He admired his sister; her efficiency, her business instinct that for a year now had been fighting to the top, her command of herself, her resource in handling her personality. He was dazzled by the new Rachel that had lately risen out of that shabby little Jewess, his sister. She could help him; she *would* help him, he knew—to the last penny. But he knew deep in his heart that it would be on her own terms.

"I like Piggy," he said doggedly. "I like going about with him and seeing the horses and the people and smelling the trampled grass. And I like coming back here, crossing the bridge in the tram and being in Cheetham Hill again. It's kind to me and familiar. Like this old dressing-gown."

"It's a disgusting dressing-gown," said Rachel, rising from

the table. "It's shabby and full of grease. It belongs to all
the things I hate, all the things I've done with for ever and
ever. I've had enough. I'm finished—finished! Do you
hear?"

Mo sat hunched in his chair, his fingers crumbling a pill
of bread. Rachel turned to him from the door, lithe and
angry as a tormented panther. "Did you hear what I said?"
she demanded.

"Yes. I'm sorry," he mumbled.

"You're sorry! There's no need to be sorry. What is
there to be sorry about? Just shake yourself out of this and
come away. I'll keep you till you get a job."

He shook his head.

"Very well. I hope you understand what I mean. I'm
not coming back here. Never again. Last night finished
me. I packed everything. My trunk will be called for
to-day. I shall write to Mrs. Moss and settle with her. If
you stay, it's on your own responsibility. I shall not pay
another penny towards keeping this house or keeping that
woman's child."

"Do you want to say good-bye to Brian? Shall I fetch
him down?"

"No!"

"Very well. I must see to his breakfast now. I shall have
to make some arrangements. . . . I don't quite know. . . ."

He remained at the table till he heard the front door
bang. Then he rushed upstairs and from the bedroom window
followed her tall proud figure with swimming eyes till she
turned out of sight into Cheetham Hill Road. He went
downstairs, boiled an egg and warmed some milk, and brought
Brian down to breakfast.

CHAPTER SEVEN

I

ANNA awoke, feeling chilled to the bone. She huddled on her
clothes and found the cupboard in which Anton kept his

coffee. She found some biscuits and condensed milk, too, and soon had a meagre breakfast ready.

Nick was still sleeping, looking like a death's head, she thought, as she stood above him with her teeth chattering and listened to the hollow rumbling of early trams in Mosley Street. She could hear charwomen, too, moving about the stairs, and managed to grin at the thought of their surprise if Anton's studio were on their round. But it was not. She and Nick had their coffee in peace, warming themselves at Anton's electric radiator.

Nick had got up in a sullen mood. He had spoken no word more than was necessary. He asked her for a cigarette, and she had none. He cursed and began pulling out drawers here and there. He was prepared to interpret Anton's hospitality in the widest sense. But there were no cigarettes.

He prowled about the studio, examining pencils, brushes, paint, with a pointless, idle busyness. He looked at the portrait on the easel and laughed cynically. He got on Anna's nerves. Dirty-looking coot, she thought, with his ravaged unshaved face and uncombed hair. She was a cheerful creature and felt that a very little of this would be enough. He was acting as though she did not exist, and she liked to exist emphatically.

He took the canvas off the easel and put its face to the wall. He found a new canvas and set it up and began to fiddle with oils and brushes. His eye took on lustre, and fumbling in his pocket he found an empty cigarette carton, flung it from him in disgust and cursed again.

" I'll go out and see if I can get some fags," she said.

He did not answer, but threw her a shilling as though she were dirt. She picked it up and flung it, hitting him on the back of the head. He took no notice of that and started whistling.

It was not yet eight o'clock when she came back, but she had found some cigarettes. She placed a hundred box grandly on the table, opened them and looked at the canvas.

Nick's coat was off, his sleeves were rolled up, and the canvas was already blurred with marks meaningless to her. He lit a cigarette without a word, and Anna took one, too.

"Don't light that," he commanded. "Take your clothes off—all of them."

"Glory be to God!" she said. "And is this an Eastern slavemarket?"

"Hurry up, you fool," he said, throwing a hand through his hair. "Anton will be here by nine."

She did not answer, but slipped behind the screen. "As a precaution," she said when she emerged, "'twould be an ill beginning to one of the Lord's own days to make the charwomen envious," and shot the bolt in the door.

Nick took hold of her as though she had been a dressmaker's dummy, and urged her towards the throne. "Arms up—right up. Like that." He propped them aloft and ran back to the easel. "D'you remember swimming yesterday morning?" he asked breathlessly.

"Yes."

"Well, remember it hard. Don't be here, for God's sake, in this mangy hole. Be there. The light's just coming. You're on the edge of the lake; you throw your arms up like that. In wonder. You're marvelling at it. It's such a glorious day. Don't look at me. Don't think about me. Get something else into your face. Think about Brian. Think of having him back. You're going to have him back to-day. Isn't that glorious?"

He mesmerised an ecstasy into her countenance, and as he talked he worked. He lit cigarette after cigarette, and was remorseless with her. "To-day! To-day!" he yelled. "Shout Halleluiah for getting Brian home to-day!"

She became tired, terribly tired; but for a long time she kept it up. Then she said faintly, "Nick!"

He gestured to her furiously to be still.

"Nick! There's blood—blood coming out of your mouth."

He wiped the back of his hand across his mouth, examined it, and rubbed it contemptuously on the seat of his trousers. He cursed, and worked again.

"Now dress," he shouted at last; and, feeling worn to a rag, Anna crept behind the screen. She was amazed at what he had imperiously taken out of her fit young body.

When she came out, dressed, he threw down his brushes and sat exhausted in a chair. She looked at the canvas with the intense curiosity of the uninitiated.

"Begod," she said. "And d'you call that me?"

"Oh, I didn't want you in particular. Any strapping wench would do."

"And is that all you ever want a strapping wench for?"

He did not answer. He had risen and was making a dab here and there at the canvas. He stood back, looking at it: the woman, the swan, the opalescent light filtering down from sky to water.

"Good enough," he said. "We'll finish that sometime."

Then he scribbled on a piece of paper: "Anton—Don't touch this or you'll damn well be shot.—Nick Faunt." He stuck it alongside the canvas.

At that moment Anton came in. "Good-morning. Sleep well?" he shouted cheerfully. Then he took in the evidences of work done: the canvas, the messed palette, the dirty brushes. He cocked his head on one side before the easel.

"Lummy, Nick. That's a good 'un."

"It is, my boy. I'll leave it here awhile for you to study. Come on, Anna. We'll go and find a real breakfast."

"You might have washed the brushes," said Anton ruefully.

Nick slapped him jovially on the shoulder. "That's all right, Anton. That's a job you *can* do as well as I can."

II

Not twenty paces from where they came out into the street there is a Lyons tea shop. Not many people were in it at that time of day, and they settled down luxuriously to fried eggs and bacon, with toast and a pot of tea.

"It's wonderful," said Anna, filling Nick's cup. "It's wonderful the way the Almighty has led me this last couple of days. Who would have thought two days ago that I would be under the patronage of a famous artist? And what are you going to do with me now? You said I'd be having Brian home to-day. Where is home going to be?"

"For God's sake don't take any notice of what I say when I'm in that state," Nick answered. "I say anything."

"Didn't you mean, then, what you said about Brian?"

He gulped down a cup of tea and drew his brows into a hard frown.

"You look as if you're going to be sick," said Anna. "Well, don't be sick on my account. I can walk out on you as easy as I walked in. After your professional examination this morning you must admit that I'm not without resources."

She said it lightly, flippantly, but he sensed the under-thought of bitterness. He rarely looked at her, but now he gave her one of his hawk's swift glances. "Would you walk out as easily as you walked in?" he asked.

"No," she said with a child's candour. "I've taken a fancy to you. God knows why. Look in that mirror."

The room was furnished in good Lyonese style with count-less mirrors. They caught and echoed and re-echoed Nick's pathetic, pitiless face. The night's restlessness had left him haggard as a spectre, unkempt as a scarecrow.

"You want someone to look after you," said Anna. "But I'm not going to apply for the job. It's not that. It's just that there's no bunk about you. I like you."

His eye flickered back from the contemplation of his own gruesome image and pierced her again. "All right, Anna. We hang together. Understand, I don't want a woman. I want a friend. I'm damnably lonely. You'll probably have a hell of a time."

"I'll chance it," she said. "And now, for the love of Mike, go and get a shave."

"Be back here in half an hour." Nick instructed her when they were outside the tea-shop. "There's something I want to do." And off he went to find a barber's.

Anna strode away in the opposite direction. For a day and a night they had not been for a moment out of one another's company. A day and a night! It seemed to her an infinity of time, and a grand time at that. A little choke of loneliness came into her throat now that he was gone. What if he should not return? The thought panicked her for a moment, and her heart gave a sickening turn over.

But she got hold of herself again. He would come back all right. She felt sure she had him weighed up. No bunk!

So with her sombrero rakishly tilted, the green broken feather more dissolute-looking than ever, her hands thrust into the pockets of her faded raincoat, Anna strutted through the blue-and-white morning. Manchester wasn't so bad to-day. Clouds were bowling across the narrow sky-line over Mosley Street and St. Peter's Cross stood out white and fair. The steelwork of the new library was etched in intricate tracery against the blue, a vast web in which men were entangled here and there like flies fatally meshed. Through a gap in the boarding she looked down into the great hole out of which the building was rising, and whistled jauntily. It was grand to look at. Men wheeling barrows, men running up ladders, men clambering about the web, walking like tightrope experts across precarious gulfs; cranes grunting and lifting and moving their tall fingers in wide arcs upon the sky; shrill whistles of command, brisk rattle of hammer on steel and slither of chains upon pulleys. All grand to look at in the blue-and-white morning.

The tilt of the wide sombrero prevented her seeing the man who stood at her side, looking down into the hole. She sensed his restlessness and shifted a pace farther away at the perhaps not accidental light touching of his knee against hers.

"A busy sight," he said. It was a pleasant voice.

"It is so," she answered, keeping her face concealed.

He shifted to her side again. "It fascinates me," he said. "I always have to stop and look when I'm passing."

She saw his hands, gloved in suede, joined on the handle of the rolled umbrella on which he leaned. She saw the perfect crease of a trouser leg, falling upon a shapely shoe. Slowly she brought her face round and looked at him. She was a connoisseur and saw what he wanted. His frankly appraising glances were not difficult to decode. More than middle-aged, perfectly dressed, the dandy coming out in the carnation at his button-hole. He had on a light-grey spring overcoat, and a good grey felt hat rested on his well-brushed hair. His face had once been handsome. It was now florid, a little too fat, and the blue eyes were a little too bright and

protuberant. He raised his hat. His hair was almost white.
Anna placed him instantaneously: an elderly rake. He was
not so sure of Anna. Accessible? Possibly. Probably.

He flung up his left arm to consult a wrist-watch. "Coffee-
time," he said in his pleasant voice. "Liar," thought Anna.
"Not for an hour."

She gave him a smile that showed her pretty teeth.
"Hardly," she said.

"Then might we meet—in an hour's time—in the Midland
Winter Garden?"

"Is there any reason why we should?"

"I find you an excellent reason."

He smiled, and she could not help liking his smile, and his
voice, clear of Northern harshness. He tapped his toe
meditatively with the point of his umbrella, awaiting her
reply.

"Sorry," she said. "Can't be done."

"Meeting someone?"

"Yes."

"Some other time, perhaps?"

"Begod, man, aren't you persistent! No. You be a good
boy, now, or you'll be getting your wife on your track. No
ill-wishes, or anything of that, but just toddle off. Nothing
doing."

He accepted his dismissal with equanimity, raised his hat
and departed, smiling. She watched him with a smile on her
own lips till he had rounded the corner of the hoarding and
faded out towards Peter Street. With the ghost of the smile
lingering in her eyes, she ran back to join Nick.

III

"D'you know what that place is?" Nick asked, pointing
across the road from where he stood outside the tea-shop.

"Is it a Hottentot you think I am, then, and not able to
read my own language? Doesn't the board tell you as large
as life that 'tis the Art Gallery? You're looking better," she

said, stroking his chin. "Your face is as smooth as a baby's bottom. You look less like a hyena."

"Thanks," he said sourly. "I'd rather look like a hyena than a bottom."

They crossed the road and went up to the pillared portico of Barry's lovely little building. Even the brightness of the spring morning could not relieve its becoming gloom. It was as black as a building cut out of ebony. A bill on the notice-board announced that the spring exhibition of the Manchester Academy was housed within.

At the turn of the stair a niched nude lady in white marble had achieved a modest disposition of her hands. "If she feels like that about it," said Anna, for the hall porter's edification, "she ought to keep on her knickers."

They clicked through the turnstiles into a room hung with water-colour, woodcuts, the miscellaneous trivia of art. Nick, without a glance at any of it, hurried through to the main gallery. One look showed him what he wanted to know.

"My God! Look, Anna, a red spot!"

He took her arm in a grip that made her wince and hurried her to the end wall. He halted her before an oil—race horses laid out hell for leather with the jockeys bobbing on them like coloured balloons and the course having the rich illusion of reeling away sickeningly beneath the flying hooves. On the right-hand bottom corner of it was a red spot, and over the spot Anna read the name "Faunt." Just that, arrogant and sufficient.

"What's that mean—the red spot?" she asked.

"Sold! And the price was fifty guineas! We'll set up house like ruddy princes!"

He waited to see no more, but rushed her downstairs again to the curator's office. "Who bought that damned picture of mine?" he shouted, flushed with excitement.

The curator shook his hand and gave him congratulations. "I'm afraid we ourselves are responsible," he said. "It's been bought for the city by the Art Gallery Committee."

The cosy office, with its bright fire and almost religious decorum, the bland, smiling curator, with his spectacles and art-shade tie, all wavered before Nick's eyes like a sand dune from which the heat visibly ripples. He pushed his hand through his hair, and all was clear again.

"Come on, Anna," he said, and took her hand. They stole out quietly together, like children leaving Sunday School.

CHAPTER EIGHT

I

Go along Oxford Street till you come to the Church of the Holy Name. Turn right or left anywhere thereabouts and you are in the region of the theatrical "digs." Pass into almost any one of these small grey houses, jammed together in rows, with doors shut like grim lips, curtains drawn like lids over eyes that keep a watchful slit, with something furtive about them all, and you will find them littered like caravan-serais with the relics of endless pilgrimage. Photographs inscribed to "Ma" in large illiterate scrawls adorn the mantel-pieces and testimonials hang upon the walls. Photographs, yellow and blotched, of boys and girls who are dust; photographs of boys and girls who are now "stars" and stay at the Midland; photographs of the latest draft in the everlasting conscription of the disillusioned and damned.

To this region, where at midnight that aphrodisiac entity the chorus becomes discrète beings concerned with porter and kippers, Nick led Anna. Amhurst Street is under the very shadow of the Holy Name, and at the end of Amhurst Street there is a joiner's yard and workshop. Nick pushed open the double doors of the yard and yelled: "Carless!"

The buzz of a circular saw faded out in the workshop, and Carless, wearing overalls powdered with sawdust, came out into the yard. He blew at a large moustache that curtained his lips, ejecting sawdust from that, too, and made towards Anna a fumbling motion with his cap, in one side of which was stuck a flat carpenter's pencil, in the other a cigarette. Each leg of Carless's overalls was patched with a pocket slap in the front, and from the pockets protruded a two-foot

rule, a square, pliers, pincers, screw-driver, and other items
that made the apparatus of his calling.

Carless took the cigarette from beneath his cap and lit it.
Nick introduced him as "the man who makes my frames."

"And is it frames to-day, sir?" asked Carless.

"No, it's not," said Nick. "I've made up my mind about
that loft."

"I knew you'd come to it sooner or later," Carless grinned.
"It'll make as comfortable a little 'ome as you'll meet in a
day's march."

"I'm going to settle down," said Nick, "with wife and
child, and the sooner we can get it ready the better."

Carless opened his eyes. "Didn't know you were married,"
he said. "I thought it was a bachelor 'ome you were after.
It mightn't be so convenient for a lady and a child."

"Oh, damn it, it's convenient enough," Nick answered.
"You've got a closet in the yard and a tap. What more do
we want? There's no difficulty about running up and down
a stairway. Can we have a look at it?"

Carless led up the outside wooden stairway that went from
the yard to the loft over the workshop. "Time was," he
grumbled, blowing his moustache away from his lips, "when
all this loft was stuffed with timber. And two assistants
down in the shop. But now—nothink—absolutely nix.
Single'-anded, and, even so, 'ardly enough work to fill my
time."

"Well," said Nick, "ten bob a week'll do you no harm,
and that's what I'll pay you."

Carless removed his cap and scratched vigorously in the
tow of his hair. "A quid I was thinking of," he said.

"Well, you can think that again," Nick answered, "when
Pierpoint Morgan is looking for a quaint old Lancashire flat.
In the meantime, you'd better leave me and my wife to look
over the place."

When the buzz of the saw told that Carless was back at
work, Anna clapped her hands with delight. "Begod," she
said, "it's like the lady of the manor I'm feeling already.
You with fifty quid for a picture, to say nothing of what the
good God sent us at Tarporley yesterday, and this palatial

modern residence thrown in. Snap it up, man, before the
news of it gets round."

"Hold your gab," said Nick, "and give me time to think."

The loft was brick-walled and the roofing slates were
exposed. "All that wants," Nick said, "is whitewash—walls
and ceiling. The floor's good. We can scrub it and stain it
ourselves and shove down a few rugs. There's a hole in that
wall for a stove-pipe to go through. We'll have to buy a
stove. Electric light's in. We can get a shade from
Woolworth's."

Anna paced the floor, listening delighted. Fourteen paces
either way she found she could give. "In that corner," Nick
went on, "I'll get Carless to shove up a light screen of wood.
Ten foot each way will do, and it needn't be more than six
or seven feet high. Cheap three-ply. We'll paint it green.
That'll make a bedroom for you and Brian. I can sleep out
here on one of those sofa things that open out. And isn't
that window made for me? Six foot high and dead north."

"Ay, it'll all be grand," said Anna, "as a first step to a
Rolls-Royce and a butler. Didn't you paint me in less than
an hour this morning, and don't you get fifty guineas for a
picture? Holy Mother of God, if you do an eight hour day
for a month we're made!"

Nick split the difference with Carless. Fifteen shillings
a week was agreed on, and Carless promised to have the walls
and ceiling whitewashed without delay.

"And now," said Nick, "we'll toast the city fathers who
bought the picture. Blast and bless 'em."

"And then," said Anna, "we'd better go and see Brian."

They took a tram to the Royal Exchange and crossed the
road into the Shambles, the last coherent fragment of the
Manchester that crouched humbly at the foot of t'Owd Church,
perched on its sandstone bluff above the Irwell. The Old
Church has become the new cathedral; the Irwell that was a
bright sword is rusted and corrupt; but the Shambles remains,
ancient and evocative.

Nick pushed open the brass-bound swing-doors of Simpson's
and led Anna upstairs to the old room that slants like a ship's
cabin in a beam sea. "Anna," he said, "you don't know yet

what you've let yourself in for. You'll probably be starving
in a month, so go ahead now and order the meal of your life.
You can leave the drinks to me."

II

At nine o'clock that morning Holy Moses and Brian Fitzgerald were busy at the kitchen sink. Moses was washing
the breakfast things, Brian standing on a box, was drying
them with grave concentrated thoroughness.

It would, Moses thought, be a useful gesture to greet Mrs.
Moss with the news that the first of her morning's jobs was
done. He was going to need Mrs. Moss as he had never
needed her before. He did not doubt that Rachel meant
what she had said down to the last word: Stacey Street would
not see her again. The problem of the child had to be
approached altogether anew. He did not think that Anna
would take him away. Anna was always talking like that,
and nothing ever came of it. What was to be done he could
not think. He was not practical like Rachel. He would have
a long talk with Mrs. Moss, let her wisdom produce a suggestion. It would have to produce one quickly, for to-
morrow was a working day and he would have to be out of
the house by seven in the morning.

Mrs. Moss, he hoped, would arrive in a good humour and
find him in the full spate of his useful activity. She was due
at nine. She had not come at half-past nine. At ten came
a note, dropped furtively through the letter-box, to say that
she would not be coming at all. She had had enough. Last
night had finished her. She would look in one of these days
for her wages. Yours truly.

A feeling of panic took hold of Moses. There was no one
he could turn to. In that grey place of the exile of his people
he was an exile even from them. He and Rachel had never
been practitioners of their religion. She, he knew, hated
more and more the thought that she was a Jewess. It was not
that with Moses. He was by nature a solitary, but he loved
his solitude to be in that crowded place peopled with the

faces of his kind. She for her reasons, he for his, had remained aloof, and now even she was gone.

A wild thought began to possess Moses that it would be a grand thing if he and Piggy White could take Brian about with them. The fresh air would do him good; he would love the horses. Then he thought of Piggy's temper on days when too many winners had been favourites, and he decided that it would not do.

Brian was at the window, catching what glimpse he could of the great white clouds sailing like galleons across the blue.

"Uncle Mo, let's go to Heaton Park," he shouted.

"We must make the beds first," said Moses. "Mrs. Moss isn't coming, and Auntie Rachel is gone away. Perhaps she won't come back at all."

"Good. Much better to be just me and you."

"No, no, Brian. Auntie Rachel's been very kind to you."

"Auntie Rachel hates me," Brian asserted stoutly. "I'd rather Auntie Mummy." So he had learned to call the infrequent Anna whom he knew but as a talkative visitor who laughed a lot.

Between Moses and Brian there was a grave, adult understanding, and they worked methodically at the bed-making as grave adults should. They did not talk much. Mo rarely talked to anybody. Particularly he did not want to talk now. He wanted to think about this problem so cruelly and suddenly thrust upon him, though he himself realised that the mere process of turning the matter round and round which was going on in his head did not amount to thinking at all. But he addressed himself fatalistically to the work of the day, hoping that if he went forward as though there were no problem at all, the problem would, somehow, solve itself.

So, when the beds had been made, he and Brian did such cleaning as rather promiscuously suggested itself to Mo's mind; and then he cut some bread and butter, slapped it into a paper bag, and put some apples in his pocket. "Now let's go," he said; and Brian, accepting these exiguous preparations as constituting a "picnic," whoopd with joy and ran to put on overcoat and cap.

At the end of Stacey Street they climbed to the closed-in

upper deck of a tram, and, at that slack mid-morning hour, had it to themselves. Up and up the tram lurched with them, shaking off the close congregation of mean streets and coming gradually out to the once-august regions where industrial aristocracy had made its imposing habitations, sitting upon the hills whence it might look down to the smoky monster that for its well-being slaved upon the plain.

But all that was over and done with; the captains and the kings of industry had departed; and Heaton Park, the grandest of all their territories, stretching upon the hill-tops in acre upon tumbled acre, was an objective for such expeditions as this of Mo and Brian.

Now they were indeed under the sky, an immensity of blue, whereon the clouds marched with the grandeur of armies, and there seemed no limit to the vast perspectives that opened out before their vision. Hill upon hill the country stretched away, and on every hill there was a crennelation of smoking chimneys—chimneys that had been smoking for generations, and for generations depositing their grime upon the seeming fair face of Heaton Park. On a day like this it was still a grand and inspiring place, though hardly one in which it was desirable to sit down if you were wearing white breeches.

But such considerations meant nothing to Mo, and less than nothing to Brian. Rabbits were still to be seen bobbing in and out of their burrows in heathery banks; and in the hall that stood in the midst of the park there was a collection of toys that assembled in one room the enchantment that had held children throughout many generations.

These things Mo and Brian explored, and they paraded with solemn faces before the outlying sections of the city's art treasures that the hall housed. Then they went outside and, sitting on the grass, consumed their meagre lunch, and when that was done they went into the tea-room and Mo drank a cup of tea and gave Brian a glass of milk.

And all the time, ignore it as he might, the problem was at the back of Mo's mind like a nagging toothache, not bad enough to take to the dentist but too bad for peace.

The fewness of his friends suddenly appalled him. Rachel

gone. Piggy White no good. Piggy was a bachelor, living in rooms, and a stray child was the last thing he wanted. Anna was in Manchester, but he did not know where; and, in any case, to appeal to Anna would mean, he was sure, the end of everything as far as Brian was concerned. And there was no one else.

Brian finished his milk and pricked the dark bubble of Mo's meditations. "Let's go in a boat, Uncle Mo."

"It'd be lovely, Brian, but I can't row."

"I'll row. You watch me. You'll soon learn."

"You'll find the oars bigger than you think, Brian. P'r'aps I'll have a try. Come on. I don't expect it's difficult."

Brian gave a whoop and shot away towards the lake. Mo followed sombrely. Athletics were decidedly not his line. Rachel had taken up tennis last summer, and in the winter had been a daily visitor to the Ice Palace. She had poise, rhythm, that shot her ahead in the sport. Mo had sat mutely in the balcony, astounded at her verve and abandon—skirt swinging, face glowing under close cap of fur. He was proud of her, but unenvious. He carried her long boots home, kept the steel of the skates clean and oiled.

Brian was already in a boat when Mo arrived. The thing seemed to him horribly frail, to wobble most alarmingly when he got into it. With prodigious caution he thrust an oar into the landing-stage, pushing out the boat inch by inch. He discovered that oars were devilish and opinionated contrivances that leapt out of rowlocks and that would not do concerted work. When one leaned lustily against the water the other would shoot across its surface. The boat went round in a bewildering circle: it was an inexplicable and unmanageable vehicle.

"Faster!" Brian shouted. "Race those people!" And he bounced his behind up and down on the seat. Moses perspired with fear. "Keep still, Brian. Keep still!" he cried, and there was angry anxiety in his voice. Damn the boat! He ought never to have come out. One oar plunged almost vertically and the boat shivered like an ill-used horse. Damn it!

"Better go in now," Mo said.

"Oh, Uncle Mo! We've only just started! You're not afraid, are you?"

Mo *was* afraid. He couldn't swim. Brian couldn't swim. He was hating the whole thing. If anything happened to Brian. . . . .

"Let me have a go," the child exclaimed and leapt up from the stern thwart. He stumbled, recovered himself by grabbing an oar and rocked the gunwale almost under.

"Damn you!" Mo snarled. "Sit still!"

Perspiration was on his forehead. His teeth were bared like an animal's. He felt like an animal with something precious to protect. The very intensity of his affection had drawn from him the snarl that made Brian wince as though he had been bitten. The deep blue of Brian's eyes went darker, filmed over with resentment. Never before had Mo spoken to him like that He sat still and glowered.

It was an impossible situation, and Moses resolved to end it. Gingerly he manœuvred the skiff round, bows to landing-stage, and gingerly pulled her in. Gingerly still, looking apprehensively over his shoulder, he saw that they were almost there; and then he sought inexpertly to hasten matters. He gave the hardest pull he could command, the bows cannoned into the stage, and Brian, unprepared for the shock and wobble, went overboard.

There was no need for alarm, no need for Moses' raving cry as he plunged in after the child. The landing-stage attendant with his boat-hook could have done all that was necessary. But there the pair of them were, thrashing like octopuses in two feet of water.

When they stood dripping on the bank the stern servant of the municipality had no sympathy to waste. He was purple with wrath. "Never oughter've took out a boat!" he exclaimed with passion. "Blimey! You bloody Sheenies!"

Contempt edged the word. Moses waited for nothing more. Flowing like a cataract, he picked up the screaming child and ran.

III

Nick and Anna, elated with Simpson's champagne, arrived at No. 8 Stacey Street, and, unavailingly, they knocked and rang. They peered through the front window and saw no one stirring. They raised the flap of the letter-box and spied down the dingy passage-way into the kitchen. No one was there. Nick cursed their luck and said they might as well clear out. They retired through the few square yards of dirty earth that were the front garden and turned into the street. Then they saw Moses and the child.

They were a deplorable pair. Most of the water had drained out of them by now. Moses was without a hat. His hair was a wet mat hanging down his forehead, his collar a sodden rag about his neck; his boots squelched as he walked. A light steam, engendered by the heat of his body, was rising from him like the smoke of a damped-down garden bonfire, and clutched in his arms was the child, still sobbing hysterically, with whom he had rushed from the tram at the end of the street.

"Begod," cried Anna, "you've been in the bulrushes again, Moses! Now, who pulled you out this time, for I'll bet my shirt Pharoah's daughter wouldn't look twice at you."

Moses did not answer. Straining the child to his breast with one arm, he fished a key from his trousers pocket and mutely handed it to Anna. She flung open the door and the four of them trooped into the narrow passage.

"Better get him to bed," said Moses between chattering teeth. "He fell in the lake."

Suddenly Brian emitted a bellow: "Uncle Mo tried to drown me!"

Anna picked him up and shook him. "Don't talk like a daft little fool," she said. "You go and have a hot bath, Mo, if there's such a thing in the house. We'll look after Brian."

Holy Moses oozed his way upstairs. Anna carried Brian into the kitchen where the fire still burned. She stoked it to a blaze and unhooked a roller towel from behind the kitchen door. She flung it to Nick. "You warm that."

She left him to the task, with the naked Brian sitting on the kitchen mat, while she made a foray upstairs to find the boy's dry clothes. Brian quickly revived in the warmth of all these attentions. He was not used to being rubbed down with hot towels or to wearing his best suit on one of the plain days of the week. He took on some importance and began to demand Nick's credentials. "Who's he, Auntie Mummy?"

"There's no Auntie Mummy about it," said Anna. "You'll call me Mummy from now on. You're going to leave here and come and live with me and Uncle Nick."

"Are you Uncle Nick?" Brian demanded.

Nick nodded, leaned back in his chair with his feet stretched out to the fire, and blew a perfect smoke ring. Then he blew a smaller one right through the first. "Can Uncle Mo do that?" he asked.

Brian cheered. "No!" he shouted. "And he can't row. He tried to drown me."

With the easy injustice of the young, he was ready to drop Mo overboard at once. The unaccustomed snarl in the boat still rankled, and Uncle Nick seemed a good sort. He began to babble the story of the unhappy adventure on the lake.

"And Uncle Mo looked like this," said Nick. He picked Brian up and dumped him in a chair at the table, sat down beside him, and pulled from his poacher's pocket the sketch-book he always carried there. "Like this," he said, drawing rapidly; and as a fantastic and ridiculous picture took shape, showing Holy Moses in a boat with a bowler hat on the back of his head and oars sticking out in awkward fashion, Brian roared with laughter and shouted, "Do more!"

So Nick embroidered the picture with swans and an island and a castle on the island, and a princess leaning out of the castle window; and Brian, his eyes aflame, marvelled at the gifts of his new uncle. Mo, rubbing himself lugubriously in the bathroom, was not aware that the position was already carried and Nick triumphant in the child's mind.

"You can't draw lions!" Brian challenged.

"Only lions with toothache," Nick conceded sadly, and drew a dejected beast with a swollen jaw and a bandage.

"Aren't you the one to get round 'em?" said Anna, who saw what was going on. "And I suppose you'll raise hell if he whispers when you don't want him to."

But she was content that Nick should win his way with the child. He certainly knew how to do it.

So Moses found them when he came downstairs. He exploded with his worst news first. "Rachel's gone. She's not coming back here any more. Mrs. Moss is gone, too."

Anna's heart leapt, but she was too wise to voice at once the obvious implications. "Then it's the good God himself sent me here to look after you this day," she said. "I suppose you and Brian are starving, you poor boobs in the wood. Where's the larder?"

She soon had out a pastry board and a jar of flour, sugar and lard and currants. "It's a grand thing," she cried, "that I've had a thorough training in the domestic sciences. Did you ever see the like of that for a bit of dough?"

She slapped a dollop of dough on the table, and Nick leaned over and grabbed it. "Now, look here, Brian," he said. "There's better uses for this than making rotten cakes."

And, taking out his pocket knife, he began to prune and slice and chip. "Trafalgar Square lion," he announced; and Brian crowed with joy as an unmistakable lion emerged above a white soggy plinth.

"It's marvellous," the child shouted. "Come and see it, Uncle Mo."

But Mo did not get up from his chair by the fire. His brooding eyes surveyed the scene: Nick's nimble fingers working miracles with that preposterous material, his head of rat's tails bent down alongside Brian's curly mop, the child's face glowing with easy appreciation of the work. Anna, her floury arms akimbo, stood above them with a secret smile in her eyes. Moses felt outside the circle, and he stayed out, almost scowling.

Presently Anna moved around the table to the pastry-board, beat on it with the rolling-pin, and shouted, "Come on, now! Are you going to keep our bellies empty all night while you play the giddy goat with that child? Hand us over that dough."

"Oh, Mummy," Brian protested. "It's a marvellous lion. I don't want cakes," and some mania had seized Nick, too, at his ridiculous task. "By God," he said, "give me ten minutes, and I'll show you a lion that'll make Landseer's look like tom cats."

"I'll give you damn all," said Anna. "Am I to go to all the trouble to display my domestic accomplishments just to have you fooling about like some damned coon on the sands at Blackpool? Give me the dough."

"Ach, to hell with the dough," Nick shouted, wild as an adder, and, smashing the lion to a shapeless lump with a blow of his first, he picked it up and hurled it across the table at Anna. She ducked, and Mo received the missile full in the face.

Mild as he was in most of the circumstances of life, Mo saw in this nothing but a premeditated outrage. He picked up the dough from the floor, threw it on to the table and leapt towards Nick with his fists upraised. His face was twisted with a spasm of violent hate, but all weapons broke in his hands when Nick lay back in his chair and roared with laughter. Holy Moses felt a shock of black loathing for that laughing face, but he could do nothing about it, especially as Anna intervened with the rolling-pin in her hand.

"Mother of God!" she cried, "be peaceful, will you, and let me get on with my work!"

And though Brian continuously roared that he didn't want cakes, he wanted a lion, she calmly ran the rolling-pin like a steam-roller over the battered corpse, cut the flattened dough into circles with the lid of a cocoa tin, and presently had them all sitting down to tea as though nothing had happened.

CHAPTER NINE

I

DURING tea-time Brian gave a snuffle, and after tea he gave a sneeze, and Anna, who wanted him out of the way, made the most of the symptoms. "Come on, you," she said. "Bed's the place for you." And it did not cheer Moses when Brian, after bellows, shifts and evasions, consented to go to bed if Uncle Nick would come upstairs and draw something before he went to sleep. So Uncle Nick drew him at top speed a racehorse leaping a hurdle, promised that if it was fine he would take him on the Heaton Park lake in the morning, and left Brian persuaded that he had made a most satisfactory exchange of uncles.

Nick suspected, when he returned to the kitchen, that Anna was prolonging her washing-up in the scullery with the intention of keeping clear of Mo until she had an ally; and, indeed, no sooner had Nick sat down and lit a cigarette than she came bustling in, wiping her hands on the tea-cloth. "Now, Mo," she burst out, "Nick and I want to talk to you about Brian. What's to be done about him if Rachel isn't coming back?"

For a moment Moses did not answer. Then, as though he and the girl were alone, he said: "He loves me, Anna. You'd think to-day he hated me, but he loves me, I tell you— loves me! And I love you. Oh, Anna——"

He slid from his chair to her feet and grasped her round the knees.

"Holy Mother!" she murmured in despair.

Nick hurled his cigarette into the fire and rose. "See you later," he said hurriedly. They heard the front door bang.

II

Nick turned out of Stacey Street into the murk of Cheetham Hill Road. Dark had come early, with a drive of rainy clouds across the sky. The roadside lamps were sizzling, and at the bottom of the hill the lights of the city were pulsing under a dome of lead.

Nick wandered down the shabby street and asked himself why, in God's name, he had hitched himself up with this woman. Peace and quiet were all he was asking for a month ago; and so little, it seemed, did he know of his own mind that a touch of the medicine he had sought had filled him with melancholia, with a maudlin readiness to cry in her apron and chatter about his loneliness. By heavens! She was quick to relieve his loneliness, with her bastard and her Jew lover slobbering over her under his very nose, with her Piggy Whites and Rachels.

He slouched into the taproom of a pub, and ordered a pint of bitter. It did him good. He began to see Anna and to see himself in a new light. After all, it was time he did something. For a couple of years now he had been a local pet, the promising Manchester boy, the adored of dear nit-wits like Anton Brune, who was sure he was as good as Augustus John. And not so far wrong, thought Nick, with satisfaction, taking a long swig and banging his pot on the table for more.

The *Manchester Guardian* could be relied on to say the right thing every time he showed a picture, though he wished to God they'd send an art critic, if they had one, to look at his stuff, not one of those damned know-all reporters, who were equally competent about Nellie Wallace at the Hippodrome on Monday, about an art show on Tuesday and a dog show on Wednesday. Still, he was all right with the *Guardian.* That was something.

But it wasn't good enough. He had to get a wider showing somehow, and the first thing was work. He would work like the devil all this summer, and in the autumn he would have that exhibition he had talked about to Anna. He pulled at his beer again, took out a cigarette, and felt virtuous at the thought of all the work he intended to do.

Anna would be useful. He wouldn't get entangled with Anna; he was sure of that. As to their irregular position, damn what anyone thought. And by that he meant what was thought at the Laurels, Fallowfield, the capacious suburban residence of Sir George Faunt, his father.

His mind bemused itself for a moment with the thought of Sir George Faunt. Let Manchester go to the devil, as it appeared to be doing as quickly as it could. That did not matter to Sir George Faunt. Damn you, Bill! I'm all right.

Plain Mr. Faunt, and no Sir George about it, had done very well before the war (which was a time Nick could but dimly remember) out of wholesale provisions, spending his days in an office behind Corporation Street, where the air was impregnated with rank odours of cheese and bacon. The war gave him just the counters he wanted for a plunge when the grand gamble called the boom cheered the cockles of Lancashire's heart as a gay preliminary to cutting Lancashire's throat. George Faunt had had nothing to do with the cotton trade before the boom; he would not be such a fool as to have anything to do with it again. He put in his hundreds at the right moment, took out his thousands at the right moment, and left others to pick up the pieces when the balloon burst. It was not long before his knighthood followed. Of such is the kingdom.

Well, Nick reflected, he had done with that lot, and now he had only himself to please. As he finished his second pint, the thought of Anna keeping the decks clear while he worked like a galley slave in the Amhurst Street loft became very attractive. The life he was to live there stretched away in an alluring rosy perspective. He called for a pony to settle his second pint, and walked out hazily into Cheetham Hill Road, which was full of a rain as fine almost as steam. It looked to Nick like a dew of pearls.

III

At the corner of Derby Street a tram ground to a standstill, a girl leapt off, and the light of the corner lamp flashed across the skates she carried. Nick followed her down the dark street to the Ice Palace.

He had never been there, and if he wanted to go he had better be quick, for the season was nearly ended. Movement was the thing he loved to capture, though the movements of machines left him cold. Horses racing; the animals, sentenced for God knows what offence to penal servitude at Belle Vue, aprowl in exploration of the narrow frontiers of their bondage; the knotted anatomies of boxers and wrestlers in the Free Trade Hall—these were his subjects. One glance at the grey floor of the skating rink made his heart jump, and then he stood, as though he were frozen stiff as the floor

itself, transfixed by the swift improvisation of beauty that
swirled and eddied before him.

The hiss of skates was a monotone underlying the startling
tonal arabesques of the artificial music. In it was something
urgent and essential; it seemed the very voice of an
apprehensive joy, surcharging with expression a fugitive
moment.

Under the lamps colour flamed; scarfs flared like banners
behind women in winged flight; pursuing males flashed in
rhythmic undulation above the searing hiss of steel. A face
with eager parted lips threaded the mazy lither; a mouth red
with laughter was seen and gone; skirts swirled in the perfection of unpremeditated grace; a woman, spinning like a
teetotum, was a whirl of silken thighs and a mad flame of
red hair that blazed like a waved cresset.

When the totality of the rich experience had passed over
him like a wave, Nick climbed the stairs to the gallery,
found a table there against the rails, and pulled his book from
his pocket. Anna and Holy Moses were forgotten; forgotten
were Brian and Sir George Faunt, as Nick's fingers, thin and
brittle almost as the pencils he used, recorded the hints and
intimations of the evanescent loveliness that flowed beneath
him.

He was tired when he had finished. He snapped-to the
book and shoved it into his pocket, and then, looking round
him, saw Rachel Rosing, alone, approaching a neighbouring
table. She was as inelegant as a swan out of water, for she
was wearing skating-boots that put a smooth leathern grip
round the calves of her legs. She slumped into a chair, and,
moved by some derisive impulse, he rose and moved over
to her table.

"Good-evening. Shall I order you something?"

His lean face grinned insolently down at her, and he was
prepared to receive again such a rebuff as had come the night
before. To his surprise her dark eyes lit with a smile. She
held out her hand and said: "That would be very kind of
you."

He was taken aback as effectually as though she had struck
him, but he retained enough self-possession to overlook the

offered hand. He called a waitress and Rachel said she would
have coffee. She pulled off her yellow gloves and he noted
the charm of her long hands, ruined by painted claws.

"Why do you choose to look like a harpy, your talons
dyed with the blood of your victims?" he asked, handing her
a cigarette.

"At any rate, it's a fair warning of my most recent occupation, isn't it?" she laughed. "You see, I don't take an unfair
advantage."

"I will paint you," he said, "ripping the guts out of Anton
Brune. A lovely but evil eagle. With a sneer in the eyes
like you treated me to last night."

"You shouldn't have mentioned that," Rachel protested.
"I hoped we might both leave it alone."

She conveyed a hint of reproof. She looked aggrieved
and penitent, and, he thought, beautiful. She was wearing
a tight bodice of blue velvet that showed off her splendid
bust, and a short blue velvet skirt edged with white fur. He
looked her coolly up and down as she sat there, one leg
thrown over the other. She seemed anxious to be friendly.

"Yes, I must paint you," he said appraisingly. "Anton
can't do you justice."

The music reached a dragging wail and died. A board
went up announcing a waltz. The floor began to clear of
all but the elite.

"Excuse me," said Rachel, rising and stabbing her cigarette
into an ashtray. "Please don't go. I will come back."

She stumped awkwardly away, turned, and threw her handbag towards the table. "I shan't want that." It fell, spilling
some if its contents under his eyes.

He craned his neck over the rail and saw her shoot out
from the promenade into the rink. It took his breath away
to see the perfection of that lovely launching, like the swoop-
ing flight of a gull. She had come with a short awkward run
out of the promenade, and then, touching the ice, was away,
one or two sharp strokes of her blades sending her into a
long swinging curve, which sped her round the top of the
rink and fetched her up, with a sudden harsh grind of steel,

upon the arm of her partner. With one toe pointed upon the ice, she stood there lightly, awaiting the music.

Only four couples stood up to the waltz, and who Rachel's partner was Nick did not know. He only knew that he had never seen such perfect movement as Rachel Rosing's as she swayed and undulated upon the harsh grey surface, her body's beauty mitigating the emphasis of its strength, its strength launching its beauty into such rhythmic improvisations as a silver birch might achieve in a vagrant wind.

The sprightlier two-step followed, to Nick a vivid embodiment of all he understood by movement—muscular and aery, earthly as the mud from which man was made, heavenly as the stars to which he aspires.

He was more deeply moved than when he had watched Pavlova at the Hippodrome.

He had not expected to be so moved, and as Rachel and her partner brought the dance to an end, hands lightly touching, each with a right leg extended backward in air, pivoting slowly to a standstill on the left, he rose and made his way into the street, crumbling in his fingers a piece of paper which he had absently picked up from the table. He did not wish to see Rachel just then. He hated her, and was resentful that she had been able to touch him so quickly.

IV

Anna heard with a sinking of the heart the bang of the front door. Damn the man! He *would* desert her just when she needed him.

"Anna!" Holy Moses, kneeling at her feet, breathed the name as though it were a saint's. His hands took hers, lying passive in her lap. She looked across the top of his head at the fire glowing in the kitchen grate. For a time she dared not look at his eyes, brown and mournful as a spaniel's. She both feared and hated their abject entreaty.

God! It was awful! If only he would take hold of her, shake her, bash her to blazes, then there would be something

in it; at any rate something to be done about it. But this
was drowning in treacle. She would suffocate.

"Anna, do you hate the very sight of me? Why don't
you look at me?"

His hands went up and took her arms above the elbows.
He did not grip her. He hung to her softly. Like those
pictures of a drowning girl, already sprouting wings, clinging to a cross that miraculously rears itself amid hissing seas.
He was a good old devil, she reflected, staring stonily ahead
—a cut above those Sheenies you saw in the Market Street
cafés with dirty eye-pupils and fat dripping from their oozy
hair. Their cheap lacquered shoes, their cheap ready-made
suits, with trousers generously fetlocked. A dirty lot. He
kept away from them. He must be lonely.

Compassion stirred in her. She loosed one arm from his
touch and placed it on his head. It unleashed all the softness
in the beggar. His head slipped down to her knee, buried
itself in her lap. Muffled words came to her ears. "Won't
you marry me, Anna?"

She spoke decisively. "No."

The word rang in his ears like a shot.

There was nothing more to be said. She knew he would
not urge what he had done as a claim upon her. He would
not say, as he might have done: "I have kept your child
when it would have starved." She had counted on that.
With a stab to the heart, she realised clearly for the first time
that she had counted on it. It had been beastly, unpardonable.
She had taken all he had to give, and, as luck would have it,
when he was at the end of his tether and could do no more,
she had come in order to bear away the fruit of his fidelity.
And she had nothing to offer in return.

A powerful temptation besieged her to take him in her
arms, to comfort him, to give him his desire. She beat it
back resolutely. She mustn't, whatever happened. She had
offended, but retribution did not lie there. An intuition of
all the necessary sorrow, all the suffering that seems to futile
in the world, touched her mind, and she was strengthened
to know that here was something beyond the puny and

insincere alleviation that she could offer, something that she must not interfere with.

So little had been said, but both knew that everything was said. She was glad it was over, so quickly and decisively. She was a little surprised at the force she had displayed. She realised now that for years this moment had been awaiting her, and she had been able, with the resolute inflection of a single word, to dissipate a miasma and see her way clearly.

Moses got to his feet. They sat on either side of the fire, each on an uncomfortable kitchen chair. Hands on knees, Moses fastened his eyes on the glow. "When will you be taking Brian away?" he asked.

"As soon as we've got a place," she said. "It should be ready in a week."

"But what will happen to the child? A week! There is no one. I must go to work. Rachel will not come back. Mrs. Moss is gone."

They stared at one another. "Nick will think of something," said Anna at last.

Mo's eyes smouldered at the name. "There is no need for Nick to think," he said. "I will think. You will stay here, and Nick can stay here if you want him. The rent is paid till the end of the month. You can sleep in Rachel's room."

Compassion wrestled with her again. "Mo," she said, "you're good. You're a good man, Mo."

She struggled for more words, but they would not come to her.

"Good, am I?" said Moses. "So Rachel has already told me to-day. It becomes monotonous. Now I am going for a walk. You will be all right?"

"Yes," she said faintly.

For the second time that evening she heard the front door bang. The silence of the house closed in on her. She could hear the tin clock on the mantelpiece ticking hoarsely, as though its rusty guts would shake to pieces. She sat still and collected for a moment, then rushed upstairs to the companionship of her sleeping son. She lit the candle and put her hand on his forehead. It had a damp heat under the tangled curls, but the child's lips were smiling like a cherub's. In his clenched fist was the drawing of Moses looking ridiculous on the lake. Anna gently removed it, tore it angrily to pieces.

She blew out the candle and moved to the window. She drew back the curtains and gazed at the blear night lying sodden and wretched along the roof-lines. Her eyes filled suddenly with tears as her mind bowed under the fact of man's splendour and misery.

v

It was nearly eleven o'clock when Nick returned.

"Where's Mo?" he asked.

"Gone for a walk. And I'm going to bed. I'm fagged out."

"Very well. I'll wait up for him. I didn't know we were sleeping here to-night."

"God help us if our sleeping depended on you," she said. "Were you expecting us to turn out with the child at this time of night and start looking for lodgings?"

"I don't know what I expected," said Nick vaguely.

"Well, you've got more than you deserve. You've got a roof over your head. No thanks to you, boyo. Wait up if you like. But Mo's not coming back."

"That's lucky," said Nick, off-handedly. "That gives us a shake-down till we move into the studio."

She flamed up at that. "Lucky, is it?" she cried. "Mother of God, what is it you're made of? Have you got any guts in you, or are you stuffed with sawdust, you dirty great galoot! A man turns out of his house to make room for you, and you think it's lucky! A man that's worth ten of you to any reasonable being."

"Does that by any chance include you?"

"No, begod, it does not, or I'd have gone with him," she said, going out noisily and banging the door.

When Nick heard her footsteps overhead, he explored the front room, seeking something more comfortable than a wooden chair to sit on. He found a thing of sagging wicker and carried it to the kitchen. He made up the fire and stretched his long legs to the blaze. Anna, presumably, had some reason for thinking that Moses would not come back. He could make a guess at what had passed between them; but he would wait up, at any rate, till midnight.

He thrust his hands down into his trousers pockets, and the piece of paper he had picked up from the table in the Ice Palace crinkled between his fingers. He drew it forth and smoothed it out. It was a fragment ripped out of the evening paper. "Manchester Artists' Work. Bought for the City."

"From the Manchester Academy Exhibition now being held at the City Art Gallery," he read, "the Art Gallery Committee has decided to purchase two pictures by Manchester artists. One is a vivid racecourse scene by Nicholas Faunt; the other a small water-colour drawing by Anton Brune, showing the work now in progress on the new Free Library. Mr. Faunt is the son of Alderman Sir George Faunt, himself a member of the Art Gallery Committee."

Nick tossed the cutting into the fire, his nose wrinkled in disdain. Glory be to God! They had bought a picture by old Anton! Well, well! The little man would be like a peacock with two tails, both spread and quivering. Who the deuce had been responsible for buying a picture by Anton? "D.I.A., I suppose," he reflected: "Design In Industry." Fitness for Purpose. All that sort of thing. Manchester was mad about it at the moment. Fitness for Purpose. Though why the devil God put spots on a Dalmatian. . . . Nothing could be more useless. Still, Anton was the darling of the Fitness for Purpose and Design In Industry gang. He was the boy for putting Art into the designs for shirtings to be worn in Bacup and Burnley. And now he had his reward. Well, good luck to him. Nick supposed the cutting had fallen out of Rachel's bag. She had culled this offering to her beloved.

And then suddenly into his mind came remembrance of her bland expectation that that snotty remark of the night before might be overlooked and that they might, for what had seemed no reason at all, be good friends. "Mr. Faunt is the son of Sir George Faunt." There it was! She was a snob as well as a bounder. He could imagine that Anton, who appeared to have talked to her pretty freely about him, had left Sir George out of the question. It was the work alone that mattered to Anton; you could at least say that for the little man. But for Rachel, Sir George's name was evidently a halo on the brow of Mr. Nicholas Faunt. Sir George Faunt was rich. Everybody in Manchester knew that. Had not his knighthood been granted for "political services?"

Nick's eye roved round the shabby room that had been for so long part of Rachel Rosing's home; took in the worn rug mat at his feet, the fly-blown wallpaper, the fixed dresser, varnished a dirty yellow, the tuppenny-ha'penny deal table, the lace curtains that looked as though they had come out of Nottingham in the happy days before the war. The fire-irons were a joblot that had probably been picked up for a shilling in the Flatiron Market in Salford, and the few pictures belonged to the vintage years of Pear's Almanack.

Nick was not susceptible to environment. He could have worked as happily in that room, completely unconscious of its hideousness, as in a light and airy studio of St. John's Wood. But though he didn't mind it, he could appraise it, he could look at it through the eyes of the girl emerging into beautiful womanhood whom he had seen so radiantly disporting herself that night. He could imagine how she loathed it, longed to shake it from her for ever. In him were resources that put it under his feet, but for her it would be a burden clinging closely to the back.

He began to understand what riches—using the word in a very comparative sense—would mean to Rachel. He could see that "the son of Sir George Faunt" was capable of disturbing her imagination. He allowed himself to wonder whether her imagination was worth disturbing.

He decided at last that Anna was right. Holy Mo would not come back. He put out the kitchen light and went upstairs. The sounds he heard assured him that Anna was in the room where Brian slept. He went to the other, and remembered when he got there that all his possessions had been left in Anton Brune's studio.

Well, it wouldn't be the first time he had slept in a shirt. Anna had nothing, either. She was probably sleeping as naked as Eve.

He noticed that the room was full of feminine knick-knacks. Rachel's, then. He grinned as he clambered into her bed. He here, and Anna must be in Holy Mo's!

A subtle essence, an emanation of femininity, powdered his senses as he drifted into sleep.

CHAPTER TEN

I

"THIS," said Rachel to herself, "is more like it."

Though there was still a little light draining out of a primrose sky, she drew the chintz curtains, switched on the shaded lamp, and stretched herself in the chintz-covered chair.

The room on the first floor was not a large one, but it had a decent carpet, walls covered with paper to which time had brought the dull sheen and restful colour of faded ivory, a simple and unobtrusive fireplace, painted olive-green, no pictures, and no piece of furniture that was not necessary.

She took her meals downstairs with her Jewish landlady. She had a bedroom as uncrowded as the sitting-room, and the bathroom was unexpectedly good.

Miriam Jacobs, her partner in Arlette et Cie, had fixed it all up, and Rachel, who had lived with Miriam for a day or two after leaving Cheetham Hill, had arrived that evening, with some trepidation, to embark on her new venture. The district was as Jewish as the one she had left. When she climbed on to the Palatine Road tram that was to bear her to the southern suburb, she knew that the trolley boys called it Palestine Road, and that Didsbury, whither she was bound, was just as likely to be hailed by them as Yidsbury.

But if Cheetham Hill was largely the land of the defeated,

Didsbury, she knew, represented Jewry triumphant; Jewry
not in squalid cottages, but in opulent houses set in the
midst of fine gardens. The very synagogue, which was in this
street where now she had her lodgings, looked different. It
was a new building, of a challenging modern style, not like
the grim black synagogues of the place of bondage.

And all about Didsbury there were trees. She loved that.
Journeying home to Stacey Street day after day she had seen
smoke and steam, steel and brick, stone and concrete, towering façades of glass, soot and grime, narrow dirty pavements
and penurious front gardens where not so much as a nettle
would grow. She had seen, in short, the damndest that man
could do to make a hell on earth.

From the top of the tram that night she hailed the trees
as soon as she came upon them. It was so sudden. The
demarcation between city grimness and suburban amenity
was as sharply drawn as with a ruler. It came at Dickenson
Road. The flat greenness of Platt Fields began at once on
her right hand; on her left were mansions in gardens, imposing stuccoed houses whence the carriages and pairs had been
accustomed, so recently as twenty years ago, to bear the lords
of industry and commerce daily to the city.

One of the houses, she knew, was the Laurels, the home
of Sir George Faunt. She was aware of a definite quickening
of interest as her eye captured a swift impression of a lighted
room, a standard lamp, a group of people composed for a
flying instant into a picture of serenity and security.

The trees were hardly interrupted after that. There were
pendent flames of laburnum, upstanding chestnut candles,
snowy smother of cherry blossom, mauve and white lilac.
And she knew that there was no end to it, that, did she care
to follow it, the road ran on and on, deeper and deeper into
the quiet unexciting heart of Cheshire.

She got off the tram at the terminus, where there was a
picture house with a cleared gravelled space before it, and
trees were growing there with lights twined in their branches
and with arc lamps shooting the opening leaves with a green
translucency. There were tables in the open air, people
taking coffee—altogether a charming if fragmentary Con-

tinental illusion. At any rate, it helped her to feel a long
way from Cheetham Hill, and that was what she wanted.

II

Rachel would have liked to spend that first evening in
lazy enjoyment of her new, distinguished status. But there
was a thing that must be done at once. She had written to
Mrs. Moss instructing her to pack all Rachel's belongings
and have them ready for a boy who would call. There had
been no reply from Mrs. Moss, and the boy, calling, had
found no one at home. She must make a final call in Cheetham Hill, gather the essential things, and satisfy her some-
what troubled mind as to how Moses was meeting his crisis.

She had hoped that Anton Brune's useful car would take
the distasteful edge off the adventure; but this happened to
be one of those nights when Anton was chained to his studio.
She tore herself out into the street, walked to the railway
station at the end of it, and took the train to the city. She
could not face the racket of a tram a second time in one
evening. Not all the way into town. She would have to
take one from town out to Stacey Street.

She dropped off the tram at the corner of the street wherein
had been for so long her home. The air was quick with
spring, but all about her the squalor of the district was
battling with the year's renaissance, battling and winning.
What in Didsbury had been a clear call, a challenge to hope
and endeavour, was here a furtive rumour, discredited, slinking down the dark cañons of the by-ways, held in countenance
only by the serenity of the terribly distant stars.

Her head went up in defiance to it all; she was done with
it. It wasn't good enough, and it was time ten thousand times
ten thousand people joined her in the shout: "It isn't good
enough!"

With something of that defiance stiffening the clean resili-
ency of her step, she approached the shabby door whose artificial " graining" looked hateful to her, and knocked sharply.
There was a shuffling of footsteps, the sick gas in the passage
was turned up, and Nick Faunt stood in the doorway.

Both of them were taken aback. Nick was still wearing his green corduroys, his grey shirt without a tie. He looked as though, if he had washed lately, he hadn't been enthusiastic about it. He wiped his mouth with the back of a hand that was a disgracefully ill-used masterpiece.

"I was just having a drink with a friend," he said with a grin. "Will you join us?"

"I should like to come in—if I may," said Rachel.

"Do. It's your house, after all."

"No, thank you," Rachel said shortly, stepping into the passage, "it's not my house. I've done with it for good."

And, indeed, when she had come in and stood under the anaemic light of the whining incandescent burner it seemed to Nick that she was extraordinarily inappropriate. He himself seemed more indigenous and assimilated. He would rather have drawn her than describe her. How describe that coquette of a hat, tiny, slightly askew, from which depended the eye-veil of a substance intangible as cobweb, yet giving to the laired eyes an aspect of dark awareness. Lipstick, applied with a mastery which he recognised and saluted, made the only colour in the pallid oval of her face. On the lobe of each ear was an artificial pearl as big as a pea. The smooth perfection of her chin rested in fur as black as her eyes. The contours of her clothes rippled down in smooth, clinging lines to her high-heeled shoes, to her silk stockings that were black, but acquired by reason of their fragile transparency an indescribable subtlety of dull grey.

"Anna is out," said Nick. "Will you come into the kitchen?"

"Where is Jacob?" she asked.

For a moment Nick did not understand. Then he remembered. "Oh, you mean Mo?" he said, leading the way to the kitchen. Flinging open the door, he shouted: "Piggy, you're not the only one on the track of the lost tribes. Here's Mo's sister asking where he is."

The foetid atmosphere of the kitchen struck Rachel in the face. The fire was blazing. Piggy White, sprawled in the wicker chair, was blowing smoke from a foul pipe. A store of cigarette ends in a saucer attested Nick's contribution to the fug. Half a dozen unopened bottles of beer were on the table. There were several empties, and as Piggy rose he drained a glass with a smacking appreciative gulp.

"Bless my soul!" he cried. "It's little Rachel in disguise! By God, whoever would've thought such a scrawny little filly would turn into a looker like you!"

Piggy held out his red, sweaty fist, beaming upon her, not displeased with his compliment. She touched it lightly with her gloved hand, sat as far as possible from the fire, and asked: "So you don't know where my brother is?"

Piggy, a bottle between his knees, waited till the corkscrew had achieved its pop. It looked as though his bulging eyes might simultaneously leap from his head. He tucked the corkscrew under the edge of his cummerbund and reached for a clean glass. "'Ave a drink," he invited.

"No, thank you," said Rachel. "I'd rather have the window open."

"Well, then, open the bloody window," Piggy said sourly, the bonhomous bubble of him pricked by her cold manner. "Indoors is indoors, I say, and outdoors is outdoors. Why mix 'em? Good 'ealth."

He slumped into his chair with his back to Rachel and put back the liquor. He belched lightly, stared moodily at the fire. Nick lounged across the room, let the spring blind fly up, and threw up the window.

"Thank you," said Rachel.

"Thank you for nothing," Piggy shouted as a keen air struck like a knife at the red roll of his neck. "If you like to spend the night on the bloody Matter'orn you can. Christ! The White 'Ell of Pitz Palu!"

He rose a little unsteadily, having clearly had enough. He stayed his bulk with one hand resting on the back of his chair as the air set blue wraiths of smoke eddying round him. He glared at Rachel through the quickly thinning fog.

"No," he said. "I don't know where your brother is. 'E ain't been near me for days. And if he do turn up, all 'e'll get is my boot right in the middle of 'is backside."

He took up half a glass of beer that was Nick's and tossed it down his throat. "Not that I blame Mo," he went on beginning to orate seriously. "That kick in the pants would be what they call vicarious, and intended, dear lady, for you. It's you 'oo've been sticking ideas into Mo's 'ead. 'E's a good ole sod if left alone. But it's you 'oo want 'im to be too big for 'is boots. Well, 'e's vanished, Gawd knows where. When you find 'im, get 'im a job as a pimp. You look as if you know the ropes. Bon soir, an' many of 'em."

Rachel sat frozen with fury as Piggy White raised his podgy hand in ironic salute and lurched out of the room. Nick went with him, stood at the jarring iron gate till Piggy was swerving well away down the dark street, singing aloud, "Jerusalem the golden, with milk and honey blessed."

III

Nick did not at once go in. Looking left along the street, he saw an occasional tramcar hurtling up or down Cheetham Hill Road like a travelling house on fire. Between these sensational appearances there was an extraordinary quiet, the profound ultimate quiet that you can get only in the heart of a great town where there are no birds or beasts, no singing rivers or sighing trees or whispering grasses. In the country, Nick reflected, the very earth seemed to have a voice, a suspiration that went out at night like the voice of God walking in the garden. But here the earth was battened down below hatches; these flagstones and cobbles and concrete slabs, all welded together and interlocked so solidly upon the breast of nature, were a vast monolithic tombstone with no chink through which the ghost of a sigh could break its way. The silence was the silence of death, annihilation under the icy indifference of the stars.

The thought re-established his irony. It whisked out of his mind a misty tinge of sentimentality which had suggested that he should go in and apologise to Rachel for Piggy White. Piggy White and Rachel and himself were all jigging on the same string; let her make what she could of it. After all, he liked Piggy, the disgusting great animal. Piggy was as natural and unashamed as a sow wallowing amid its litter. He was going to see more of him, and he was going to draw him. He was not so sure that he liked Rachel.

He found her sitting where he had left her. Her hands were knotted in her lap; her tight lips were a vivid wound in the drained indignation of her face. He offered her a cigarette, and she shook her head, fluttering the little veil that seemed now to put her eyes into mourning.

"Then you don't know where he is?" she said at last.

"I'm sorry. I have no idea. Anna and I came to take Brian away. I went out that evening. It was the evening I met you at the skating rink. When I came back, Anna said that Mo was gone. I have an idea that he proposed to her and that she turned him down. She has said nothing to me about that, but that night she was as touchy as a bear with a sore behind. She seemed to know that he would not come back—and he hasn't come back. So we're hanging on here till a place we're getting ready is in order. It will only be a few days now. You don't mind?"

"Why should I mind? I don't care if a herd of buffaloes comes and fouls the place. I never want to see it again. After to-night I never will see it again. It's loathsome."

She was silent for a moment, staring unseeingly before her. Then she asked: "Are you Brian's father?"

"Do I look," he asked, a grin deepening the grooves of his dark, cadaverous face, "do I look as though I could beget anything so lovely?"

"Goodness knows what a man can do when he tries," she said. "You haven't answered my question."

"The answer is No. I had not seen Anna in my life until a week or so ago."

"Why do you take up with a girl like that—a man of your family?"

"My family is the only thing I will thank you never to throw in my teeth."

"It's the only thing that would make me look at you," she answered frankly.

"Then I advise you to avert your gaze."

"Is Anna your mistress?"

"Scandal is one of the few joys of life. I refuse to rob you of an opportunity."

She got up. "You're clever, aren't you?" she said. "Well, I know that girl, and she's clever, too. Now, if I may, I'll go to my bedroom and take the few things I want."

"Don't let my pyjamas disturb you," he said. "I'm afraid they're on your bed, probably unfolded. Otherwise, everything is as you left it."

She came down in a quarter of an hour, carrying a small handbag. "If you will be good enough," she said, "to let Anton know when you have finished with this place, I will arrange about the sale of the furniture."

"I'll do that," he promised. "Would you like to see Brian before you go?"

"No, thank you. During the last five years I've seen more than enough of Brian. You have a treat in store."

"I think he's a good kid. He's very fond of me."

"That *is* lucky. Good-night."

"Shall I carry your bag as far as the tram?"

"Why should you? I'm more capable of carrying a bag than you are. You want to look after yourself."

She went with great serenity, leaving him feeling rather small. It might have comforted him to know that civil war was rampant behind her placid façade, that her head ached violently all the way home, and that even the cool sheets in her wonderful new bed did not bring sleep easily. She felt bitter towards Anton. Surely he might have stretched a point. If only he had been with her, what humiliation she might have been spared!

CHAPTER ELEVEN

I

NICK and Anna always spoke of the home that was being prepared for them in Amhurst Street as The Loft. Preparations for the occupation of The Loft went forward quickly. Anna saw to that. Nick's high resolve to make this a summer

of intensive work did not include such a detail as preparing
a studio. He mooched about Anton Brune's place, sorely
trying the temper of that earnest worker; he went to the Ice
Palace every day of its closing week, filling a book with
sketches; he drew ducks in the parks, greyhounds at Belle
Vue; and one day, when Anna missed him from morning to
night, he was at Dunham Massey Park, whence he returned
with a dozen drawings of shy lovely deer. They are now all
in one private collection.

His days went in a sort of idling activity. A group of
navvies driving a wedge into a road, the rise and fall of their
sledge-hammers weaving a rhythm perfectly interlaced, would
bring him bounding down from the top of a tramcar; and
he shivered through the whole of a freezing night on a
tramway track, where, under the intense irradiation of
acetylene flares, men laboured like gods to tear up and renew
between midnight and dawn.

But in the midst of all this Anna kept him to what was, to
her, the essential task. He raised fifty pounds from Anton
Brune on account of the picture that the city had bought,
and began to look about the furniture salerooms in the neigh-
bourhood of Albert Square.

On his first visit, Anna, with Brian holding on to her fist,
accompanied him. Up and down the dusty corridors the
wreckage of a hundred homes deployed before them the
misery of dissolution and decay. Bedroom suites that had
still something of the delusive gloss of Tottenham Court Road
neighboured the solid mahogany that seemed to have stored
in itself the privacies of many generations, but now was
public as a bed in a film. Forks and fenders, bird-cages of
tarnished gilt, and billiard cues of doubtful balance; chan-
deliers that no one would have use for any more; family
portraits surviving the family portrayed; mountains of books,
dirty and dog-eared; grand pianos and upright pianos and
pianos that were played by pieces of perforated paper; gramo-
phones and wireless sets; chairs, tables, chamber pots to which
Burslem and Etruria, disregarding all fitness for purpose,
had contributed a startling efflorescence; cruets, carpets and
vacuum cleaners, parapets and parados of such-like stuff made

up a trench system through which Nick and Anna threaded their way with Brian in the rear, a trench system haunted by the ghosts of the defeated.

The place was dim, and dust was over everything. An old man closely buttoned in a antique frock coat, and wearing a battered silk hat, was furtively testing a tuning-fork, glancing round like a child, fearful lest someone should forbid his play; a pair of obese, indecent-looking women were bouncing experimentally the springs of a divan, cackling with pleasure.

Brian, lingering behind on private exploration, let out a cry that set the ghosts flying. His rich young voice seemed out of place in that dreary catacomb. "Mummy! Fruit!"

"For the love of God, Brian," Anna said, scurrying back and scolding in a hoarse, subdued voice, as though she were in church, "have some respect for the place you're in and don't attract people's attention. I'll get your Uncle Nick to tan your backside if you can't control yourself."

Brian merely called attention once more to his discovery. "Fruit!" he said in sepulchral tones, pointing to a glass cover on an oak sideboard. Beneath the cover, pears and grapes, apples and bananas, reposed with a deceptive hue of health upon their waxen substance.

"Well, what about it?" Anna demanded. "You can't eat that stuff. It's wax."

"Don't want to eat it," said Brian. "Want to have it."

"Well, you can't have it. You've got very large ideas, young man."

"Why can't he have it?" asked Nick, strolling up. "I think it's gorgeous. He *shall* have it."

And in that moment the "Victorian" atmosphere of The Loft was born. It came over Nick all of a sudden; and thereafter Anna did not need to urge him on about the furnishing. He went to it with a burst of tom-fool energy and quickly created the room that astounded Anton Brune on the night of the house-warming.

II

The fine spring weather had suffered a set-back, and as that evening came down there actually was frost in the air. Anton Brune, looking up at the tower of the Holy Name as he hurried to The Loft, noticed that its dark magnificent mass was thrust among stars that seemed to crackle in the sky.

Anton was uplifted by a great happiness and depressed by a great sorrow. The exhibitors at the Manchester Academy exhibition had been bidden to a reception at the Town Hall; and that was pure joy, especially as a real slap-up affair was promised by the discreet line at the bottom of the invitation card: "Decorations and academic robes."

Anton figured himself flatteringly as he looked forward to that occasion; but he could not be as gay as he would have wished, for Rachel Rosing had been inclined of late to be captious and fault-finding.

It had begun when she had discovered from an evening paper that Nick Faunt was Sir George's son. "If you had only *told* me," she protested.

"But what does it matter?" Anton objected. "Who his father is happens to be last thing to interest Nick."

"Oh, Nick, Nick," she almost shouted at him. "Have you got the man on the brain? Am I to hear nothing but Nick? It's not what interests Nick; it's what interests me that I'm talking about. Doesn't it matter to you that you permitted me to make a complete fool of myself that night at the Bassoon Club?"

"Nick would hardly notice that," Anton said.

A freezing calm settled upon Rachel at that. "Very well, then, Anton. If you're incapable of seeing anything but what *he* would notice. . . ."

"Well, he's a damn good painter, anyway," said Anton lamely, flustered and embarrassed by the whole fuss.

That was the beginning of a coolness; and the frost had thickened after that night when Anton had been unable to take Rachel to Cheetham Hill. They met as often as ever, but something was gone from their companionship; and when

Nick, inviting Anton to the house-warming, said, "Bring anyone you like," Anton had decided that perhaps it would be as well not to ask Rachel. She seemed to hate Nick so. He had often told her, truthfully, that he would be working late; it would not hurt, in the interests of concord, to lie for once.

He plunged into the dinginess of Amhurst Street with his corn-coloured beard sunk into his turned-up coat collar. It seemed to symbolise a shrinking into himself that the expansive fellow was not accustomed to. At every step his abhorrence of the district deepened. Why Nick didn't work like anyone else and make a decent living, why he should choose to pitch his tent in that sordid desert, he could not imagine.

He found the place at last, with a dam-fool oil lantern tied to the top rail of the outside staircase. Little enough light it gave. He stumbled up and banged on the door. At first he did not recognise the man who opened it. A second glance showed him that it was Nick.

"I didn't know it was fancy dress," Anton apologised.

"Fancy dress my foot," Nick answered. "This is a genuine Victorian household. Be careful of your language."

A great white choker swathed round and round with a black cravat was the first impression Anton had gathered of his host. The side-whiskers were clearly false. Running his eyes downwards from this daunting beginning, Anton took in the foppish coat, the sprigged waistcoat, the check trousers that grasped the legs tightly and were secured by straps beneath the boots. An ornate seal protruded from the fob.

Anton was by now inside the door, confronting an ancestral and aldermanic portrait which had cost five shillings and which Nick introduced as Old Jolyon, our Founder. There were two other pictures: A child with sorrowful eyes asking a collie with eyes even more sorrowful, "Can 'oo talk?" and "The Thin Red Line"—British bayonets upholding the Empire on some foreign field.

The stove, unfortunately, could not pretend to be a Victorian fireplace, but from a high-backed horsehair chair

alongside it an unrecognisable Anna rose to greet her guest.
Her hair had become miraculously grey and a little white cap
was upon it. She peered at Anton over steel spectacles,
fumbling with some knitting as she advanced. Finally she
put the knitting down on a spindle-shanked table on whose
centre the waxen fruit rested upon a stout, clasped family
Bible, with a coloured wool mat interposed between them.
She held out a hand elegant in black mittens.

From a replica of Anna's chair, on the other side of the
stove, a great coarse-featured man, who Anton had never seen
before, shouted: "Ain't it a damn rum do? A bloody
caution I call it, a bloody masterpiece." And he rolled so
vehemently with laughter that there seemed grave danger
that the slippery horsehair would glissade him to the floor.

Nick introduced him as Piggy White, and Piggy wrung
Anton's hand in a warm perspiring vice, shouting: "They're
corkers, the pair of 'em. It's a bloody knock-out. Pleased
to meet you." He produced a capacious cigar-case and offered
it to Anton and Nick. Nick refused, taking up instead a
long-stemmed churchwarden pipe.

That set Piggy off again, and he nearly choked in the
smoke of his own cigar. Anton found time to look about
him, to wonder at the bamboo bookcase in which had been
assembled *Eric, The Basket of Flowers, Jessica's First Prayer,
The Wide, Wide World, Queechy, Birds of the Holy Land,
Ministering Children,* and many another masterpiece; at the
photographs of strange women with whalebone necks and
little round buttons, such as page-boys affect, down the convex
fronts of their bodices, all framed in plush; at the epergne
gay with paper poppies and maidenhair fern that stood on
a fretwork bracket nailed to the wall.

A few nondescript people began to drift in; some of the
hangers-on from the Press Club and the Bassoon Club; and
Piggy White, who had been placed in charge of the bar,
was kept busy pulling corks, squirting soda, and chuckling
confidentially to every newcomer that it was a bloody eye-
opener. Nick and Anna refused to move. They sat in their
straight-backed chairs, one on either side of the stove, Nick

smoking gravely and reading Emerson's Essays, while Anna peered through her spectacles at a stocking that made little progress.

Their sheer immobility moved everyone to laughter, till Anna asked in a quavering voice: "John, dear, shall we call Willie?"

Willie had evidently been waiting for his cue behind the partition that marked off Anna's bedroom. Without giving John time to reply, he emerged and came self-consciously down the room, wearing a Little Lord Fauntleroy suit, with the charming addition of frilled drawers that reached below the knees.

"Now, Willie," said John dear, hoisting disguised Brian on to a chair upholstered in yellow plush. "Mamma and I have asked all these gentlemen from the church to supper to-night. It would be nice if you recited your poem to them. Mind now! No mistakes."

Willie piped up: "The Sparrow's Christmas Eve. Or Waste not, Want Not:

> Huddled in their humble feathers
> Underneath the castle wall,
> Thinking of their hungry nestlings. . . ."

Nick stood behind Brian, one foot on the chair, one hand in the small of the child's back, the other twisting his head this way and that.

"Oh, Arthur Prince!" Piggy moaned. "Oh, Coram and Jerry! Stop 'im, someone. 'E's too rich."

But the recitation went through, and just as it was finished Anton, quietly opening the door to a knock, discovered Rachel standing in the light of the guttering lantern.

Anna was pushing Brian into bed, and a reporter who had brought a gramophone stuck on a record. "Here's 'ow!" Piggy White was shouting to someone, and the gramophone said, "Happy Days are Here Again!" Anton doubted it.

"My dear! How surprising!" Rachel said, and swam past Anton into the thick blue waves that surged towards her. Piggy, cummerbunded like some gorgeously-banded amor-

phous creature of the deep, wallowed forward, a strict inter-
pretation of duty supplying his hand with a full glass. It was
of his essence that he should expect the memory of their last
encounter to be gone from her mind. Her smile suggested
to him that it was. It was Nick who intervened, diverted
the glass of Guiness to another quarter, took Rachel to a
chair, and produced sherry from a cupboard.

"It was like my cheek to ask you, wasn't it?" he said.

"I'm surprised that you thought it necessary. You might
have assumed that Anton would bring me."

"I *was* assuming that, till he told me this morning how
much you hated me and that you wouldn't come. He
apologised for you most charmingly. So I slipped the note
into your shop."

She looked at him steadily over the top of her glass.
"What was the idea—to surprise Anton agreeably or humili-
ate him?"

He grinned back at her, unabashed. "That decision may
be left to you."

She turned a glance of slow insolence round the room.
"Do you know," she said, "if it weren't for all this drink and
your disgusting company, these surroundings would suit you
perfectly. You've no idea how natural you look as a Victorian
bourgeois. Did you make these wax fruits? Or are they a
wedding present for you and Anna? I can picture you two
leading a model life here. I suppose you've insured Brian
with the Prudential?"

"And hasn't the good God sent a pussy cat to purr on our
hearthrug on the very first night?" Anna said appearing at
the back of Rachel's chair. "An omen, I call it. Brian's
just been saying his prayers: 'God bless Auntie Rachel, and
make her a good girl.' I don't think. But, begod, you'd
better be. Come and dance, then. We don't want ornaments.
Piggy White'll make you a grand partner. Look at the old
hound—all on fire round the middle. The rings of Saturn.
Thank God I've dipped into astronomy. Come on, now."

Someone put on "The King's Horses," and Anna seized
Anton, lugubrious in a corner, and pulled him to the middle
of the floor. "Come on, now, you blond hero," she said.

"You look like the Vikings after Brian Boru had given 'em hell an' all. An' that was at Clontarf, in case you don't know. Dance it out of your system. Piggy White won't hurt your girl. You've only to look at the man to see he's an ascetic."

Piggy had advanced to Rachel, his paw gallantly on his heart, and over Anna's shoulder Anton beheld him, cigar in mouth, like the Michelin balloon-man sagging across the floor with a vivid Paquin fashion-plate.

Nick, smarting from Rachel's thrust, had torn off his side-whiskers, retired behind the partition, and reappeared in his green corduroys. He watched her venomously, wondered why he had asked her, marvelled at the grace of her body, which even Piggy's obstreperous embrace could not turn wholly from the expression of some fundamental rhythm. She danced as well as she skated.

The record skirled to an end just as a theatrical gossip writer arrived with two chorus girls from the show at the Hippodrome.

"There's no more beer," Piggy announced from his improvised bar.

"Then I call this no damned party," the gossip writer said. "Come on, children; we'll find something wetter." And they were gone as briskly as they had come.

"That's a pity," Piggy said. "We want more girls."

"I'm an educated woman, may the good God be thanked for it," Anna exclaimed, "and your words remind me of Longfellow's *Excelsior*. I'd like to see you, Piggy, bearing your strange device on a banner in Market Street."

Thereupon a youth with an e :llent baritone voice and an eye which for some time had been glazing, started suddenly to life and began to sing *Excelsior*, using Piggy's slogan instead of Longfellow's. "We want more girls. We want more girls. We want more gur-urls, we want more girls!" Only his voice came alive; his eyes remained dead. The rendering was spirited and deprived him of the last of his senses. He fell back and went to sleep.

The party began to sag. They, indeed, wanted more girls if there was to be dancing, so there was no dancing; and the drink was done, so everybody began slowly to deflate. Anton,

who had been melancholy all the evening, took up a portfolio
and spread Nick's drawings round him on a table. A group
gathered about them, discussing and criticising.

"Take one each," Nick invited grandly. "A memento of
this marvellous year. By December, Anton, you'll want a
bronze plate in your studio to say I slept there once."

"Well, there's no bronze plate in *this* studio to say that a
maniac lived here who gave away his bread-and-butter."

Anna swept the drawings together from under snatching
fingers. "A guinea apiece," she shouted. "Any offers?"

There were none, and she put the portfolio away in a
drawer.

"How lovely," Rachel said, "to have some entirely disinterested person to look after you."

"Disinterested, my armhole," Anna retorted briskly. "I
haven't got a shimmy to my back, and it's time I had one."

CHAPTER TWELVE

I

THE striped awning was out in front of the Town Hall.
Handsome cars stopped with perfect breeding dead to the
inch, discharged their occupants, and slid away with marvellous self-control. Taxis chugged up and stopped with a shock,
shot forward again with a bone-shaking rattle.

Silk hats, white silk scarves, velvet, lace, a waft of perfume,
a flash of "academic gown." The occasion assembled itself,
passing bit by bit beneath the striped awning.

Nick and Anna walked. The card had invited "Mr.
Nicholas Faunt and Lady," and if there had been a fireplace
in The Loft Nick would have thrown the card upon it. But
there was only the stove, and as he lifted the flap to post
the card to hell, Anna snatched it from his hand.

"You'll be in on this," she said.

"I'll be in on nothing," Nick answered. "What d'you
think I want with that damned gang?"

"You want all they can give you."

"And what would that amount to?"

"I haven't the least idea. But don't you be a fool. You've got to live by selling, and you've got to meet your customers."

"I'll look a bright beauty among all those blasted peacocks."

"Then peacock yourself and look as good as they do."

"I'll see 'em in hell first."

"See 'em where you like, but go to the show first. You can't get anything out of a guy in hell. You've got to catch him on the way. For God's sake be practical!"

Nick smeared butter on his bread, gulped some tea, and sneered. "Rachel was right. You're looking after me, aren't you?"

Anna disdained to reply. She opened the door and called down the wooden stairs into the yard: "Brian! Are you going to be all day in there? Get on now to school, will you?"

"And why d'you want to send Brian to a Catholic school?" Nick continued to grumble inconsequentially.

"D'you give a damn where I send him?"

"No, I don't."

"Then shut your gob."

The drone and whine of Carless's circular saw came up from below. Anna gathered the breakfast things together, cursed the necessity of taking them down to the yard to wash up, decided to leave them unwashed, and pulled on her black sombrero.

"I'm going to buy a hat," she announced at the door, "because when this affair comes off I'm going with you."

It was a discouraging day. The sky had slipped and was crushing down upon the roofs. Nick went to his easel—a house-warming present from Anton—and looked despairingly at the half-finished picture that stood upon it. He had made innumerable studies of Piggy White, and here was their synthesis: this great bawling vulgar figure, bowler thrust to the back of the head, mouth gaped in a shout, face red with the lust of gain and cunning with greed. Nick had indeed seen Piggy, but Piggy had not seen himself. He loved the picture.

Nick stared at it gloomily. The light was shocking. He could do nothing. He sat down with his head in his hands, listening to the circular saw. Dro-o-o-o-ne, as Carless pressed his wood upon it, and then the glad released whine, like a gnat in sunlight, when the burden was lifted. Drone . . . whine. Drone . . . whine.

He sat for a long time doing nothing, then he slung out of the room, down the stairs and into Carless's workshop.

"Carless!"

"Yes, sir."

Carless moved out into the open, removing a cigarette end from his cap, glad of an excuse for a whiff.

"I'm going out with my wife on the fifteenth. We'll be late, and we can't leave the boy. Could you and Mrs. Carless put him up for the night?"

"Ay, glad to do it, Mr. Faunt. We never goes out anywhere, and there's a spare bed. We're only five minutes away, and I can bob 'im back to you for breakfas'."

"Right-o," Nick said. "Put it on the rent bill."

"Oh, no. I meantersay . . ."

"Put it on the rent bill," Nick said.

No harm in saying that, he reflected, and walked away down Amhurst Street.

Anna was turning out of the main road. She swung towards him jauntily. The drab morning air was stabbed by the bright pink of a pork-pie hat she wore on her head.

"Now, begod, you needn't be ashamed to be seen walking with me," she cried, her black eyes sparkling. "Is there a hat to match it between here and the dear God knows where?"

"I should say not," Nick conceded gloomily. "Where did you get it?"

"In the little shop opposite All Saints, and it's a saint I'm feeling myself with a new halo fit to go straight to glory in."

"And where's your old hat?"

"In the dustbin, I hope. I left it in the shop."

"H'm."

"H'm to you, you sour-looking old devil. You don't deserve a woman with a sense of chic."

When Nick came back at midday he flung Anna's old hat, green broken feather and all, on the table.

"I'm taking you with me on the fifteenth," he said, "and you'll wear that."

Anna turned from a hissing frying-pan at the stove. "You like it?" she said, wiping her hands on her apron.

"It suits you," Nick conceded briefly.

"Glory be to God!   He likes something about me!" She snatched up the new pink hat and banged it through the flap of the stove.   "Now you do something worth while and warm a good man's sausages!"

II

They walked to the great reception, Nick in green corduroys, Anna belted taut into her old raincoat and crowned with the black sombrero. They walked down Oxford Street, and when they came to God's most gloomy tabernacle—All Saints Church—rearing its carbon mass as though it were carved out of the very heart of the black misery of Hulme that lay behind it, when they came to that, standing in its ghoulish churchyard clotted with foul tombstones and withered witchlike shrubs, they paused, attracted by the knot of idlers grouped around an orator whose box was placed outside the iron wall of a public urinal.

Apathetic men, who looked as though they had been dead a long time, preserving solely the living ability to spit occasionally and feebly towards their planted feet; youths whose cheap fleshiness was more awful and frightening than faded decency could ever be; a few women, their arms folded within their shawls, listened unemotionally to the impassioned voice that preached the gospel of Moscow.

But not the crowd or the speaker nailed the attention of Nick and Anna. What brought them up was the face of the youth leaning flaccidly against the urinal wall, holding in a thick white hand the staff of a crude banner bearing the symbol of sickle and hammer. The holding of the banner seemed a purely automatic action. The man was holding it in a dream. The staff looked like a stick jabbed through a dollop of dough. From out of the white full moon of his uneventful face his eyes looked through the men and women before him upon God knows what picture of misery and despair. A torrent of hot eloquence poured down upon him from the speaker's brazen mouth, but he was icy and inaccessible in some grievous world of his own.

It was weeks since Nick and Anna had seen Holy Moses. Both shuddered as though they had seen a ghost. Nick took Anna's arm and hurried her away. "Come," he said. He did not feel capable of saying another word.

III

The stairway twisting up to the Lord Mayor's apartments had been banked with palms and hot-house flowers, blooming in pots whose shameful earthiness was concealed by green foliage, craftily arranged. The air was impregnated with dank and heady perfumes of jonquil and narcissus, but here and there the yellow shine of daffodils suggested Proserpine, arrived indeed, but still vestured with the deathly odours of the underworld.

"Holy Mother of God," Anna whispered, clutching Nick's arms, "what do we want but a few candles to have a grand wake! Would that be a duchess, now, whose backside is like a beer barrel? I prefer them small and switching from side to side. There's seduction in that. Are you sure this old hat's all right? They won't boot me out?"

Nick grunted, and plodded steadily up the stairs in the wake of the vast velvet posterior that had attracted Anna's attention. On the landing a great crowd was assembled, and the air hummed with conversation as though all the bees on the tessellated pavement were in full buzz. Shirt fronts gleamed; here and there the jewel of a decoration flashed; the blue and scarlet of learned garments added their note to the flowers which had spread out into a garden.

Nick and Anna came to a stand. Nick, with his hands thrust into his pockets, glared offensively about him. Anna

D

was overwhelmed by a spectacle such as she had not looked
on before.

"What do we do now?" she whispered.

"By and by," said Nick gruffly, "we'll be presented to the
Lord Mayor. Then I suppose we'll eat something. Then
probably there'll be a bit of jaw, and then, thank God, we'll
be able to go home to bed."

"I say, look at our Rachel! Put on your beautiful
garments, O daughters of Zion! Begub, I'll bet that goes
back into stock to-morrow in her shop. Oh, why did you
make me burn my little pink hat! That would have been
something."

Anton, in tails, his golden beard shining as though it had
recently been burnished, was advancing adoringly at the side
of a tall, straight, indifferent Rachel. She was in a casing of
ivory satin, tight almost to the knees, then flowing out, exquisitely graceful, into a little train. Her hair was dressed
in Spanish fashion. There was a comb stuck in the back
of it, and a furled fan drooped negligently from her hand.
For all her banter, Anna felt a sick shock of envy, and turned
her face away.

"Ach, why the hell did I ask you to come here?" she said.
"I didn't know it would be like this."

"What's wrong with this?" Nick said, his thin claws
raking his untidy head. "I think it's amusing. There are
about six people here worth a damn. The rest are what their
shirts make 'em. They tickle me to death."

"Ah, well, I don't like it," Anna said. "I feel like a lousy
old hen at a peacock show. They'll take me for one of the
attendants in the women's lavatory."

"Don't be a fool. You're the finest-looking woman in
the place."

"Fool yourself. If this was the Garden of Eden I'd be in
the running. But these people aren't looking at women.
They're looking at clothes. Use your brains, if God gave you
any. There you are! What d'you make of that?"

Anton and Rachel had drawn abreast. Anton had half
made to stop. Rachel, head in air, swinging her fan, walked
steadily forward, dragging her escort with her.

"And that's the bitch that was swigging our beer the other night," Anna hissed with venom.

Nick's haggard face tinged suddenly red. His eyes went hard and dangerous. Leaving Anna standing where she was, he strode leanly in pursuit of Anton, elbowing the crowd rudely. It was a restless, chattering, moving crowd, and it swallowed up him and his quarry almost before Anna realised that she was alone.

She stood there for a moment with wondering eyes, super-cilious eyes, amused eyes, shocked eyes, deprecating eyes, looking her up and down, dismissing her, rejecting her, passing on. She suddenly felt appallingly, indecently con-spicuous. She felt as though everyone there had come for no other purpose than to stare at her, to jeer at her, to laugh covertly or openly at her old faded raincoat, her battered hat with its drunken feather. She could have carried it off with Nick at her side, but now she was without resource. There was not a friendly look anywhere. Stony indifference, icy disapproval, open hostility, seemed to pierce her raw con-sciousness from every side. Nick was gone, lost completely in the shifting, coloured sea. She couldn't stand it. She turned and fled towards the head of the grand staircase. A man was ascending, slowly, elegantly. She almost collided with him. A monocle dropped from his eye and swung against the distinguished cut of his white waistcoat. He adjusted it and looked at her quizzically. "So we meet again!"

Anna felt as though a heavenly creature had deigned to stoop down to the pit of her humiliation. She halted, looked at him puzzled. She could not place him, though the face was not unknown. He helped her, holding out a hand that was still trim, though inclined to be puffy.

"The other morning, my dear, by that great big hole, where they are planting the tree of knowledge."

The encounter flashed back to her memory: the ageing philanderer on the new library site, the invitation to coffee.

"Oh, yes," she said helplessly, and contrived a wan smile. And rather breathlessly she added, "I'm just going."

"But why so early—before the fun begins?"

"Ach, to hell with the fun," she said, recovering her balance a little. "The fun isn't for the likes of me. D'you ever see the equal of this damned old crazy hat?"

He looked steadily not at the hat but into Anna's black eyes. "No," he said, and his smile was disarming. "Never. Let me buy you a new one."

She allowed the challenge to pass. "Are you going to the jamboree?" she asked.

"I never miss a free jamboree in the Town Hall," he smiled. "It's one of the few compensations for being an alderman. The municipal sherry at least is excellent. That is the one point that unites all parties."

"So it's an Alderman you are?"

"Yes, dear young lady," putting an arm confidentally through hers; "and an alderman must not dally on the stairs. A city father must get to his duty, which is to help to entertain the children."

She found herself being gently returned the way she had come. She took a sidelong glance at his rosy cheeks, exquisitely shaved, and had the feeling that he had just come out of a warm bath. She felt, too, as she had done when last she met him, that she liked him. He couldn't surprise her; she had him weighed up; she knew the type. It was a type she could be very comfortable with.

They were back on the tessellated landing, but a change had come over things. The bubbling coloured sea had subsided into a river set in one direction. Towards the door of the Lord Mayor's apartments, and in the distance Anna could hear a decisive voice announcing names.

"There's no hurry," her alderman said. "Let us rest."

He led her to a bench bowered in palms and ferns. "You were going to the show?" he asked as the stream flowed determinedly by them.

She looked round for Nick, but he was nowhere to be seen. "Yes, but I've lost the bloke that's got the ticket."

"You will permit me to deputise for the lucky bloke?"

"Looks as though I'll have to. But really I ought to clear out. Look at these bloody clothes! I can't go in like this."

"Everything is permitted, my dear, on an artistic occasion

You are an artist? You have an artist's hands—and an artist's freedom of speech."

He sought to possess himself of one of the hands as though to consider its artistic proneness, but good-humouredly desisted from pursuing the quest when she drew them away.

"Well," he said at last, "shall we go in now?"

They joined themselves to the rather dejected tail of the procession. "Your name?" he asked. "We will have to be announced. You can hear that, can't you?"

Anna could, indeed, hear that. Like an archangel's on the judgment day the decisive voice was ringing out ahead.

"Anna Fitzgerald," she whispered.

Now they were passing through carpeted rooms whose tall windows, despite the light within, shimmered with the violet irradiation of the arc lamps in Albert Square. It came to Anna with a little shock. Albert Square just beyond the window, the streets she knew and the sort of people she was accustomed to. Piggy White, Holy Moses. . . .

She glimpsed the ivory pillar that was Rachel moving stately down the long room, between the high dingy walls inflamed with a few fine canvases.

Now they were there themselves. Beyond the last door she saw again the coloured tumultuous crowd, caught the sudden shock of its hot, concentrated breathing, the clack and whinny of its discord. A scarlet figure, gold-chained, was smiling and bowing in the doorway. The archangel's voice clamoured: "Alderman Sir George Faunt and Miss Anna Fitzgerald."

She felt as though all the movement had ceased, all the voices gone suddenly still. Grasping the Lord Mayor's hand, she said breathlessly, "Jesus!"

The Lord Mayor winked at Sir George Faunt and said quietly: "She's mistaken your identity, George."

Then they were beyond the last door. The noise and movement seemed to swing suddenly at her again, like after the two minutes' silence.

IV

The great hall beyond the tessellated pavement was open, but almost deserted. A hidden organist was breathing the very ghost of music out of his pipes, a gentle flutter of sound like doves under the high dim vaulting. The place was almost dark. One or two people peered at the half-seen splendours of the Madox Brown panels on the walls.

As Nick flung open the door he saw Rachel and Anton pacing slowly side by side. They were almost at the far end of the hall, and in that twilight Rachel was as tall and straight and indifferently beautiful as a lily.

When the door swung behind him, Nick stood still for a moment, and he could hear his own breath coming in quick, gusty spasms. Then he strode swiftly down the room to the end where no one was save Rachel and Anton. He put himself in their path, his eyes glowering, hot and red, in his white bony face.

They looked at one another for a moment, Rachel enigmatic as a death-mask, Anton flushed and uneasy.

Presently Anton said, " Nick——"

Nick raised his hand. A sharp, flat-handed blow stung Anton's cheek and cut off the word. The sound was startling in the quiet. Anton recoiled, his eye brimming, not at the blow but at all that it meant.

He came forward, his hands beseeching. " Nick——" he said again.

Nick did not speak, but, raising his other hand, he struck again, and the sound was like a twig snapping in frosty weather.

Then he rushed away to the other side of the hall and sat down on a rickety cane-bottomed chair. He leaned his face upon his arms stretched along the back of a chair before him.

He sat there for a long time as though he were praying in the dusk. The homeless music crept round him, and it was too dark for anyone to see that he was crying.

When he went out the landing was empty. He could

hear the far rumour of the party; and, damning God and man
in fierce undertones, he fled from it down the flowery
escarpment of the staircase.

v

Anna discovered that a guest without a wedding garment is
not so conspicuous to other people as to his own self-con-
sciousness. She soon forgot that she was dressed differently
from everybody else, and once she had got over the shock of
finding that her gallant was Nick's father, she enjoyed herself
very much indeed.

Sir George was a good host. He was at home, and knew
that she was not. He bridged all her gaps and kept her at
ease. He saw that she drank no more than a wise quantity of
sherry. He was attentive with sandwiches, jellies, fruit, coffee,
cigarettes. Talk raged round them, but it might not have
existed. He kept her isolated, the sole object of a perfect
unobtrusive solicitude. The occasion might have been
arranged by him as a little spree for her alone.

Not that Anna was deceived. He knew how to go about
a job, but she knew what job he was about. Nevertheless,
she was ready to concede her admiration to his artistry.
Nicely warmed with wine, her tongue was slippery, and
presently she said what she had been thinking.

"It's a rum thing you being Nick's father."

Then she thought: "Now you've done it, you fool." And
then again she thought: "Well, it'll be amusing to see where
we are, anyway."

Sir George took a red carnation from the vase on the table,
twirled it in his fingers, considering his reply. He snapped
the stalk and put the flower in his button-hole before he
answered, allowing, judiciously: "Yes, I suppose it is."
Then: "So you know Nick?"

"In a sort of a way. I've heard him talked about. They
say he's a wild hooligan."

"Yes, you might call him that."

"But they think he's a grand painter."

"I'm told so, too, but I know nothing about these things."

Sir George permitted himself to consult a wrist-watch, as though the subject bored him. "So that's that," thought Anna.

"Do you like speeches?" Sir George asked.

"Not if there's anything better to do."

"There's always something better to do. The speeches are about to begin."

He led her skilfully through the crowd which was drifting from the supper-tables, and inconspicuously but resourcefully left them to their idea of fun. An attendant appeared with his hat and coat, and a moment later, as he and Anna stood under the striped awning, a Daimler slid to the pavement edge.

"I don't know whether I could drop you anywhere?" Sir George said.

"Well, if you could chuck me out at the corner of Dickenson Road——"

Something defensive in her suggested that Amhurst Street had better be left out of the conversation.

The chauffeur put a rug over their knees, and the big car moved away on velvet. Ten minutes, Anna reckoned, should bring them to Dickenson Road. After all, you were pretty safe with a chauffeur driving.

Sir George sat quietly and decorously as they sped smoothly along Oxford Street. As they were passing the Infirmary he took her hand as he might have taken his daughter's and said, "Well, we'll meet again, of course?"

"Shall we? How do you know?"

"Oh, one does."

And as the car slowed to a standstill he leaned over and kissed her on the cheek.

"Begod, no more pep in it than if he were kissing the baby good-night," Anna reflected as she watched the car disappear. Then, climbing on to a tram that would take her back to Amhurst Street, she remembered that from Nick she had not received even so chaste a salute as Sir George's had been.

CHAPTER THIRTEEN

I

BRIAN was not sure that his exchange of uncles was so satisfactory as he had hoped it would be. Vividly present in his memory was that day which had begun with Uncle Mo trying to drown him and had ended so charged with hot colours and bright sensations. He recalled the warmth of the fire as he was being dried, the cosiness of the kitchen, the thrill of seeing the pictures that Uncle Nick could draw. He hadn't known that anyone could draw pictures like that; he had thought that they were simply things that came in books. Then there was the lion that Uncle Nick had made out of dough, and there was the grand moment when it had been thrown and hit Uncle Mo in the face.

Those good days were over. There was no Uncle Mo to throw things at, and Uncle Nick was not always the cheerful man he was that first night. Sometimes he was horrible. Uncle Mo had never been horrible, except that day on the lake. But you never knew how you were going to find Uncle Nick.

Brian recalled how he had been scooting along to St. Joseph's, the Roman Catholic school just round the corner from Amhurst Street, and how he had collided with a filthy old man who seized him by the collar, shook a fist under his nose, and said, "Look what you're doing, blast yer bleeding 'ide!"

The old man's face filled Brian with loathing, but his words were rich delight. Released with a shove, he sped like a bolt from a catapult, the lovely rounded oath ringing through his head. His mind was not yet fully accustomed to Catholic images, and when he saw the great figure of Jesus in the school, with his breast torn open and a red heart exposed, he murmured, fascinated, "Bleeding 'ide."

When he got home to dinner his mother and Uncle Nick were already at the table. Uncle Nick had a tin-opener in his hand and was working at a tin of salmon. He was half-way round when his hand slipped and the half-lifted jagged cover sliced his flesh. Blood spurted, and Brian yelled: "Look what you're doing, blast yer bleeding 'ide!"

Uncle Nick dropped the tin-opener, wrapped a handkerchief round his hand, and roared with laughter. Brian was delighted with the success of his remark, and repeated in ecstasy: "Bleeding 'ide!" A flat-handed blow from Anna sent him reeling.

"Don't let me hear that sort of word on your tongue again, or I'll flay you alive," she threatened.

"Uncle N-Nick l-laughed, anyw-way," Brian blubbered.

"More shame to him," Anna stormed. "Your Uncle Nick's got a funny idea of a joke."

And then Uncle Nick knocked the salmon tin over, squirting juice all over the table, pushed back his chair, jammed on his hat and went out.

There was another occasion, a wet Saturday, when it was impossible to go out. Uncle Nick had not been in since breakfast, and Mummy had helped to send the Woolworth engine round and round its track a thousand times. Brian had looked at all the pictures in all the books. He had made towers out of the wood-blocks that Carless sent up for him, building them to the limit till they toppled, then building again and again.

And still it rained, and at last there seemed nothing more to do, and the world was just a great boring wilderness.

Brian yawned and said: "I wish we had a dog."

"Well, we can't have a dog. Where would we put a dog in a place like this?"

"Why can't we have a house like Uncle Mo used to have?"

"Because we can't. That's why."

"I wish we had a cat."

Anna groaned.

"I wish we had a brother."

The rain on the roof was pattering in Anna's brain. "For the love of God, stop wishing," she shouted. "You'll drive me mad." And then, her mind flooding with inspiration: "Here. Come and learn to paint like your Uncle Nick."

Occasionally, but not often, Nick painted in water-colour. Anna found his box of colours and his brushes, and took a volume of the *Strand Magazine* from the Victorian bookshelf. She filled a tin mug with water, and settled in her chair with peace flooding her.

Save for the rain-tattoo, there was silence in the room. Brian bent his dark curled head happily over his task, enlivening Sherlock Holmes's dressing-gown with scarlet stripes and ennobling Watson's unimpressive visage with a golden beard. The leopard changed his spots and the Ethiopian his skin, and Brian thought he had never before found so fascinating an occupation.

Then Uncle Nick came in, with rain shining on the lean angles of his jaws and his boots making a squelching sound on the floor.

"Look, Uncle Nick, look!" Brian shouted. "Blue camels!"

Uncle Nick looked. Then he lifted Brian out of the chair and dumped him on the floor. He took the brushes and washed them. He shut the colour-box with a snap. Then he put everything away where it belonged and turned upon Anna with an angry bark. "Those things are mine! Understand? Mine!"

And he began to furrage about with the tea things.

So you never knew where you were with Uncle Nick.

II

Seeing that Anna was inclined to sigh and grow weary whatever he did, and seeing that Uncle Nick, though he might laugh one day, might bark the next, Brian began to look elsewhere for solace, and found it in the friendship of Mick Murphy.

Mick Murphy was seven, two years older than Brian. His ginger hair and impudent freckled face were to be seen any day bobbing in and out of a house in Amhurst Street where his mother let rooms to ladies of the chorus. Mick was sharp at picking up the songs which he heard the ladies singing; and it had become the thing for one lady of the chorus, recommending Mrs. Murphy's digs to another, to say, "And, darling, you *must* get Mick to sing to you. He's the sweetest kid."

Thus Mick, at seven, was a very assured individual. He would stand by the piano in the parlour with his incredibly blue eyes shining amid his freckles, and his incredibly ginger hair blazing on his head, and, as one of the young ladies played, he would sing: "I lift up my finger and I say, 'Tweet, Tweet.'" or, "When you're all dressed up and there's no place to go." And then the young ladies would laugh uproariously, ruffle his hair and kiss him, which many a maturer vocalist would have regarded as a splendid reward; and on Saturday mornings they would wander down to Woolworth's and add something more to the formidable array of railway lines and tin rolling stock that Mick Murphy had accumulated.

It was merely the accident of their turning into Amhurst Street together that gave Brian the friendship of this desirable boy. It might not have developed into friendship if Mick had not stopped, when Brian turned into Carless's yard, and watched him mount the outside wooden staircase. The idea of going up an outside staircase in order to get home struck Mick as a strange, romantic proceeding. If only it had been a ladder that you kicked down when you were up, it would have been perfect. But even an outside staircase was sensational enough. Seeing Brian standing there as at the top of a ship's accommodation ladder, Mick burned to know what was on the other side of that romantic door. He was a man of swift resolution. He was into the yard and up the ladder like a monkey, and before Brian could touch the knob Mick was standing at his side, holding his hand meekly.

"Please, Missus," he explained to Anna, "I've brought your Brian home, and could I come and play with him to-morrow?"

"Where are you going to play?" Anna demanded. "Are you going to take him to Platt Fields?"

"No. Here," Brian explained with authority.

"I'm afraid there's not much to play with," Anna fenced.

"I'll bring my things," said Mick. "I'll be here at half-past nine."

And, having thus arranged matters to his satisfaction, he scuffled away before more could be said.

He was punctual the next morning. As though his hair were not enough, he was wearing a red jersey that moulded itself to his sturdy body. He did not knock; he kicked. He kicked because both hands were full. From one arm depended a vast suit-case made of cardboard, with imitation leather corners and rusty locks; the other clamped to his side a cat as red as himself.

"I've brought our Ginger," he explained, smiling disarmingly into Anna's eyes.

"It's a devil a lot of peace there'll be for me this day," said Anna prophetically. "How long are you staying?"

"How long'll you have me?" asked Mick, flashing his smile once more.

"Come on in," Anna said. "I know your sort. You've got a career before you."

So Mick Murphy came in and dropped Ginger to the floor; and Ginger at once arched himself against Anna's leg, tail up, sound-box vibrating.

"Ach, you're another of 'em," Anna said. "Come on and have some milk."

"What are we going to play?" Brian asked.

Mick had clicked back the locks of his suitcase. "Trains," he said, and shot on to the floor a clattering collection of engines and coaches, lines, signals, tunnels, stations—all the love-gifts of his young successful life.

"We'll have to clear a big space," he explained to Anna, seizing the table. "You give a hand and shove. And my mother says she don't care if she don't see me again to-day."

"It sounds as if I'm lucky," said Anna. "Well, get hold of it and lift."

"You've got a gramophone," Mick said warily, casting his eye to the portable shoved in a corner.

"Yes, we have, but you don't want a gramophone to play trains. Now you get on with your game."

"We'll talk about that by-and-by," said Mick. "Come on, Brian. You help to make this track. There's miles and miles of it, and it goes through forests.   Look at those names on the stations."

It was not much use for Brian to look He could not read; but Anna took a glance out of the corner of her eye, and saw that familiar English names had been obliterated by strips of gummed-on paper, and on the paper Mick had put names from his own romantic geography. " Oziboomba," one read; another quite simply was " Oom "; and the third, incredibly, was " Bethlehem."

" And where's all these places, Mick?" she asked.

" All over the world," Mick said vaguely.   " Oziboomba's wild and rocky.   There's lions at Oom.   That's why I brought Ginger.   Ginger's always lions.   And at Bethlehem you get out and see the crib and the Blessed Mother with her Babe. She's all dressed in blue and he sits in her lap no bigger'n Mrs. Finnigan's baby.   But he never wears anything, and Mrs. Finnigan's baby's all wrapped up.   I've wheeled his pram.   I know."

Mick gave these explanations casually over his shoulder as he crawled about the room, fixing rail to rail.   The system soon sketched itself in, sweeping in voluptuous curves and loops into the most inconvenient places. " Oom " was under the table, and as Mick fixed the station name he said inconsequentially: "Because if you let a gramophone nearly run down and then put the needle on, it makes a strange whine, and you could have that for lions in the distance.   I always have a glass of milk at eleven."

" We'll talk about eleven when eleven comes," said Anna.

" And now we're at Oom we ought to talk about lions in the distance," said Mick, emerging on all fours from under the table, with an impudent grin disturbing his freckles.

"Yes, Mummy, let Mick do it," Brian pleaded.

"Very well, have it your own way," said Anna.   "It's a good thing your Uncle Nick's out.   He'd give you lions in the distance."

" You haven't got a bit of meat, have you?" asked Mick. " Because if you have we could put it under the table, and then Ginger'd stay there to eat it and be lions at Oom.   If we worried him he'd growl."

But this delight was denied him, and Ginger, asleep on a chair by the stove, seemed indisposed to give local colour to the occasion.

"Now you just get on with it," said Anna, "and leave me to do my own work."

"Well, come on, Brian," said Mick, "let's have some head-on crashes to start."

So for half an hour they played the simple game of starting an engine simultaneously at each end of the track and yelling with glee when they collided and toppled over in a whirr of running-down cogs and springs.

"Now, look here, Mick Murphy," Anna said at half-past ten. "I'm going out shopping. Can I trust you to look after Brian?"

"Yes," Mick said confidently. "Leave him in my hands, Missus. That's a grand hat," he added, as Anna tugged the sombrero down over her eyes. "I like that green feather. I know a song, 'All round my hat I wear a green willow.' I'll sing it to you."

"Not now you won't," Anna said, taking up a basket. "You'll have your milk when I come back, if you've been behaving yourself."

"Who's to judge?" Mick asked.

"Now, for the love of Mike don't drag me into the depths of philosophy," said Anna. "That's a big question you've started. Now I'm going."

"*Au revoir*, darling. Be good," Mick admonished.

"Now, quick, Brian," said Mick, as soon as the door was shut. "Let's get the clothes off the bed and make some real caves at Oom."

They were not long about it. They trailed the blankets along the floor, and the blankets swept up a froth of engines and lines and signals, but that did not matter. The great thing was that Oom soon became as dark and fateful as its name. The blankets were draped over the table; they hung down to the floor with just enough aperture at two corners to permit the trains to run in and out; and the gramophone was allowed to slow down to the point of producing the

most excruciating groans. Then it was pushed into the
darkness under the table.

"You go in," Mick ordered, "and see what it's like. Oom
ought to be horrible. Is it horrible?" he demanded, as
Brian's legs vanished through the gap in the blanket.

"Yes, very horrible," Brian said. "I'm coming out. It's
dark."

"Of course it's dark. It's midnight, and the lions are
coming down to their water-holes."

"Not while I'm in there," said Brian wisely.

"We'll have to put Ginger in. We must have a living
lion as well as sounds."

So Ginger was put in, and Ginger at once came out again
and went back to the stove.

"What do we do now?" Brian asked.

"Tie him up," said Mick. "If he won't stay in, we'll tie
him by the leg to the table. You find some string while I
hold him."

But Ginger decided not to be cast for a lion at a waterhole.
He eyed Mick warily, jumped to the floor and picked his
way nicely but swiftly through the debris of rolling-stock.
Mick followed less delicately, crushing flat a Pullman coach
with one false step. Ginger had reached the partition that
screened the bed. There he stood, looking back over his
shoulder, his tail moving in slow angry sweeps. When Mick
was nearly upon him he gave one spring of exquisite elasticity
and landed on top of the partition. He seated himself contemptuously on the thin edge, and his tail hung down, twitching with annoyance. His eyes peered down at the boy out
of a head that seemed to achieve the length and flatness of
a snake's.

Mick's ruddy face flushed at this defiance. "Come down,
Ginger!" he commanded. But Ginger yawned and switched
and looked wary. But for all his wariness he was not ready
for Mick's next move—a swift and sudden grab at the
twitching tail. Down came Ginger in a spitting, scrabbling
heap, and Mick went down to the floor in surprise at the
red beast's sudden fury.

"Catch him!" he shouted to Brian, and Brian did his best.

He pulled an antimacassar from a chair and tried to net the cat. But before the gain of a good throw could be consolidated by Mick, now risen to his feet, Ginger was off, antimacassar and all, leaping grotesquely from point to point. He landed on a spindle-legged table, took off thence for a wall-bracket, and from the wall-bracket achieved the top of a wardrobe, where he settled down, feeling safe, and proceeded slowly to unwrap himself from the antimacassar.

All this would not have mattered so much if the spindle-legged table had not contained the glass-encased wax fruit, and if Ginger in his frantic flight had not sent the whole outfit to the floor—table, glass case, fruit and all—as the back-thrust of his hurtling limbs took him to the wall-bracket. It was the crash of glass that hurried Anna's feet up the last steps of the outside staircase.

With one furious sweep of her eye Anna took in the devastated area before her: the wreckage of the railway system, the smashed table, the splintered glass, the bedclothes trailing on the floor, a picture knocked askew on the wall where Ginger's searing progress had passed. Up on the wardrobe was the wild red cat, who had seated himself on his haunches and looked an interesting invalid with a shawl draped over his head to keep out the draught. He yawned into Anna's face.

Anticipating what he could hardly expect to be delayed, Mick Murphy was on the floor, the suit-case open beside him. He was shovelling in his toys as quickly as he could.

"You're soon back," he said, without looking up. "I don't think I'll stop for my milk. Thank you for having me. If you leave the door open, Ginger'll find his way home."

"It's marvellous," Anna said. "You think of everything. Brian, get a dust-pan and brush and sweep up this glass. And you, Mick Murphy, when he's done that, just get hold of these blankets and help Brian to put them back where they came from. And look slippy, the pair of you, or you'll get the broom-handle across your behinds."

They jumped to it, and soon the place had a semblance of order once more.

"And to think," said Anna, "that I went out of my way

to get half a pound of ginger biscuits especially for a pair of little devils like you. Well, come and sit down now and eat them."

They all three sat round the stove and ate ginger biscuits and drank milk.

"Will I sing to you now?" asked Mick. "I'll sing the Lily of Laguna. We've got Eugene Stratton's photo in Ma's parlour with his name written on it."

"Go on, then, and sing. It looks as if that's what the good God meant you to do."

So Mick stood on the bit of carpet by the stove, threw back his red head, and with his blue eyes shining sang "She's my lady-love."

Anna crooked her arm round him when he had done, and said, "Ach, it's a shame the old halls are done for. You'd have made a grand fellar on the halls. Lancashire was the place for 'em. All the best of 'em come from Lancashire. Well, now, go along home and disappoint your mother."

Mick pulled down his red jersey, picked up his suit-case, and repeated, "Leave the door open and Ginger'll find his way home. Thank you for having me. I suppose Brian'll be walking?"

"What d'you mean, walking?"

"Whit Friday—walking."

"Oh, that. We'll see."

Mick departed, and no sooner was he through the door than Ginger, disengaged from his wrap, made a leap to the floor, knocking out of himself a thick furry exclamation as he landed, and hell-for-leather he flew after his lord and master.

CHAPTER FOURTEEN

I

A VISITOR to Manchester, walking down Market Street, stopped at the window of Arlette et Cie, and saw there the very thing she wanted. She entered the tiny carpeted shop,

tasteful and unencumbered, to make the usual heart-breaking
discovery that the very thing was not precisely of the fit she
had hoped.

"But if Madam is staying in Manchester for another day.
. . . The tiniest alteration . . ."

Madam was staying at the Midland Hotel and would be
there till noon the next day.

And so it came about that, exactly at that moment when
Anna and Mick Murphy and Brian were gathered round
the stove munching ginger biscuits, Rachel Rosing was
pressing the lift bell in the Midland Hotel, taking in person
the dress to the valued client.

Nick, lounging past her, did not recognise the neat back
in its tweed suit. But Rachel recognised Nick. She saw
the surly droop of his shoulders go towards the octagon
court, saw the insolent way his eye raked the well-dressed
crowd seated at their morning devotions on the pale green
lacquered chairs.

Then the lift was there, silent and deferential. In the
short transit to the third floor she had time to be surprised
by the tumult of her feelings.

She had not seen Anton Brune since the night of the
assembly in the Town Hall. She had guessed that Nick
would be there, though Anton had said nothing about it. In
self-defence, Anton had for some time shut his mouth about
Nick, and that pleased Rachel no more than his babbling had
done. She was in a mental and emotional quandary about
Nick. He fascinated her, and yet she could not resist the
temptation to prick him with rudeness when they met, to
goad him to self-revelation.

She had not intended to cut him dead. But the sight of
Anna with him had been too much. That woman! That
hat! No, Rachel could not face it; and even as she propelled
Anton past the strange couple she realised that unconsciously,
without premeditation, she had done the right thing. Now
he would have to do something about it! Now we should
see!

And then so swiftly she had seen. The sound of those
slaps in Anton's face was in her ears for the rest of the

night. She knew they were meant for her as well as for Anton. So! He felt it as much as that!

If Anton had knocked Nick down that would have been the end of Nick. But Anton did nothing, and that was the end of Anton.

Rachel said nothing. She took Anton's arm and led him quietly away. In a daze she took her place in the procession surging through the Lord Mayor's apartments. She did not hear when Sir George Faunt's name was called, so strangely coupled with Anna's, nor, divided from them by the length of a long room, did she see those two come or go.

She stayed through it all. She listened to the Chairman of the Art Galleries Committee patting himself on the back at securing for the city a remarkable work by Mr. Nicholas Faunt whose pictures, doubtless, in a few years' time you would not be able to snatch for a few guineas. She listened to a great man from London, who had begun his studies at the Manchester School of Art, congratulating the city that the channels of its genius were not running dry. Evidence this picture by Mr. Faunt. Anton, with the smart still in his cheek, loyally cried, "Hear, hear!" whenever Nick's name was mentioned. Rachel said nothing. She continued to hear those two sounds like the snapping of twigs in a winter wood; continued to see the lithe tautness of a shabby tiger, tortured to the pitch when it springs.

He had obsessed her imagination from that moment, till she began to think of him almost literally as some gaunt and hungry animal crackling its way through frozen woods, and she on its track, though it might turn and destroy her. She did not conceal from herself that he had first appealed to her as a rich man's son, nor that she had burned with a desire to separate him from Anna Fitzgerald, with her bastard, had been so horribly knit up with that life which, because it was still so dangerously close to her, she pushed away with the more shuddering earnestness.

But now it was the man himself, fierce and elemental, who was diffusing his image through her consciousness, spreading like a cloud impalpable but irresistible, into all the nooks and crannies of her being.

She could not forget, as her client turned and twisted before a long mirror, that he was down there, that she might see him if only this woman would quickly have done.

"Of course, Madam, it isn't everyone could wear a gown like that."

(Oh, take the thing and go to blazes and let me get downstairs!)

Thank God that was over! She flew soundlessly along the carpeted corridor, whose many uniform doors looked as though they led to padded cells. The chastely-lit silence was pathological. A chambermaid, slummocking along with a jangle of great keys, loomed in the distance like a wardress. Not the lift. The stairs led down to the far end of the octagon court. She could walk right through it and spy out if he were still there.

She came to the last turn of the staircase and slowed her pace, alarmed at the thumping of her heart. She saw him sitting alone in a corner, a strange sight amid the Levantine elegance of his surroundings. He was wearing the only suit he seemed to possess—that atrocious outfit of dark green corduroy, and his shirt flared open at the neck.

She sailed across the lounge amid appraising glances and stood before his table.

"Good-morning."

Nick looked up at her with a sulky eye.

"You've got a damned nerve. One day you cut me dead, and the next you pick me out for this remarkable favour. Why me?" He waved a hand round the lounge. "Look at 'em. God knows they're looking at you. Why me?"

"Won't you ask me to sit down while I apologise?"

With his foot he pushed a chair in her direction. "Sit down if you want to."

"Thank you. Would you order me some Russian tea?"

"You can imagine what a pleasure it is to do anything for you."

She sat opposite him, her elbows on the tiny table, her chin cupped in her hands. Her thumbs were behind her jaw-bone. From above the eight almond points of her finger-nails, dipped in blood, her black unfathomable eyes regarded his, a foot away. He could not but be aware of the texture of her skin, a creamy satin, the perfect artistry of her plucked eyebrows, the lustre of her hair, blue-black like a crow's head. The subtlety of a faint perfume was about her.

Nick beckoned a waiter and ordered the tea.

"I've got no excuse," she said. "I don't know what made me do it. I'm sorry."

"And if you met me and Anna in the same circumstances to-morrow, I suppose you'd do it again."

He saw her eyes harden. "Anna!" she said. "Yes, I daresay I would if you were with Anna. I hate that woman!"

"Why, what have you got against Anna? She's a damned good sort."

"Is she? A vulgar, hateful creature! I'm not going to talk about her. You don't understand. I want to finish with all that sort of thing—Anna and her five shillings a week, Piggy White, Brian. . . . It's all hateful to me."

"So you were cutting dead the memory of your disreputable past—not me. Is that it?"

"Something like that. But I don't expect you to understand what I was doing. I only want you to forgive me."

"And to take care that Anna's not about when we meet?"

She nodded. The waiter brought her tea, and Nick weighed her up carefully as she sipped it. He didn't know what she was getting at, but she was very clearly contrite, anxious to be friendly. And, by God, she was beautiful. The sort of woman he imagined at some grand court function in the days of the Tsars. Impossible to believe that Holy Mo was her brother. Strange creatures, these Jews: ugly as sin or beautiful as the stars. He noticed, as she put down her glass of tea, that her hand shook. The glass clattered lightly on the saucer. She was looking at him as if she feared him. Her eyes had a shining film that disturbed him queerly.

"What do you put in your eyes?" he asked bluntly.

"Tears," she said. She took a tiny handkerchief from her bag, rose hurriedly and went away, dabbing at her eyes.

11

Nick waited for a quarter of an hour. Then he went to the telephone and rang up Rachel's shop. "Will you have lunch with me?" he asked.

"Yes."

"Thank you. I'll call for you at one o'clock."

Nick left the hotel and strolled across' St. Peter's Square into Mosley Street. It was a glorious morning. Monday would be Whit Monday. Already here and there the municipal barricades were stacked, ready to be put out for the Anglican Sunday School procession on Monday—the celebrated "walking" that made the heart of Manchester for the best part of the day as inaccessible as a besieged city. Then on the Friday they would have it all over again—the Roman Catholic's turn. That was the "walking" that Mick Murphy had mentioned to Anna. Well, it looked as though it was going to be fine for them, Nick reflected, thinking of the times when he himself, preposterously dressed in white, had formed a unit of that grand parade, carrying a basket of cowslips or hanging on to the cord of a banner that the blithe spring wind wanted to fling as a gay challenge across the gloomy warehouse roofs.

There was a feeling that the long northern spring was really over, that summer was come. "A day to be in the country, this," Nick thought. Yes, a day to be in the country. . . . In the country. How would Rachel like the country? Did Jews appreciate natural beauty? They seemed such a towny crew. Still, he had only known the ghetto type. Perhaps there were others—like the people who wrote the Psalms. But even they didn't seem to love nature—only to find in it some attribute of a God whose thought put the wind up them. Nomads, I suppose, he reflected. In the desert at night under the big stars. Yes, you could understand it.

He ran up the echoing wooden stairs to Anton Brune's studio. "Day of universal forgiveness," he grinned to himself. But what if Anton were not in a forgiving mood?

What if Anton kicked him out? After all, he deserved it.

He put his head round the door. No one but Anton in the big room. Anton was working on a poster—Blackpool without any bowler hats or gin shops or tripe saloons. Svelte girls with long brown legs, laughing dogs, a man with an Oxford college blazer and a monocle. Anton was engrossed in this production and was not aware of a visitor till Nick, bending down and protruding his posterior at a provocative angle, said, " Come on Anton. I've come to be kicked. I give you full permission. Good and hard, now ! "

Anton laid down a brush and said simply, " Don't play the giddy goat, Nick. Shake hands."

" Not till you've kicked hell out of me. Hurry up ! The waiting's the worst part."

Anton took a ruler and lightly laid it across Nick's behind. " Arise, Sir Nicholas," he said.

Then they shook hands, Anton looking rather foolish, Nick unabashed in brazen bonhomie.

" I was a pig to cut you," said Anton.

" I was a swine to hit you," said Nick.

" Well, then," said Anton, " that's that."

" That's that."

Nick sat on the table, swung a skinny leg, and gazed about him.

" Hello ! " he said. " I'd forgotten all about that ! "

Standing against the wall was the canvas he had done of Anna in the nude. " I reckon that still looks pretty good."

" I reckon it looks marvellous," Anton said. " You leapt on something that morning, Nick, and got it—absolutely. Don't touch it. Leave it as it is. As a sketch, it's a grand thing. I tell you, honestly, I've never seen anything of yours I like better."

Nick stood off and eyed the canvas critically. " D'you really like it as much as all that?"

" I do. It's fine."

" Well, look here, Anton, you keep it. I've never given you a picture You keep it."

" Oh, no,' Anton protested. " Damn it, Nick, we paint

to live, don't we? You know how I'd love to have it, but I
can't afford what it's worth."

"Put like a courtier, my lad," said Nick. "But all the
same there it is. It's yours. After all, it's your canvas and
your paint. I did nothing but introduce the one to the other.
Give us a brush and a spot of carmine."

Anton continued to protest, but Nick took a brush, put the
canvas on an easel, and brushed in "Faunt" in the proud
colour and flaunting caligraphy he used for his signature.

"There you are! Good-bye!"

And he rushed down the stairs and out into the bright
morning with a mocking devil in his head demanding to know
what was behind it all. Why this flame of generosity? What
was he going to do to Anton?

III

Nick and Rachel lunched at Lyon's Popular State Café,
which is popular because it is stately. Contraltos are apt to
break into a deep stately baying there at any moment, and
a band plays stately music, and a little boy, dressed like a
chef, trundles a wagon of hors d'œuvres among the tables
in the most stately manner you could imagine. There are
lions on all the crockery—Joseph and his brethren. Upstairs,
you dance. Rachel knew it all inside out. She liked the
place. It symbolised what she was trying to escape to. The
table napery was spotless; the manageress, dressed in decent
black, called you "Madam," and found you a vacant table.
When you yourself had been humbly calling people "Madam"
all the week, it was enchanting to be "Madam" yourself—
and to look it, too. She drew off her gloves and laid them on
the table beside her with a contented sigh.

"Well, here we are," she said brightly.

"Here we are," said Nick, and for the first time since she
had known him he smiled at her. It was a grim and hungry
smile, rather like the one the wolf gave to little Red Riding
Hood, but it pleased her. She leaned across the table and

laid her hand on his thin, agile, monkey's paw. The contact gave her a thrill. She pressed his brittle bones. "Make a good meal," she said.

"And after the meal," said Nick, "what shall we do?"

"I hadn't thought about it," she confessed. "I had nothing but the lovely feeling that half-day closing on Saturdays is heavenly."

"I suppose you have to work very hard?"

"I should say I do. The town's full of little dress shops, and to start a new one and make it pay takes a bit of doing. But we're all right, Miriam and I. We're beginning to make money."

"You deserve a holiday now and then," said Nick. "This is a lovely day to take one. It'll be glorious in the country."

His hand closed on her wrist and under his thumb he could feel the urgent blood in her pulse.

"But what should we do in the country? I've never been in the country except in cars."

"Then you know nothing about the country. Let's walk."

"Walk! But I've never walked in my life—not in the way you mean."

"It'll do you good."

"But in these!" She stretched out her foot, indicating shoes that were inadequate.

"You'll manage all right," said Nick.

"Right! Then we'll walk. I shall enjoy it. Where shall we go to?"

"Woodhead. But you've never heard of it."

"You're right. I haven't."

"Well, here's Nippy. What's it to be?"

It was all very good and unadventurous: soup which undoubtedly was thick, as it claimed to be, and Lancashire hotpot, and Stilton cheese. They had a bottle of white wine, too. "Oh, any sort," said Nick, "that doesn't tear out my palate or go sour in my stomach. God save me from becoming one of those people who can't have a drink without mewing as though it were a sacrament." And then they had coffee, smoked a cigarette, and walked along to London Road Station.

Whatever idea the name Woodhead may have called up in Rachel's mind, she was surprised by the reality. Woodhead is up on the bony spine of England. What Rachel knew of " country" was mainly the deep fleshy pastures of Cheshire. Here the earth was without depth, a skin drawn taut over the knotty vertebrae of the Pennines. Moorland stretched away on every hand, seamed with stony gullies, ruptured with harsh protuberant rocks, achieving for its gayest effect a clump here and there of silver birch, dwarfed beneath the immensity of the sky which, that day, was a shimmering blue suffused with milk. The tenderness of the sky, arched above the inchoate jumble of that feral landscape, had the nature of a miracle of kindliness.

A gritty road between unmortared stone walls thrust forward to the heart of desolation.

"Does it lead anywhere?" Rachel asked; and, indeed, it seemed as though you might for ever move forward through that tingling, winy air and not come to the end of your journey. Here and there you glimpsed the road, miles ahead, like a long white finger beckoning over the rounded shoulder of a hill, and between you and it was the primeval chaos of this land that had never from the beginning of time submitted to the rule or residence of men.

The walls petered out, and the road ran on, a narrow cut through gorse and heather and chunks of millstone grit, whence, occasionally, grouse rose with a harsh scuttering cry. In the blue, skylarks were shaking down their songs. Whin pads, thick and resilient as spring cushions, thatched themselves like eaves over the shallow sandy acclivity on either side of the road.

"Sit down," said Nick; and they sat on the whins, the surcease of their foot-beats on the road plunging them into the mysterious heart of silence. "What do you think of it?"

"I can't imagine any sort of country that would suit you better. D'you mind my saying it? I felt a bit ashamed of you in that old suit in the Midland this morning, but here I feel a bit ridiculous myself, and you seem right. Not only your suit—you. I can imagine you love all this."

"Don't you?"

" I don't know. You see, I've always lived in Cheetham
Hill, and my wildest dream of difference from that was a
house in the suburbs with a laburnum tree in the front garden.
This is a bit overpowering."

" Yes, I know. A laburnum tree makes nice pendants in
nature's ears, and in the suburbs you've got the dear lady all
tailored and permanently waved. Here she's in the nude—
and she's a savage-looking piece. Don't you think?"

Rachel nodded dubiously.

" But, by God, she's a beauty! Some day I shall go to
London, and this is what I'll miss. I'll go for walks in the
Home Counties and see farmyards with every straw in place,
and great barns with roofs the colour of Maidie Scott's hair,
and well-behaved little streams. The very pigs will all be
as clean as clean, and even in winter a stripped wood along
a skyline will look like a charming piece of lace. And I shall
be sick to death of it, and my mind will keep all this to crawl
back into at such times as other people want to pray."

Rachel slipped a hand through his arm and turned on him
her dark smile. " My dear! I didn't know you were good at
speeches."

Nick grinned back sheepishly. " Ah, well, to hell with
talking. But that's how it'll be. Come on. Let's walk."

They walked for miles and never saw a soul. Nick loped
along tireless as a wolf, and Rachel, with her inappropriate
shoes, and unused as she was to tramping the moors, felt
strained, but resolute to follow. All the same, when a twist
of the road showed them suddenly an inn set amid a cluster
of cottages, she exclaimed: "Thank God! Now we can sit
down and have a cup of tea."

They could, as it happened; and the water came out of a
furry old kettle that all the afternoon had been squatting on
the fire like a salamander hatching eggs. And when Nick
damned the smoky taste of the tea, Rachel comforted him
with the remark that no doubt all over the Home Counties
they knew how to make tea for gentlefolk.

" Blast gentlefolk," he answered tersely.

They had the room to themselves. The window was small

and heavily curtained. They were in a sudden warm twilight, duskily inflamed with the glow of the fire. After the eager exultant air and clear daylight, they were glad to sink back on their chairs, accepting relaxation. The tea was at least hot and had what Nick called plenty of body, and there were hearty slabs of Dundee cake.

"I couldn't have gone much farther Rachel said, when she had finished her tea. She moved to a rocking chair near the fire, and with one foot prised the shoe off the other. "I believe I've skinned my heel."

She put the shoeless foot up over her knee and nursed it in her hands. Her long graceful legs in their silk sheaths looked very beautiful. Then she said, "I really must look at it," and, pulling her skirt back on to her thighs, snipped open her suspenders.

Nick crossed to the fireplace and knelt on the mat as she pulled off the stocking. "Let me see," he said, and was surprised at the huskiness of his own voice. He took her foot in his hand, dropped it suddenly, and buried his face in the glowing flesh of Rachel's thigh.

He felt the sudden swoop of her lips upon his bowed tangled locks, felt the urgency of the kiss she pressed upon his head, as though she would at once draw virtue out of him and urge him down to a deeper mingling with the flesh whose tender resilience throbbed under his hot breath. Then she sat up and her two hands lifted his face towards her own. He saw the firelight staining with red the pallor of her cheeks and pricking with sparks the blackness of her eyes.

"Nick! You mustn't!" she whispered. "Get up! Get up! Someone will be coming."

When they left the inn and set their faces in the way they had come, the sun was behind the ridge to which the moor ran up on their left. It dyed the sky an angry smouldering red which slowly drained away, leaving the firmament a great bowl that had light but no warmth. It was light equally all over, from zenith to nadir, clear and metallic, the colour of green copper. Nothing broke the integrity of that magical expanse save the evening star, suspended over the abyss in

which the sun had been extinguished. In the greatness of
the silence you could almost hear the hiss of its expiring
embers.

Nick and Rachel did not speak. He handed her his old
ash stick, whose end was frayed like a worn shaving-brush,
and, side by side, obeying some instinct of avoidance, they
went forward.

Then, like a lesser dawn, moonrise began to throb behind
the ridge that rose across miles of moor to their right. They
stood still as veil after veil of silver luminescence dissolved
itself into the vast bowl of the sky till a great expanse pulsed
with a fan of radiance. Then the moon came and gathered
those skirts about her, and slowly climbed.

They did not go on. Rachel suddenly drew nearer to Nick.
He put an arm round her, and, supporting one another, they
went blindly forward into the heather. They stumbled over
tough roots and stones; they crushed the fingers of the bracken
whose fists were slowly unclenching. They stopped and faced
one another, drew swiftly together and kissed with passion.
Then they blundered forward again, till they seemed lost in
a wilderness awash with the dilute silver of the moon.

Their feet felt a great bed of heather growing under the
loom of a rock. There they stopped again and stood laced
together in one another's arms. Nick took off Rachel's hat
and kissed her perfumed hair, and she strained back her head
to give him her lips again. He fastened upon them with
ferocity, and upon the lids of her closed eyes. She slipped
half swooning out of his arms and lay upon the heather. The
moonlight fell on her white face and on the whiteness of her
breasts, which with one gesture she had bared.

Nick cast himself down beside her and ringed each breast
with kisses, then kissed the swelling nipples. She placed her
hands behind his head and pressed his face upon her exulting
flesh.

The earth swung down from under the heel of the moon
till the shadow of the rock was stretched across them, but
still they lay unheeding the moon or anything else till cold
whispers of wind began to run furtively about the moor.

CHAPTER FIFTEEN

I

ON Friday in Whit Week an incredible Mick Murphy ran up the wooden stairway of The Loft. He was wearing a white sailor suit with a blue collar, white cotton gloves, a sailor hat which lyingly associated him with H.M.S. Ganges, and white sand-shoes. His scrubbed face shone as though he had looked on God.

He tapped at the door, and Brian, who for some time had been impatiently awaiting that signal, flew to open it. Attired like Mick, he took Mick's hand, and the pair of them went circumspectly down the stair. It wanted a few minutes to eight. Anna, casting an anxious look at the sky, saw grey clouds, heavy and unbroken, above the chimneypots of Amhurst Street. A cold breeze was stirring.

She gladly shut out that chill premonition of a poor day for the "walking," and returned to the comfort of the stove, near which Nick was squeezing a last cup of tea from the pot.

"It's a bad look-out for all those poor little devils," Nick grumbled. "I wonder when people will have the sense to see that it's cruelty to children?"

"Ach, shut your gob. It's a heathen you are," said Anna. "Who enjoys it more than the kids themselves?"

"The priests. This is the day when they wallow in religious exhibitionism. A better show than the Anglicans had on Monday—that's all they want."

"And they'll get it, too, with Brian there. Anyway, are you going to see it?"

"Yes. I'm going to do some drawings. I've got two tickets for the Town Hall."

"Well, I'm not going to the Town Hall. I've bought a seat on a lorry, so that I can shout to Brian as he goes by."

So Nick made his way alone to the Town Hall, and looked down on Albert Square from one of the tall windows of the apartments which he had failed to reach on the night of the great reception. The square was a huge black reservoir, and into it bright tributary streams were flowing from all the streets that had it for centre. Gay flaunting banners, blaring bands, innumerable little boys dressed like Nick and Brian, boy scouts, girl guides, graceful nodding borders of girls in Mary's blue, floating veils, tiaras of blossom, children who could just toddle dressed in bright stuffs—pink, white, blue —long, broad ribbons reaching down from the poles of banners and grasped in tiny fists.

Soon the square was awash with the agitation of all that restless youth and colour, the wind taking the banners and filling them out like bellied sails, and making the veils to stream and the slender shepherds' crooks, tufted with posies, to sway like beds of blown flowers. The grim effigies of Mr. Gladstone and John Bright rose sheer out of the fluctuant beauty that hemmed them in tighter and tighter with every moment. For when it seemed as though the reservoir was full to the brim with children and flowers and gay glowing stuffs, still from distant streets the bugles blew under the grey lowering sky and more and more solemn priests led in more and more schools: girls bearing great sheafs of lilies, more and more of Mary's blue, and finally, sweating beneath their burden, swarthy Italians carrying on their shoulders a great Madonna.

All round that animated picture the black façades of Manchester raised their monstrous unscalable walls, so that it seemed as though the exercise yard of a prison had for once been taken over for a riot of joy.

In vain Nick allowed his thoughts to dwell on the pinchbeck quality of all these coloured stuffs, on the skimping and scraping in poor homes to buy these costumes and put them together, and on the sad state the cheap white shoes and thin white cotton stockings would be in if the rain-clouds got to work. The corporate beauty of the scene for the moment checked all other thought, and, taking out his sketch-book, he picked his crumbs from that gorgeous feast.

Then when all were present and the prayers and singing were done, the dispersion of the great host began. School by school, with banners flying and bands playing, the children moved off to make their procession through the city streets. In all those streets no shop was open. On the pavements, wedged tight as they could be, the citizens had assembled behind the police barriers that guarded the sacred roads. As clear and inviolable, those roads, on Whit Monday and Whit Friday, as for a royal cavalcade. No one dared cross save at the appointed places. Where side streets ran into the procession's route lorries were parked, furnished with benches, and here the fortunate might buy a seat. And what with the crowds and lorries, all the heart of Manchester was sealed and impassable, so that a stranger, knowing that elsewhere business was going on as usual, would be amazed to find here one of the great cities of the world which, for a week shut up shop, and for two days of that week made it impossible, unless you were an expert in side streets, even to pass from one railway terminus to another.

At nine o'clock the procession began, and it would not be till noon that the last school left the Square. That was the thought that was uppermost in Nick's mind as, at last shutting his sketch-book, he saw that a fine rain was beginning to fall. Three hours for some of those poor little devils to stand round, with their cheap finery soaking, all to gratify the damned parsons. He turned from the window. Nothing more to see there. The sight now was along the route where the rapturous mothers would be cheering their bedraggled young.

At the door he collided with a corpulent figure hurrying into the room. "Nick Faunt! Well!" And Piggy White held out the palm that was always greased with a faint sweat. "I wangled a ticket, an' I've on'y just managed to get through the blarsted crowds. I never misses this show. Uster walk in it meself. Would yer believe it? When I was as big as them tiddlers with the barskets of flowers. An' now I'm 'oary in trespasses an' sins. Poor little sods! What do they know about life? An' it's rainin' for 'em, too."

Piggy sorrowfully contemplated the sky that was by now bulging down upon the roofs. "Poor little sods," he repeated. "I'd give 'em a grand day if it was my business."

E

Nick grinned at the thought of Piggy as providence—a radiant, benign Piggy White, scattering good things from his bookie's satchel. "Well, I'm going," he said. "There's nothing more to be seen here. What about coming along to The Loft, Piggy? A quiet morning to work. Brian's somewhere in this show; and Anna's sitting on a lorry waiting to see him go by. We could get on with your portrait."

"Good enoughski," Piggy agreed. "There's damn all else to do in Manchester to-day."

He hooked his arm through Nick's as they paced a long corridor that let them out to a back street. "So Anna's watching her little cherub, is she?" he continued. " 'Ow d'you get on with 'er, Nick?"

"Well enough," Nick grunted, giving nothing away.

"Well enough, eh? 'Struth, I'd do better than that if I 'ad the chance. One of the best is Anna; a bit free with 'er mouth, but one o' the best. Arsk 'Oly Mo. Now, there's a bloke that's breakin' 'is bleedin' 'eart for 'er. Seen 'im lately?"

"I caught a glimpse of him the other night at a Bolshie meeting."

"Ay, bought with Red gold," said Piggy dramatically. "Orf 'is bleedin' napper. Gawd knows 'ow 'e's livin', unless 'e's 'andlin' tainted money. But I know *where* 'e's livin'. With a real, red-'ot Lenin-'ound in 'Igher Broughton. I've called for 'im once or twice an' taken 'im out for a drink. 'E's as blue as the bloody Danube."

"He asked Anna to marry him," said Nick briefly.

"Ay, I know. And not once, either. 'E misses the kid, too. Anna saw damn little of it. Rachel 'ated it. It was old Mo's kid more'n anybody's. 'E's absolutely loopy about Anna takin' it away."

"Well, there it is," said Nick wearily. "There's nothing to be done about it."

They had reached The Loft. He threw some coke on to the stove and handed Piggy a couple of bottles of beer. "Open these," he said.

"It's my vocation," said Piggy, beaming.

II

Brian Fitzgerald and Mick Murphy, so startlingly indivi-
dualist as they went down the stairway from The Loft, were
now as unremarkable as two daisies in a field white with
thousands. They did not know how astonishing was the
picture of which they made part. Jammed in the very middle
of Albert Square, they could see nothing save the upper part
of the Town Hall's black face, the grille incarcerating the
Prince Consort as though he had been found wandering and
put in the public pound, the sky composed of various shades
of grey, a banner or two, and a squad of boys alleged, like
themselves, to be attached to one or other of His Majesty's
ships.

But, though they could see so little, they were aware of a
great emotional stress that tightened their throats and caused
Mick to hold Brian's hand very hard. They could hear all
about them the neighing of trumpets, the zoom of drums,
the stir and murmur of the multitude. They were swayed
hither and thither. Already their shoes that had been so white
had been trampled on a hundred times, and mixed with the
exultation which their young hearts drew from the community,
was a fear such as might have assailed them had they been
lost in a forest filled with inimical crepitation and terrifying
roars.

The prayers and singing unified the host, and they took
heart, though they could not see the mouths whence the
prayers proceeded. Then at last the purposeful stridency of
the first band to move away told them that things were on the
march. The great coloured skein was being slowly drawn
into a thread that soon would be miles long, twisting in and
out of the city streets.

The rain had begun. At first it was no more than a thin
grey drizzle, but it seemed at once to bring all the winds to a
standstill. The banners drooped; the sound of the receding
band came back as though it were heard through a shut door.
But there were dozens of bands in Albert Square that day,
and soon another kicked up a lively noise, and then another.

The rain became a little heavier, and the granite setts on which Mick and Brian uneasily shuffled their thin-shod feet took on a film of greasy moisture which is characteristic of Manchester on a wet day. The children felt that it would not be so bad if they were moving. But their turn to march was a long way off; they stood, and got wet. They stood and saw white veils, that lately had been waving in the wind, gummed like draggled dish-clouts round thin shoulders; they saw flowers of rag and paper go limp and sodden, smeared like tear-stained cheeks, they saw all the children about them go limp and sodden, too, as the poor finery that had been stitched in pride wilted and shrunk at the touch of adversity. Only here and there a sheaf of real lilies shone with godly splendour in the ruin of that make-believe garden.

Brian, with a cold trickle at his neck, began to whimper. Mick Murphy, his bold blue eye hardening under the blows of fate, said, " Shut up, Brian! What's the good of sniffing? Will I sing now?" Shine or shadow was to Mick an equal incitement to song.

Disconsolately Brian nodded his head, and Mick opened his throat and began to sing: " When you're all dressed up and there's no place to go." No one bade him desist. The children round about took up the song, and they all felt the better for it.

But by the time their own band went like a prow of brazen sound cleaving a way for them through the darkening morning, they had been standing in the rain for more than an hour, and, paddling along in their sopping shoes, they felt as though they were literally following in a ship's wake. Brian's hands were cold; his teeth were chattering; his feet sucked and squelched. It was a dispiriting progress, with the black, cliff-like faces of warehouses shutting them as into a cañon over whose glimpsed top the grey battalions of the clouds went in a slow, relentless march.

Endless as the procession itself, the crowd hemmed in the marching children. Thousands and thousands of them, drab, black banks on either side of the flowing stream. Now and then the bank would crumble as someone fainted and was borne away to one of the many points where ambulance men were ready. Now and then the bank would break into a clatter of cheers as a "tableau" of especial beauty moved along. Now and then some shrill individual voice would pitch a greeting to a child or raise protest against the misguided possessor of an umbrella who sought to use it.

But to Brian it was all black and inimical, a multitude without a friendly face, hedging a dolorous way. He lifted his tired feet mechanically to the lilt of the band; and, when a halt jarred all along the line, lifted them still, marking time on the hard wet road. Then forward blindly again between the tall black buildings, under the grey unfriendly sky, through the close border of black dresses and white staring faces.

Never in his life had he felt so friendless and forsaken as amid that multitude. Mick's hot hand was no comfort, brought no assuagement to the shivers and tremors that took hold of his body. The way seemed endless, and the bands, imperiously calling from in front, relentlessly hounding from behind, jarred his head as the hard road jarred his sodden feet.

They had marched a long way. They had come round the great open space of Piccadilly and were heading along Market Street when once more the draggled army shuddered to a standstill. Brian lifted his feet, flopping his now pitiful shoes sop, sop, upon the roadway. Tears were in the eyes that searched the close ranks on the pavement. Suddenly he disengaged his hand from Mick's, rushed to the pavement's edge and gave a great shout: "Uncle Mo!"

Holy Moses, hunched in a soaked overcoat just within the barrier, ducked and pulled Brian under. He fought his way through the crowd, squeezed between a lorry and a wall, and in the quiet of a back street picked up the child and pressed him to his breast.

"Brian! Brian!" he mumbled. "You're wet, my dear. You're cold. Poor little chap! You're soaked to the skin."

He opened his overcoat and pressed Brian closer. The child shivered, sneezed, snuggled into Mo's body. Mo walked sightlessly down the street, so strangely empty, with its locked doors and shuttered warehouses; a dead backwater behind the great river of the procession. He felt strangely moved, dazed by what had happened, not knowing what to do. He stood still in the leaden vacancy of the street. A cat, sleeked with rain, the only living thing in sight, came from a warehouse door and arched itself against his leg. In that stygian alley Mo felt uplifted and happy. The child had run to him and was now warm on his breast, and a cat was purring against his leg. He looked up at the sky of dull pewter as though it were a river of stars.

Then he went on, full of a sudden resolve. In and out of the side streets he went till he had crossed the heart of the city and come to St. Ann's Square. There he found a taxi and gave his address in Higher Broughton. His progress, carrying the child, had been slow. The cat had accompanied him all the way. It rubbed his leg as he stood at the taxi door. He stooped and lifted it into the cab, then followed with the child. Brian was fast asleep, his face hot and flushed. Moses removed the ridiculous hat and pushed the damp curls back from Brian's forehead. The cat coiled itself on the seat and purred. So they came to Higher Broughton.

There was no one at home in the small house where Moses lodged. He took Brian upstairs, undressed him and put him into his own bed. Then he went downstairs and warmed some milk. Brian drank it, threw his arms round Mo's neck and kissed his pale lips. Then he lay back, with a hot spark glowing in each cheek. Moses sat patiently by the bedside, holding the child's hand, and when, soon, Brian slept, he stole down to the kitchen and washed the saucepan and tumbler. With the cat on his knee, he sat quite still, his coffee-brown eyes fixed on the fire.

CHAPTER SIXTEEN

LIKE most shops in Market Street, the shop of Arlette et Cie was shut throughout Whit Week. Although she would have no other holiday that year, Rachel Rosing did not go away. Ends were precariously meeting; there was no money to burn.

It was, at first, holiday enough for Rachel to lie late abed in that room of unaccustomed daintiness, to see the laburnum chains shining like golden icicles outside her window, and to hear, what she had never heard in Cheetham Hill, the morning songs of blackbirds and thrushes.

But the glory of her freedom had palled a little, for, though Rachel was at home, her landlady was not. Whit Week was her holiday week, and so Rachel's liberty was mitigated by the need to do her own cooking, clean her own rooms, and make her own bed.

On Whit Friday morning she delayed as long as possible the performance of those tasks. She could see through the opened curtains that it was not a propitious day. It would probably be an indoor day; and indoors might as well be in bed. She stretched her arms above her head, yawned wide-mouthed as a cat, and gave herself up to the luxury of thinking about Nick Faunt.

She had broken the back of the obsession. The ardour of his love-making was still near enough to cause her to tingle at the recollection, and she would willingly have renewed the experience which she had herself invoked; but she was realistic enough to know that something more had now been added to her feeling. She knew that she had surrendered to her own passion, not to his; that she had taken, not given; and she wondered how much more Nick would be prepared to give. The little shop in Market Street was all very well; but Rachel did not want to regard that as more than an insurance against a spinsterhood which she hoped to avoid. Anton Brune had faded out with a completeness which annoyed her, though she had contrived it. She would have liked a reluctant retreat rather than the rout which suggested to her touchy imagination a willingness to be done. It was one thing to disengage Anton; it was another to come to terms with Nick. She sensed enough of his character to know that an explosion of grand passion under the moon was as likely to burn out all that was between them as to light a candle by which she might see her next step.

She got out of bed, aware that some complicated man-œuvres were before her, bathed thoughtfully, and sat for a long time before the array of tubes and stoppered bottles on her dressing-table. She brought her black hair to a lacquered brightness; she worked carefully at her finger-nails with an emery file; she touched and retouched the lips whose brightness was enhanced by the dull creamy pallor of her skin.

She breakfasted frugally on tea and dry toast and an apple. Then she lit a cigarette as she sat before the electric fire. It was an expensive cigarette. Cosmetics and cigarettes were things which Rachel, in the wisdom that had lifted her out of Cheetham Hill, knew must not be cheap.

She rustled open the *Manchester Guardian;* not that she wanted to read it. There was nothing in the Manchester papers, anyway, during Whit Week. Simply for the luxury of being herself, Rachel Rosing, a woman who had risen leisurely, breakfasted intelligently, and now, well-dressed, sat down to read a newspaper without hurry.

Luxury! A car, and the most expensive unguents and lotions, silk stockings at a guinea a pair, stalls at the theatre, plenty of clothes, servants, holidays abroad. Rachel remembered the glimpse she had had that night from the top of the tram as she passed Sir George Faunt's house: the lighted interior, a man-servant, a car waiting at the porch. Certainly Nick, for reasons of his own, did not at the moment fit into the picture; but Rachel was not distrustful of her ability to work miracles.

Well, the first thing was to see Nick again. He showed no haste to come to her, so she must go to him. In Rachel's mind there were no qualms or hesitancies about that. Anna might be there; but some eyewash could be found if she were. An inquiry about Moses. Did they know where Moses was living now? That would do very well.

But Anna was not there. It was nearly noon when Rachel reached The Loft, trim and collected, with a white mackintosh, burnished by rain, belted about her waist. From halfway down Amhurst Street she saw Piggy White come out of Carless's yard. She lowered her umbrella hastily before her face, and was pleased, when she cautiously raised it a moment later, to see that Piggy had disappeared in some other direction. Piggy White, Anna Fitzgerald, Brian; she ticked off in her mind the odious obstacles that must somehow be eliminated.

She ran, neat-footed as a gazelle, up the steps, knocked, and popped her head round the door. Nick was alone, his right hand rootling among his dark hair as he contemplated the picture of Piggy. In his left hand was a daubed palette.

He turned at the sound of her coming and gave her anything but a welcoming look.

" What a dreadful person to paint," she said gaily. " Whoever would want to buy a picture of Piggy White?"

" Anyone who knew a picture when he saw one," Nick answered sourly. He turned his back to her and went on with his work. She sat on the table, lit a cigarette, and swung her long thin legs.

" What's brought you here?" he asked presently, without looking round.

Rachel blew a smoke ring thoughtfully before answering. " One likes to see one's lover now and then."

" Oh," he grunted, standing back again and surveying the picture critically. " And who's your lover?"

" Technically, according to all the best novels, you have the pleasure."

" You must read very old-fashioned novels. It would serve you right if my father sued you for seducing his son. That's what it comes to, isn't it?"

Rachel dropped her ash carefully into a tray. " He would be well qualified to judge whether there was a case, I understand," she answered.

Her cool, mocking eyes were unable to measure the effect of her shaft. Nick kept his head averted. " You'd better let me draw you," he said. " That will keep your mouth shut."

She was satisfied with the admission that she had touched him.

" Take your hat off," he said, " and sit in that chair. I only want a head."

" I am flattered," she said. " I gathered in the Town Hall the other night that you are the greatest artist in Manchester. Does that mean anything?"

" As it happens, it does," Nick said, putting Piggy away by the wall. " But that's something you wouldn't understand."

That wounded her deeply, because he said it as a plain

statement of fact, and not as a thing meant to wound. She took off her hat and sat down, feeling as she had felt that morning in the Midland Hotel when her heart panted after something removed and strange in him. He sat at the table with a block of paper before him and looked at her as icily as if she were a dummy. He drew, and tore up, and drew again, his thin jaws seeming to hollow more and more, and a vein in his temple ticking till it seemed that the beat of his brain was visible. She felt an appalling helplessness, a sense of his remoteness, as though all that had happened between them meant no more than a row of pins.

It was thus that Anna found them, entering presently and vigorously swishing her sombrero to and from to rid it of raindrops.

"Begod, an' it's an honour to our humble home," she exclaimed. "Put a window round her head, Nick, an' a little red thread hanging down, and call it Rahab the Harlot. It's a grand thing to be a Biblical student. I suppose you didn't dream of putting the kettle on, Rachel my darling? I'm dying for a cup of tea."

Nick rose, crushed into a ball all he had done, and threw it into the stove. "No go," he said. "Never mind, I did a good day's work on Piggy White."

"And what's wrong with what you've done on me?" Rachel demanded.

"Ach, don't argue," Anna exclaimed. "Don't you know Nick's an artist? He's not like the bloke on Blackpool sands who draws heads for sixpence. Look at Piggy there! Can't you see the wicked old devil's evil life grinning all over his face? Now that's what Nick has to get—the inside of 'em. You see what a hell of an art critic I am already, and only living with the man a few weeks. Isn't that it, Nick? You couldn't make her look wicked enough?"

Nick did not answer. Instead he asked a question. "Has Piggy White got much money?"

"Glory be to God," said Anna. "What a thing to ask about a bookie; It depends on the day of the week. I've known him rolling in it, and I've known him bust."

"Well, we'll be bust soon," Nick said, "if we don't get

some money. Piggy's dying to have that picture. Says when he buys a pub he wants it in the snug." He reached for his hat. "Piggy's asked me to have lunch with him at the Midland, so apparently he's not broke at the moment. I'm going to try and raise fifty pounds out of him for that portrait."

"Put another gold chain across his belly an' charge the old hound a hundred," Anna suggested. "Then we can go to the pictures. Rachel will be delighted to come in and look after Brian for us. She's as good as his mother."

Nick was gone. Anna raked the stove, put on the kettle, and placed cups and saucers on the table. "Now you're here, you'd better have a cup of tea," she said. "Though what you're here for I don't know. I had a suspicion that you were trying to heave me right out of your beautiful life. Isn't that so? Excelsior and to hell with Anna."

Rachel looked her most amiable. "Well, Anna," she said, "something had to be done about Brian, hadn't it, with me and my brother both at work? But why you should think I didn't want to see you again I don't know."

Anna clattered a plate of hard scones on to the table. "Oh, we just get these ideas, I suppose," she said. "Did you find Nick agreeable this morning?"

"Perfectly."

"You're lucky. He's a sour old devil."

"How did you come to know him?"

"Oh, just picked him up. You know the way with us bad women."

"Well, you picked up a bargain, my dear," Rachel said sweetly. "He'll be rich some day. His father's one of the richest men in Manchester."

"Ay, and much good that'll do us," Anna answered. "Rich or not, Nick would as soon cut his throat as look at him. It's as much as my job's worth to mention the old man."

"Your job?" Rachel dropped the question with most disarming candour. Anna took it up with frankness.

"What are you trying to get at?" she asked. "D'you want to know if I'm sleeping with him? I'll tell you: I'm not.

But I mean to one of these days. Now, is there any other detail of an intimate character——?"

"But, Anna, I didn't mean to suggest——"

"Ach, don't be so damned delicate," Anna broke in. "I'll tell you some more. He's painted me in the nude, so he knows he's got something worth bothering about. Not that that seems to matter to him. He looks at you as though you were a jelly-fish, not a fine figure of a woman with every modern convenience."

"Well, you've certainly given me your confidence," Rachel laughed. "I feel flattered."

"I don't want you to feel flattered," Anna replied. "I just want you to know where you're not to put your foot in. See? I'll tell you one more thing while we're on the subject. I happen to be in love with him. You probably think that's funny, but keep it right in your head. It's important."

Rachel took out a cigarette with ostentatious unconcern. "It may be important to you, Anna," she said, "but it can hardly affect my beauty sleep."

"Sleep, is it?" said Anna. "I thought your beauty came off a chemist's shelf in the morning? Oh, well, have some more tea. I must say you put it on very nicely, Rachel. You'll do for a few years yet, though Jewesses don't last as a rule."

Rachel's ivory face flooded with colour at the crude insult. She crushed out her cigarette in a saucer and spoke quietly: "Anna, you're just a bragging fool. You always have been and you always will be. You're insulting me because you think I've come here after Nick. Very well. I have. You can keep the job you've got. You can go on washing his pots and cleaning his boots. It suits you. But a lot of good it's doing him. A bright pair of fools you looked the other night at the Town Hall, didn't you? That's your idea of looking after him. All you're after is a roof over your bastard's head. Well, keep it, if you can, and good luck to you. But look out!"

She was pulling on her gloves as she spoke. At the last word, her face livid with the passion she had kept out of her voice, she was gone.

CHAPTER SEVENTEEN

I

THROUGH streets made difficult by the draggled remnants of
the Catholic procession finding their way homewards, Rachel
went with what haste she could towards the Midland Hotel.
She had no clear idea what it was she intended to do. She
only felt that Anna's insults had catapulted her towards Nick.
She would lay hands on him by hook or crook. She would
face even the leering, bottle-nosed Piggy White, carry
Nick off from under his eyes. As she hurried along, she
prayed that they had not gone in to lunch; but when she
reached the hotel there was no sign of them in the winter
garden, the octagon court, or any other place where men
might drink a cocktail. There was only left the American
bar; and she decided that she had better not intrude into that
male sanctuary.

A little breathless, and excited with anger, she sat down at
last in the octagon court, hoping that she might see and
waylay her man when his lunch was ended. She opened her
bag, carefully retraced the carmine curve of her lips,
powdered her nose, and in her mirror glimpsed, behind her,
an interesting face. She prolonged her toilet that she might
study the face more closely. There was no doubt the man
was interested in her. Through a monocle he was quizzing
the charming shell of her ear, the close-drawn ivory skin on
the high boss of her cheek-bone. A pity he was behind her.

There were four little chairs at her table. On the seat of
the one opposite her, a *Manchester Evening News* had been
left. She crossed over to pick it up, and found it tiresome
to return. So she sat there and held the paper before her
face.

The name that was niggling like an irritant at the back
of her mind leapt to her eye upon the page:

"Sir George Faunt, who has given £100 to our White
Heather Fund."

141

There was Sir George—photograph by Schmidt, Manchester
—debonair, monocled, infinitely charming. Rachel's heart
gave a fierce kick at her ribs. With the picture printed on
her eyes, she brought the paper down from before her face,
and let her gaze rest with frank curiosity on the man opposite.
So this was Nick's father! Well, they certainly had not
much in common. Sir George raised a plump, dimpled hand
to twirl his neat moustache. An elegant ring flashed on his
middle finger; neat gold links secured the cuffs of his stylish
shirt. As he twirled his moustache, he contemplated Rachel
openly but unaggressively. He gazed at her pensively, as
though she were not there. But Rachel was experienced
enough to know that gaze. It was not the annihilating gaze
that Nick had turned upon her an hour ago in The Loft; it
was a gaze that would respond to encouragement. She made
up her mind to administer the encouragement. This was
something worth trying. She realised with blinding clearness
that always, behind Nick, she had envisaged this man, his
father. And now that she saw the man he pleased her. The
clean-cut trim of him, the smooth rubicund cheeks, the cut
of the perfect clothes, the silken ankle that might have
belonged to a boy, the silver-headed malacca cane on which
his left hand rested—it all appealed to something fastidious
in her. She took up the Martini that the waiter had left on
her table, and as she held it to her lips she smiled. It was
the slightest imaginable, but still a frank and unmistakable,
salutation.

Sir George came and sat at her table. "That smile," he
said in a voice which Rachel thought as attractive as his face,
" is the best thing I've seen in Manchester in the whole of this
deplorable week. It deserves the reward of a drink."

He summoned the waiter and gave the order.

"You are alone?" he asked.

"I was waiting for a friend," Rachel answered; and then
blushed to recollect in what dubious circumstances that answer
must, hundreds of times, have been given. She wondered
how often Sir George Faunt had heard it.

"His absence," said Sir George, with heavy gallantry,
" suggests that he is my friend rather than yours."

Rachel smiled. "Your friend, indeed!" she thought. There was, for some reason she did not understand, little enough friendship between this elegant sire and his haggard, shabby son.

Absently Sir George took her fingers in his and absently fondled them. "Was it your intention to wait much longer?" he asked.

"It *was*," she answered, flashing at him an understanding and brilliant smile, "but I'm not sure that it matters."

"I see, I see," Sir George said. He continued to fondle Rachel's fingers, but he was uncertain how to proceed. She intrigued and stirred him. Her dark beauty, shot through suddenly by that electric smile, was exciting even to so experienced a philanderer. But he was uncertain of her status. He did not want to bungle things with his next remark. He looked at her appraisingly, and thoughtfully twirled his moustache. She sensed his trouble and helped him out. "I'm not a prostitute," she said, and gave him again her radiant smile.

Sir George smiled, too, happy to be so frankly released from his dilemma. "Thank you," he said. "It was brave of you to say that so honestly."

"Not at all," Rachel answered. "I could see it was worrying you."

"Would you care to tell me your name?"

"Why should I care? Rachel Rosing."

"I like that. It's a nice name. Jewess?"

"Yes. Do you mind?"

"Why should I mind?"

She shrugged her shoulders with faint expressiveness.

"There," Sir George said, smiling, "that's one of the reasons why I don't mind. Very few English women could have made that little gesture in just that way, so perfectly. I like a woman with unconscious, perfect gestures."

"You seem to like a lot about me—my name, my gestures —very quickly."

"And why not? Do you mind my liking you?"

She put her hand frankly on his and turned on him again her illuminating smile. "No," she said. "I don't mind a bit. I'm glad, because I like you, too. And now I must be going."

She gathered up bag and gloves and stood up.

"But this is absurd, my dear Miss Rosing," Sir George said. "Please sit down again." Rachel sat down. She had counted on being asked to do so. "We can't just meet, and say we like one another, and then say good-bye. Not quite so quickly as that. Why, you haven't even asked who I am."

"No, Sir George."

"Ha!"

She turned over the newspaper beside her and indicated his photograph.

"Oh, I see," he said. "No good giving you a bogus name."

"No good at all. And why should you?"

"I have done it before to-day," he said, smiling with almost childish frankness.

"I don't doubt it for a moment," said Rachel, smiling, too, with perfect understanding. "But it's no good with me."

"You're a woman of the world, eh? Very experienced?"

"On the contrary," Rachel answered. "I'm so inexperienced that I'm very careful."

"So inexperienced that you haven't even had lunch out of me. Have you had lunch?"

"Yes," Rachel lied, desiring nothing less at the moment than to come face to face with Nick and Piggy White.

"Then it must be dinner. Will you have dinner with me to-night? Say yes, please. I'd love it. Then we could go to the show at the Palace."

He looked at her with a boyish eagerness erasing the lines of age from his face. She found him extraordinarily fascinating. What manner of man he was she could only guess. She guessed that he was a gallant, accustomed to easy conquest; yet an astonishing freedom and youthfulness wiped out anything that might jar upon her.

"Very well," she said briefly.

He patted her hand enthusiastically. "Now, that's better," he said. "Now we can part more cheerfully. I'll call for you —if you don't mind?"

"Not at all." He wrote her address in a little note-book.

"Mind," he warned her gaily, "I'll be dressed up to the nines."

"All right," she smiled. "I won't disgrace you."

She kissed her fingers to him lightly, and went away. Sir George sat for a while tapping his lacquered shoes meditatively with his malacca cane. He suddenly looked his age. He looked lonely and a little despondent. He felt like a child who has done another of the silly things he ought to have grown out of. "Ah, well!" he sighed, and, thinking of the aching emptiness of the city in this damnable Whit Week, decided to go and sit by the fire in his own big, lonely house.

II

The tram, which went with an iron jangle along the rails to West Didsbury, could not go quickly enough for Rachel Rosing. "The theatre," she reflected, "begins at half-past seven. That means dinner at half-past six. He will call for me at six o'clock. It's already half-past two. Hurry, tram!"

They hurtled past Platt Fields, and from the upper deck Rachel looked hungrily at Sir George Faunt's house. How little time ago the grey skies and dingy walls of Cheetham Hill had shut her in! Now, incredibly, she was out of it, and was about to dine with the owner of that house. Look at it! That great big house with the gravelled sweep skirting its lawn and running under the portico that enabled you to get out of a car without soiling your shoes! Done with the hideousness of Mrs. Moss and Brian and Anna. Oh, Anna! Keep your Nick now!

She flew from the terminus to her rooms, and spent a wonderful hour deciding what she should wear. There was not much to choose from, but if M. Worth's headquarters had been at her disposal she could not more fastidiously have chosen and rejected. When she had laid out on her bed the slenderest step-ins and petticoat, the most fragile stockings, her dress of faded ivory and her only cloak, she made herself some tea and toast, and then, for the first time in her life, allowed herself the luxury of a second bath in one day. She

threw in a handful of bath salts, lay back, and luxuriated
amid the scented vapour. She dried herself, rubbed the
steam from the long mirror with a sponge, and surveyed
herself critically from the arch of the instep that was slender
as a deer's to the crown of her perfectly-poised head.

Anna's sneer came back to her mind. "Jewesses don't
keep." Anxiously she examined her figure, front and sideways. No fat anywhere. Not an ounce! She gave her flank
an approving smack. "Fit for a king," she said proudly,
and got on with her dressing.

Humble devotee of the luxury she had never attained,
Rachel had a quick eye for a car. She responded as to something worshipful when a Rolls-Royce, Daimler or Hispano-
Suiza slid past her in the street; the pretty lines of a Chrysler
made her heart dance; and even when she had been crushed
into Anton Brune's antique Morris two-seater she had felt as
though she were at least on the lowest rung of Jacob's ladder.

Therefore when, from her spy-hole behind her first-floor
curtains, she saw a Daimler slide silently and powerfully to
the front gate, her heart gave an ecstatic bound, and the bell
that shrilled through the house seemed a summons to an
incredible magnificence. She had never ridden in a Daimler,
a Rolls-Royce or a Hispano-Suiza!

She carried herself down the stairs with a slow majesty,
as though each step were ten feet wide, exquisitely balustraded.
Sir George was on the doorstep, a white silk scarf snowy
under the pink chubbiness of his chin. He gave her a long
appraising look and said: "I did not think it would be
possible to look so much more beautiful than you did this
afternoon."

Rachel turned on him a slow glance from under the lids
that looked as though they had been stained with a faint
damson dye. But they were innocent of anything save a
remarkable transparency that seemed to permit the darkness
of her eyes to show through. Her heart was mad with excitement and happiness, but she controlled herself as though she
had spent a lifetime in the exercise of rigorous conventions
and courtesies.

A chauffeur wearing a grey uniform stood with his left

hand on the door handle, a rich rug over his right arm.
Rachel bowed her head devotionally and got into the car.
Sir George followed, took the rug and spread it over their
knees, and the car slipped away so smoothly that Rachel
hardly knew they had started. She leaned her head back on
the dove-grey upholstery. There was no vibration. They
might have been lying back in clouds.

So this was travelling in a Daimler! She wondered which
she liked the better: the most lovely motion in the world,
which was waltzing on the ice with a perfect partner, or this
most glorious of immobilities. She couldn't decide; but she
knew, at any rate, that this bliss, which she had now by one
miraculous and sudden stroke attained, was something which
she must not lose if she could help it.

They swung effortlessly round the corner where the lights
outside the picture house were gaily entangled like coloured
fruits glowing amid the branches of the trees. Now, somehow, it looked to Rachel a little cheap and flashy. And so
recently it had seemed to her incredibly romantic when the
arc lamps stained the air with a violet shimmer, pulsing
under the indigo dome of the withdrawn night. She learned
that things looked different from the inside of a Daimler.

The great car pushed forward with a proud consciousness
of its own strength. It seemed unhurried, yet slipped easily
past everything before it. With a polite and honeyed gurgle
from the horn, it would give a rhythmic extra push, then
drop again, the object overtaken and left behind, into its
strong unhurried pace.

Sir George said nothing. He knew she was enjoying herself, and was content to let her do it. Her presence at his
side gave him a deep sense of contentment. He was never
happier than when he had a pretty woman in tow, and he
was connoisseur enough to know the impassable gulf between
prettiness and beauty. Rachel was beautiful. Beautiful she
had been when he saw her in the hotel, but he had not
been prepared for the perfection of her beauty when it
was arrayed and paraded, out to kill, as beauty could. He sat
well away in his own corner, studiously avoiding any contact
with her, but headily aware of her and of the perfume of her

that filled the car. Sir George had picked up many a woman;
but it was an increasing wonder to him that he had picked up
Rachel Rosing. It was incredible to him that he should feel
nervous of a woman he had so casually acquired; but mixed
with his contentment there was a diffidence to which he had
long been a stranger. It had impressed him, as they walked
together down her brief garden path, that Rachel in her high
heels was taller than he.

On the rubber entry to the hotel the car stopped as gently
as though it had kissed a buffer of air cushions.

Rachel, who, like many another, had never used the Midland Hotel save for the supply of a cup of coffee or an
occasional drink, now entered its redundant magnificence
with a splendidly proprietorial air. Here, at last, were steps
up which she could walk as though from their foundation
they had been designed for her splendid stage; and, seeing
her imperial carriage and the attention that she instinctively
commanded, Sir George could not resist the pleasure of taking
her arm as they ascended the short flight that was gay with
well-dressed women whom Rachel's passing dimmed.

Rachel was amazing herself. That stormy joy which had
rocked her heart when first she saw the great car waiting for
her had not abated; rather had increased; but save for the
kindling of a lambency beneath her ivory pallor, not lighting
it but lending it an unaccustomed warmth and richness, it
left her in the cool and undisturbed possesion of all her
resources. She was using them efficiently to carry her through
the exigencies of a situation that was to her completely novel.

Looking at her sitting there, with the glow of their golden
table-lamp lending something mysterious and rich to her
loveliness, Sir George never guessed, so self-possessed was
she, that she had never before sat down to eat in those conditions. She tactfully left to him the ordering of everything,
praised the excellence of his discernment as each course was
served, and, with a mingling of dignity and friendliness that
was perfectly calculated, kept in a good humour a waiter who
obviously fretted under Sir George's brusqueness. And Sir
George, weary with the stagnation of that doleful Manchester
holiday week, told himself that it was many a long day since

he had enjoyed a meal as he was enjoying this one. Their table was isolated in a window recess, and upon it was a great bowl of double tulips, their broad faces wide-opened by the warmth of the room. They were of the same golden ivory as Rachel's complexion, and, like it, were faintly suffused with a colour that seemed never to have come through to the surface of their substance.

Sir George twirled lightly by the stem the glass that contained still a rinsing of amber wine that flashed in the light, and looked from Rachel to the flowers and from the flowers to Rachel. He told himself that he was feeling damned sentimental.

"You're looking at those flowers as though you were a poet," said Rachel with a laugh. "You make me wonder whether it's from you your son inherits his talents."

Sir George started. She had thought he would. "Oh," he said, "I didn't know you knew my son."

"I don't," Rachel lied calmly. "But I read the papers. To judge from the talk in the Town Hall not long ago, he's Manchester's greatest genius."

"I believe he is," Sir George answered surprisingly. And then curtly he added: "He doesn't live with me. We have nothing to do with one another."

Tenderness and regret darkened Rachel's eyes as she stretched a hand across the table and squeezed his fingers lightly. "I'm sorry," she said. "You must forgive me. I didn't know."

Her look was of miraculous languishment and would have reached a heart much less susceptible than Sir George's. He returned her sympathetic caress, and asked her permission to smoke. He waved away the solicitous waiter, and himself put a match to her cigarette. Then, wistfully contemplating the glowing end of his cigar, he said: "Of course you couldn't know. It was a foolish affair. You see . . ."

"Please," Rachel interposed, her dark eyes still dewy, "please don't tell me about it if it would distress you."

But, mellow as he now was with wine and sentiment, Sir George was not to be stopped. He waved a vague circle in the air with his cigar and continued: "There's no reason why

you shouldn't know. I'd like you to know. It all began
when Nick was seventeen. He was still at the School of Art
here—you now, that mausoleum near the All Saints grave-
stones. We had a maid—a girl called Jenny Kepple—and—
well, to tell you briefly, he put her in the family way. There
was a horrible shindy. Nick's mother was very religious,
you know. She was full of ideas about doing the right thing
by the girl. So was Jenny Kepple. She knew she'd got us
on a stick. If Nick didn't marry her she'd bring a bastardy
claim, drag our names in the mud—you know the sort of
thing. . . ."

Sir George drew steadily on his cigar and exhaled a thin
spiral of smoke. " Blame me if you like," he said, " but I
came down on the side of the rest of them. It took me a long
time to do it, because I saw Nick's point of view. He took
a violent hatred for that wench, which I can quite understand. But there it was. I wasn't knighted then. The
Faunts weren't such big bugs at the time, and there was no
real reason against the marriage on that score. At the same
time I was on the City Council, I was a magistrate and this
and that, and frankly I didn't want a stink. The long and
the short of it was that we jawed and we bullied and drove
him into marrying the girl. I was to allow them so much a
week till he could earn for himself, and to keep things quiet
they went to London and got married there in a registry office,
and Nick studied in the Slade School.

" And the joke of it was," added Sir George, pouring out
coffee, " that there wasn't a child at all. There was only a
miscarriage. As soon as that happened Nick told Jenny
Kepple that he was done with her, and he wrote home and
told the family that he was done with us. I think he'd had
a few months of hell. Anyway, I know that Nick and I
haven't spoken from that day to this, and that every month
my solicitors make a payment to Jenny Kepple."

He emptied his coffee cup. " There you are," he said.
" Now you know. Let's get on to the theatre."

" Thank you for telling me," Rachel said. She smiled at
him alluringly and patted his chubby hand as though he had

been a good child. "But tell me: How did Ni—your son manage to live? I suppose this was some years ago?"

"Yes, it's a few years now. Nick's mother was never happy after he'd gone. I never heard the last of it. You would have thought I was the complete villain who had driven the boy from home. She was an ailing woman, and she didn't live long afterwards. She left what personal property she had to Nick. It didn't come to much—a few hundred pounds. It kept him in Paris for a couple of years, and then he drifted back here. But he's never been near me. That's all I know about it."

And that was all Rachel wanted to know about it. Sir George did not guess from her composed and sympathetic face that her heart was singing a Te Deum. How near she had been to making a complete fool of herself with Nick—poor devil, with his Jenny Kepple in the background! And Sir George was a widower! She had wondered about that. She felt like a general who at any rate knew his battlefield, what he had for him, and what against him.

They could have walked to the Palace Theatre in five minutes, but the Daimler was waiting for them. Rachel snuggled like a warm and well-fed cat into the resilient upholstery. "I can hardly believe," she said, "that eight hours ago I'd never seen you."

"There are things that happen suddenly and things that take time and patience," Sir George said sententiously, his mind ranging over episodes that fitted each category. "But," taking one of her hands between his two, "we do seem to have liked one another, don't we?"

Rachel did not answer. She merely raised his hands to her lips and kissed them lightly. At that moment, to Sir George's regret, a commissionaire opened the door of the car. He hardly knew what to make of the girl's caress. There was something—well, almost protective, about it. But he would have liked time to discover exactly what it meant.

CHAPTER EIGHTEEN

I

THE strong elation that had upheld Holy Mo, nerving him
to a deed unparalleled in his flat and law-abiding existence,
gradually oozed away. His mind began to be tormented by
images of Anna missing the child, tearing her hair, going
into hysterics and calling in the police.

If Brian was seriously ill, if he was too ill to talk, to say
where he lived, what on earth was to be done about it?
Moses had no idea where Anna was living. At one moment
he went cold at the thought of having a stolen child on his
hands; the next he was puffed with sudden resolution, flown
with strange and unaccustomed blatant thoughts. He would
take Brian right away as soon as he was well—right out of
Manchester. He would get a job in the country and live
happily with Brian. After all, who had a greater right to
Brian than he had? No one, he told himself conclusively.

And then the cold fit came on him again. Get a job!
Yes, it sounded likely! Manchester was not lousy with jobs,
nor was anywhere else. Wasn't that the whole song and
substance of Joe Kepple's everlasting rigmarole?

Holy Moses regarded Joe Kepple with mixed feelings. He
had not the faintest idea what Joe was talking about half his
time. Joe's mouth was full of nerve-shattering phrases:
"The ideology of Marx incarnated in the politics of Lenin."
"The proud tide of bourgeois tyranny shattered against the
rock of proletarian solidarity."

Standing alongside Joe Kepple and holding his banner,
just as he had stood alongside Piggy White keeping the
ledger, Moses listened to Joe's words washing over his head
in as raucous a blast as any with which Piggy had called the
odds.

But against his bafflement at what Joe was getting at, he
set Joe's kindness and rough hospitality. It was when every-

thing had fallen to pieces about him, when Rachel had
suddenly quit and Anna had sailed away with Brian, that he
first met Joe Kepple. On an old croft, the hard-beaten play-
ground of generations of slum children, he saw, as he wandered
disconsolately, a crowd listening to the outpourings of Joe's
brass mouth and iron lungs. He edged right up to the box
on which the man was standing, holding his banner with
one hand and gesticulating with the other. Suddenly Joe
looked down and saw him and impatiently thrust the flagstaff
into his hands.

"Here you are, comrade! Hold that for me. And be
proud to hold it—the hammer that will batter down the
citadel of privilege and possession, the sickle that will reap
rich rewards for the toiling proletarian masses. Hold it up,
lad! Don't be ashamed of it! Now, comrades. I want to
make it clear to you why you are no better than a flock of
sheep, shorn to the skin for the benefit of the bourgeoisie.
And now that they're down to the skin, the next thing will
be that they'll flay the very skin off your backs, and then they'll
proceed to suck the marrow out of your bones."

It was when the meeting was over that Joe, thanking his
standard bearer, invited him to come and have one in a
public-house that neighboured the croft. A small, dark-eyed
woman wearing a great flowing cape and no hat joined them.
"Comrade, this is Olga," Joe explained; and Olga shook
hands with Moses and the three of them jostled through the
swing doors into the pub. They sat at an iron-legged round-
topped table. Olga drank gin and ginger beer, Joe Kepple
whisky, and Moses beer. It was near closing time. The air
was whirling with eddies of blue smoke, and a few disputants
had brought arguments with them from the croft.

"Cheers!" Joe cried in his ringing voice. "Here's to the
overthrow of capital!"

"All bloody well, mate," said a red-faced man with a dirty
white scarf tied round his neck. "Wot about the national
beverage? Could I go in an' order a pint in Russia? Could
I 'ell as like! Wot about the child prostitutes? Wot about
the bloody Ogpoo?"

"Comrade," shouted Kepple, holding up a fist like a sledgehammer, "you've been lapping up the poison disseminated by the capitalist press."

"Oh, well, let me lap up my beer. Oo arsked you to come in 'ere? Go an' drink vodka."

"In this so-called free country I drink what I like," Kepple retorted.

"An' that's more'n you'd bloody well do in a country where freedom ain't so-called," said his antagonist, wiping his sleeve across his mouth and turning his back to Kepple's table. "Same again, miss," he commanded.

"Similar, you mean," said the barmaid, bright even on the stroke of closing-time.

"Same or similar, it's all the same to me so long as it's beer." And, turning irritably, he launched himself at Kepple again. "Stands to reason, you bleedin' cuckoo, if someone's up someone's down. Wot do it matter to me whether you call 'em capitalists or bolshy commissars? Someone runs the roost and someone lays the bloody eggs. An' they're never the same people."

"Oh, shut up, Charley," came from another part of the bar. "Shut yer mouth and give yer arse a chance, for Gawd's sake."

Charley allowed himself to be pacified, and when Joe Kepple, unruffled by the encounter, shouted: "Well, here's to your very good health, friend," he raised his can in amicable acknowledgment.

It was not long before Joe Kepple had got the ins and outs of Mo's predicament. "Well, comrade," he bellowed, "you're no more than a typical representative of the victimised masses. No job, no home, your face ground into the dirt by the bourgeois jack-boot."

Mo swigged his beer and brooded, saying nothing. He liked the look of Olga. Her strong iron-grey hair stood out evenly round her shapely head and had the well-ordered contour of a new mop. Her features were all small and fine, her teeth small and white, her eyes kind and sensible. They had the slightest possible upward and outward slant and the thick brows above them had a queer attractive fly-away curve. And all there was in her face belonged to her face alone. No brush or pencil had added to it; no tweezer had taken from it.

"I've got nowhere to go to-night," Moses said.

"Then you'll come with us," Olga answered promptly; and that was the only word Moses heard her speak till they were in the house in Higher Broughton.

They slogged along through the misty evening, Joe carrying his box and Moses the banner; and Joe poured out the tale of his life, as he was willing to do on the slightest provocation. Shorn of its bombast, it was a tale characteristic enough. Joe was an engineer, and, until the war, he had been content with the capitalist organisation that permitted him to earn a decent wage, keep a wife and child, follow Manchester United in the winter, put in an appearance now and then at Old Trafford in the summer, and play the cornet in a good brass band.

"Ay, all was fair enough, lad," said Joe, "but I soon learned that all this was nothing more than the smile on the grinning mask of social corruption."

In other words, Joe joined the army, did his bit with the best, enjoyed a lot of it, hated a lot of it, feared a lot of it, and learned at last to damn and blast the whole of it and everyone responsible for it from top to toe.

"The death-spasm of capitalism. That's what was happening under my eyes, comrade, and out of it rose the Russian phœnix with healing in his wings."

All this had not come to Joe at once. The doubts and fears that had clouded the end of the war for him were dispelled in the happy warmth of what he now called "Capitalism's Indian summer," in other words, the boom years. Joe's wife died, but he could hardly blame the bourgeoisie for that; and, as he had good work and good pay, he was happy enough.

"And then, comrade," said Joe, who had said it many a time before on his box, "the Indian summer faded out. The awful realities of the world economic situation could no longer be hidden."

Joe lost his job, and he never got another. If Moses had been quicker-witted than he was he would have glimpsed the story of a decent man driving on blindly through year after year of humiliation, asking for nothing but hard work and hard living, and turning at last in disgust upon a society that could not meet so elementary a need.

They had reached Higher Broughton by the time Joe's recital was ended. "But how are you living now?" Moses asked simply.

"I'm keeping him," Olga answered cheerfully, taking off her great cloak with a flourish and hanging it on a hall-stand peg. Now, you two, go into the dining-room and I'll get a bite of supper."

It was a good bite, and Mo was glad of it—cold meat and pickles and cheese, hunks of bread and a wedge of butter and a huge pot of tea. After supper they drew sagging wicker chairs up to the gas fire and Joe Kepple lit a big briar pipe. He had pushed off his boots and sat with his stockinged feet thrust contentedly towards the warmth. He looked rosy and well-pleased with life, nothing of the dangerous firebrand about him.

Mo's eye ranged the comfortable room, taking in the books that filled, and fell out of, and lay in front of, a big book-case, and the planks on trestles that made a long table in the bow of the window. Inkpots, envelopes and bills littered it from end to end.

"This is the workshop, comrade," Joe explained benevolently, "the anvil for the forging of a new society. All you need you'll find in that bookcase, from Robert Owen to Karl Marx and Lenin."

"Give Lenin a rest," said Olga. "You'd better go to bed, Moses. You look worn out. You don't mind if we call you Moses?"

Moses got up and shook his head, smothering a great yawn. Olga led him upstairs, followed by Joe's bellow, "Sleep well, comrade," and ten minutes later he was sleeping like a child.

From that day he had lived with Joe Kepple and Olga, and even his bemused apprehensions had realised that in Olga was the driving force that kept Joe bellowing on his way. It was Olga who was always bringing new books to the house

and making Joe read them and showing him how their
arguments could be laced into his speeches. It was Olga who
kept both Joe and Moses hard at it addressing envelopes. It
was Olga who settled the pitch where Joe should blast forth
and who interviewed the occasional frowsy, furtive individuals
who called.

But to Moses she was kindness itself, and Moses guessed
that to Joe she showed more than kindness. She was always
up first in the mornings; she was punctual with ample and
well-cooked meals; and, realising that Moses, who held the
flag at the meetings and did whatever else he was told, had
no more interest in the "cause" than her boot, she was quick
to shut up Joe when his long-winded disquisitions flowed
over from the street corner to the hearth. Joe needed no
more than one word. He would push his hand through his
tumbled mane of black hair in a puzzled way and rumble,
"As you wish, dear comrade," and bite hard on his gurgling
pipe.

II

Moses never got to know what was the source of Olga's
income, or what it amounted to, but it was enough to keep
the house going comfortably, and even to permit Olga to run
a ramshackle car, which had been out of commission on the
night when Moses first came to the house. They used it to
get to and from their meetings, and on the day of the Whit
Friday procession it was being used for another purpose.
Getting up early to avoid the congestion of the streets, Joe
and Olga had gone off to Blackpool for the day. "Just like
a burgeois married couple," Joe grinned, happy as a school-
boy, his great pipe sticking out from under the peak of a
black and white check cap. Olga, hatless as usual and
wrapped in her immense black cape, did not fit into Joe's
hearty picture.

And now, with the child lying in a fever upstairs, Moses
sat there awaiting their return, tortured by doubts about their
attitude, full of vague ideas concerning proprietary gestures,
such as having tea ready or a good whack of envelopes

addressed. But they might have had tea, and they had left no instructions about envelopes, so Moses just sat and dithered till a ring at the doorbell startled him to his feet.

But it was not Joe and Olga. Standing on the doorstep was a young woman swinging a cheap cardboard suitcase in her hand. A tiny knitted hat was slapped down on to one side of her head, permitting Mo to see that her hair was arranged in bleached metallic corrugations. Her lips were very red, and she had on a tight little black fur coat that hardly reached her hips, whence a skirt of vivid emerald green swung down to stockings that had the same bleached metallic colour as her hair.

She treated Moses to a long impudent stare before drawling: " And who may you be, if I may make bold to ask?"

" I'm staying here with Mr. Kepple and Olga," Mo explained.

" Olga?"

" Yes; this is Olga's house. Did you want to see her?"

" Oh, it's Olga's house, is it? And what sort of job has Mr. Kepple got in it? Stud groom?"

Moses stared at the shining furrows of hair and the coral lips.

" Well, gangway for a naval officer," said the young woman. " I'm coming aboard, lad. Jenny Kepple my name is and it looks like time I was seeing what the old man's up to."

With that she thrust past Moses, banged her suitcase down in the passage, and proceeded, uninvited, into the sitting-room. " If Dad's not in, I guess I'll wait," she said, lighting a cigarette and sprawling into a chair. " And if you've got such a thing as a cup of tea, for God's sake save my life."

Moses obediently shuffled into the kitchen and put the kettle on the gas-ring. He was wondering whether to put one cup or two on the tray—would this smart young woman resent his sharing her tea?—when the rattling of a key in the front door announced the return of Joe and Olga. Moses put his head into the passage, shouted, " I'm making tea, Joe," and slapped four cups on to the tray.

Joe shambled into the living-room, dazed with fresh air,

and yawning cavernously. He caught sight of Jenny, flicking ash into the fireplace with complete nonchalance, and the yawn remained fixed, a gape of amazement.

"Well?" said Jenny, yawning in turn, and stretching her arms luxuriously. "Glad to see me back?"

Joe collapsed into sentimentality. "My little girl!" he cried. "Olga, this is Jenny, my little girl. I've told you about her—a victim of bourgeois morality."

Olga considered Jenny critically. "She don't look so little to me," she said, "or so much of a victim, if it comes to that. Ah, Moses, thank you."

Olga ostentatiously picked up the bag and gloves that were lying on the table and dropped them upon Jenny's lap. "Here, Mo—on the table."

Mo put down his tray, and burst out: "And, please, Olga, I've got a baby upstairs."

Olga looked swiftly from Moses to Jenny, then dismissed the idea as biologically improbable.

"Oh," she said. "What is this—an asylum?"

"He's very ill—shivering and hot," said Moses. "It's Brian. You know about Brian."

"I know about Jenny," murmured Olga. "I know about Brian. Has anyone else turned up that I know about?"

Joe looked comically from Moses to his daughter, his stubby fingers scratching the crown of his head. "It's a rum do," he said—"a reight rum do."

"You're helpful, Joe," said Olga, swinging her great cloak on to a chair with one magnificent gesture. "Sit down, all of you. Let's have some tea."

Jenny passed the bread and butter with manicured tinted claws. "If the child's ill, I'll look after it," she announced calmly.

"You!" Joe said thickly, champing a mouthful.

Jenny nodded complacently. "I'm the very person. You don't know what I've been doing the last few years, do you?"

"That's a fact, I don't," Joe answered. "You've taken damned good care to keep your old Dad in the dark."

"Well, when that dirty skunk left me," said Jenny, "I started training for a nurse—God help me for a fool."

"Well, it would have been a trade to your 'ands," Joe said. "Why didn't you go on with it?"

"Why? Because this is a free country, not a damned nigger-driving spot of the tropics. The Lady with the Lamp, I don't think. That's all mush for suckers. You know, dear parent, they've got a National Register, and when you're on it you're fully qualified for the chain gang. Britons never will be slaves. I don't think."

Jenny put down her cup and lit a cigarette, blowing the smoke copiously down distended nostrils touched with rouge.

"District nurse," she said. "That's about the best you could hope to be. And what does that come to? Sweating your guts out for years on end, at the beck of every wench that has a bastard at one o'clock on a cold and frosty morning, and all for the wages of a parlour-maid. And then, when you're all withered skin and bone, too old to do any more and with not a penny saved, the dear ladies of the local committee decide to make you a presentation. A marble clock, twenty quid, and the order of the boot. Not for Jenny!"

"Ay, that's the organisation of the capitalist state all over," Joe rumbled. "Haig that threw thousands of our lads into the bloody shambles of the Somme—turn a tap and let the blood flow—that's all he knew about being a commander-in-chief—he gets a hundred thousand quid and a country home from a grateful nation. Don't be vague—give all the bloody dough to Haig. That's capitalism," said Joe, bringing his mightly fist down with a slam that set the tea-things ringing. "And the workers on the battle front of humanity—what do they get? A marble clock and the blessed Order of the Boot!"

Already his eyes were beaming with gratitude to Jenny who had contributed so excellent a point to his next oration; but Olga asked rather coldly: "But you have learned enough to look after this child?"

Jenny rose contemptuously and took a thermometer from her bag. "You," she addressed Moses, "just take me to him."

"And come straight back here," said Olga.

Moses humbly preceded Jenny up the stairs and stood aside for her to enter the room. Brian was tossing on the bed, one clenched fist rubbing into the curls matted on his forehead. Jenny's manner surprisingly changed. She shook her thermometer vigorously, placed a hand on the child's hot head and slipped the thermometer between his lips. She looked at Mo over her shoulder with a smile that washed all the artificiality out of her face. "Go down now," she said. "Don't worry. He'll be all right."

Moses felt exquisitely comforted. "Thank you," he said. "Thank you so much."

He slid out of the room, and half-way down the stairs felt a soft velvet vibration against his leg. "Oh, Olga," he burst out, entering the living-room. "I forgot to tell you: I brought a cat home. You're not angry with me?"

Olga looked at him with a harsh pretended frown corrugating her brows. Then laughter broke through. "Here, give him this," she said, pouring milk into a saucer. And as Moses bent down to place the saucer before the fender she rubbed her hand affectionately in his straight lank hair.

CHAPTER NINETEEN

I

SIR GEORGE FAUNT sounded all very well; but what about Sir George Faunt, Bart?

Sir George, easy-going and pleasure-loving, was nevertheless ambitious. The Manchester City Council was riddled with knights; the Town Hall seemed to be a spawning-ground for them; and Sir George would have liked the little extra flick that lay in the word "Bart."

He was tired, too, of a widower's status. A series of shady and rather shameful adventures had come his way since Lady Faunt died; or, rather, since then they had become more numerous. It was a good time, he had been thinking, to regularise his life. All the fortunes made in the boom years had not been dissipated. He knew of one or two that were now in the hands of fortunate widows. Amalgamated with

F

his own considerable fortune, one of them would make a
number of things possible. Everyone knew that titles were
not bought, but, still, if you dropped a coin in the right slot
you never could tell what might be delivered.

Some very nice Cheshire estates were coming into the
market, too. The Ashburys had had to clear out of Codham
Hall. In these days the place would go for a song. Sir
George liked the idea of himself as Sir George Faunt, Bart.,
of Codham Hall. He had turned the matter over so carefully
in his mind that he had even decided on the warm widow
whom he would invite to participate in the further steps to
grandeur that he had in contemplation.

But, alas, turning and turning in his bed when he got home
from the theatre, he realised with a sickening certitude that
she was warm only in the Northern sense of having a well-
lined purse—in that sense and no other. No, damn it all,
her neck was a twist of ropes, and her bleak, white nose was
all feminism and no femininity. Against her spectral
attributes, melting them to nothingness, burned in Sir
George's brain the illusive and alluring flame of Rachel
Rosing's beauty.

Sir George had been conscious of pride as she sat at his
side in the theatre. Often enough, sitting it out brazenly
with some picked-up woman, he had known the prick of
shame when someone he knew had had the bad taste—the
malice, perhaps—to hail him. But Rachel had given him
nothing but pride. He could not analyse it, but he was
aware of some racial fineness, something ancient and august
in her marvellous profile and perfect skin, to which he himself was a stranger. And yet there was the fact which you
could not get over that the girl had almost winked at him
in the Midland that morning. Damn it, thought Sir George,
baffled and uneasy, she had deliberately *got off* with him; yet
here she was now, smooth and inaccessible and beautiful as
an ivory tower.

The utmost decorum had marked their homeward journey.
At her door she had thanked him demurely for the evening's
entertainment, and almost before he knew it the door was
shut and the fanlight leapt awake.

At 2 a.m. Sir George, sleepless, touched the switch over his head and flooded his bed with mellow amber light. He lit a cigarette and, feeling very wakeful, got out of bed, slipped on a dressing-gown and strolled to the open window. A glorious night had followed the dreary day. A big moon was high overhead, and the young leaves of the trees in his garden and in Platt Fields were silvered scales under its serene radiance. A waft of lilac scent came through the window, and Sir George crushed his cigarette on the sill and leaned out as though he would bathe his face in its impalpable essence. He could almost hear the insurgence of spring threading the night with ardour. A tram, super-charged with light, striking violet coruscations from the overhead wire, roared through the stillness and, so far from breaking his mood, confirmed it. He felt it right and good that big vital things should be hurtling about, and he followed the tramcar's progress down the road as eagerly as a boy. He knew with an overwhelming certitude that he was in love. God, he cried to himself, to think that he had been playing with dull and stale ideas of safety and fortune! Safety! He was safe, anyhow—rich, rich, rich! Oh, how glad he was that he was rich! He could buy Codham Hall without feeling it, and he had been so near to a beggarly compromise between paying out a little and gathering in a lot!

He left the window, lit another cigarette, and walked excitedly up and down the room. By George, he said to himself, he could understand even that damned fool Nick to-night! He felt ready to burn boats, destroy bridges, do anything irrevocable and final.

He sat down at a small writing table and dashed off a note. " Please don't have any engagement to-day. I am calling for you at eleven.—GEORGE FAUNT."

" By Gad," he said, " I'll run her out to Codham." And he knew that Codham was as good as bought, that he was tearing along as tempestuously as the lighted tramcar. Then he got into bed and slept like a log till his man waked him at seven. " Tell Jarvis to have out the car and deliver this note at once," said Sir George; and with tingling satisfaction he sipped his tea and flicked open his *Manchester Guardian*.

Sunlight was streaming through his window and in the garden
thrushes and blackbirds were calling. Sir George didn't feel
a day older than twenty.

II

Rachel was not surprised when she found Sir George's note
on the doormat. She was a sensitive register of male ardour.
That Sir George had refrained last night from any overt
demonstration of excitement did not disturb her. She
reckoned it, rather, a favourable symptom. The pouncing
men who were so damnably sure of a woman were apt to
sheer off as quickly as they had come aboard. She felt certain
that she had left Sir George in a simmer, unappeased and
full of anticipation, and that was the best thing. A note
coming thus hot from his restlessness was the happiest possible sign.

She bathed and dressed in a serene and conquering mood.
She prepared her sparse breakfast and noted with satisfaction
the perfection of the day. From the angle of her window
she could enfilade the street with a glance, and she observed
the red and white hawthorns, the laburnums and guelder roses,
and one or two snowy domes of cherry. Overhead was the
sky's tender blue, mottled with woolly clouds teased out by
a light warm wind to the utmost tenuity. Here and there
clumps of daffodils were like flambeaux stuck in the dark
earth.

Splendid, thought Rachel. Not that the beauty of earth
or sky meant anything to her, and if she observed the weather
it was never for any other reason than to know what she
ought to wear. All the same, she was not unaware of the
importance of natural conditions to a plan of campaign. She
had put on a coat and skirt of blue tweed, and a blue tweed
hat. Sir George, she felt, would want to make this a country
day.

This assumption was borne out when Sir George appeared
in a low open two-seater, enamelled bright red. Observing
his arrival from the window, Rachel commended his sense
in doing without a chauffeur. She shouted to him out of

the window not to get out of the car, and, running down the
garden path, inserted herself dexterously into the negligible
space of the seat beside the driver's. A perfect vehicle for
abduction. She liked Sir George's lit-up, excited look. His
handsome pigskin gauntlets lay lightly on the wheel. "Just
a bit of a run in Cheshire," he shouted as the car zipped along
the perfect road and took the Mersey bridge. "There you
are! Now we're in Cheshire. Lancashire one side of the
bridge, Cheshire the other."

The noble trees of Wythenshawe were hazed with green,
clamorous with rooks. They slowed down through Altrin-
cham, zoomed towards Knutsford, and missed it on their left.
This was something like being in the country, Rachel
reflected, and smiled at the reminiscence of Nick's raptures
amid the bare bones of the moors above Woodhead.

For miles they ran along the palings of great parks, for
miles they ran alongside pastures, through little red-brick
villages, glimpsing here and there the ancient seats of the
gentry with which the country is thickly strewn, the reedy
meres, the patient unaspiring churches, inns and resting-
places of an unexacting God. They hardly spoke. Sir George
was buoyant with the vivid sap of the day, eager for Codham
and the journey's end; Rachel was content to be lying back,
moving in swift comfort without lifting a finger. The
stinging air made her feel deliciously sleepy. She thrust her
long legs down to their farthest reach and eased her body in
a prodigious stretch.

A long red brick wall, blotched with sulphur-coloured
lichen, livened with ferns unfurling from their pockets, the
parapet a-dance with wallflowers trembling against the blue
sky, trailed along their left hand as Sir George slackened
speed. "We're going to make a call in here," he announced;
and, as Rachel instinctively opened her bag and began to
powder her nose, he added with a laugh: "Don't bother about
that. There's no one at home. The place is empty."

The wall was pierced by a wrought-iron gate of elaborate
and intricate loveliness. An old woman came out of the
lodge and Sir George greeted her with ready affability. "Well,
Mrs. Fiddon, I told you you'd see me back before very long."

"You did, Sir George," Mrs. Fiddon answered. "And I must say how anyone can see that beautiful place and not buy it right away is more than I can understand."

"Hard times, Mrs. Fiddon, hard times," said Sir George. "Well, if you'll let me have the keys, perhaps this time it'll get me down."

"Would you like me to come with you, Sir George?" the old woman asked, returning with the keys.

"No, thank you. If you'll trust me not to steal the spoons, I'd rather go alone."

The back of the house was towards the wall and the road. The car moved slowly along the gravel drive and came to the great gravel sweep at the front. There Sir George alighted, helped Rachel out, and almost forgot her. He had never seen Codham look so lovely. It almost took his breath away.

Codham was a half-timbered house of immense antiquity. In the bright light of that morning it looked as though it were compounded of snow and ebony. It made three sides of a square, and the recess was paved with great cool squares of stone. Leaded windows looked out from all sorts of improbable positions, generation after generation having imposed its fantasy upon the house, while respecting its essential integrity. Behind its roof-line the green plumes of the beeches stood up, and one white dove, its tail fanned, strutted on pink toes along the ridge.

Sir George crunched across the gravel and examined with new wonder the carvings, quaint, beautiful and innumerable, upon the beams. Then he turned and said simply: "Look at that."

There were no flower-beds in front of the house. Where the gravel ended the grass began, running in a slight and cleanly-shaved decline down to a tiny mere, in which the green heads of rushes were beginning to thrust up through the sere battalions that had stood their ground through the winter. A little red-tiled boathouse sheltered under willows at one end; and beyond the water the countryside ran on in gentle undulations to the blue ambiguity of the horizon.

"I like this," Sir George said. "I was here once when old

Ashbury gave a garden-party. There was a big marquee down there on the grass by that mere. I'd like to do that myself. Get the local Conservative Association people to come."

Sir George was shaking himself out of his first startled vision and getting back to the facts of life. He took the great key from his pocket. "Let's have a look inside," he said. The door creaked on its hinges, and Rachel followed Sir George into the dark splendour of the hall, fighting as she had never fought before to maintain her poise, to be unsurprised at any hazard.

She found it difficult. She was forcing herself to believe that Sir George Faunt was seriously thinking of buying this house whose beauty she was not concerned with, but whose implications were immense. She had to act as though she accepted that belief as calmly as the belief that she would eat bread-and-butter for tea. She stood and contemplated the ancestors of the Ashburys looking down from the panelled walls upon her strange incursion.

Sir George spoke in a whisper. "Old Ashbury says they'd take the pictures and the personal things, but all the rest is being sold with the house."

Everything shone: the floors of solid oak, the panels, the mirrors in frames of tarnished gilt. There were fresh-cut daffodils on the gate-legged table whose surface gave back their golden beauty.

"Mrs. Fiddon knows her job," Sir George said. "I'll keep Mrs. Fiddon."

"I don't understand," Rachel prevaricated. "You said we were making a call."

She fiddled delicately with a daffodil and watched a beam of light shattered into iridescence by the cut edges of the Waterford bowl. Sir George looked at her standing there, framed by the door open behind her; and all the sunlit countryside seemed to enhance her beauty and vindicate the sanity of what he was about to do. He found his heart thumping, and his knees were unsteady.

"You don't understand," he said; and, hearing the huskiness of his voice, she did not look up, but continued her con-

templation of the flowers. "There isn't much to understand.
This house is for sale. I'm going to buy it if you'll marry
me."

She did not answer, and Sir George went on: "Don't think
I brought you out to show you this for a bribe. But you're
so lovely, Rachel, I wanted just to see you in this lovely place.
You're the sort of girl who ought to be proposed to where
everything is beautiful. But if you don't like Codham, say
so; and if you don't like me—well, say so."

She looked at him across the gleaming oval of the table.
"But I do like you, Sir George," she said, "and I love
Codham."

"You like me and you love Codham. Well, I could wish
you had put it the other way about."

She went round the table and put her arms round his neck.
"That was clumsy of me," she said. "I'm not good at saying
what I mean. But I mean you're a darling."

She smiled into his face, and seeing the provocative depths
of her eyes, the cool seeds of her white teeth gleaming
between her red parted lips, and the rich sheen of her skin
like ivory satin, Sir George crushed her to him and felt her
body abandon itself in a long surrendering sigh. It felt to
him that she was melting in his arms, and he crushed upon
her lips kiss after kiss, which she received but did not return.

"And now," he said, putting her gently from him at last.
"Tell me something about yourself. You see how mad I am.
I'm going to marry a girl I met yesterday and I don't know
the first thing about her."

Rachel straightened her hat and smiled enigmatically. "I
am no one," she said. She waved her hand gracefully towards
the portraits upon the walls. "These people make me feel
small."

"Don't let them," said Sir George. "We are alive and
they are dead. It's our innings."

III

They lunched at an inn, and Rachel told Sir George all
that he ought to know. She was a poor, hard-working

woman. Not destitute—oh, no. The dress shop was going ahead. She would soon have been comfortably off. She allowed Sir George to understand that a shop conducted with the impeccable *chic* that she could impart was an opening bud of affluence that would soon have been in most profitable bloom. And Sir George, who had seen the little Jewish dress shops come and go with pathetic regularity up and down Market Street and Oxford Street, patted her hand protectively, and knew all about it, and said how, doubtless, it was a shame to snatch her away from the hatching of such golden eggs.

There was no one, she told him no one but herself. Her father and mother were dead; no sisters, no brothers, hardly a friend. And Sir George was secretly enchanted that there would be no complications of that sort, and began to feel more like providence than ever. He was pleased to discover that there would be no religious difficulties. Not that religion meant anything to Sir George, but he had been a little apprehensive that she might insist on some queer fooling in a synagogue. He didn't want to be circumcised, or anything. But all that sort of thing seemed to mean as little to her as to him. It would be a straightforward registry-office affair.

"And now, Lady Faunt," Sir George smiled, when he had lit a cigar and had his legs stretched out comfortably under the table, "admitting that this business of yours was a gold mine, and all that, just treat me for a moment as a business man. How much are you in debt?"

"Well," Rachel hesitated, "we had to begin on borrowed capital——"

"Precisely," said Sir George. "I know how these things are done, my dear. I want you to make one more visit to your little shop. You will have two things to do there: one is to settle up with whoever financed you, and the other is to buy all the clothes you want. Understood?"

Rachel nodded and seized his hand across the table. "George, you are good," she said. "You are a very good man."

"You love me?" he asked.

"Yes," she said, and hoped that some day she would.

Sir George bought a great sheaf of daffodils from the inn-garden. "Take these to your rooms," he said. "But I'm not allowing you to stay there this evening. You must come and have dinner at my house. I'll call for you at seven."

"You darling," said Rachel. "Please don't bother to come. You can send the car."

She thrilled as the words summoned back to her mind the downy delights of the great silent Daimler.

"I will call," Sir George repeated, slamming the door as he settled in the driver's seat; and the red car zoomed away towards Manchester like an angry excited gnat.

CHAPTER TWENTY

I

THAT same morning Holy Moses woke uneasily on his made-up bed. Jenny Kepple had been occupying his room all night. Mo slept on the living-room couch. Jenny had turned out to be surprisingly efficient in a sick-room. "I love it," she said, "but the pay's lousy, and they let you rot in your old age." She scorned the idea of calling in a doctor. "Give me two bob and tell me where there's a chemist's shop," she said. What she bought with the two bob she did not condescend to explain. "Light a fire in the bedroom, give me an easy-chair and something to read, and I'll earn my night's keep."

These orders Moses humbly carried out, save the provision of reading matter. "Strike me blooming well pink," Jenny said, casting her eye over the book-case. "Pa, you're going barmy. Isn't there anything by Edgar Wallace or Berta Ruck? Here, Mo, go down to that newsagent's on the corner and get us a few *Pansy's Papers*. I'm not going on night duty with Karl Marx. I wouldn't mind Groucho, but no Karl."

And the last thing Mo saw of his bedroom that night was the fire burning gaily, giving the place a warmth and personality it had never known before, the light, shaded towards the child, falling on the gleaming corrugations of Jenny's head as she sat stretched comfortably in a wicker chair thumbing number one of her three *Pansy's Papers*.

" You're very good . . ." Moses quavered.

" Good! Believe me, boy, this is the cushiest billet I've had for a long time. Now get out, and don't worry. I'll snooze off and on, but I'm on the spot."

Moses went away, filled with a tremendous confidence and respect. No one before had taken trouble like this about Brian—not Rachel, not Anna—no one.

In the morning he sat up, stiff and cold, though almost fully dressed, on the couch, and noted with satisfaction the smell and the sound of frying sausages. He shuffled into the kitchen, where Olga, already looking fresh and rosy, her mop a cloud of fine burnished steel wire, was bending over the frying-pan.

" Why didn't you call me, Olga?" he said. " I'd have lit the fire for you."

" Well, light the fire in the sitting-room," said Olga, " and throw up the window. Then you can have a wash and lay the table. Look nippy, and root out Joe and tell that daughter of his to come down. These sausages won't wait much longer."

Mo shuffled off on his jobs, and in a surprisingly short time everyone was seated at the table, Joe Kepple in his shirt-sleeves with his shave postponed till after breakfast, Jenny looking as though she had had eight hours' sleep and an hour's ministrations from a lady's maid. Mo looked with awe at the petrified perfection of her head, the vermilion of her lips, and the carefully-applied peachbloom of her complexion.

" Good-morning, Jenny," Joe rumbled. " How's the child?"

" His temperature's normal, and he's asleep," Jenny replied. " He'd better stay where he is for a day or two, but he's all right."

Olga thudded the teapot on to its tile. " A day or two,

eh?" she said. "Look here, Joe, hadn't we better have an inquest?"

Joe looked uncomfortable. "You know what Olga means, Jenny," he said. "After all, this is Olga's house. A strange baby and a strange young woman all in one night—I suppose Olga thinks it's a bit thick."

"Olga does," said Olga with emphasis. "Now, Mo, first of all about Brian. I can understand your snatching him up in that way, for goodness knows we've heard often enough what you think of him. But what are you going to do about it? You'll have to take him back. Where does he live?"

"That's the point," said Jenny. "It's a cert he doesn't know himself. I asked him, and all he can say is 'The Loft.' I asked him what street, and he doesn't know any street. 'It's not a street—it's a loft,' he says, and I don't think you'll get any more out of him."

"Don't you know, Moses?" Olga asked.

Moses shook his head in glum dismay. "No, Olga," he moaned, "I don't know. Anna took him away from me and went off with Nick Faunt——"

Joe and Jenny exploded like simultaneous pistol-shots. "Nick Faunt!"

"Yes," said Moses. "Do you know him?"

"Do we know him!" cried Joe. "Why, that's the bloody bourgeois that got Jenny into trouble!"

Moses turned a chapfallen face upon Jenny. "Trouble?" he said. He could not imagine trouble touching the splendour that confronted him across the table.

"Pa, cut it out," Jenny commanded sharply. "Don't talk punk. I never had a happier night than the night when I got into trouble, as you call it. Look here, Moses: the fact is, Nick Faunt is my husband, but I'm not living with him. The dirty twister cut and run. Now have you got it?"

Holy Mo tried hard to get it; and what he got was an almost suffocating sense of hatred for Nick Faunt. He could feel the blood surging up behind the pale immobile mask of his face. Vague thoughts assaulted him of the damned and double-damned villain: the man who with clever fingers stole Brian's childish liking; the man who had whisked Anna away with a word; the man who had wronged and deserted this other woman whom he liked so much, the woman who had sat up all night with Brian and could report with such comforting confidence, "He's all right." Mo sat for a time staring moodily down at his plate, then he said tensely: "I'll kill the sod." He raised his smouldering eyes and looked slowly at the three startled faces before him: Joe with a mouth opened amid his stubble; Olga looking as pained as any bourgeois at the unseemly outburst; Jenny just surprised, as she might have been by some unexpected accident. Mo looked from one to another without speaking; then he took up his knife by the haft and brought it down with a swift jab on the table. The steel snapped, and the haft thudded on the wood. "I'll kill him," said Holy Mo.

Jenny was the first to ease the situation. "You'd better not," she said with a laugh. "If Nick goes, my income goes, too."

Joe Kepple cleared his throat with a rasp and boomed in like a good wind intent on dissipating a bad atmosphere. "Yes, that's the trouble, Mo. You'd better not cut Jenny off with a shilling."

"I'll wait," said Moses.

"Yes," Olga advised, "and wait a long time. And now, where has this all got us about the child?"

"Well," said Jenny, "if the child's mother is living with Nick, I'll call on Nick's father. He'll know where they are."

"Call on Sir George Faunt?" Joe cried, aghast.

"Lummy, and why not?" Jenny demanded. "After all, whether he likes it or not, he's my Pa-in-law, and don't you forget it."

"Well, we can't keep the child here," said Olga, "and it seems to me the only way."

"And for the moment," said Jenny, "Jenny's all right. You'll get rid of me when I've got rid of the kid?"

"We'll see," Olga said briefly.

"We will," said Jenny. "If you want a razor, Pa, I can lend you one. Rather small——"

"Bah!" said Joe. "It's a pity I never used the strop on your behind."

II

The one splendid dress that Rachel possessed—the ivory dress that fitted her almost as a scabbard fits a sword—shimmered in the light of the standard lamp that stood beside her chair. She was well pleased. Her first glimpse of Sir George Faunt's house showed her that it contained all she needed for complete satisfaction.

A *chic* maid had preceded her upstairs, shown her into a splendid bedroom, and indicated a dressing-table superbly furnished.

"If there is anything you require, madam——?"

Rachel said that there was not, though she would have loved the girl to say again in just that same deferential way: "If there is anything you require, madam——?"

The girl took the cloak that slipped from Rachel's shoulders, laid it on the bed, and with one admiring glance at the tall figure caught in the gleam of the firelight, departed noiselessly over the deep carpet.

The noiselessness was what fascinated Rachel. The whole house ran with the noiseless efficiency of perfect service. She sat in a chair and listened. You could hear nothing. Yes; you could hear the rustle of the fire in the grate, and the muffled roaring of the trams in the street without; but the roaring was remote and withdrawn, emphasising the charmed, islanded security of the lovely room.

She noted, and was thankful for, Sir George's consideration in having a fire lighted just for her comfort while putting off a cloak, and later putting it on. She noted the flowers on the dressing-table, and, with an anticipatory eye, noted the deep alluring proportions of the bed. Yes, said Rachel, this was all splendid. This was what she wanted: this luxury on the edge of turmoil, this security with the noisy street tearing past its doors; town, theatres, shops. Not Codham. No. There was something disturbing about that place. She shuddered to think how it would look now, facing across that little mere, not a light anywhere, and owls calling. She hoped Sir George would not buy Codham, or that, if he did, he would keep this place as well. Perhaps she would make it a condition. Was she strong enough to make conditions? She wondered, patted her hair absently and sailed with all her grace downstairs.

In the hall Sir George stood with his back to the fire awaiting her. He offered her his arm. Her hand lay along it like a lily as he led her into the dining-room. It was a large room with a massive table in the middle, but they dined at a small round table near the fire. The same smooth perfection of service. The dishes came and went. There was a golden wine from a tall slender bottle. They talked but little, but Rachel sensed in Sir George a deep content which emanated from him to her and was a subtler tribute than chatter. " Or perhaps he's always like this at meals," she thought. " Perhaps he enjoys his food too much to want to talk when he's eating it."

" I'll join you in a moment in the drawing-room," said Sir George, rising; and Rachel found a presence, till then unseen, removing her chair, escorting her across the hall to the drawing-room. So there she sat before the hearth of old Dutch tiles, with the light of the standard lamp falling upon her, and again the uncanny but soothing silence of the house settled around her like folded wings. She lit a cigarette, stretched herself in the chair, and gave herself up to the glow of good wine and firelight. She had had an exhausting day. For nearly ten hours on end she had been radiating femininity. This was where, if this house were already hers, she would slack up, put her toes to the fire and sleep. But her task for the day was not ended.

Then she heard a bell peal loudly through the house. A moment later there were voices in the hall. Notably, there was a woman's voice, shrill and discordant coming upon that peace. Presently she heard Sir George's voice, too; and then the door opened and Sir George said : " Will you excuse me, my dear? This is unexpected. Something I must attend to at once. But I'll be with you very soon. Quite comfortable?"

He patted her hand and smiled benignly; and she said yes, she was quite comfortable, thank you. But the acuteness of her discomfort was indescribable, for the opening door had shown her Moses standing there in the hall, with a woman she had never seen before. She was superb under the blow. She didn't betray its force by the wink of an eyelid.

"Don't be long, darling. I'm dying to talk," she said.

"And I'm dying to kiss you," Sir George whispered gallantly.

She smiled, relaxed in the chair, and the moment the door clicked behind him she was up, taut as a tiger, her cigarette crushed into an ashtray. A swift stride took her to the door and, listening intently, she heard what was said.

"Well, Jenny," that was Sir George's voice. "I don't know that I can do anything for you, but you'd better come into my study and tell me all about it."

"Very well, father." The flippant, disrespectful voice stung Rachel to the quick. So that was Nick Faunt's wife! Father, indeed, the saucy little bitch. No wonder Sir George wanted to get her away to his own room where they could talk in privacy.

"You wait here." That was Sir George again. "Brewer!" Rachel could imagine the silent Brewer springing into being. "This man will wait here. Bring him some sandwiches and a glass of beer."

This man. . . . A glass of beer! That was the shabby courtesy her brother got; and that's what she'd get, too, if she were ever associated with a scarecrow like that. A tumult of apprehension shook her. My God, what a sketch he looked, dirtier than ever, gormless, shambling, cringing. What had he come about? Was it some sheer fluke, nothing to do with her at all? Was it better for her to keep out of it altogether? She stood behind the door, tortured with indecision. She couldn't chance it. She must see him. She crossed to the fireplace and rang the bell.

"Yes, madam?"

"Oh. . . . I thought when Sir George opened the door just now that I recognised the man out there. Is the man still there?"

"Yes, madam."

"Oh. . . . Will you ask him if he is clerk to Mr. Charles White?"

Brewer was back in a moment. "He says he *was,* madam."

"Ah, I know Mr. White. There is something I want to speak about to this man. Ask him to come in here."

She stood clutching the mantelpiece with both hands, her shoe on the fender. "Thank you, Brewer," she said without turning her head, and waited through the eternity that seemed to pass before the decorous shutting of the door. Then she turned round and confronted Moses, standing there flabbergasted at this unexpected summons, a glass of beer in one hand, a half-eaten sandwich in the other. At sight of her his hand shook suddenly and a spill of beer dribbled over on to his fist. He was too amazed to speak, and she saw that she must manage everything for herself. She drove her nerves sternly to action stations. She spoke quickly.

"Did you know this was Sir George Faunt's house?"
Moses nodded.

"Did you know I was here?"

He shook his head, still speechless at the wonder of her appearance there.

"I know who the woman is—the woman you came with. Does she know anything about me?"

"Not a thing," Moses croaked.

"Well, that's something to be thankful for. Put down that beastly stuff for goodness' sake."

Mo threw the sandwich into the fire and placed his glass inside the fender. Rachel seized him by the lapels and talked into his face.

"I'm going to marry Sir George Faunt. Do you understand that?"

"But, Rachel——"

"Oh, man, don't argue. You'd love me to marry someone rich, wouldn't you? Wouldn't you, Jacob? I'll have cars, and furs, and servants. I'll have money. I'll be able to help you, Jacob. I want to do something for you."

"Yes . . . well . . . you'll be able to, won't you?"

"Yes, I will—once I'm married. Do you understand? *Once I'm married.* Sir George doesn't know anything about you. He *mustn't* know anything about you. Do you understand, Jacob? If I'm to marry Sir George, you must keep out. Do you understand?"

She shook him by the lapels and gazed at his dull, lacklustre face. "After I'm married you'll be all right, Jacob—really, you will. But now you must keep out. You mustn't know such a person ever existed. Don't mention me to that woman, or to anyone else. Oh, God! Can't you speak? You do understand, don't you?"

Moses gently removed her passionate hands from their clawing at his lapels. He put her down into her chair as though she were something he had done with.

"Yes, Rachel," he said. "I understand. Don't worry. Tell me something. Where does Nick Faunt live?"

"Nick Faunt. What the hell has Nick Faunt got to do with it?"

"Nothing to do with this—nothing at all. That's done with, Rachel. I told you. As you said, I must never know such a person existed. But where does Nick Faunt live?"

"Oh, well, if you must know—in an old loft over a carpenter's shop in Amhurst Street."

"Thank you. I'll get back where I was." He was halfway to the door when he returned and took his glass from the fireplace. "Mustn't compromise you, must I, Rachel?" he said. "You look grand. Good-bye."

She leaned her forehead on the mantelpiece and gazed into the fire, her dark eyes stormy. She felt riven, torn to pieces, but she murmured: "Thank God! He'll do it. He's as safe as houses."

CHAPTER TWENTY-ONE

I

"AND you're keeping quite well, Jenny, are you?" Sir George asked with charming friendliness. "That's right. That's fine.

You're certainly looking splendid." But in his heart he was thinking what a cheap little piece she really looked compared with the superb woman who was awaiting him in the drawing-room. He was impatient to rejoin Rachel, but he was never a boor with women, and he did not allow his impatience to be apparent.

" I'm sorry I can't be of any use," he went on. ' But there it is. I know no more than you do about Nick's movements. I believe he's in Manchester. That's all I can tell you. Anyhow, I advise you not to go near him. You're getting your allowance regularly?"

"Yes."

" Splendid, splendid!" Sir George joined the tips of his fingers judicially. "Then I shouldn't worry Nick—perhaps not even his father—'m?"

Sir George rose on that hint, and Jenny rose, too, swigging swiftly the remains of the whisky and soda which had been her chosen drink. "All right, all right," she said pertly, "I won't worry him or you, don't you fear. It's not money I'm after. It doesn't matter to you what it is. Well, bye-bye. Sorry you can't help."

She held out a hand cheaply gloved in cotton. Sir George shook it warmly, took her by the arm, giving it a little paternal squeeze, and led her to the door.

"You *are* a bit of all right, you are," she said, looking up smilingly into his face. "I always thought you were the best of this bunch." And Sir George accepted the compliment as an assurance that he had conducted the interview just as he would have wished. And, having stood at the door as a good host should till she and Moses were well away down the drive, he turned then and mopped his face and murmured: "Dreadful little slut! I wonder what she's after now," and strode with glad release towards the drawing-room.

II

"Well, Moses, my lad, it looks as if you've got to keep that kid," Jenny announced as they turned into the highroad, their faces towards town. "His lordship knows nothing about my beloved husband—so that's that."

"I know where Nick is," Moses said; and added with astute diplomacy: "I asked one of the servants. They know, but they're keeping it from Sir George."

"Well, of all the cock-and-bull stories!" Jenny burst out. "If I thought that old bum was fooling me I'd go back and play hell's delight." She half turned as though to carry out her threat.

"Please!" Mo appealed. "He wasn't fooling you. He doesn't know—really, he doesn't."

"All right, Mo; I'll take your word for it; but there's something fishy about it. Is Nick's place near here? Can we get there soon?"

"In ten minutes on the tram," said Moses.

"Lummy! It makes me feel queer. I haven't seen Nick for years. I'll have to have a drink to screw me up to it. Come on in here."

They had reached the public-house on the corner of Dickenson Road. Jenny took Holy Moses by the arm and urged him towards the steps. Moses resisted. "You've had something already," he said, and added with inelegant honestly: "I can smell it on your breath. Are you used to it?"

"No, I'm not," Jenny answered with an impatient shake of the head. "But for God's sake don't preach at me. I feel I want a drink, and I'm going to have a drink. I spend a night looking after someone else's brat. I'm worn out with sleeplessness, I traipse across Manchester on your business, and, damn it! you grudge me a drink to pull me together. If you don't want to come in, sit on the step and wait for me."

"I'm sorry," said Moses, contritely, and they swung through the door.

Moses ordered beer. Jenny, who did not know that it was the last thing she should touch, ordered port. She had never drunk it before, but there was a picture of a Spanish grandee wearing a stylish cloak who somehow made her feel that port was a drink no one should miss. So she ordered port. And when she had drunk it she ordered another port, and Moses, who felt crushed to the ground because he had been ungrateful for all she had done, paid for them, and asked if she would like another port. She said she would, and when she had drunk it they went out. Jenny thought the picture house across the road looked extraordinarily vivid and yet unreal. She missed a step and recovered herself with a grab at Mo's arm.

Moses suggested that they should get on to a tram, but Jenny's stomach said no. She thought she would rather walk. So they walked, and to Jenny's feet the pavements were erratic cushions and there was a subdued, persistent buzzing in her head. She wasn't sure, as she made the street crossings, whether she was taking risks or exercising an absurd caution. The red length of the Royal Infirmary, which suddenly opened before her, seemed infinite, and then, to her surprise, it was gone, and Holy Moses, to whose arm she was clinging, had switched her to the right down a side street.

"Soon be there now," he said. "How are you feeling?"

"Wanna sit down," she answered thickly; and then, to her annoyance, found that, instead of sitting down, she was going up a flight of steps—queer, tricky steps that trapped her toes and seemed to go on and on. At last she refused to have anything more to do with them; she wanted to sit down, and she sat down. Then a light stabbed out suddenly, hurting her eyes, and she was looking into a room.

"Holy Mother of God!" said Anna, not seeing at first the heap on the floor, but fixing her eyes on Moses. "Homo! It's like a corpse from the cemetery you're looking. You're bringing some dreadful news!"

Like a corpse, indeed, Moses felt. Daft and dithering at the best of times in Anna's presence, he found himself now cold and trembling. He had not seen her for so long. She seemed to him supernally lovely, but haggard and bereft. Her eyes were red with crying, and her face was a mask of sorrow. He knew that he in his folly had brought this on her, and the woman he had hoped would explain everything, make his part seem not so dreadful as he now felt it to be,

sat there silly with drink at his feet. Anna's eyes had now
taken her in, huddled on the top step, her elbows on her
knees, her face cupped in her hands.

"Begod, Mo," said Anna, "you're a bit of a shock, but
your lady friend's a knock-out. She looks as if she's passing
away."

"Gotta headache. Wanna cuppertea," Jenny mumbled.

"Ach, tea!" said Anna in disgust. "It's a quiet corner
and a ho-heave-ho you want, my girl. That's all that'll do
you any good. Bring her in, Mo. My God, look at her hair!
Like Blackpool sand varnished. Where did you get her?
Who is she?"

"She's Nick Faunt's wife," said Moses simply, helping the
suffering Jenny across the threshold. He did not see the
swift spasm of Anna's features or hear the sudden intake of
sharp breath. By the time he had settled Jenny in her chair,
Anna was taking tea-things from a cupboard. She handed
the kettle to Moses. "Here, Mo. Go down to the yard and
fill this. You'll find a tap there."

Moses was amazed. He had been ready to curse himself
for his blunt announcement. He had expected an outcry, a
passionate scene. Now she was giving him calm orders in
the way he liked. He slid off, docile, obedient.

Anna crossed the room and looked down at Jenny, slumped
in a chair, eyes closed, head sunk. So that was it! It
explained a lot. She looked at the metallic pantile of yellow
hair, the nails crudely dyed, the complexion of a cheap doll.
"Poor little devil," she murmured. "And poor Nick!" She
felt no anger or resentment. Her thought dived unerringly
upon the truth about those two: some poor, trashy, but
disastrous contact. Nick hitched up to that ha'penny lolli-
pop! It was enough to make you cry. No wonder he was
like a bear with a sore backside.

Moses came shambling into the room. "So you knew,
Anna, all the time?" he said, putting the kettle on the stove.
"You knew Nick was married?"

"Of course I knew. There's no secrets between me and
Nick."

"He's not living with her now."

"That's a fact, he isn't. He's living with me."

Anna busied herself with the tea. "What did you come for, Mo?"

He yammered and stuttered upon his confession. "Oh, Anna, I can see you've been crying your eyes out about Brian. It's no good standing there pretending, as though nothing had happened. You know you've lost him."

She put down the tea-pot and came towards him in a terrible calm. "Well? What do you know?"

"Oh, Anna—I've got him safe! I stole him, but I've got him safe."

She took him by the shoulders, blazing. "You stole him! You stole him, you crazy fool! Where is he? What have you done with him?"

"Temrashur's normal," Jenny said thickly. "No nee' t'worry."

"Has he been ill?" Anna demanded savagely, shaking the sagging Moses like a sack.

"You ler him 'lone," said Jenny, trying to get up from her chair. The bells rang in her head, and she desisted. "Mo's a' ri'," she said. "Ler him 'lone."

Suddenly Anna felt all the strength ooze out of her, and she sat down lest she should be shamed by showing her weakness.

"Mo, come here," she said, and she stroked his hands as he stood before her. "Make us a cup of tea now. I was just mad, and I'm sorry."

"It's all my fault," Moses moaned. "I never ought to have done it. But I saw him in the procession, wet and tired, and he ran to me, and then I found him all feverish and took him home. Honest to God, Anna, it was just a mad moment, and then I didn't know where you lived to bring him back. We've only just found out—honest to God, Anna."

"All right, Mo, all right," said Anna, feeling terribly tired now that the spirit that had kept her up had retired, no longer needed. "Don't talk about it. But I haven't been to bed since Thursday night, and I've been calling on the police and the hospitals and the priest and the neighbours, and I'm just dead, that's all. Ach, now, for the love of God say nothing more. I'll come and bring him home, and let that be the end of it. Keep him to-night, because I'm tired and I want to sleep."

She leaned back in her chair and closed her eyes; and, tiptoeing, terribly subdued, between the two sagging women, Moses made the tea.

They stirred themselves at last and came to the table, and after a few gulps at her tea Jenny began to come alive.

"Where's ole Nick?" she demanded. "Wanna see m'husband."

"Now, shut your gob and drink your tea," said Anna, "and get out as soon as you can. It's bed I'm wanting."

"You got no ri' go t'bed with my husband," Jenny said morosely. "Not gonna let anyone go t'bed with Nick."

"Mo, you'd better get her out," said Anna. "Just leave me your address, and I'll come for Brian to-morrow. Now get her away."

Jenny took a tight hold of the seat of her chair. "Not goin' 'way," she said resolutely. "Gonna see m'husband. Keep 'way from Nick, says S' George. Thinks he'll stop the blurry money. A' ri', let him." Then suddenly she rose, truculent. "You gerrout. You're a dirty whore. Whaddyer mean, eh? Whaddyer mean sleeping wi' my husband?"

Moses took her arm. "Come on, Jenny," he said. "Come on, now. Your father'll be wondering what's happened to us."

Jenny shook him off and landed him a smacking backhander in the face. "Let him blurry well wonder," she crowed. "He's gotta fancy woman. Nick's gotta fancy woman. Wha' 'bout li'l Jenny? Everybody goin' sleep with someone 'cept li'l Jenny. I'm gonna wait for Nick. I'm gonna bed with Nick. I'm gonna get ready."

She flung off her hat and her close little black skin coat and began to fumble with the skirt of emerald green.

"Show you bitta stuff worth gonna bed with," she muttered.

Then Anna pounced suddenly. Choking with rage, she pinned Jenny's arms in a grip of iron. "Whore, am I?" she muttered in a fierce undertone. "I'll give you whore, you cheap, nasty little trollop. Married to Nick you may be, but begod if I hear his name on your dirty lips again I'll choke you. You're not fit to breathe within a mile of him, and don't do it—d'you hear? Don't do it, or, by all the saints in glory, you'll know who you're reckoning with. Married! You little tuppenny trickster. It doesn't need Scotland Yard to see how you got married. Now, out with you! Take that coat, Mo—and that hat—and off you go, the pair of you. Sleep with Nick! You've got as much chance to sleep with St. Patrick."

She hustled the astonished and trembling Jenny to the door, flung it open and hurled her into the arms of Nick. Mounting the stairs behind him came Piggy White, with a few bottles under his arm. Piggy's face beamed. "Any more, Anna?" he shouted. "Chuck us out another—one for Piggy! What you got, Nick? A good 'un?"

Jenny squirmed in Nick's arms. "You lemme go" she said. "You hate the sight o' me, you do. You lemme go."

"It's you, is it?" said Nick. "Get inside, Piggy. We can't stand here raising hell on the doorstep."

They scuffled into the room, Nick still holding Jenny in his arms. With his boot he slammed the door behind him. He put Jenny down in a chair, and she relapsed into stupor. Moses slipped furtively into a quiet corner. Anna faced the two men truculently.

"And where have you been since Friday?" she demanded. "D'you care a damn whether I live or die?"

Nick twisted his fingers restlessly in his lank hair. "Don't make me laugh," he said. "I can't see you dying of a night without me. Talk about something that matters. What's Jenny doing here? How did she get here? What's she want?"

"Never mind Jenny," Anna retorted hotly. "You listen to me for a bit. D'you know that Brian didn't come home last night, and you didn't come home, and I was all alone and distracted and worried out of my life and not sleeping a wink——"

"Now, see here, Anna me darlin', let me explain," Piggy began, smoothing the scarlet constriction of his cummerbund, but Anna cut him short.

"You! Let you explain! For God's sake don't *you* start throwing out ballast, or up you'll go through the roof, you damn great gasbag. Anchor yourself down with a drink. Get some glasses, Mo."

"What do you mean—Brian didn't come home?" Nick asked.

"Begod, is it Dutch, then, I talk?" said Anna. "Are there two meanings to it? Brian didn't come home."

"Is he home now?"

"Temrershur's normal," Jenny murmured. "Pay's lousy, but temrershur's normal."

"My God, Piggy, open those drinks," said Nick. "We've drifted into a lunatic asylum."

"Boy," said Piggy brightly, "you've named the recipe for sanity. Mo, give me that glass. Here! Damn it, what are you doing? Give us that glass!"

Mo, with his eyes turned in smouldering hate upon Nick Faunt, was clutching the glass till his knuckles showed white through the skin. Suddenly he raised his hand. "Duck, Nick!" Piggy yelled. The glass passed over Nick's head and splintered on the wall behind him. In the silence which followed, Moses sagged into his chair and hid his face in his hands.

"Why didn't he come home?" he sobbed. "Why did he leave Anna all alone? He comes and t-takes her away, and then he l-leaves her all alone—miserable."

Piggy wiped a hand across a brow beaded with sweat. "Ker-rist!" he said. "I'm out of my depth." He drained a glass of beer.

Nick went across and knelt by Holy Mo's chair. He put his arm round his shoulder. "Look here, old son," he said, "it's all right. Understand? All right. I know how you're feeling. Don't you worry about Anna. I'll look after Anna. I ought to have let her know I wasn't coming home last night. I was a fool. But it's all right. Understand?"

Mo's sobs subsided. He nodded his head and got up,

rubbing his sleeve across his eyes. "I'm going," he said. "I'll take Jenny home. Anna'll tell you about her."

"Anna knows no more about her than the man in the moon," said Anna with a resigned sigh. "But for the love of Mike, Mo, some of you start clearing out. I want to go to bed. Give us your address, and tell us all about her when we come for Brian to-morrow. That all right?"

Mo nodded. His eyes were enormous after his tears. Piggy looked at him piteously, dived a hand into his pocket, and brought it up jingling with coins. "Take a taxi, Mo," he said. "She's not fit to go in a tram. You're not, neither." He counted three half-crowns into Mo's hand. "You'll find a taxi by the King's Head," he said.

Piggy raised Jenny from her chair. She had fallen asleep and blinked stupidly as she stood on uncertain feet. Anna got her hat and coat on to her, and Nick opened the door as Moses and Piggy, one on either side, led her from the room. A last flicker of strength flared up in her. "Kickin' me out, are you?" she shrieked. "Kickin' me out! A' ri'. I'll go. I'll come back, but I'll go now. I'll go, I tell you," wrenching herself free, "an' I'll go on m' own. On m' own."

She dived erratically towards the door, through it, and came up heavily on the unsteady banister of the outside stairway. Anna threw her hands up before her eyes. "Jezus!" she said softly. When she looked again Mo and Nick and Piggy White stood there with their eyes glued on the spot where the rail had been. They had heard no more sound than if a sack of corn had hit the ground down below.

CHAPTER TWENTY-TWO

I

JENNY KEPPLE'S body was carried to the Royal Infirmary, which was conveniently near, and a reporter who made his night calls not long afterwards learned of the strange death of a woman named Faunt. It happened that he knew Nick, and had indeed enjoyed his hospitality when the house-warming took place at The Loft. "Didn't know Nick was married," he murmured, and decided to go along to The Loft and see what he could find out. On the way he called at the Bassoon Club. You never knew Nick: tragedy or no tragedy, he might be there. He wasn't there, but Anton Brune was.

"Anton, did you know that Nick Faunt was married?"

Anton scratched in the golden corn of his beard and considered his questioner.

"Well," he said, "since you seem to have got hold of it anyhow, I don't mind confessing that I did. Why?"

"There's been a tragedy. He's a widower."

"That's not a tragedy, Tommy," said Anton heartlessly. "It's a blessed release."

"Oh, like that, was it?"

"Yes, like that. What happened?"

"I don't know exactly. I'm going along to find out."

"I'll come with you."

They found a knot of grim sightseers, including Mick Murphy's mother, loitering in Carless's yard, drawing a queer satisfaction from the contemplation of the broken rail at the head of the outside staircase. Piggy White and Homo were gone; Anna, worn out with sleeplessness and emotion, had fallen into bed and relapsed into stupor. Nick was shambling up and down the room, his hands thrust into his trousers pockets. He wearily told Tommy all he knew. "Yes, she was my wife. I wasn't living with her. Haven't seen her for years. I was out all day to-day. When I got back she was here. Don't know where she came from or what she wanted. She was as tight as a newt and fell against that bar. I didn't know it wasn't safe. That's all. Inquest on Monday. Now get out, Tommy, for God's sake."

Tommy went, murmuring sympathetic words.

"Well, Anton."

"Well, Nick. This is a rotten do."

"Yes, poor little bitch. Come and have a drink."

"Where?"

"Press Club."

"Right you are—if it would set you up."

They went out through the gaping group in the yard. "That's 'er 'usband," Mrs. Murphy whispered. "Pore thing —flattened out dead on the ground, and 'im livin' with another woman up there."

"Hear that, Nick?" said Anton when they were out of earshot. "You've got to leave this place. They'll give you and Anna hell if you don't."

Nick grunted, shuffling along with hunched shoulders. At the end of the street they got on to a tram. They were alone on the upper deck.

"I suppose you think," Nick said with a harsh laugh, "I'm a pretty heartless devil coming out for a drink after that?"

Anton murmured non-committal words.

"But she meant *nothing* to me—nothing at all," Nick went on, spreading abroad his gaunt hands in protest against the senselessness of things. "Dead or alive—nothing."

"She's going to mean a pretty considerable stink, old boy," Anton explained wisely. "That's what I want you to see. You can't keep Anna's name or your own name out of the inquest. Your name's going to be mud in Manchester. Why don't you get out of it?"

"I'll get out of it in my own time," Nick answered stubbornly. "D'you think I care what a pack of lousy hyænas say about me?"

Anton shrugged his shoulders despairingly. "Where are you going to live? You heard that crew in Carless's yard. Anna can't stay there. You can't stay there yourself now. Your little arrangement with Carless was all very well so long as you could keep it quiet, but you can bet your boots you'll have the housing authorities down on you now. A man and woman and child living in a loft with no water, no closet—they won't have it, my boy. They've got you nobbled now."

They found a quiet corner in the Press Club. "Buy me something to eat," said Nick. "I'm starving."

Anton cheerfully obeyed. "You can get out of Manchester right away if you want to," he said. "I've got something fixed up that you can step straight into."

He pulled a bundle of papers out of his pocket. "Industry's moving south," he announced as though he were opening a lecture, "and the industrial artist must move with it. Ever seen the Great West Road, Nick? You know, running from Brentford to Slough."

"Oh, yes, I've seen it," Nick growled. "A lot of damned little conservatories of steel and glass where they make laxatives, and anti-smell muck for sweating flappers, and headache powders and cosmetics. Industry! God, Anton, you could swill away the whole shoot of it in a decent-sized Lancashire mill closet."

Anton winced and pulled at his tankard. "I rather like the Great West Road," he said.

"Well, well, Anton, like it if you must. There's something *to* Lancashire. Its foulness is like the seams on a man's face, wounded in a war that mattered. But the Great West Road—pimples on a hobbledehoy."

"Anyway," said Anton, spreading out his papers, "there's a good job going down there. I could wangle it for you."

"What d'you want me to do—draw pretty pictures of nice little girls exclaiming brightly: 'All men used to shun me after a hot game at tennis'?"

"Well, I'm sorry, Nick, if you take it like that. I've got an option on this job, but if I turn it down I could get you in. I was going to take it myself, but when I saw how things were fixed with you, I thought it would be a way out."

"Anton, take no notice of my poor attempt at humour. You're a good 'un. I appreciate your offer, but honestly I don't appreciate what you offer me. No, no. You take it. I'm not looking for a bolt-hole. Not yet."

"It's cars," Anton said, still hopefully, "all the publicity drawing for a fine stylish make. I know you like movement, Nick. Think what you could put into cars."

"No go, Anton. I'd put so much movement into 'em that no one would see the latest chromium-plated gadgets.

You're the boy for that. Go to it. And I'll be sorry. That's honest."

Anton looked at him shyly out of his innocent blue eyes. "Really, Nick?"

"Honest to God, Anton. What about that girl—that Jewess?"

"Oh, that," said Anton, blushing. "That's off, Nick. It never was much, you know. She treated you pretty badly, didn't she? I didn't like it."

"That didn't worry me," Nick answered, forgetting that blind passion in the Town Hall. "It'd take more than that to come between us, Anton."

"Yes," said Anton, simply. "Anyway, I'm glad I'm going."

"Because of her?"

"Well—partly. And the job's attractive." Impulsively he added: "You are right not to take it, Nick. It's all right for me. For you—no. But stick at it, there's a good feller. You're not working enough, Nick."

Nick patted his hand affectionately. "All right, Anton. I'll work—when I feel like it."

II

A Sunday newspaper, which came into Sir George Faunt's hands at breakfast-time, gave him plenty to think about. There was the story of Jenny Kepple's end; there was a photograph of Nick, "the well-known Manchester artist, the deceased's husband, and the only son of Sir George Faunt." There were sufficiently broad hints of unhappy marriage, of the errant wife's return home, where, it was perfectly suggested without anything that you could lay a finger on, Mr. Faunt was living with another woman. Sir George also gathered that a well-known bookmaker had been present as well as a certain Jacob Rosing.

His mind immediately flew to that obscure Jewish figure that had accompanied Jenny the night before; and he broke out in a cold sweat as he imagined the man in the witness-box.

"Where had you been with the deceased that night?"

"To the house of Sir George Faunt."

God in Heaven, Sir George reflected in panic, he might have to give evidence himself! He could imagine the ironic ghost of Jenny Kepple smiling at the thought that she was achieving, dead, the scandal she had threatened when alive.

Jacob Rosing—Rachel Rosing! Sir George's heart slammed painfully into his ribs. There couldn't be any connection. No, no. Hadn't she told him she had no relations at all?

Sir George drained his coffee cup, hurled the accursed paper from the table, and went to stand with his back to the fire. He nipped a cigar and stuck it in his mouth, pondering. He'd got to keep out of this. He simply could not have Rachel knowing that this wretched woman had been there a few hours before she died, with this—this Rosing fellow. Strange! Jenny had come to him for Nick's address. He hadn't known it. And now Jenny had given it to him. There it was in that paper. "A loft over a yard occupied by a carpenter and joiner named Carless." It wouldn't be easy to talk to Nick after all these years, but it had got to be done. He'd get this fellow Rosing's address out of him and see if he could persuade him to shut his mouth. After all, what did it matter to anyone where he'd been before the wretched woman killed herself? Except to him, Sir George Faunt. To him it mattered a lot. Better take the car. He might have a long way to go. But not the chauffeur. No, he decided with a wise smile, not the chauffeur.

As Sir George turned his red two-seater into the main road he cursed the fate that had dealt him this blow. Before him stretched the awful aching emptiness of Manchester on a Sunday morning. The sky was clear; the elm trees at the roadside were gaily green low down their boles. There were a few newly-arrived swallows over Platt Fields, cutting the air in great arcs like aerial skaters. One of life's mysteries. Why do swallows go to Manchester, with all the world to choose from?

Everything was right, Sir George reflected, except this blasted city and the errand he was on. It was a day to be out—out with Rachel. It was lucky he had made no arrangements with her.

Well, here was the street, and here was the yard. He winced as he noticed the curious women gathered there, gazing up at The Loft. He screwed the glass firmly into his eye, gave a pull to the peak of his cap, and ran swiftly upstairs. Knocking, but not waiting for an answer, he lifted the latch and walked in.

Anna, with her shabby raincoat belted round her, was adjusting before a mirror her green-feathered sombrero. The sound at the door swung her round, and Sir George, removing his cap, came forward affably. "Haven't we met before?"

Anna regarded him with surprise. "Begod," she said at last, "you're a coughdrop. Doesn't anything ever knock you off the perch? Own up, now—I'm the last person in the world you expected to find here? And you're as cool as a cucumber. I suppose you're looking for Nick?"

"Yes," said Sir George, taking her hand with his inimitable fatherly affection.

"It's honoured he'll be," said Anna ironically. "You'd never believe how he's been looking forward to the return of his prodigal father."

"Well, my dear," Sir George purred blandly, "I don't know what your—er—status is in Nick's household—whether he would mind my asking you a question? If you can answer it, I shall be able to postpone the pleasure which I am sure Nick would feel at seeing me."

"Love-a-duck! You don't half hum and haw. I'll answer you if I can. Come in and have a shot."

"Well," said Sir George, "I'm anxious to get hold of the address of a young man named Rosing."

"Rosing—Rosing? Oh, you mean Holy Mo! Whenever I hear Rosing I always think of his sister Rachel. Oh, yes, I can tell you where Holy Mo lives. Matter of fact, I'm just going there. Going to collect my kid. Not Nick's. Don't have evil thoughts."

"So the young man has a sister?"

"Who? Holy Mo? Oh, yes. And such a sister! Believe me, you can't see her behind for dust. Well, coming?"

G

"Yes," said Sir George, "if you will allow me. I've got a car outside."

"Seems a habit of yours. Well, come on."

They went down to the car, and the group of women in the yard hustled them close. "That's 'er!" one shouted, and another demanded truculently: "Wot's this?" Another of yer fancy men?"

Sir George lost no time in getting away. "Begob, you're blushing," Anna accused him. "Ah, well. I suppose that sort of thing will go on till I slosh one of 'em in the kisser. And that won't be long. What do you want to see Holy Mo about?"

"Well," Sir George answered, as the car throbbed before the red lights at Whitworth Street corner, "it's—er—something I want you to help me with. I want you to get him alone with me if you can manage it."

"I'll manage that all right," said Anna confidently. "It's a lucky thing I like you. I do, you know, you old rakehell."

"Thank you," Sir George said as the car hurtled forward. He was thankful for any sympathy he could get at that moment.

As it happened, no diplomacy was needed to get him and Holy Mo together. Joe Kepple and Olga were out. Moses and the child were in the living-room. Brian was wrapped in a shawl—a woolly cocoon—and propped in an easy-chair. Moses was busy with a pencil and a writing-pad, trying to draw amusing pictures. They were no good, and Brian told him so. He wasn't wet and weary now; the intuitive burst that had carried him from the procession's ranks into Mo's arms operated no longer. He was exacting and critical.

"You going to take me back to Uncle Nick, Mummy?"

"Yes, Brian," Anna answered, taking him very calmly now that she had got him again.

"And will Uncle Nick draw pictures? Uncle Mo's pictures are rotten."

"Uncle Nick's more likely to give you a hiding for running away, you little devil," said Anna. "Come on, now, kiss your Uncle Mo and thank him for looking after you, and come on."

"I don't want to kiss Uncle Mo. Uncle Mo tried to drown me."

She took him up and shook him till all his drapings fell loose. "Ach! It's an ungrateful little devil you are," she chided. "Don't take any notice of him, Mo. Good-bye, and thank you."

"You must take him home in a taxi, Anna," Moses protested. "He's been ill, and you can't carry him with all those wrappings." He pressed into her hand the money that Piggy White had given him last night and bundled her out into the passage. It was only then that she remembered Sir George, waiting in his car. "Oh, Mo," she said. "There's someone wants to see you. I left him outside. You're getting in with the nobs, my boy. It's Sir George Faunt. I'll send him in."

III

Sir George said how sorry he was that Anna would not wait for him to drive her back. Yes, he agreed it would be bad for the child to be in an open car; and fervently in his heart he thanked God for it. He did not want to face those pushing women again, especially with the child. He could imagine that they had a name ready for it. He gaily waved Anna away and went up to the dingy front door.

Holy Mo's obtuse mind had reeled when Anna mentioned the name of Sir George Faunt. All night long he had lain awake thinking of Rachel's passionate face as she shook him, holding on to his lapels. He was not to know, she said, that such a person as herself existed. And now, here was this inquest. Very well, he knew what to do. He would stick to the story he had already told Joe and Olga. He had met Piggy White, and Piggy had happened to know Nick's address, so they hadn't called at Sir George's after all. He need not mention Piggy's name at the inquest. He would just say that he and Jenny had had a few drinks together and then gone on to Nick's. That would keep Sir George Faunt's name out of it, and he was sure that was what Rachel would want him to do. He would do that for her because he had promised, and then she could go to the devil. He hated her after last night.

And now, when his slow mind had at last got a scheme cut and dried, here was Sir George himself upsetting everything. Had he guessed something? Had he come to question him about Rachel? Mo came to the conclusion that for Rachel's sake he must know nothing—not even Sir George himself. With a face as white and blank as a full moon he received his visitor.

"Sit down, please," he said. "Anna tells me you are Sir George Faunt, Nick's father."

Sir George looked at him with sharp surprise. "Yes, yes," he said. "You know that, of course. You called on me last night with this poor woman who has killed herself."

"You are mistaken."

Sir George's glass dropped from his eye. "But, damn it," he cried impatiently, "surely I can be trusted to know a man who was in my own house less than twenty-four hours ago!"

His outburst fell shattered before Mo's white uncomprehending stare. "Jenny Kepple and I had a few drinks, and then we went on to Nick's place. That is what happened last night."

Sir George polished his eye-glass with eager irritation. This man was mad. He looked towards Mo's lack-lustre gaze, bent unwaveringly upon him. Suddenly illumination burst in his mind.

"So that's the story for the inquest, is it?" he asked sharply. "You're keeping—me—out of it?"

"That is the truth," said Mo doggedly, "as I will tell it at the inquest."

Sir George rose. "Thank you," he said. "I made a queer mistake. I apologise."

Moses bowed awkwardly. "We all make mistakes at times," he said.

"Yes," Sir George answered bitterly, "we do."

He did not return at once to his house in Fallowfield. He drove out into the country, whizzing his car along like a red hornet. "He's keeping me out of it," a thought was crying in his mind. "Why? Why?"

He knew the answer well enough. Anna's voice was in his ears. "Whenever I hear Rosing I always think of his sister Rachel. Such a sister. You can't see her behind for dust."

Sir George was obsessed, as he whirled through the grand spring day, by the vision of a squalid ghetto crew crowding upon him from behind the lovely form of Rachel. Damn it! He couldn't chance it! She'd lied to him. Said she was all alone. She was lovely!

Damn it! Damn it!

CHAPTER TWENTY-THREE

I

THE brief sensation of Jenny's death fizzled out. There could be but one verdict: accidental death. The coroner permitted himself the pleasure of saying a few words about Nick's dangerous housing arrangements; but it was upon Moses that the hottest censure fell. He had contrived an impression of himself and Jenny spending that Saturday night in a colossal pub-crawl, and the coroner said that everyone's sympathy must be with Mr. Faunt in the misfortune that had befallen him through his wife's association with so undesirable a character as this man Jacob Rosing. He hoped the unhappy woman's death would be a lesson to Rosing and teach him to think of those responsibilities that decent citizens recognised and that he appeared to have so shamefully neglected.

Holy Mo stood up during the homily, fixed his blank white stare upon the coroner's face, gave his awkward bow when it was over, and then slipped quietly away. He had not gone far when a voice bellowed behind him: "Whatcher, Mo!" and Piggy White, red and globular, rolled alongside.

"Well, my lad," Piggy teased him, "you see the trouble

you get into as soon as you leave yer uncle. When you coming back, Mo?"

"I'm all right where I am," Mo grunted.

"Come an' 'ave a cup o' cawfee an' don't talk so damn soft," said Piggy, urging Mo through the doorway of a Lyons tea-shop. "All right where you are, be blowed! You leave them Bolshies alone, my lad. Look at Russia!" He planked himself down at a marble-topped table, his body seeming to wallow in bulges outside the confines of his chair. "Wot's Russia? Nothing but a lot o' bloomin' Bolsheviks. Any 'orse-racin' in Russia? Is there my foot! I was readin' in a paper the other day that on their days orf the Russians go to palaces of culcher. Fancy that! 'Ow'd you like to go to a palace of culcher instead of the November 'Andicap?"

There seemed to Piggy no answer to that question. Certainly Moses made none.

"Two quarts o' bitter, miss," said Piggy, facetiously, "with my compliments to Joe Lyons, and if 'e don't run to it, make it two cawfees. And religion," he went on, turning to Moses again. "Anti-Gawd. Wot d'yer make o' that? It's not right, Mo. Give the Almighty a sportin' chance, I say. Leave 'im in the runnin'. It looks to me too much like scratchin' the favourite. Thank you, miss. D'you believe in Gawd?"

"We don't discuss such matters in working ahrs," said the young woman haughtily. Not for nothing had she won the medal that swung upon her chest.

"Well, wot abaht a slight discussion after workin' ahrs?" Piggy inquired indomitably, but a retreating nose raised in disdain was all he got for it.

"Something about Lyons' waitresses, Mo, that I don't understand," he complained. "They all seem set on medals and the 'igher life. Never got orf with one of 'em yet. Give palaces of culcher to people like that and old England's dished. Wot we want, my boy, is 'umanity—man and woman gettin' together—not culcher. Well, good 'ealth. 'Eere's to openin' time."

He drained his mug from force of habit, and, leaning his elbows on the table, spoke confidentially. "Now, look 'ere, Mo, I got a solid proposition to make. You've often 'eard

me say I was goin' to give up the old umbrella an' satchel.
Well, boy, it's come. Whadyer think o' that?"

"I'm glad, Piggy. You ought to settle down."

"Ay, an' wot about you settlin' down with me? Now,
now——" he raised his great fleshy hand that looked like a
bunch of bananas as Mo opened his mouth in objection——
"you listen, me lad. You remember Sat'day night in The
Loft when Anna started layin' into poor ole Nick about not
bein' 'ome the night before? Well, where 'ad 'e been? With
me to a little pub not so far from Tarporley. The True
Lover's Knot. Wot about that, Mo—eh? The True Lover's
Knot." Piggy mused over the words, twiddling the short
spikes of his moustache. "Real pretty, I call that. And a
pretty 'ouse, too. Right on the 'ighroad 'an not too far from
the racecourse. Once a year we can 'ave a look at the ole gee-
gees. You an' me, Mo—just like we used to."

Moses continued to look glum and non-committal. "I'm
not pressin' you, Mo," Piggy went on. "I'm only tellin' you
I'd like it. I'd like it no end, Mo, if you could come. It's
all right, believe me. A little garden at the side and bloody
great roses all over the front. A fair picture. Like wot I
was readin' in the *Dispatch* by Willermina Stitch. It's not
a tied 'ouse, either. All me own. An' the money paid down.
I'm just 'angin' on till after the November 'Andicap, and
then the True Lover's Knot is my address. You think it over,
Mo. There's no future in Bolshevism, but there is in British
beer."

"Right you are, Piggy, and thank you. I'll think it over,"
said Moses.

"That's the stuff, Homo. I know your sort. When you
start thinkin' you don't stop. You're one o' the bleedin'
deep 'uns. An' turn this over in your mind. A li'l bar
parlour, all oak panels, pewter cans an' a damn great fireplace. An' over the fireplace that picture of me wot Nick
painted. 'E's a caution. I thought I'd get that picture for
a fiver, an' 'e twisted me for fifty. 'An' you'll soon be able
to sell it for five hundred,' 'e says. 'E don't arf think 'e's
someone, that lad; an' the funny thing is, I gotter sort of
believe 'e is, somehow. An' to look at 'im you'd think 'e was

of no more importance than Jimmy Maxton. Always makes me think o' Jimmy Maxton. Well, Mo, me lad," he concluded, "think it over."

He rose, tucked his thumbs into his cummerbund, and with his fingers played an approving tune upon the barrel of his belly, he looked with benevolence at Mo's crumbling figure. "Don't be bought with Red gold," he advised solemnly.

II

A week later Nick and Anna sat at their last breakfast in The Loft. "How much money have we got, Anna?" Nick demanded.

"Now, the good God be praised Who has put one common-sense thought into the man's head," Anna exclaimed. "Let's have a look under the clock."

Under the clock were three one-pound notes, and in Anna's purse were a few silver pieces and some pennies.

"Call it three-pounds-ten altogether," said Anna. "There was fifty pounds you got for your picture, and there was what we snaffled at Tarporley. We spent the fat end of it on altering this place and buying the junk for it. And now we've got to leave it. If you get a couple of quid for all you're leaving behind you'll be lucky."

Nick drew a wad of notes from his pocket and threw them across the table. "There's fifty pounds. Look after it."

"Now, isn't that just how things happen in the Duke of York's house!" Anna exclaimed. "Here, Duchess, here's fifty pounds! Buy yourself a few handkerchiefs. The good God leads me still. I shall not want. Where did you get it?"

"Worked for it."

"I'll never leave a man capable of such a lovely gesture. 'Here's fifty pounds.' Begob, I'm overcome. Is this the week's allowance, or just to see us on to tea-time?"

"Stretch it—stretch it like hell," Nick advised her. "It'll probably have to be getting us tea in six months' time."

He went to the door and yelled down the stairs: "Carless!"

"Yes, Mr. Faunt?"

"Got that truck ready?"

"Yes."

"Good. We're just coming down."

He went back into the room and heaved on to his back a bundle of bedding tied in a quilt.

"Would you not allow me to buy a bit of a new hat now?" Anna wheedled. "'Tis a damned old thing this, with its fool of a feather."

"It's the only becoming hat in Manchester," said Nick. "Put it on and bring down something in your hand."

The bedding and the easel and Nick's painting things were piled on the handcart. Anna's scarlet suitcase, Nick's rucksack. Crockery, towels, kettles. All the big things were left behind.

"Now you come, Brian," Anna shouted; and Brian came and was dumped on top of the bedding. Nick took the shafts and ran the cart into the road. Anna trudged at his side down Amhurst Street, singing, "Good-bye Piccadilly; farewell, Leicester Square."

A few contorted faces appeared at windows. A few fists were shaken. One front door burst open and a shrill voice yelled: "Good riddance to bad rubbish."

Anna changed her tune. As the cart went leisurely towards Oxford Street she sang, "Thank you, sergeant-major, and the same to you," and Nick, shuffling along in his dirty green corduroys, hatless, tieless, incredibly unkept, suddenly began to intone hoarsely: "Any ole rags, bones, bottles, jars!" Brian leapt on the bedding, yelling: "Gee-up! Gee-up!" And so they headed for Cyril Street.

Cyril Street is a dubious thoroughfare on the other side of Oxford Street from Amhurst Street. Here they had booked two rooms, a bed-sitting room for general purposes and for Nick to sleep in, and a bedroom for Brian and Anna. This time they were a brother and his widowed sister with her little son.

Mrs. Haworth, their landlady, received them with cold, suspicious sniffs. Her hair was drawn tight upon her head, ending in a knob that looked like the handle by which the

torturer might give an extra twist to its drastic pull. It
seemed to have dragged all the skin of her face back with
it. There was nothing but a taut strained film on her bones.
She looked at Brian and she looked at Anna, young and
radiant and insolent. "Your 'usband must 'ave died very
young, Mrs. Fitzgerald," she said.

"Yes," Anna answered gaily, "poor little Brian never knew
a father. He just had time to put me in the family way
before God took him. But there you are. That's how it is."

Mrs. Haworth sniffed more emphatically. "I'll expect a
week in advance, of course," she said, eyeing the bedding
and few sticks contemptuously.

"Pay her a month and have done with it, and then come
and give us a hand," shouted Nick, who was wedged half-way
upstairs. Anna flew up, heaved upon him, and precipitated
Nick and bedding on to the stale-smelling landing. They
stuck again in the narrow doorway, but heaved and bounced
the bedding through, and when everything was in, Nick ran
gaily back with the empty handcart. "Don't expect me to
lunch," he shouted; and Anna exclaimed to the greasy
passage: "Now the day of miracles has come! That's the
first time he's told me whether to expect him or not."

From Carless's yard, which he hoped he would never see
again to his dying day, Nick walked to the Stoat Restaurant
in Hurlingham Street, where he had arranged to eat a farewell lunch with Anton Brune. To startle the Great West
Road, Anton had bought new tweeds, hairier than ever, as
golden as his beard. He moved into the restaurant like a
small haystack, with his crimson tie burning brightly. He
was sentimental, and talked about the old days when he and
Nick had been together in the Grammar School and then in
the School of Art.

Nick told him he had left The Loft, and Anton approved.
"Now, work!" he adjured him. "If you'll only work, Nick,
you'll walk over everybody in Manchester."

"I know all about that, Anton," Nick boasted. "There are
only two painters in Manchester with any guts at all—L. S.
Lowry and myself. And I'm the better man of the two."

"Well, go on and prove it," said Anton.

"Prove it!" Nick blustered. "Doesn't that picture they bought for the Art Gallery this year prove it? Doesn't the picture of Anna that I gave to you prove it? Doesn't my portrait of Piggy White prove it? What more proof do you want?"

Anton soothed him. "I thought you were going to have an exhibition this year."

"So I am."

"That's the stuff. Good boy. Now, you get busy on the pictures for it. I'll tell you what I'm going to do. I'm going to lend you my studio. It's a yearly rental. I've paid till December. Now you get up there and work."

"Oh, but look here, Anton," Nick protested. "I'm not going to have you keeping me. Damned if I am."

"You'll pay for it all right," Anton threatened. "I'm not giving. I'm only lending. When you can spare the rent, pay me back. But the studio's yours till December. Hang it, man, you gave me that picture of Anna. That's worth more than the rent."

"Yes," Nick readily agreed. "I suppose it is. Oh, yes; much more."

III

On the morning after Jenny died Rachel Rosing opened the same Sunday paper that had shocked Sir George Faunt, and she was shocked as profoundly as he. It spoiled everything. She had got up, made some tea and toast, placed them on the bedside table, and got back into bed. She was looking forward to an hour's delight, lying propped up there, thinking of the beautiful evening she had spent, and savouring in anticipation all the mornings when she would get up in this same leisurely way—except that she would not have to make her own tea and toast. A maid would see to that. A maid would come in and draw the curtains and say that madam's tea was ready. No—your Ladyship's tea. Rachel felt a slow burning blush of pleasure mount to her face as that thought sank into her mind. Strange, but it had not come to her before. The whole thing had been so incredibly swift. She had

imagined the "madam" with pleasure enough. But "your
ladyship." She murmured the words to herself, and all the
warm beatitude of snobism flowed through her like honey.
Lady Faunt!

And then she read of Jenny's death, and fear tore her to
pieces. The paper shivered in her hand as though she were
holding it in a wind; she felt deathly cold. All those names
that were crowded together there on the page: Faunt, Kepple,
Charles White, Jacob Rosing, Anna Fitzgerald. She had a
presentiment that the unravelling of that knot would be her
undoing.

A bitter calm succeeded her agitation. Moses and Piggy
White and that damned Fitzgerald girl—how they had
always to her been evil stars! She cursed them as the sym-
bols of all that she wanted to leave behind; and now, when
the millionth chance was hers, they had wrecked it between
them. Her reddened talons hooked up the paper. She tore
it across and across, and hurled the fragments about the room.
She lay down and gave herself up to the bitterest imagina-
tions.

Half an hour's reflection restored her practical sense of
tactics. On the larger issue she had the realism to see that
she could do nothing but wait on events. But that was no
reason why she should not be ready for events as they arose.
Sir George might call, and therefore she must be bathed
and dressed and radiant as he would want her to be.

But all the time as she prepared herself she felt that Sir
George would not call that day; and he did not. Well, then,
there was to-morrow. He had said she was to make only one
more visit to Arlette et Cie, but now that must not be taken
too seriously. She must not be such a fool as to throw her
hand in there. That was the only ground from which she
could spring again if she had missed this time.

In the shop on Monday she read with the keenness of a
K.C. every word of the long report of the inquest in the
evening papers. Sir George hadn't come into it, and there
was no word that could connect Moses with herself. Dared
she ring up Sir George or make any move in his direction?
She decided that she couldn't. She told herself with bitter

vulgarity that she had nothing on him. They had spoken of marriage, but there was no witness, no ring, no letter. She had dined intimately with him—that was all. She imagined she was not the only one who had done that.

There was nothing to do but wait till the next step was under her nose and keep her wits about her. And then, dramatically, there it was. As she stepped from the shop into Market Street, Sir George sauntered towards her. He looked attractive with his light-grey hat, his white silk scarf knotted with careless elegance under his plump pink chin, his well-fitting overcoat. Rachel felt her knees unsteady, and the directness of his attack took her off her guard. "Is this man Jacob Rosing any relation of yours?"

"Well—I——"

"Is he?"

"He's my brother."

"I thought so. And Nick's my son. Shall we try to live them down?"

His eye twinkled behind his eyeglass. She put her hand swiftly on his arm, afraid she would fall.

CHAPTER TWENTY-FOUR

I

IN July there was a picture in the *Manchester Guardian* which delighted a number of people. It showed Nick Faunt standing in the little exhibition gallery of the Bassoon Club surrounded by the works he had on show. Anna was delighted because she was in the picture. She had just been standing round, eaten up with a fierce pride that Nick was to be photographed. The picture that was to appear in the paper meant more to her than all the pictures that were on the Bassoon Club walls. And just as the photographer had got his camera ready, Nick hooked out one of his long arms, pulled Anna to him, and slipped an arm through hers.

"Ach, now, Nick," she protested, "don't be a fool! They

don't want me." And with all the animation of her protest still on her face she appeared in the *Guardian*, but unnamed.

Piggy White was delighted, because Nick's portrait of him, which had been loaned for the exhibition—"Charles White, Esq."—came out beautifully in the paper. He bought fifty copies. "I'd make it a hundred if the damn thing didn't cost tuppence," he said. "Tuppence—an' no tips! Gawd! What a paper!"

Sir George Faunt was delighted. He was prepared to be delighted by anything. He had bought Codham. He had settled Rachel's affairs with Arlette et Cie; he was enjoying every moment of his springtime. He thanked God he had overcome the scruples that assailed him when Rachel's deceit became clear. Poor little Rachel! Such a little lie, so easy to understand. He had made her tell him of all her struggles, and a warm wave of benevolence engulfed him. How she must have feared, hanging there by her finger-tips, heaving herself up out of the pit! It was just that fear of falling back when he, Sir George, seemed attainable that had prompted the one and only lie he was ever likely to hear from her lips. Damn it all, thought Sir George with some satisfaction, when it's a question of her love for me, can I wonder that she slipped up, fearing to lose me? And, buoyed up by the confident belief that it was himself she loved, he pushed resolutely into the back of his mind any whisper that it might be the things he possessed.

Results seemed indeed to justify this blind magnanimity. Never again, he knew, would life receive this illumination that was in all his days. This was the last affair that he might ever hope to call a love affair. He was not a novice lover, eager for nothing but a marriage-bed. He did not fix a wedding-day. He was content to savour for a time this happy illusion of youth, this last adventure in courtship.

Rachel was all that he had hoped she would be. His infatuation deepened. He was delighted by her air of thoroughbred ancestry, the bored courtesy which she accorded to some of the semi-precious jewels whom she met among his Town Hall acquaintances. He had been a little hurt by her obvious lack of feeling for Codham. But she had not pressed the objection. He was glad of that, because he wanted her to live there a good deal. His solicitude made him apprehensive about a lassitude which she reluctantly admitted, a pallor which was not the rich natural pallor that sat so beautifully upon her.

But these things did not seriously alarm him. They gave to his care a tenderness that it pleased him to exercise; and Codham, when the time for it came, would put that all right.

So he was ready to be delighted; and when he saw Nick's picture in the *Manchester Guardian* that was incorporated in the general body of his delight. Damned good boy, Nick! Clever. All these people couldn't be wrong. He hoped, now that that wretched Kepple affair was ended, that he would settle down and make something of his life. Sir George stood in his favourite attitude—with his behind to the fireplace, twirling his cigar with his tongue to the corner of his mouth. And here was Miss Fitzgerald again! Cute little piece, if he knew anything about women. He wondered how Nick had picked her up. Had she let on that he had himself made advances? Not, he decided again, if he knew anything about women. Just as well, too. Nick was a wild devil. What might he do in revenge? Get off with Rachel?

Sir George chuckled at the delicious absurdity of the idea, and, struck by a sudden impulse, thought: "Damn it! I'll take Rachel to see the boy's show. Why not? Perhaps we can patch something up. I don't mind, if he doesn't. Anyway, he may let me buy a picture. Give him a leg along." And right away he rang up Rachel, whom he had had put on the telephone.

Rachel was lying down. She was wretched. She wished to God that they were already married, or that she might die. Anything. She couldn't stand this horror any longer. She put back the telephone on to its stand and buried her head in the pillow. All right. A little show—a surprise—that he wanted to take her to in town. Then lunch at the Midland Hotel. All right. She'd have to stand up to it somehow.

She put all her skill into taking the deathliness out of her face. She was once more a creditable picture when he arrived with the Daimler—just that touch of interesting tiredness was about her that caused him to take her hand with a little special petting pat as they leaned luxuriously back in the cushions.

"Rachel, your eyes are beautiful. They're bigger and darker than ever. And yet I'd be able to see them in the dark."

Rachel snapped at his poesy: "I look like a cat?" And when he replied with no more than another soothing pat, she exclaimed, almost on the verge of tears: "Sorry, darling; I'm a bundle of nerves. Forgive?"

And Sir George kissed her behind the ear.

The car stopped outside the unpromising doorway of the Bassoon Club. "Well, what little surprise can be here?" said Rachel "I know this place."

Sir George pointed to a hand-printed bill on the wall. "Exhibition of Pictures by Nicholas Faunt. Bassoon Club. Take the lift."

"My son," he explained, not without a touching trace of pride. "We'll see what he's up to."

"No!" cried Rachel, with sudden startling clarity. "No! I don't want to go."

She stood rigid on the pavement, and Sir George turned to her and spoke with the first hint of frost she had ever heard in his voice: "My dear!"

Rachel closed her eyes. Darkness seemed to engulf her, and in the midst of the darkness she had a sickening sense that something was turning over inside her. Sir George was looking at her apprehensively.

"Are you unwell?" he said.

She took his arm. "It was nothing," she said. "Let us go up."

II

It had been a bad morning for Anna. She had arrived early at the Club with Nick, and they had worked hard at rearranging the pictures. They had all been arranged overnight, but, seen in the morning, they failed to satisfy Nick's

crochety taste. The strong light of the July day produced
all sorts of effects that he had not imagined when he saw
the pictures by artificial light. They sweated at the job for
an hour, and then the catalogues hadn't come. Anna was
sent running like an errand girl charged with violent and
vituperative messages which Nick well knew she was capable
of delivering. She brought back the catalogues, and Nick
damned them lock, stock and barrel. The paper was rotten
and the printing was lousy. Damn and blast it, he wanted
to know, through the telephone, did they think he was
auctioning the bankrupt stock of a Yid jeweller? Well, then,
they knew what they could do with the bill instead of sending
it to him.

Anna began to realise that an exhibition of the works of
Nicholas Faunt was not going to be the calm and academic
occasion that she had imagined. It was a hot day. Nick
came back from the telephone with his lank hair glued by
perspiration to his forehead. He glared at the table placed
at one end of the room and checked off the items upon it.
Cigarettes, matches, catalogues, a little tray of red tabs, a
visitors' book, pen and ink.

He scowled at the tabs. "You know what to do with
those," he said. "If anyone buys a picture, stick one on like
blazes, and see you get the buyer's address. And you can
offer the cigarettes to the buyers. You needn't offer them to
anyone else; they'll take 'em. And that's all. I'm going out
for some coffee. You look grand in that hat. It grows on
me."

"Holy saints," said Anna, "you can't go off like that, man.
You've got to have an opening. I thought you'd be having
a chairman and a bit of jaw, and me sitting there among the
nobs—the artist's inspiration."

"Well, if you want an opening, that's soon arranged," Nick
said. And, mounting a chair, he addressed the empty gallery.
"Here is the finest collection of pictures painted by any
Manchester man or woman in the present century. If I sell
one, it will be a marvel. If I sell two, it will be a miracle.
If I clear my expenses, I'll eat my bloody hat. The show is
now open."

Anna cried, "Hear, hear!" And Nick slouched off to get his coffee.

Anna sat gravely on her chair behind the table, the spittle increasing uncomfortably upon her tongue as she looked at the red tabs and yearned to lick them vigorously. She looked longingly towards the door, praying that someone might come in and shout, "Shop!"

"Certainly, sir. Can I show you a few pictures? This is me, painted in the nude, with swan in background. Rather chaste? This is Piggy White—not for sale. I'm sorry. He often is, but not on this occasion. Half a pint is his usual price. . . ."

"Ach! I'm going potty," Anna exclaimed aloud, and, getting up, she began to stump about the room. Not a soul. It was getting on her nerves. You'd think Manchester was a city of the dead, sitting there in that quiet room. She walked to the window and looked down on the crowds jostling their way along the hot pavements of Oxford Street. Manchester was lively enough, but not a soul out of all those hundreds seemed to give a single curse whether Nick had a show or not, whether he had butter on his bread or starved. Anna felt herself growing livid with unreasoning hate as she watched the ant-like figures moving along beyond the clanging trams and hooting motor-cars. Three-quarters of an hour had gone by, and not a sound had disturbed the quiet of the gallery, when Anna, with something like a sob, tore open the window and yelled down to the street: "Come on up, you Lancashire bastards! Come on up!" But the uproar of the traffic received the thrown pebble of her voice into its maëlstrom and not a head was turned.

But when Anna looked back into the room she saw a young man, nervously clutching a felt hat to his bosom, just inside the door. "I beg your pardon?" he said.

"Oh, I was just saying a few words," said Anna. "D'you want to see the pictures? Here, have a catalogue." She kept her hand over the cigarettes as she handed him the catalogue. He drifted like a nervous ghost round the room, looked at the nude for rather a long time, and, after completing the circuit of the gallery, came back to it timorously.

"That's me," said Anna. "How d'you like it?"

"Oh, beautiful—a beautiful piece of work. So——"

But then there were some newcomers, and as Anna swung round to take them in the young man escaped.

"I don't seem to be a success," she mused. "Better shut my gab." And she returned to her seat behind the table.

There came a thin dribble of people: some who stood back and looked wise for a long time in front of one picture; some who scampered casually round as though they had come in to kill five minutes; some who earnestly studied each picture and its name in the catalogue as though that would help them to understanding. Fragments of whispered conversation came to Anna's ears. "I'm so glad the artist isn't here. I hate to see them about when I *know* I'm not going to buy anything. They hover round, trying to appear unconcerned, poor devils."

"Yes. Who wants originals these days, with the Medici so good, and all those German prints. Still, this is the stuff, you know. Jolly good."

"Yes, but still——"

And another pair escaped towards the lift.

Anna sat with a face of stone. She lit a cigarette and contrived to look at nobody. She had almost achieved a state of coma when a figure, halting at the table, startled her to awareness. The man held a catalogue in his hand. "This picture—twenty-three," he said. "D'you mind putting a tab on it for me?"

Anna seized the tray and rushed to the picture. "Begod," she said, "I'll put twenty tabs on if you like. I'll scatter it so's it'll look like a church porch after a wedding."

She looked hastily at her catalogue and saw that the picture was marked ten guineas. She rushed her customer back to the table, gave him pen, ink, cigarettes in a single comprehensive gesture. "Put your name and address in the visitors' book," she invited, striking a match. "We'll send the picture after the show."

She surrounded him with an aura of homage and admiration; and the man, who had never bought a picture before in his life, went whistling to the lift, feeling no end of a fellow

—an amateur, a collector, an initiate of the secrets of the cognoscenti. He halted before the lift, swung back on his tracks, and announced blithely: "I might as well make out the cheque now."

"St. Patrick himself never had a holier thought," Anna breathed, offering him another cigarette; and off he went, whistling more happily than ever.

Anna pulled off her sombrero and fanned her face. "Begod, now," she said, "if that's not salesmanship, what is? Ten guineas in the first hour, and an eight-hour day. That's eighty guineas. A six day show . . ." She scribbled some figures on the back of her catalogue. "Holy angels! We're up to the eyes—rolling in it!"

She longed for Nick to come back so that she might burst the news upon him, like a glorious bubble smashed upon his head. She went to the window again and looked down more tolerantly on the passers-by. It was an uplifting thought that any one of them might dash in, sign a cheque for ten guineas, twenty guineas, and stroll out again, whistling casually as though it were all in the day's work.

Anna began to whistle herself, suddenly as care-free as a blackbird, but stopped short and sat down bravely as footsteps without spoke of more visitors. And then her hands gripped tight on either side of the table as Sir George Faunt and Rachel Rosing entered. Her thoughts dashed like lightning through her head, and like lightning she reached her decision. "Anna, my darling, this is where you know nothing and nobody unless somebody knows you first."

But nobody knew Anna. She rose and bowed and handed a catalogue to Sir George and another to Rachel. Sir George raised his hat and thanked her without batting an eyelid; Rachel accepted hers with the frozen dignity of a snow-queen. Neither of them was surprised to find Anna there; both in their hearts were glad that Nick was absent.

Anna offered the cigarettes. Sir George took one, but Rachel said: "Please don't smoke, darling. I couldn't stand it now."

Anna made a mental note: "Darling! What ho, she bumps!"

With Rachel's hand resting on his arm, Sir George made a slow tour of the gallery. He knew nothing about pictures, didn't pretend to know anything about them; but he was going to buy the most expensive picture in the show, and let Nick think what he darned well liked about it. Fifty guineas. It was a lot of money. The young devil must think a bit of himself to stick his prices on like that. All the same, though he knew nothing about pictures, he liked this one. Pretty startling, but, by gad, you could see those people moving. It was an oil that Nick had elaborated from his drawings in the Ice Palace: an extravaganza of colour, red and green and yellow skirts flaring across the silver-grey ground of the ice, woollen caps of many hues, long white boots, a glare of light from the ceiling, and in the midst of all, like a pillar of fire round which the movement and colour swirled, was a teetotum of a woman, rotating upon her skates, her skirt whirling waisthigh about her silken thighs, her untrammelled red hair blazing like a wind-blown cresset.

"That's a good picture," Sir George said. "I like that. And I'm dashed if one of those women isn't like you, you know."

"I shouldn't be surprised," Rachel answered coldly, "seeing that it's an Ice Palace picture and I used to be there nearly every evening."

"Good," cried Sir George. "All the more reason for buying it. Here—young woman—we like this picture."

Seizing the tab-tray, Anna ran forward, but Rachel intervened. "No, please, my dear. You may like it, but really I don't."

"Oh, what a fool I'm being!" she cried to herself. "I'll give myself away. Have the picture and shut up about it—forget it." But at the same time she was revolted at the thought that something to remind her of Nick Faunt would hang in front of her eyes every day of her life.

Anna gritted her teeth and groaned in spirit. "Oh, the measly bitch! Fifty pounds! Oh, God, make him slosh her. Make him have his own way."

But Sir George merely looked queerly at Rachel, shrugged his shoulders with some annoyance, and said: "Very well, my dear. Let's see if we can find something else. Here you are. What about this? If you don't want an indoor scene, what about an outdoor one? Looks too cheap to me, though. I wanted to do Nick a good turn. H'm. Six guineas. What's the catalogue say? Woodhead. Ah, yes. I've been up in those parts with the Waterworks Committee people. Looking at the reservoirs. Very like it. Just the wild romantic——"

But Woodhead—the memory of that night with Nick—was too much for Rachel. "Oh, don't chatter!" she shrieked. "Let's get out of this place. I hate the pictures—hate them!"

"Look out!" Anna shouted; and Sir George was just in time to catch the swaying Rachel and carry her to a chair.

"Would you mind getting me some water?" he asked.

"Like a shot," said Anna. "But, begob, 'tis a midwife she'll soon be wanting, not water."

Sir George's head flung up, and he gave her one wild look.

"Ach, you needn't look so startled," said Anna. "Take or leave it, but it's a fact. Don't I know those crochety symptoms. I was like it myself before Brian came."

Sir George groaned aloud, covering his face with his hands.

III

"Begod," said Anna, when Nick returned, "it's time you were back. Grand doings there've been here; ten quid in the till, fifty quid gone west, and Rachel Rosing great with child."

"What are you burbling about?" Nick answered off-handedly. "You're daft." And then, more thoughtfully: "Rachel . . .?"

"Yes, Rachel," said Anna; and, jocularly: "Do you know anything about it?"

And then, seeing him standing there, abstractedly scratching the back of his head, she cried: "You do! You do know something about it! Oh, Nick! Wasn't I good enough? Why didn't you have me?"

CHAPTER TWENTY-FIVE

I

SIR GEORGE FAUNT leaned on the rail at the head of the swimming bath. A girl in a green, skin-tight costume raised her arms, browned almost to coffee-colour, and dived perfectly, cutting into the water a hole with no ragged edges. A few more girls, young and beautiful, sat on the edge of the bath, dangling their toes. One of them dropped feet-first like a stone just abaft a friend swimming through the green translucency. "Race you!" she shouted as she hit the water; and off they went, lovely as hamadryads.

Sir George sighed. He got no kick out of the spectacle. It left him feeling as flat as everything else did these days. Slowly and sorrowfully he polished his eyeglass, stuck it in his eye, and went out on deck. The glittering horizon sawed up and down across the rail. Nothing in sight but blue shimmering water and a blue, burning heaven. With a step that had lost its jauntiness, Sir George promenaded up and down, up and down. He wished the blasted cruise was over. Still, it was one way of forgetting Manchester, forgetting what had happened in Manchester. Hot, this promenading. Better take it easy. He lowered himself down to a deck chair in a shady spot, put back his head and tried to go to sleep. He was tired. "I'm not so young as I used to be," he murmured.

II

The September evening was very soft and bloomy on the city. It had been a warm day, but now the air was gratefully cool, and up and down Oxford Street the arc lamps were spilling a violet radiance that rubbed off crude edges and spread a romantic patina upon the workaday face of shops and offices.

Piggy White emerged from his favourite grill-room, not

215

far from the Palace Theatre, and sniffed the air like an old
horse. The smell of the air always suggested a race-meeting
to Piggy. The eager air of spring put Tarporley in his mind;
and some sluggish residue of romance furnished a picture
of the village gardens with snow-on-the-mountain foaming
among the mauve of aubrietia. Not that Piggy knew or
cared for these names. He only knew that there were some
damn fine flowers knocking about Tarporley in springtime.

A sniff into the oven-breath of a midsummer day whisked
Piggy's thoughts to Epsom, and the gypsies, and the downs
packed with people like Blackpool beach when Oldham wakes
were on.

And this September evening, standing there smelling on the
Oxford Street pavement, Piggy caught an intimation of
Michaelmas daisies and the St. Leger; with a colder, damper
tang just round the corner: the Manchester November Handicap, on that foul course where you could bet on catching a
frog in the throat from the mist rising off the Irwell.

That one sniff of a scarcely-palpable cold breath brought
to a head all the meditations in which Piggy had been indulging as he sat over his steak and chips, his gorgonzola, and his
beer. Even with the cheerful splutter of the grill to gladden
his eyes and ears, Piggy had sunk into a morose self-pity.
Now that he was committed to the True Lovers' Knot beyond
all hope of drawing back, he began to see the implications
of the venture. He began to realise that he would stand on
his box and bawl the odds no more, that his grand days were
over—and, by God, he told himself, some of them had been
grand days. He had his tankard refilled, glowered into the
flaming grill, and fell into a maudlin reverie. He wished
he had a pal with him; he wished old Mo was with him—
good old devil, Mo, for all his glum ways. Well, it was something that Mo had consented to join him at the True Lovers'
Knot. That was fixed now.

He wished he was going to finish up on some gorgeous
course. Newbury—that was a bit of all right. Or Chelten-
ham. Could you beat that? But there it was: he would
finish up with the stink of the Irwell in his nose.

He swigged down his beer, and went out into the street

and sniffed. Like an intimation of mortality, that touch of
a breath from off a distant glacier flared his nostrils and
caused him almost unconsciously to turn up the collar round
his neck.

"Well," said Piggy to himself, "there's only one thing for
a man to do when he's feeling like this." And he went
leisurely towards St. Peter's Square.

Up and down the pavement of the square between Oxford
Street and Mosley Street the women were walking with slow
provocation, singly and in pairs. You could always be waiting
for a tram there, and Piggy joined the few other loiterers who
out of eye-corners were passing in review the sparse parade.
There was one mysterious figure aloof in the shadows where
Dickenson Street joined the square. She stood there, tall,
unmoving; somehow, to Piggy, magnetic. He squared his
shoulders and strolled towards her with all the unconcern he
could muster. She hissed at him as he drew near: "Go away!
I don't want *you*!"

"By God! Rachel!" Piggy cried, suddenly sober.

"Go away!" she repeated, stamping her foot.

"But, damn it all, Rachel," Piggy persisted, "you can't do
this, you know."

"A fat lot you care, and the likes of you," Rachel sneered.

"Well, supposin' I don't care," said Piggy, "an' I don't
know that you've ever give me any reason to feel tender-
'earted—what about Mo? He'd care all right."

"You dare!" Rachel cried with flaming eyes. "You dare
to mention a word of this to him. You're not fit to touch
him with a pole."

"Come to that," Piggy answered ruthlessly, "I don't know
as you are. And it's because I feel as I do about Mo, that
you're goin' to stop this damn nonsense. See? Stop it. You
come and talk things over with me, or Mo'll know all about
it before you can say knife."

Piggy puffed himself up, tried to look and feel important;
but his heart was in his boots. He did not think he would
prevail. He had always been uncomfortable in Rachel's
presence, felt that she disliked and despised him. She had a
style that daunted his cheerful vulgar egotism. And now

to all that was added the puissance of a great sorrow that
seemed to put her further than ever beyond his reach. Taller
than he, she stood there looking down into his eyes that
wavered and shifted. Hers were burning and steady, but
aloof as stars.

"Well?" he said huskily.

Unexpectedly her eyes dropped. She touched his arm
with her gloved fingers. "I'll come," she said.

They turned into the darkness of Dickenson Street, and
there, more unexpectedly still, Rachel suddenly stopped,
placed her face upon her arms which she propped against a
wall, and shook with terrible sobs. "Piggy," she said, "for
God's s-sake get me out of this."

Piggy, who had turned bright and jaunty the moment she
said, "I'll come," was cast down again by this unlooked-for
outburst. That the splendid and unapproachable Rachel
Rosing should be weeping almost on his bosom left him
feeling grotesque and inadequate. There was nothing in
Piggy's rules to meet a situation of this sort; and so he let
the rules go hang and did the first thing that came into his
head. He swung her round clumsily, put his red flaccid paws
behind her head, pulled it down to his face, and gave her a
smacking kiss. "There, there, Rachel!" he said comfort-
ingly. "Don't you cry now," and to his amazement and
satisfaction she sobbed: "Bless you, Piggy!"

Piggy would not have been surprised had she bitten him.
Instead, this grateful, "Bless you, Piggy." He was filled
with amazed delight. Never in his life had he felt so pleased
with himself. To be a success with Rachel Rosing was
something he had never expected. Gone were the maudlin
thoughts of half an hour ago. He was a conqueror sitting
on top of the world; and, since feasting throughout the ages
has gone with conquest, his thoughts turned to feasting now.

Rachel was wiping her eyes, and the fragment of cambric
that fluttered like a white butterfly in the darkness set Piggy's
heart fluttering, too. "Food, eh, Rachel?" he proposed
succulently. "I've 'ad enough to fill an 'ollow tooth already,
but I call this an occasion to celebrate—eh?"

She patted his arm, and said, "I'm hungry."

"Well, then," said Piggy magnificently. "Midland, eh?" Nothing so splendid as an appearance at the Midland with Rachel on his arm had ever happened to him. But Rachel said, "Thank you, Piggy, but if you don't mind let's go somewhere quiet."

It was a disappointment; only a cosmic gesture would have expressed Piggy's mood; but he said gallantly, "Anywhere you like, Rachel." And ten minutes later he was back in his favourite grill-room. With his steel pince-nez on the end of his nose he was studying the menu, when the waiter who had so recently dismissed him appeared at his elbow with a knowing and confidential grin. Piggy regarded him across the quivering pincers, and said severely : "Wot's the matter with you, my lad? You better learn some manners or you'll get a sock in the snout."

Rachel's face burned and she laid a protesting hand on Piggy's sleeve. He threw down the menu and said : "Order what you like; and you"—turning to the waiter—"'op to it quick. I'll 'ave a pint o' bitter. Nothing to eat."

Rachel ordered an omelette, and French rolls and butter, and a pot of coffee, and fruit.

"Lor' lummy," Piggy protested, "I thought I was orderin' supper for a 'uman bein'. Looks to me more like a midmornin' snack for an 'ummin'-bird."

"It's all I want, Piggy," said Rachel, "and thank you for it. You're very kind."

He sat back comfortably, one thumb tucked in the armhole of his waistcoat, the other hand inelegently employed with a toothpick, and considered her closely. Now that the light was on her he could see that she was changed. She had always been lithe of form and delicate of feature; but now she was thin and shrunken-looking, and even Piggy's inexpert eye saw that the cosmetics were a concealment of deficiencies rather than a heightening of endowments. He was a little shocked to feel what he had never expected to feel for Rachel Rosing—a stab of pity.

Without consulting her, he called the waiter. "An old

brown sherry, my lad, p.d.q.," he commanded; and when it came he placed it before Rachel. "That won't 'urt you, my dear," he said, "and it might do you good."

She sipped it delicately. "It's lovely," she said.

Piggy's gallantry urged him to retort obviously: "So are you," but he couldn't. Damn it, there was a ghastly change in her somehow; she wasn't lovely; she was gone all to bits. The cheerful pride of possession oozed out of him. He asked himself why he should bother anyway with a woman who had always made him feel like dirt. "By God," he said to himself, "She looks down in the dirt herself all right now." And, although he felt no desire for her, he liked her better. He sat and swigged his beer and watched her eat, and was glad to be able to stand her a feed.

He had no diplomacy. Bluntly he asked after a while: "Well, Rachel, how long you been on the knock?"

She shuddered and said: "I haven't been. This was the first night."

"Holy smoke!" Piggy cried gleefully. "Fancy me turning up as the instrument of Providence! D'you want to tell me all about it? Don't, if you don't want to. I don't see much of Mo nowadays, and when I do see 'im 'e don't mention you. I thought you were all set up—runnin' a dress shop an' coinin' money."

"So I was," she said, "and then I got engaged to be married, and I gave up the shop."

"Oh, yes, I heard something about that. It was that artist bloke, wasn't it?" 'E was at Nick's party in the Loft—beard an' tweeds, an' a red tie."

"No," said Rachel. "I was never engaged to him—but I might have been."

Piggy did not miss the bitterness of the tone. "An' you wish you 'ad been—eh?"

"My God—don't I wish it!" she said. She put down the fruit she was paring and gazed, wide-eyed, arcoss the room.

"But I let it go." She came back to a consciousness of Piggy's presence. "Then who was it?" he asked.

"Sir George Faunt."

Piggy put down his tankard with a clatter, and his mouth

gaped at her foolishly. "Nick's father? Why, 'e's one of
the richest blokes in Manchester! That's why I can't understand the way old Nick goes on. There's all that dough lyin'
under his fingers if 'e knew 'ow to play 'is cards, and
yet . . ."

"Oh, Nick, Nick!" said Rachel in a dead voice. "Why
must you talk about him? Anton Brune was just the same.
Nick this, Nick that. Is there anything so wonderful about
him?"

"Well, 'e painted a damn good picture of yours truly," said
Piggy with innocent pride. "But lummy, Rachel, to think
you might 'ave been Lady Faunt! Struth, I always thought
it was a fire escape for you, not a step-ladder, when you started
to climb, but I never thought you'd back a winner at those
odds." He looked at her with respect. "Wot 'appened?"

He gave her a cigarette, and she exhaled a thin spiral of
smoke before answering calmly: "He found out someone
else had been there first and left a baby behind."

Again amazement parted Piggy's lips. "Gawd, Rachel,"
he said, "you been livin'! You are a one! I'll bet the old
boy said a thing or two."

"He said nothing at all," Rachel answered. "The day he
found out he took me home in his car, handed me politely
over the doorstep and raised his hat. But I'm not half-
witted, Piggy. I know when a thing's over."

"Well," said Piggy, twisting the brief skewers of his
moustache, "I don't see that a very bright intelligence was
called for. Who was the villain?"

"That's my business."

Still Piggy could not see the end of the matter. "But,"
he asked, perplexed, "what about the——?"

Rachel cut him short with a quick gesture of the hand that
held her cigarette. Without looking at him, she said:
"There are ways and means. They are not pleasant."

Not pleasant. No, thought Piggy, looking with new understanding at the clear evidence of something broken, ruined,
in the girl before him. Not pleasant. He felt less satisfaction in the thought that Rachel had wept upon his bosom and
permitted his kiss. This was not the Rachel he had known.

She had experienced things that were not pleasant, and after them even Piggy White might seem not so bad.

There seemed to Piggy little more that could be said; and as, in those circumstances, one could always fall back on the offer of a drink, he said, " Wot say a brandy?"

Rachel looked past him, shook her head, and stubbed out her cigarette. Piggy contemplated her with the pathetic eyes of a spaniel, sucking thoughtfully at a hollow tooth. " What about the dress shop?" he asked. " Can't you go back there?"

She spread her thin ivory hands with a gesture of finality. " Finished. I quarrelled hopelessly with Miriam. I was— well, uppish, I suppose. She's got a new partner. No, there's nothing—nothing."

" There's Moses."

" I wonder." He did not understand her faint ironical smile. He did not see what was before her eyes: the picture of herself, arrogant, dominant, clutching the lapels of Mo's shabby coat, shaking him till his big daft head was rolling, hissing: " You don't know me! Do you understand? You don't know me!"

She looked at Piggy with a hard, unsentimental eye. " No, Piggy," she said, " it's no go. I know just where I am. I've been pretty good at fooling other people, but I can't fool myself. Most people can, I know, but I'm not made that way. I've never made any friends. I've only made steps of people, and now they all know it. And I know it, and that's that."

Piggy cleared his throat and twirled his moustache and looked tremendously wise. " I understand you, Rachel," he said. " We're a pair, we are. I can never fool myself either. I see where you stand."

Rachel laughed aloud. " You dear old clown," she said, " I suppose you believe every word of that. You're the simplest old thing I've ever met. You're about the only person I know whom I haven't tried to fool and use, and that was because I didn't see what good you could do me."

Piggy blew out his cheeks, coughed and went purple.

"I'm a man of the world, Rachel, understand that," he said. "You'd want to be pretty fly to put anything across me."

"Bless you, old thing, you'd do anything I asked you."

"Well. . . . Perhaps. . . . I'd do a lot for you, Rachel."

"Would you give me the price of a night's lodgings? It's as bad as that."

"You're trying to trap me now," said Piggy, looking very cunning. "You want me to say, 'Yes, I'll give you the price of a night's lodgings—for the usual consideration.' Then you turn round and say, 'There 'e goes, dirty 'ole 'ound, just like the rest of 'em.' But that's where I've got you, see Rachel. I can be as generous as the next man, specially to old Mo's sister. I'm not goin' to treat you like a tart, so don't you think it." He fumbled with a wallet. "So take that—and that—and that," he said, slapping pound notes on to the table as though he were dealing cards. "Now, then, what d'yer think o' Piggy?"

Rachel folded the notes delicately. "I think you're too good," she said, squeezing his paw. "My bag, with all I've got, is at the station. Now I can go and get it. Good-bye, Piggy, and thank you."

She rose, but Piggy urged her back into her seat. That touch upon his hand left him reluctant to close the matter there. After all, Rachel was Rachel, the glorious woman whom his lecherous old eyes had so often caressed at the Ice Palace and in many another place. So inaccessible she had been then, so remote, so scornful. And now that touch upon his hand—that look in her eyes. "Damn it all," Piggy thought, his head more than a little befogged with liquor as his mind was with sentiment, "she's under the weather, but the weather will change. Our Rachel'll be all right again one of these days if she gets the chance. Give 'er the chance, you old barboon." And, transient but sweet and exciting, there flashed across Piggy's vision a Piggy not quite so—well, not quite—so—Piggy—walking in a garden full of darned great roses with a Rachel at his side—not this Rachel—a resplendent Rachel, lovely as a filly going to the tape for her first race. And this other Rachel would be looking at that other Piggy with a look which told everyone: "This is all your doing. If it hadn't been for you . . ."

"Garcong!" Piggy shouted hoarsely. "Two old brandies."

"No," said Rachel. "Please!"

"Yes," said Piggy in what he felt was a new, masterful manner. "Sit down, Rachel. I'm gonna talk."

He waited for his brandy, swung it in the goblet and flared his broad nostrils above its heartening aroma. Then cupping his hands about it, he leaned across the table and said, "You know, Rachel, I'm givin' up racin'. I'm gonna settle down. Me an' Mo. Yes—that's a fact—me and Mo in a little pub. Can you imagine it? As snug as two bloody little kittens in a basket of 'ay. Ain't that news?"

"That'll be fine," said Rachel without enthusiasm.

"Fine! I'll say it is," Piggy cried. "An' you should just see that pub. In the country. Roses! All roses outside, an' inside shelves of glasses—shinin' like 'orses shoes as I've seen 'em flyin' over Becher's Brook. Twinklin' in the bl—in the firelight. But that'll be in the winter. 'Ow d'you like the sound of it, Rachel? An' it's got a name as sweet as Fanny Adams—the True Lovers' Knot. 'Ow d'you like the sound of it?"

Rachel sipped her brandy and looked at him steadily across the rim of her glass. "Are you offering me a job?"

"It's yours for the takin', Rachel—safest billet you ever been offered."

"What sort of job?"

Piggy gulped down all that was left of his brandy. "What sort of job would you like, Rachel?"

She smiled with cold self-possession at Piggy's beaded anxious face. "You don't want me to share the basket of hay?"

"Oh, Rachel——"

"Be honest. Do you? Is that what you're talking about?"

Piggy took out a large silk handkerchief and mopped his brow. "You make me uneasy," he said. "You make me see pictures, Rachel." He fluttered a fat hand before his eyes. "Vivid pictures. Details."

"Well, listen to this," said Rachel, "and see it as vividly

as you can. I haven't got a penny in the world except the money you've given me. I'm down and out because I've fooled so many people. So I don't want to fool you. I'll come to your True Lovers' Knot. When are you going?"

"After the November 'Andicap."

"Very well. I'll come because I want a roof over my head. I'll work for you, and I'll work hard. But I'm not sharing the basket of hay. Is that any good to you?"

Piggy nodded, speechless.

"And one of these days. . . . Who knows? Let's leave it at that."

"Rachel," said Piggy, his voice thick with fervour, "I'd make you a good 'usband."

"Husband! I didn't know you were thinking of that!"

"Neither I wasn't. You led me up to it."

"When I came out to-night," she said with a hysterical catch in her voice, "I didn't think I'd meet an offer of marriage."

He patted her hand, and the contact of his hot gross flesh sent a shudder through her body. Her glance came at him again, cold and calculating.

"Well, let's leave that, shall we, Piggy? Let's just say for the time being that you're offering me a job. Believe me, I'm thankful for it. You don't know what may come of it, do you? We'll see a lot of one another—and who knows?"

Piggy pushed up a great sigh from the very pit of his stomach. "Well, I guess that's all, Rachel," he said.

"No," said Rachel. "It's still two months to the November Handicap."

"Ay," he said. "I forgot. You gotta live. What can you live on?"

"Two pounds a week," she answered readily.

"Eight twos are sixteen," said Piggy, calculating. "All right, Rachel. I'll do it."

"And after the November Handicap I'll work for eight weeks for nothing—just my keep."

"You'll do nothing o' the sort."

"I will."

"You won't."

"We'll see."

"I'm yer boss," Piggy grinned. "Don't you start arguin'
with me."

"You don't mind where I live till then, do you?"

"Not a bit," Piggy cried generously. "Go where you like.
Pick up. Get bright. Got any ideas?"

"Yes. I know some rooms in Blackpool. I'll send you
the address."

"Grand! I'll bring the ole car over some weekend an'
we'll 'ave a dance at the Tower. Ever danced with a blarsted
ole sea-lion before? Believe me, it's an experience."

He rose, hilarious, feeling buoyant, and fumbled into the
overcoat that was held for him. He was aware that Rachel
had shaken his hand, then that she was already down the
vista of the room—going—gone. She looked superb: the
old radiant disdainful Rachel—skating rink—swinging velvet
skirt, fur-hemmed—lovely legs——

He gave the waiter a generous tip, pressing his hand.
"Buy li'l kittens," he said, "two li'l kittens in barsket. Ha!"

CHAPTER TWENTY-SIX

I

ON the trestles stretched under the living-room window of
the Higher Broughton house there was an array of brushes
and ink-pots and oblongs of white cardboard. Under Olga's
instruction, Homo was transforming these materials into the
banners of an army. Olga drew words in pencil upon the
cardboard, and Moses brushed them in in ink, red and black.

"Down with the Nationalist Government," Olga wrote;
and "Down with the Baby-Starvers"; and "No Means Test."
On another piece of cardboard she drew a crude hammer and
sickle; and as Mo inked in her work, she took what he had
done and nailed the cards to the tops of poles. These she
stood in a corner. Forty or fifty of them were already there.

"You ever been in Russia, Olga?" Moses asked.

"No."

"Your name sounds Russian, but you don't seem Russian."

"If anyone calls me a Russian I'll poke him in the eye,"
Olga laughed. "Nay, I'm a Bacup lass, and for fifteen years
I ran a boarding-house in Blackpool. I gave that up a year
ago. I had a brother who went to the United States. He
never married, and when he died he left me all he had.
Not a lot, mind you; but it means ten pounds a week without worrying, and that's worth twenty that you grizzle your
guts after. And as for Olga—well, I just called myself that
for a lark when I went Red. My name's Ramsbottom."

"Why did you go Red?"

"Mo, my boy, there's one thing I'm not going to do with
you, and that's talk politics. I *am* Red, and let that be
enough. If I thought I could make you a Red I'd have a shot
at converting you. But you'll never be red or blue or pink,
and if I were you I'd thank God for it. You just get on with
that job and leave politics alone."

"What are all these for?" Mo asked.

"For the demonstration next week. We're going to march
to the Town Hall—thousands of us. We're going the day
the City Council meets, and we're going to demand to see
'em and tell 'em a few home truths."

"Ay," said Joe Kepple, coming in from the kitchen,
where he had been washing in the sink, "we will an' all! If
we can get anywhere near the lousy bourgeois lot, we'll tell
'em. Not that I expect to. So don't you be disappointed.
Olga. I know what's likely to happen. Mounted police, that'll
be it, the paid Cossacks of the capitalists. They'll have a shot
at breaking us up. They oughter give 'em knouts and have
done with it. You keep out of it, Mo. It ain't going to be
a picnic. Oh, look at that blasted cat now! Walking all
over those wet letters. Why the hell d'you keep the thing,
Mo? How often have I told you?"

"And how often have I told you it's nothing to do with
you?" Olga demanded. "This is my house, isn't it? And
I've given Moses permission to keep the cat. And, what's
more, you know *why* he likes to keep it."

"All right, all right, Olga. You're boss," Joe grumbled;

and Moses seized the black skinny culprit and slid off with it
to the kitchen.

"I'm surprised at you, Joe," said Olga, when he was gone.
"You know what a queer creature Mo is, and you know he's
just barmy about that cat. He brought it here with that
child, and the child and the cat are all mixed up in his mind.
You know what wool his mind is. I've heard him talking
to the beast as if it *was* the child. So just leave him alone.
He's harmless and he's useful."

"All right," said Joe, "All right. Let's get on with the job.
What about something original? What about this?"

And, like a boy playing pirates, he roughed a skull upon
the cardboard. "That ought to put the wind up the petty
bourgeois," he said with a grin.

"Give it a meaning," said Olga; and, seizing a brush, she
scrawled beneath: "Must we starve? What has the Labour
Party done for the Unemployed?"

"That'll do for to-night," Joe said. "Come to the pictures."

II

The banners looked impressive enough when they turned
out on parade the following Wednesday. Throughout the
week Joe and Olga, dodging about the city in their ramshackle car, had left them here and there, in ones and twos;
and now they all began to assemble behind Ardwick Green,
trembling above the heads of a great concourse of cheerful,
shabby people. Shawls and caps and mufflers, leaky shoes,
frayed coats, stubbly chins, Woodbines, chatter, chatter, the
impatient tap of a drum, the *Daily Worker*. . . . "News
of the Mass Resistance to the National Government. . . ."
Clumsy bobbing banners on the ends of sticks, the roar of
the trams on the other side of the Green, the stunted trees
and the grim grey grass, the War Memorial of the 8th
Manchesters.

Nick Faunt stood on the pavement and drew: the lean
angle of a hungry face, the queer glint of an eye, a group
here, an individual there, the jaunty impatience of the drum-

mer . . . tap, tap . . . *when* will we march? . . . stolid, glum Lancashire faces, fanatical faces that looked like alien imports, the crude swaying banners.

"And begod," said Anna, squinting at his drawing block, "you look the dirtiest coot of the whole parade. Put yourself in to show how the workers are starving."

Up at the tossing head of the procession Holy Mo stood with pig-headed stolidity between Joe Kepple and Olga. He had insisted on coming, but he had small notion of what it was all about. He stood with his eyes brooding upon his boots as Joe and Olga exchanged hot words with some members of the City Council. He didn't know what the argument was about; he was confused by the crowd that closed in, shouting and gesticulating.

"Take my tip," one of the councillors shouted. "Don't try to march on to Market Street. The police have laid down your route. You go left when they want you to, or there'll be trouble."

"Aren't we citizens?" Joe roared through his brassy lungs. "Isn't this our city? Aren't these our streets? We've got the right to walk where we like." And as an angry buzz of assent rose from the impatient crowd one of the leaders leaped on to the railings of the Green and yelled: "Comrades! Your leaders have chosen a route for you, and the police have chosen a route. Which will you follow?"

"Forward!" the crowd roared. "Forward, comrade! Go where you like." And the impatient drummer permitted himself a long inciting roll.

Then a few fifes found voice, and suddenly the vast unorganised gathering was shuffling shabbily forward, with a squad of fresh-faced friendly constables vainly trying to impose some sort of order and formation upon its advance. Some of them shouting with braggart voices, most of them sheepish, almost furtive, the poverty-stricken army ambled by. Far ahead, behind the fifes, Olga's grey aureole swayed above her swinging cape and below the skull that Moses held aloft. Just there, some spirit was in the step, some resolution lit the eye; but the tattered tail, gathering tributaries from side streets, was a murky uncertain affair.

Anna looked at them with wonder and pity. "Holy Mother of God!" she cried, seizing Nick's arm. "They don't know how to sing. Come on! We must make them sing!"

"Keep out of it, you fool," said Nick. "I've got all I want. This outfit's heading for trouble."

He stood where he was, but Anna dashed into the procession, and he saw the green feather swept along far ahead on the black scum of the stream. He stood irresolute for a moment, then ran. As he drew near, he heard her shouting: "Sing, comrades; for the love of God, sing! Isn't there anyone knows 'I'm a hobo?' Listen to this." And her penetrating voice rose above the dull shuffle of shoddy leather.

> " To hell with the toffs, and to hell with the Czar,
>   And Ramsay MacDonald, the Tory hussar."

And Nick joined in the great roar of the chorus:

> "Halleluiah, I'm a hobo!
>   Halleluiah, amen.
>   Halleluiah, put your hand down,
>   Revive us again."

"That's the stuff, comrade," a voice shouted; and a lout slapped Anna approvingly on the back. Nick was surprised to find himself suddenly aching to slosh the man in the jaw; but he looked at Anna's laughing face and felt ashamed. "She loves this," he thought. "She loves people. She loves being alive." And he thought: "My God, if anyone in this crowd hurts her I'll kill him." And then he shouted as Anna had done: "Sing!" And everybody sang as the despairing banners rocked forward over the tramlines, between the dingy shops and shabby roofs of London Road.

III

Impasse. Moses looked stupidly right into the red distended nostril of a horse. He could feel the heat of the animal's breathing, hear the faint crepitation of leather as the policeman shifted in his saddle.

Gathering force yard by yard, the procession had come to the testing-point. Under the echoing arch of the railway bridge they had passed, and there the fifes and the drum became silent. Singing ceased. The pace of the procession slackened, for ahead, blocking the road, was this barrier of mounted men. The barrier was just beyond a street turning left. Go left, procession, and trouble is ended. The procession slowed, knowing it had no intention of going left. Uneasily, doggedly, silently, it crept forward.

Between the horses and behind the horses were policemen on foot. The members of the City Council who had hopefully elected to lead the procession turned left. A few of the processionists trailed after them. For a moment it looked as though all would be well; then there was an obstinate stop, and Moses, hemmed in to right and left, found himself considering a horse's nostrils, and the green-grey spume that soiled the bit.

The processionists on the road, the sightseers accompanying them—and these made a solid army on each pavement—piled up slowly into a mass that thickened before the rigid barrier of the police, and above them their banners waved their demands.

A queer dogged silence fell. The front ranks of the marchers glowered at the police; the police sat like equestrian statues.

Then arms began to wave; voices were unfrozen; the banners pointed forward. But nothing happened.

For ten endless minutes Moses looked at the horse's nostrils. Joe and Olga had been squeezed away from him. His doughy hands held aloft the skull under the policeman's nose, and the policeman did not look at him, did not look at his banner, looked straight ahead over the jammed mass, his gloved hands lightly on the horse's neck, his behind occasionally shifting to comfort in the creaking saddle.

Then Moses was aware of a figure rising out of the mass on his left, a man struggling to the shoulders of his fellows. His appearance was the signal for the band to play "The

Boys of the Old Brigade," and through the music came a shout
for twenty volunteers. They sprang forward, Moses among
them, and the movement unleashed the crowd's passion.
With one simultaneous leap they hurled themselves after
the volunteers. The silence was ended by a deep roar. All
the forward ranks were propelled, willy-nilly, upon the barrier
of men and horses.

In a second the cross-roads were a welter of fighting men,
of horses pushing through the struggling confusion, of policemen hitting right and left with batons, of marchers retaliating
with stout sticks to which their banners were nailed, with
stones, bricks, coke seized from a cart beleaguered there in
the heart of the affray.

More in panic than with passion, Moses laid about him.
The first wave of the assault hurled him between two horses,
but, as he passed, the rider of one of them smashed at him
with a baton. The blow grazed his temple, knocked off his
hat, and filled his eye with blood. Then the horses were
gone, and policemen on foot, pushing, striking, seemed all
about him. His pole was too long for effective swinging,
so he lunged and pushed with it, till someone shouted in his
ear: "Put that blarsted thing down. Use yer fists." Moses
obeyed, and, mixed up in a tangle of marchers, thrashed out
right and left. Suddenly a blow across the wrist sent a hot
pain searing through him; and as he paused, agonising, a
sharp hissing sang through the air, and he found himself
lying in the road, spluttering, gasping for breath, soaked to
the skin.

"It's the fire brigade—the barstards!" someone shouted;
and the rout began. Stampeding feet trod upon Moses as he
lay in the road, blinded by blood, saturated by water, whimper-
ing with the agony of a smashed wrist. A horse charged by,
missing him by inches; and, staggering to his feet, he saw
that now there was room for horses to charge. Hoses were
quartering the wide space of the cross-roads like machine-
guns, and all about lay a litter of broken banners, broken
sticks, hats, caps, policemen's helmets, bricks, stones and
shattered glass. Here and there a man was lying still or
crawling towards the gutter. But the crowd was gone.

As if by magic, they had melted away down side streets and back alleys, and Moses, more frightened by his isolation than he had been by the roar of the conflict, took to his heels and made off under the bridge at a shambling trot. With his left hand he clutched the swinging wrist of his right, and felt sick with pain. Joe Kepple and Olga were nowhere to be seen. He did not know that Joe was in gaol and Olga in the Infirmary.

He blundered away down a turning to the right, making for Oxford Street, and it was when he had nearly reached the University that Nick and Anna, homeward bound, saw him. Groans breaking between his lips, his vision obscured by congealing blood, his clothes soaked with water and foul with mud, he went loping sightlessly past them, when Anna stopped him with a cry. He heaved-to dully in his tracks, turned towards them, and then stood still with hanging head. "It's my only suit," he said stupidly.

Nick and Anna looked at the awful wreck: hatless, bloody, sodden. Nick was speechless, twisting his lank forelock in his fingers. Anna suddenly wept. She leaned on the shabby railings of a house and shook with sobs. "He's such a baby. He's such a child," she moaned.

"I'm all right, Anna, I'm all right," said Mo. "Don't worry about me. I'm going home."

"You stay where you are for a moment," Nick commanded; and, running across to the University, he called a taxi. They all bundled in, Moses with his death-white, blood-streaked face; Anna crying her eyes out; Nick with flaming anger against dim, uncertain foes. "God in Heaven!" he shouted out loud. "God in Heaven! What a world we live in!" And he shook his skinny fist out of the taxi window against all whom it might concern.

IV

"If you think I'm going to take that into my house, you're greatly mistaken," said Mrs. Haworth.

She stood plumb in the middle of her dismal passage, her

arms folded, her bearing militant, her taut skin almost burst-
ing under the upthrust of her cheek-bones. She barred the
way to the stairs with resolution.

"But the man's ill. We want to wash him and get in a
doctor—that's all," Nick protested.

"Oh, that's all, is it? Well, you're not going to wash him
in my bath—that's flat. I don't want drunks in here."

"He's not drunk," Nick cried with growing exasperation.
"He's been marching with the unemployed."

Mrs. Haworth's eyes narrowed sharply. "Ah, that's it, is
it? A police matter. Now out you go. I'll have no trouble
with the police in my house."

Mo leaned groaning against the varnished wallpaper.
"I'll go," he said. "I'll go. I'm not going to be a worry."
And Nick turned to Anna with a despairing gesture. "Well,
what are we going to do now?"

"Do!" cried Anna, blazing forward and sticking her face
aggressively into Mrs. Haworth's. "Why, leave the rotten
old witch, and take Mo home. Look at her! I'm thankful
I'm not a nursing mother or my milk would turn to vinegar.
Begod, a starving cannibal would go vegetarian at sight of
her. Old boiling fowl! Brian!"

Brian's bright eyes had been staring over the banisters, and
now he bounded down the stairs. Anna seized his cap from
a peg and stuck it on his head and bundled him into his
overcoat. "And, remember," she said, shepherding her three
men towards the door, "those rooms are paid for till Saturday.
I'm particular about who uses my bedding. None of your
passers-by. I've got my suspicions about this house."

Mrs. Haworth gave an outraged gasp, stalked into her
front room and banged the door. "Boiling fowl!" Brian
hooted, and Anna promptly clipped him in the chops.
"Cheeky little brat!" she said. "Where do you pick up your
manners?"

So once more they found a taxi, and Mo directed them to
Higher Broughton. There was no Olga, no Joe; but Moses
had a key; and Nick took him to the bathroom and helped
him to undress; and as he lay comfortably in hot water Nick
rummaged in the chests-of-drawers till he found one that

contained Joe Kepple's clothes. He was back and bathed Mo's broken head and found there was nothing to worry about. He dried him and dressed him, put his arm in a sling, and conveyed him, white and patient, down to the sitting-room where Anna, as calmly as though the house were hers, had prepared tea. "And now," said Nick, "as soon as there's a surgery open we'll see about that wrist."

They did, and the doctor was very cheerful. "Nothing broken," he said, when he had made Mo squirm with pain, "but there's terrible bruising, and the tendons are badly sprained. What have you been doing with yourself?"

"We've been playing football," Nick explained improbably. The doctor grinned. "Seen the evening paper?" he asked. "Take it away with you." And when they got home they read that Joe was in goal and Olga detained in the Infirmary.

"Lucky for us," said Nick heartlessly when Mo had gone to bed, complaining that he felt bruised and tired. "For one thing, I don't fancy meeting Jenny's father. For another, we've got a roof over our heads. You didn't think about that, did you, when you bounced out of the house?"

"No; I always bounce first and think afterwards."

She sank into one of Olga's sagging wicker chairs, exhausted by what she had been through that day. Nick threw some coal on to the fire, drew the curtains, and sat opposite her. Brian had been put to bed, and was long since asleep.

"You'd better go and give Mo a hand," Anna said.

Nick rose wearily. He, too, was tired out. He found Moses struggling patiently with his clothes.

"Sorry, Mo," he said. "I forgot you'd be in difficulties. Anna sent me up to give you a hand."

One of Mo's rare smiles lit the pale round of his face. He said nothing, but allowed Nick to undress him and put him to bed as though he were a child.

"D'you want the light left on?" Nick asked, hesitating at the door.

"No, thank you." And then, from the darkness: "Nick."

"Yes?"

"It was kind of you and Anna."

"Oh, that's all right, Mo. Good-night."

"Nick."

"Yes?"

"She doesn't love me. She loves you."

"I know that, Mo."

"Then—then, I suppose that's all right?"

"Yes, Mo. Don't you worry. That's all right."

He heard Mo rustle down into the blankets. He shut the door quietly and went downstairs. Anna was sitting where he had left her, fallen asleep, her head thrown back on the chair, the light of the fire-flames pulsing on the taut white column of her neck. Her lips were a little parted; her eyelashes were like fine brush work on ivory.

Nick sat on the chair facing hers and watched her for a long time, smiling at the innocent-seeming of that dynamic being. Then he took a drawing-block, and when he had finished working at it, he wrote: "Anna: the day she said she'd marry me."

He propped the drawing against the clock on the mantelpiece, then quietly took the hand that hung down alongside the chair. Anna started up, instantly wide awake.

"I've been drawing you," said Nick.

"Begod, is that all? And me asleep. I'm lucky."

Nick pointed to the picture. She got up to look at it, and turned from it swiftly with her eyes shining.

"D'you mean we're going to stop living in sin?" she demanded.

"Who's been living in sin?" Nick growled.

"Ach, if thoughts are sinners, I've been damned for months."

She grinned up at him with happy impudence. "And to think I don't even know how you kiss," she said.

And then she saw that he was not laughing, that he was suddenly grey and grim and hungry-looking. All that was in her leapt to answer his passion as his bony arms went round her with a strength she had not suspected.

CHAPTER TWENTY-SEVEN

I

ANTON BRUNE had come down from London overnight, and in the morning he went to his old studio, hoping to catch Nick Faunt at work. And there Nick was, with a picture all but finished on the easel.

"Well, what d'you think of it?" he asked, when he and Anton had exchanged greetings. He stood back looked at the work, and then truculently at Anton as though daring him to find spot or blemish.

"It's the most restful thing you've ever done, Nick. Something new for you, isn't it?"

It was Anna, asleep in the wicker chair. She had come to the studio and posed day after day, and now Nick was putting in the finishing touches. The old affectionate admiration lit up Anton's eyes. He slapped Nick on the back. "You're there, old soldier. Nothing can hold you back now, you know." He looked again at the picture with something wistful and envious in his eyes.

"It's my wife," said Nick.

"What! You're never married!"

He seized Nick's hand and began pumping, whereon Nick became rather surly. "No demonstrations, Anton," he commanded. "We just slipped into a registry office. That's how we wanted it, and we don't want any shouting about it."

"All right. Can you leave it now and come out? Come to the Midland and drink some coffee."

They went to the Midland, which was full of racing men, and tweed overcoats, and glasses slung on shoulders, and sporting editions rustling open at the hopeful predictions of the tipsters.

"I'd forgotten," said Nick. "November Handicap to-day. And see who's here! Well, Piggy, you're looking brighter than the morning star."

237

Piggy White rolled alongside, a paradisal figure, in a grand check suit and white spats and a new grey bowler. A red carnation bloomed in his button-hole before a few sharp spikes of foliage.

"Well, well, you're a grand sight for your last day," said Nick, shaking hands, with a grin. "You know Anton Brune. Isn't he a treat, Anton? No one'll take you for a bookie to-day, Piggy—not till you open your mouth. Either an owner or a trainer."

"Ah, well, they won't take me for a jockey, anyway," said Piggy, looking complacently at the protuberance that concealed his spats. "That's one good thing—we can eat. Come on."

Nick and Anton declined to eat. Piggy ordered a great plate of beef sandwiches and expressed his view of the licensing laws.

"I'm waitin' for 'Oly Mo," he explained. "Arranged to meet 'im 'ere. 'E's comin' to keep the ole ledger for the last time. An' as soon as the show's over to-day off we go. I've got the car, an' we'll tootle along by road. An' don't you forget, Nick—or you, Mr. Brune—any time you're passing the True Lovers' Knot, drop in an' 'ave one on the 'ouse. 'Ow do I look for a landlord, Nick? Bought all these togs in honour. Pretty good?"

"They'll come in from miles round, Piggy, just to have a look at you. You'll have to wear something else when I'm about, or we'll never have a chance of a quiet drink. Well, there's Mo, looking as hangdog as Judas Iscariot. You'd better give him a shout, Piggy, or he'll slink off."

Mo was standing at the entrance, nervously wringing his hands. Piggy waved his bowler ostentatiously, and Mo came slinking forward ill at ease.

"Well, 'ow's the ole wrist?" said Piggy. "Up to the job?"

"Yes, thank you. It's much better," Mo answered. "It doesn't hurt much now."

"Well, come on," said Piggy. He stood up, smacked his stomach approvingly, spun his bowler between thumb and forefinger before placing it on his head, and hitched his glasses round to a more elegant angle. "*Au revoir*, boys.

See you sometime." And off he went, his spats twinkling among the tables.

"Who's the Jew-boy?" said Anton.

"Piggy's clerk—Rachel Rosing's brother."

"Good God!"

"Why, what's the matter, Anton? Not a snob, are you?"

"No, I don't think I am. But still. . . . She always told me she was without a relative in the world. Her father was dead—used to teach languages in London. That's what she told me."

"Oh, well, forget her, Anton. I expect she's told a few tales in her time. I don't know that I blame her, either. If people are such fools that they can't stand the truth, why, you've got to feed 'em with something else. First lesson in politics, sonny."

"Damn politics. Let's talk about something clean. You, for example."

"Thank you kindly, guv'nor."

"Well, it's you I want to talk about, anyway," said Anton. "That's what I've come for. How did the exhibition go?"

"So-so. Marvellous notice in the *Guardian*——"

"I saw that. What did you sell?"

"I did better than most people do. I cleared twenty pounds after paying expenses."

"Pretty good. But that's not all you did, my boy, if you only knew it. D'you remember a chap called Holliday who bought one of the pictures?"

"Can't say I do. What was the picture?"

"A gouache thing: a big white horse straining like blazes on a hill, with a bright green dust-cart behind it."

"Ah, yes. Damn good picture, Anton."

"I know. What did you get for it?"

"Twenty quid."

"Would it amuse you to know that it's been sold for thirty-five?"

"Like hell it would. That's the sort of thing that tickles me to death."

"I've seen your picture. There's a room built round it. It belongs to Peggy Ashburton. You know, the girl who's

playing in *Pop Goes the Weasel*. That's Holliday's job—
selling beautiful things to the only people who seem to have
any money nowadays—successful actresses and film-actors,
and all those sort of thim-thems. Peggy loved her gee-gee
at sight. 'Oh, Mr. Holliday, you must make me a room for
it.' See—that's how things are done nowadays. And Holliday
obliges, repeating the green of the cart in hangings and
carpet, and the colour of the horse in the white leather arm-
chairs."

Nick was torturing his forelock. "I'd like to see that,
Anton. That's the first of my pictures to get to London."

"Well, don't be a fool. See that it's not the last."

"Do I gather that you've got something up your sleeve?"

"Yes. I've got an offer for you to go an join up with
Holliday. He'll find a use for lots of your work. He's only
a beginner, and he's anxious to hitch up with some good
men. He could give you all sorts—mural work, designing
textiles——"

"Textiles!"

"Damn it, don't be sniffy, Nick. Duncan Grant designs
textiles."

"We—ell. He's pretty good."

"Nearly as good as you, eh?"

"Nearly."

"Well, then, what about it? Holliday was pretty well
knocked sideways by your show. He's dead keen. He says
you've got the makings of the greatest painter in England."

"The *makings*! Tell him too look again, silly ass."

"Silly ass yourself, Nick. Come off the high horse and
jump at this chance."

Nick glowered at him silently, twisting his hair round and
round his finger. Anton was quiet for a while, then broke in
on his meditations. "Holliday asked me to make you an
offer. One of the big hotels is having an ice rink put in.
He's collared the decoration. There was a picture in your
show of the crowd at the Ice Palace. He says, 'Tell him I've
got to have that. I'll put it in the best place in the vestibule,
where it'll hit 'em silly. He had it priced fifty guineas. Tell
him not to be a damn fool. He can take that price off and

leave it to me.' That's the sort of thing Holliday's going to do for you, Nick."

Nick's hollow cheeks ticked and twitched. "Anton, you've been pushing me down this bloke's throat."

"Don't you believe it. What's got him all set up and whooping is that you're his own discovery. Anybody'd think you'd never been heard of before."

"Well," said Nick fiercely, "have I? Have I? Not a yard outside this blasted town. But, by God, I will be. I will be, Anton! D'you hear?"

He shot out his claws and seized Anton's plump wrist. "Well," said the little man, at once pleased and uneasy, "well, that's that—eh, Nick?"

"When you go back," said Nick, "you will take that ice-rink picture and give it to this man Holliday with my compliments."

"You fool, Nick," Anton laughed. "When will you learn sense? Here, boy! Telegram form."

And Anton wrote: "Have secured ice-rink picture. Terms not settled. Faunt accompanying me London Monday for discussion.—ANTON BRUNE."

"It seems to me, old horse," he said, shoving the telegram under Nick's nose, "that I've got to take you to the water *and* stick your nose into the trough."

"Have it your own way," said Nick morosely.

II

"Wot the 'ell's that?" said Piggy White, as his dilapidated car snorted towards Castle Irwell. "It keeps on."

"It's my cat, Piggy," Mo answered. "In that basket at the back."

"Cat! Oo d'you think you are—Dick Wittin'ton? Take the bloody thing out, Mo. I can't stand cats. I'm like Lord Kitchener—they gimme the creeps."

He drew the car in to the kerb and came to a stand. "Come on, now, Mo, 'op out and let the blarsted animal go. I tell you I can't stand 'em."

Piggy was really upset. He felt cold shudders go along his spine. He rootled among the miscellaneous luggage at the back of the car till he found a bottle of beer. He opened it with a pocket corkscrew and swigged through the neck. "That's better," he said, throwing the empty bottle over a privet-hedge into a raddled front garden. "Now, then, Mo. You let 'im out. I can't abear to touch 'em."

Mo remained sullen in his place. "I don't want to, Piggy," he said. "I want to keep him."

Piggy looked at him with amazement, and the cat mewed protestingly from the basket. "There it is again! I can't stand it, I tell you! Wot the 'ell d'you want a cat for? No good comes of cats. Vermin, that's wot they are."

"This one isn't," said Mo. "I want to take him with us."

"Wot! To the True Lovers' Knot?"

"Yes."

"Now, Mo, 'ave a bit o' sense," Piggy pleaded. "'Ow can you do that, seein' that cats get me all worked up with the willies. Look at that! I won't be able to drive in a minute."

Piggy held out his red paws, and sure enough they were trembling. "Cats!" he spat. "They're worse than ghosts to me, Mo. No, ole feller, we can't take 'im. You didn't oughter've done this, Mo. You oughter've told me. They're evil—that's wot cats are—evil."

"Well, what are we going to do?" Mo asked, sitting stubbornly in the car.

"You just 'op out, Mo, there's a good feller, an' open that barsket and you'll see 'im buzz orf like a witch on a broomstick. An' that'll be the end of it."

"He won't go if I do open the basket."

"'E will, Mo. You come an' 'ave a try. We gotter get on, Mo. Come on, now."

Mo clambered down reluctantly and pulled the basket out of the car, murmuring endearing sounds. "Shut up!" said Piggy. "That's not fair."

Mo took out the skewer that held down the lid, and the cat pushed out its head—a flat, snake-like head that made Piggy recoil and brought out beads of sweat on his forehead. Then the beast heaved up the lid and leapt lightly on to the pavement—a skinny, black, evil-looking bag of bones, with tail lashing and belly slinking to the ground. Piggy stood farther back and shouted: "Shoo! *Allez!*" and stamped with his fat, spatted feet. But the cat did not run. It snaked around for a moment, than sprang to Mo's shoulder, curled itself round his neck, and leered with yellow eyes at Piggy.

"You see!" Mo cried triumphantly; and Piggy fanned himself with his bowler. Then he made a mighty effort to overcome his fear. He stole slowly towards the cat, put out a hand with clicking fingers, and crooned, "Puss! Puss, then!"

The cat drew up its gaunt vertebrae into a warning arch, opened wide its mouth of dirty pink, and hissed faintly. It held aloft one paw, heraldically, all the claws protruding, and its ears went flat on to its head. Piggy sprang back, and he was aware that his knees were trembling. He wiped his face with his handkerchief. "Drive the damn thing off, Mo," he shouted. "I can't stand it. It hates me."

But Mo laughed and raised a hand to stroke the cat, and the cat sunk its back slowly, and drew in its claws, and rubbed its head against Mo's ear.

"You see," he cried, pleased as a child, "he's quite tame, Piggy. Come and stroke him now."

Piggy did not accept the invitation. He strode to the car and climbed to his seat. "Mo," he said, "we're meetin' Rachel on that Blackpool train at the Exchange Station to-night. See you there. Make up yer mind about that bloody animal between now and then. I'll find a clerk for this afternoon. Plenty of fellers glad of a job. So long."

He slammed the car door. The car kicked, exploded, and shot away as violently as though the devil were after it. To Piggy, wiping one clammy hand after the other on the knee of his trousers, the idea did not seem far-fetched.

Moses stood for a moment stupefied on the pavement. He watched the car as long as it was in sight, hoping that Piggy would stop and wave to him to come on. He did not know that he had struck the one snag over which he and Piggy could never come together. He felt that he could not be happy without the wretched creature that was now purring like a dynamo at his ear; and Piggy knew that in the inscrutable laws of life it was written that he and cats were not on speaking terms. A dog, yes. And recoiling from the shuddering that even now afflicted him, Piggy began to think happily of dogs. Dogs would be grand at the True Lovers' Knot. He would give Mo a dog. That would please him. A damn great St. Bernard—like wot those monks trained to carry brandy about. And toying with the idea of making the True Lovers' Knot a unique hostelry where the brandy was served by large, pained-looking St. Bernards, Piggy recovered his spirits, tootled his horn happily, and plunged on to Castle Irwell.

III

Moses put the cat back into the basket and turned his face towards town. He had plenty of time. No need to take a tram. He and Piggy were to meet Rachel in the early evening. Piggy reckoned that they ought to be at the True Lovers' Knot by nine o'clock. There had been several excursions to the place, and everything was in order. Nick's portrait of Piggy hung in the private bar with prints of King Edward leading in Minoru, a jumble of 'chasers going over the first hurdle at Aintree, Pretty Polly looking every inch a queen. Piggy's name, as pretty as paint, was over the door—that door whose trellis-porch was newly green, though the roses on it were not at the moment much to look at.

Moses was sure that he was going to enjoy life at the True Lovers' Knot. He had been upset when told that Rachel was joining the party. Rachel's conduct had shocked and wounded him; but Piggy talked him round. Moses did not know what had happened to Rachel. He knew that that amazing fairy-story about her marriage to Sir George Faunt had somehow withered out of existence, and that things had altogether gone badly with her. He had come round to the idea of forgiving her, but he had not yet seen her.

He pondered these things as he went slowly towards town;

pondered the fate of Joe Kepple, still in gaol for assaulting the police, and of Olga, out of the Infirmary but walking with a limp. Mo had explained to Olga how Nick and Anna had thrown up their lodgings in order to look after him; and Olga had consented to their remaining in her house—at any rate till Joe came back.

A rum business—a rum, upset sort of year it had been altogether, Mo reflected. Things hadn't gone straight ever since that spring morning when he first met Nick Faunt— the morning when he was going to Tarporley Races with Piggy, and Nick and Anna seemed to spring out of the ground.

Well, it was all straightening out now. Once he had made Piggy see sense about the cat, and they were settled down in the pub, things should be all right again.

He decided that he would leave the cat in the left-luggage office at Exchange Station. Then he could pick it up in the evening when he and Piggy met Rachel. He was obstinately convinced that he would be able to make Piggy accept the cat as a member of the family.

When he reached town, Mo bought some odds and ends of meat, stuffed them into his pocket, and made his way to the Exchange Station. He crossed the long bridge to the station and paused near the taxi-rank. He must put the meat into the basket before leaving the cat. He drew out the skewer of the lid, and the cat forced its skinny body through the aperture. A taxi at that moment back-fired like a gun, and, with every hair angrily on end, the cat leapt in the air as though it were shot. Then like a black arrow it whizzed across the bridge, back the way Mo had come.

Mo dropped the basket and ran in his shambling awkward fashion after the cat, but from the first flash the creature was out of his sight among the busy traffic of legs and wheels. he ran, nevertheless, his brown opaque eyes searching this way and that, affectionate moaning calls coming from his lips. People turned to stare after the daft-looking unkempt fellow; but Moses did not see them. Not till he came out on the Cathedral side of the bridge did he pause, looking in con-

sternation at the grinding wheels of trams and buses and
motor-cars. Straight into this world of crushing heartless
things the cat had rushed, and disappeared.

He stood still at the end of the bridge and sobbed. The
Cathedral bell-ringers were having one of their mad merry
days, and all the air of the town's heart was a rush of flying
melody. The bells could not have beat more cruelly in Mo's
head if he had lost a love child. He stared up at the tower,
blocked darkly against a pewter sky, and tears flowed down
his cheeks.

He didn't know what to do, till suddenly he bethought
him of an old story that cats always make their way home.
He was not far from the dreary back streets where he had
picked up the cat that day when Brian had burst out of the
procession, wet through. With a new hope in his heart, Mo
hurried thither. It was a Saturday, and the street was as
empty as it had been the last time he saw it : grim and gaunt
as a prison yard, hard as a miser's face, but filled with the
clamour of the bells.

Up and down Moses prowled on the hard granite setts of
the road, searching in the locked doorways, peering behind
dustbins, as lost and lonely as the mangiest cat could be. A
sleek yellow beast shared the street with him. It came purring
to his legs. He stooped and stroked it mournfully; but of his
own cat there was no sign.

Back, then, he went to the bridge, and as he crossed it he
looked away to his left, where, within a short stone's throw,
a second bridge crosses the river of scum that is the Irwell.
And on that bridge Moses saw a small, excited knot of people
shouting and pointing down to the river. He stopped and
looked, and his heart stood still. The bridge that faced him
was carried on one wide arch springing on either side from a
sheer wall, on one hand of brick, on the other of stone.
Between those walls, that had not a handhold or a foothold
anywhere on them, the black and noisome river poured
towards the great dark vault beneath the bridge. Low down,
where the left-hand side of the arch took its spring, there
was a small buttress, smooth and rounded so that no hand
could grip it, no man get a stance upon it; but it was good

enough for a cat, and there, just discernible in the grey light
of the November day, soaked and pitiable and looking like
nothing better than a dirty dish-clout, was the cat that had
brought the small crowd together. And Mo was certain that
the cat was his.

A minute's run brought him to the second bridge, where
the cat's fate was being eagerly discussed.

"'Ow the 'ell they gets there fair beats me," a little man
with a green baize apron was saying. "But they do. It's a
reg'lar performance. Every month or so some silly sod goes
over an' gets drowned tryin' to save 'em."

"Yerss. The p'lice oughter forbid it. It's suicide."

"But 'ow *do* they get there?"

"Search me! Falls in or scrambles in somewhere 'igher
up and gets carried down. Then they just makes it on that
buttress, and there they're stuck. Nothin' for 'em to climb
up, and if they gets orf they're done for. An' so they could
be, for all I care."

Moses listened with his heart pumping noisily. "But they
do get rescued," he said. "I've read about it in the papers.
How do people get at them?"

"Wiv ropes," said the man in the green apron. "Silly
devils. Fair suicide, that's wot it is. The p'lice oughter
forbid it."

Moses clawed the parapet of the bridge, heaved himself
up and peered down to the river. It was a long way below
him. He saw the oozy rubbish carried under the bridge at
a frightening pace, saw the cat, crouched on the buttress with
its fur flattened to its thin, shivering body. As he looked,
the creature stood up and opened its mouth in a plaintive
cry that he could see but not hear because of the clamour of
the bells. Seagulls were diving at the river's garbage.

He dropped back on to the pavement. "Where can I get
a rope?" he asked.

At the demand the small crowd became animated and
alert. If someone was going to be such a fool . . . well, let
him. But cat-rescuing over the Irwell bridge was one of
Manchester's specialities and it behoved everyone to assist.

"Ropes! Where'll we get ropes, Bill?" The green-baize

man became keen and business-like, and as if in response to
the quickening interest a lorry rolled up, laden with a builder's
impedimenta. Bill held up his hand, and the lorry stopped.
Green-baize, his eyes sparkling with interest spotted the ropes
neatly coiled in the back.

"Spare a minute, mate," he shouted to the driver, "and
lend us a rope. Another cat marooned. This bloke's going
over."

The crowd was thickening, and eyes turned with interest
upon Mo standing there glowering at the pavement, listening
to the bells filling the air with a crazy rush of sound.

"Come to the other bridge," a boy shouted. "You get a
better view from there. I've seen this before."

A knot detached itself from the crowd and scampered off.
The rope was paid out. Bill and the green-baize man and
the driver of the lorry gripped the end. Trembling with
fright, Mo climbed the parapet, and heard a cheer from the
other bridge.

"When you get him," said Green-baize, "give a shout,
and we'll haul in gently."

And then, as though for a few moments his conscious life
had ceased, Mo came to himself, and with a shock that turned
his stomach over realised that he was going hand over hand
down a rope. Before his eyes gaped suddenly the black
chasm that was the underside of the bridge's arch. Below
his feet, still a long way down, was the swift flow of the river,
black as the arch itself. He dared not look up. He was
suddenly, inexorably, alone, swaying gently in mid-air.

He stopped climbing, and held on desperately. Before
him stretched a field of filthy stalactites growing out of the
arch; to his ears came the suck and gurgle of the black water,
audible even above the jubilation of the bells. Suddenly
there was a throb and flutter in the rope as though it were
living and struggling in his hands. The arch vibrated and
roared. A tram was passing over the bridge.

He gave himself a moment to recover, then slowly went
down, hand over hand. He tried to look at nothing but the
rope, and then found his boot full of water. He twitched
violently, hauling up his leg, and saw the water swirling

round him. The disturbance threw up sharply into his nostrils its foetid odour. He hauled himself up a notch, and held on, sweating. He shut his eyes and put his forehead against his fists, but a heavy, creaking, beating sound forced him to look up, and a seagull almost fanned his face as it plunged towards him through the arch. He saw the red-tipped yellow of the curved beak and the cold unwinking eye. A fear such as he had never known gripped him as he thought of that beak pecking at his hands.

The rope turned slowly, and hanging on with hands that were beginning to feel hot and sore, Holy Moses turned with it, like a joint on a spit. So, presently, down there where most of the light of day was strained into a foul twilight, between the sheer walls, over the rushing, stinking water, he came face to face with his cat. The cat was alert, standing on its precarious ledge, watching him with eyes that glowed in the dark. But Moses could not reach the cat. He was too far out over the water. He called the beast, hoping it would leap out and mount to his shoulders, as it had done so often; and no one heard his voice—not even the cat. The sound was paralysed in his throat by the fear that held him.

Slowly the rope swung him round, away from the cat. He thought of the meat that was in his pocket, bits and pieces considerately chopped up. Gingerly, in an agony of apprehension, he took his right hand off the rope, hugged his knees round it, and felt in his pocket. At any rate, the cat should not starve. As he swayed round again towards the cat he threw a piece of meat. It hit the slimy buttress and slid down towards the river. A gull swooped with a cackling laugh and caught it. Mo threw again, and again, and soon the poor fool was surrounded by wings beating white in the darkness; he was dazed by harsh voracious screams. They were all about him, throbbing round his head, dizzying him, filling his ears with their clamour. He struck at them with his free hand, and suddenly a black horror engulfed him. He forgot the cat, forgot every thing but the gurgling water, and the beating wings, and the mad shouting of the bells that seemed to come from some remote heaven miles away from this dark cañon where he fought with winged devils, chuckling and screaming. He let out a great cry of agony which they heard on the bridge, and they began to haul him up. Exhausted, he changed hands on the rope, felt a searing shock flame into his wounded wrist, and plunged down through the white wings, through the stinking air, through the black oily water. He came up under the arch, heard the majestic thunder of it as a tram stampeded by, and from a distance that seemed to be infinite the bells wavered out the last sound that reached his ears.

CHAPTER TWENTY-EIGHT

I

AT the appointed time Piggy White reached the Exchange Station. There was no Moses to meet him; and as there were ten minutes to go before the Blackpool train came in, he went into the refreshment room and stood himself a couple of bottles of beer. Then he went out to the Blackpool arrival platform, puzzled and worried about Mo, wondering how Rachel would look after her long spell of sea air. He felt pretty good himself. Though the favourite had won the November Handicap, it hadn't been a bad day for him. He pushed his grey bowler over to a cocky angle, sniffed his carnation, and approved his spats.

The train came in, and a wave of passengers swept towards him. A man accosted him. "Mr. White?"

"That's me."

"Thought so. I was given your description."

The fellow grinned impudently, as though the description had not been a flattering one, stuck an envelope into Piggy's hand, and in a twinkling was lost in the crowd.

Not too well pleased by the brief offensive encounter, Piggy stared as long as there was anything to stare at. Then he put the letter into his pocket, and, with growing uneasiness, scanned the faces of the few people still dribbling off the train. Soon there was no one. The platform stretched away emptily to where in the blackness beyond the station lights of red and green were winking. Porters were pulling up windows, salving newspapers, banging doors. No Rachel. And there had been no Moses.

Perhaps she had come by an earlier train. Perhaps Mo was knocking about somewhere now. Piggy prowled about the station, thinking of the festive meal which was to be served at nine o'clock at the True Lovers' Knot. He prowled for half and hour. No Moses. No Rachel. He went into the refreshment room and ordered a drink, and thought of the letter in his pocket.

She did not call him "Dear Piggy." She did not call him anything. She began straight off with a blow between his eyes: "I shall not be turning up to-night." She told him of the man she had met, and of course she was going to be married, and it was useless for Piggy to try and find her. She had already left Blackpool.

"Find her! My Gawd!" said Piggy under his breath. "No, no, Rachel, my girl. No private inquiry agents on your track. Well, Gawd 'elp some poor devil. Twenty quid of my good money. Put not thy trust in bitches."

He was rather incoherent as he stumbled out of the station and got into his car. No Rachel. No Mo. It didn't seem worth while to drive through the night, alone, to the True Lovers' Knot.

He went to his grill-room, rang up his pub, and told them to wash out the night's festivities. He felt rotten, low and dispirited. The day was ending so differently from what he had expected. He went to the grill and chose his steak; then sat in his favourite spot near the fire where he could smell the good things that were to come to him. He called for an evening paper and balanced his pincenez on the end of his nose.

He read of the death of Holy Mo. The paper gave no name; "a youth of foolhardy daring" was all they could find to call him. But Piggy knew, and as he read the bald account of Moses clinging to the rope over the foul river he had a sudden access of insight and imagination. He understood the fear that had been conquered, the horror that had been

crushed back; and he felt horribly and bitterly worthy of
shame because his own fear had sent Mo to that ghastly end.

He pushed back his chair noisily and countermanded his
order. He felt that food would choke him. He went out
into Oxford Street, where a thin drizzle had begun to fall,
and was overwhelming lonely and sad among the jostling
crowds. Because he could think of nothing else to do, he
walked up and down several times between All Saints and
the Midland Hotel. Then he went to his rooms, where his
landlady was surprised to see him. He went straight to bed,
but he couldn't sleep, and as his gross body heaved restlessly
from side to side he was filled with purer emotions than he
had known for many a day. His clothing of them was
perhaps grotesque, for he resolved that if Mo's body was
recovered he would see that he had a slap up tombstone. " I'll
bury 'im at Tarporley," he said. " Jew or no Jew. I'll wangle
it some'ow. 'E was a better Christian than I am. An' I'll
give 'im a damn great tombstone that'll let 'em know wot
I thought of 'im."

And in the course of time Piggy achieved all those things.

II

It was the First of January. Joe Kepple and Olga had
gone in the car to Blackpool. Blackpool air, Olga said, was
the stuff, summer or winter, for a man who had just come
out of gaol. They had been gone for some days. " Well,
you'll have cleared out by the time we get back," Olga had
said. " Good luck to you. And thanks for what you did
for Moses. He was one of the right sort."

" He was a simple proletarian hero," boomed the incorrigible
Joe. " Do a thing like that in a capitalist war and you get
the V.C., with a month's leave to come home and lure some
more lambs to the slaughter. Do it in these times of so-called
peace and you're a foolhardy youth who ought to have more
sense."

" Well, come on," said Olga, grinning at him affectionately.

"You have the sense to keep your hands off the police in future."

She limped away on her stick. "Good-bye, Nick. Good-bye, Anna. See you in London sometime."

That was a few days ago; and now breakfast was finished, Nick's old rucksack was packed, and Anna's scarlet suitcase stood alongside it on the floor. In the front room Brian had his nose glued to the window, on the look-out for the taxi that was to take them to the station.

Anna opened the morning paper and gave a cry of delight. "Begod now, that's what I call a game old cock! Your father's engaged, Nick. Here you are, in the Court and Personal. 'The engagement is announced of Sir George Faunt of Codham Hall to Mrs. Sanderson, widow of the late Mr. James L. Sanderson, who was a member of the firm of Sanderson and Briggs, cotton merchants and manufacturers.' Glory be to God, I've got a mother-in-law. Is she nice?"

"Nice! I know her, my girl. Rich as hell; but I don't envy him the job of tickling the old trout."

Anna let out a shrill whistle. "And that's not the end of it. Look at this: 'New Year's Honours. Baronets: Sir George Faunt.' Nick, that's hereditary, and praise the saints, I know a grand word like that. It's a cultured woman you married. You'll be a baronet, Nick, and I'll be Lady Faunt! Now, why did that mare kick my old Dad in the guts! It's a proud man he'd have been this day."

Nick snatched the paper from her hand and glowered at it. "It's true!" he said with a harsh laugh. He looked Anna up and down, standing there trim and taut and excited. He sank back into a chair and laughed uncontrollably. "Sir Nicholas and Lady Faunt. My God, Anna, it's a scream!"

"A scream is it, you great grinning galoot. Begod, it's a bit more gracious you might be for the gifts of Providence. And what about Brian? When you're Sir Nick, what'll Brian be?"

"Now you're asking," said Nick solemnly. "I don't know how many billions of worlds there are, but Almighty God chose this one in order to make a special demonstration of his love. And in this favoured place, the one thing no thinking being dares to ask is what'll become of a little child. Feed my lambs. Hell! It makes me laugh."

"Begod, what's biting you now?" Anna demanded. "I don't know what you're blethering about."

"Well, then, you're lucky. Don't think about it, or you'll go further off your chump than you are already."

He tilted up her chin and kissed her.

"Taxi!" Brian shouted.

Nick jammed the old sombrero upon Anna's head. "Come on, then!" he said. "Let's live while they let us!"

The green feather teased her cheek as they scrambled together along the passage.

THE END

Howard Spring

In 1938 his most famous book, *My Son, My Son*, was published; it was a world-wide success. Since then all his books, without exception, have been best-sellers and have earned Howard Spring a high reputation as an author of universal appeal.

'Howard Spring is a novelist of solid and considerable talent, whose ability to tell a story, sense of character, craftsmanship and industry should put hollower and more pretentious novelists to shame.' *Spectator*

'He is not afraid of stark drama, and he writes with real feeling.' *Sunday Times*

I Met a Lady

A Sunset Touch

Winds of the Day

These Lovers Fled Away

My Son, My Son

There is No Armour

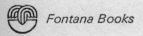 *Fontana Books*

Fontana Books

Fontana is a leading paperback publisher of fiction and non-fiction, with authors ranging from Alistair MacLean, Agatha Christie and Desmond Bagley to Solzhenitsyn and Pasternak, from Gerald Durrell and Joy Adamson to the famous Modern Masters series.

In addition to a wide-ranging collection of internationally popular writers of fiction, Fontana also has an outstanding reputation for history, natural history, military history, psychology, psychiatry, politics, economics, religion and the social sciences.

All Fontana books are available at your bookshop or newsagent; or can be ordered direct. Just fill in the form and list the titles you want.

FONTANA BOOKS, Cash Sales Department, G.P.O. Box 29, Douglas, Isle of Man, British Isles. Please send purchase price, plus 8p per book. Customers outside the U.K. send purchase price, plus 10p per book. Cheque, postal or money order. No currency.

NAME (Block letters)

ADDRESS

While every effort is made to keep prices low, it is sometimes necessary to increase prices on short notice. Fontana Books reserve the right to show new retail prices on covers which may differ from those previously advertised in the text or elsewhere.